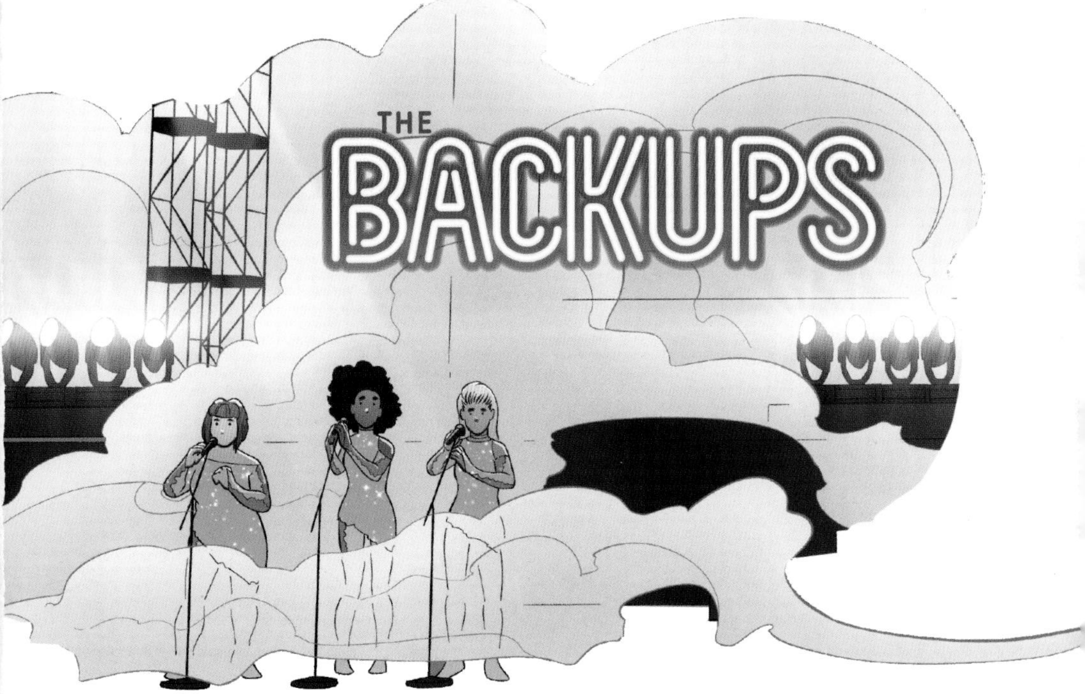
THE
BACKUPS

[Imprint]
MAKE YOUR MARK

A part of Macmillan Publishing Group, LLC

120 Broadway, New York, NY 10271

THE BACKUPS. Text copyright © 2021 by Alex de Campi.
Illustrations copyright © 2021 by Lara Kane, Ted Brandt, and Dee Cunniffe.
All rights reserved.
Printed in China by 1010 Printing International Limited.

Library of Congress Cataloging-in-Publication Data is available.

Our books may be purchased in bulk for promotional, educational,
or business use. Please contact your local bookseller
or the Macmillan Corporate and Premium Sales Department
at (800) 221-7945 ext. 5442 or by email at
MacmillanSpecialMarkets@macmillan.com.

Inking by Ted Brandt

Coloring by Dee Cunniffe

Paper doll artwork by Ashe Samuels

Imprint logo designed by Amanda Spielman

First edition, 2021

Paperback ISBN 978-1-250-21259-7
10 9 8 7 6 5 4 3 2 1

Hardcover ISBN 978-1-250-15394-4
10 9 8 7 6 5 4 3 2 1

fiercereads.com

Why would you steal
what you can borrow for free
from the magical shelves
of your neighborhood library?

THIS BOOK IS FOR EVERYONE
WHO HAS A DREAM.
—ADC

FOR MY MOTHER,
WITHOUT WHOSE SUPPORT I WOULDN'T BE DOING THIS.
AND FOR RO, WITHOUT WHOM I'D BE LOST.
—TB

FOR MY BACKUPS—
CIARA, CONOR, TARA, AND FIONN
—DC

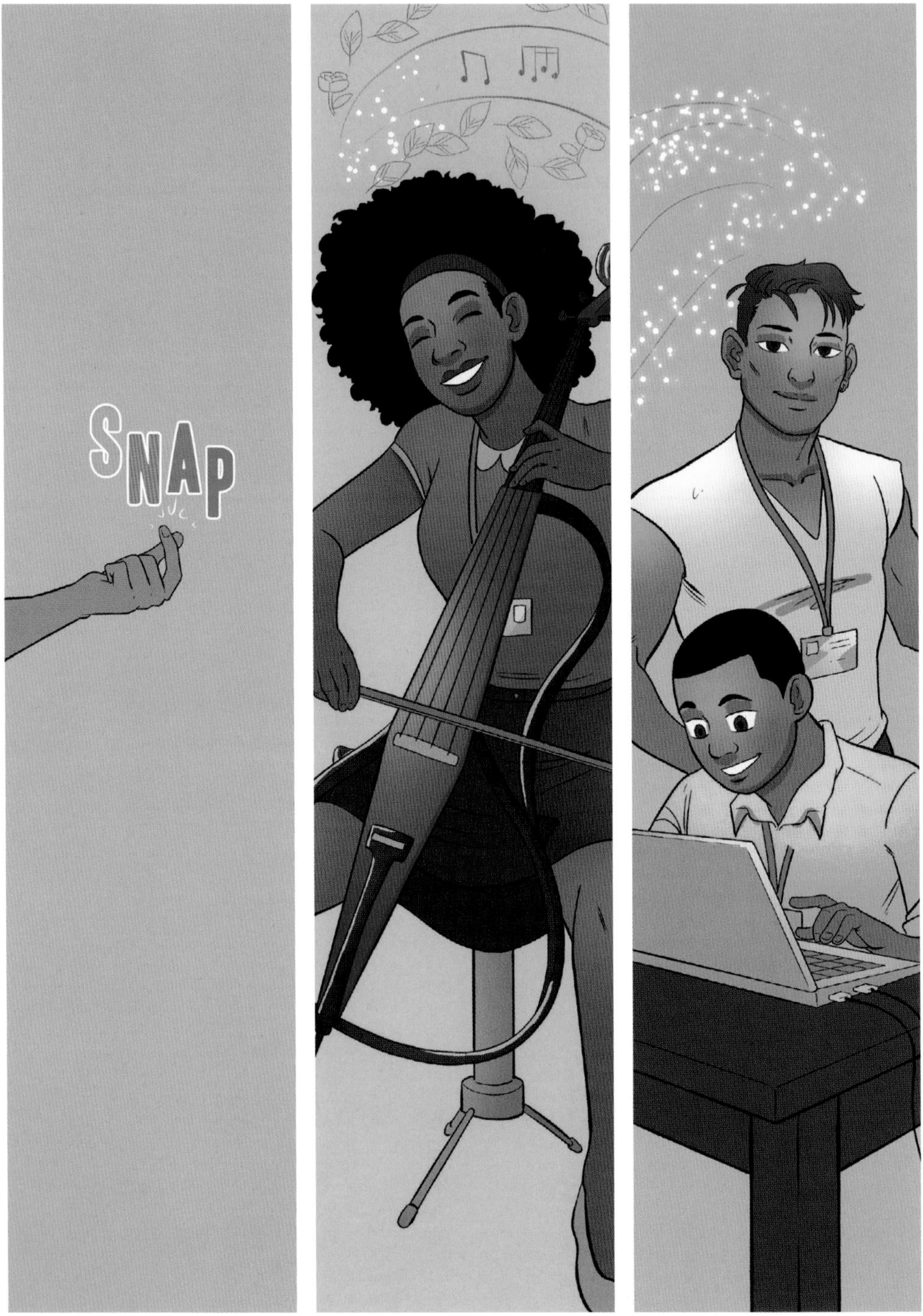
SNAP

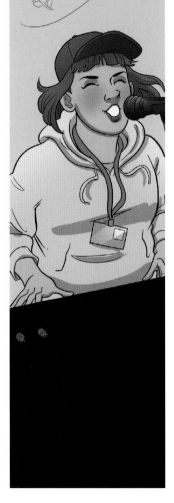

THE BACKUPS

A SUMMER OF STARDOM

Alex de Campi

Illustrated by

Lara Kane,

Dee Cunniffe,

and Ted Brandt

[Imprint]
MAKE YOUR MARK

NEW YORK

PROLOGUE

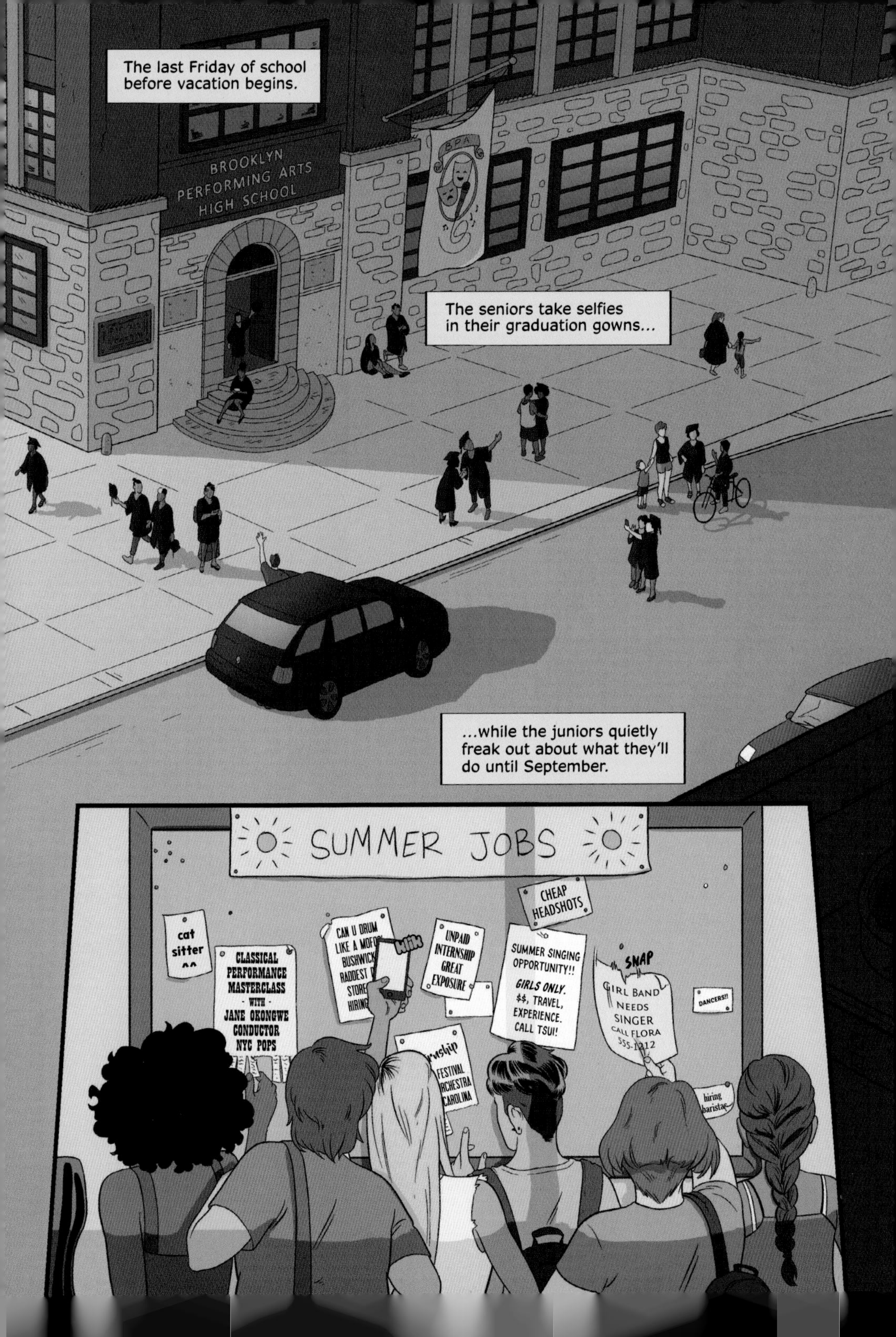
The last Friday of school before vacation begins.
BROOKLYN PERFORMING ARTS HIGH SCHOOL
BPA
The seniors take selfies in their graduation gowns...
...while the juniors quietly freak out about what they'll do until September.
SUMMER JOBS
cat sitter ^^
CLASSICAL PERFORMANCE MASTERCLASS - WITH - JANE OKONGWE CONDUCTOR NYC POPS
CAN U DRUM LIKE A MOFO BUSHWICK RADDEST D STORE HIRIN
klik
UNPAID INTERNSHIP GREAT EXPOSURE
CHEAP HEADSHOTS
SUMMER SINGING OPPORTUNITY!! GIRLS ONLY. $$, TRAVEL, EXPERIENCE. CALL TSUI!
SNAP
GIRL BAND NEEDS SINGER CALL FLORA 555-1212
DANCERS!!
FESTIVAL ORCHESTRA CAROLINA
hiring baristas

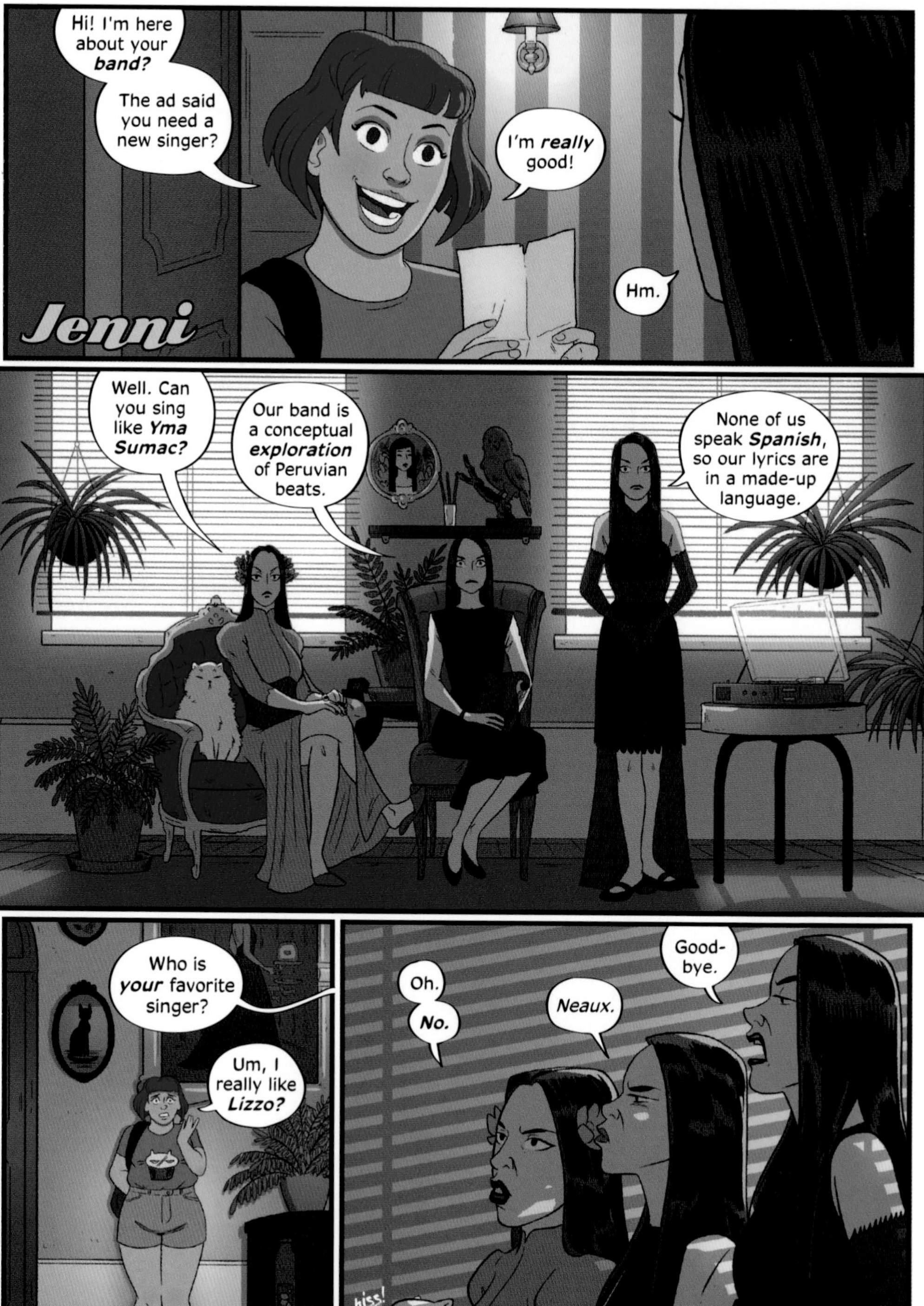
Hi! I'm here about your **band?**
The ad said you need a new singer?
I'm ***really*** good!
Hm.
Jenni
Well. Can you sing like ***Yma Sumac?***
Our band is a conceptual ***exploration*** of Peruvian beats.
None of us speak ***Spanish***, so our lyrics are in a made-up language.
Who is ***your*** favorite singer?
Um, I really like ***Lizzo?***
Oh.
No.
Neaux.
Good-bye.
hiss!

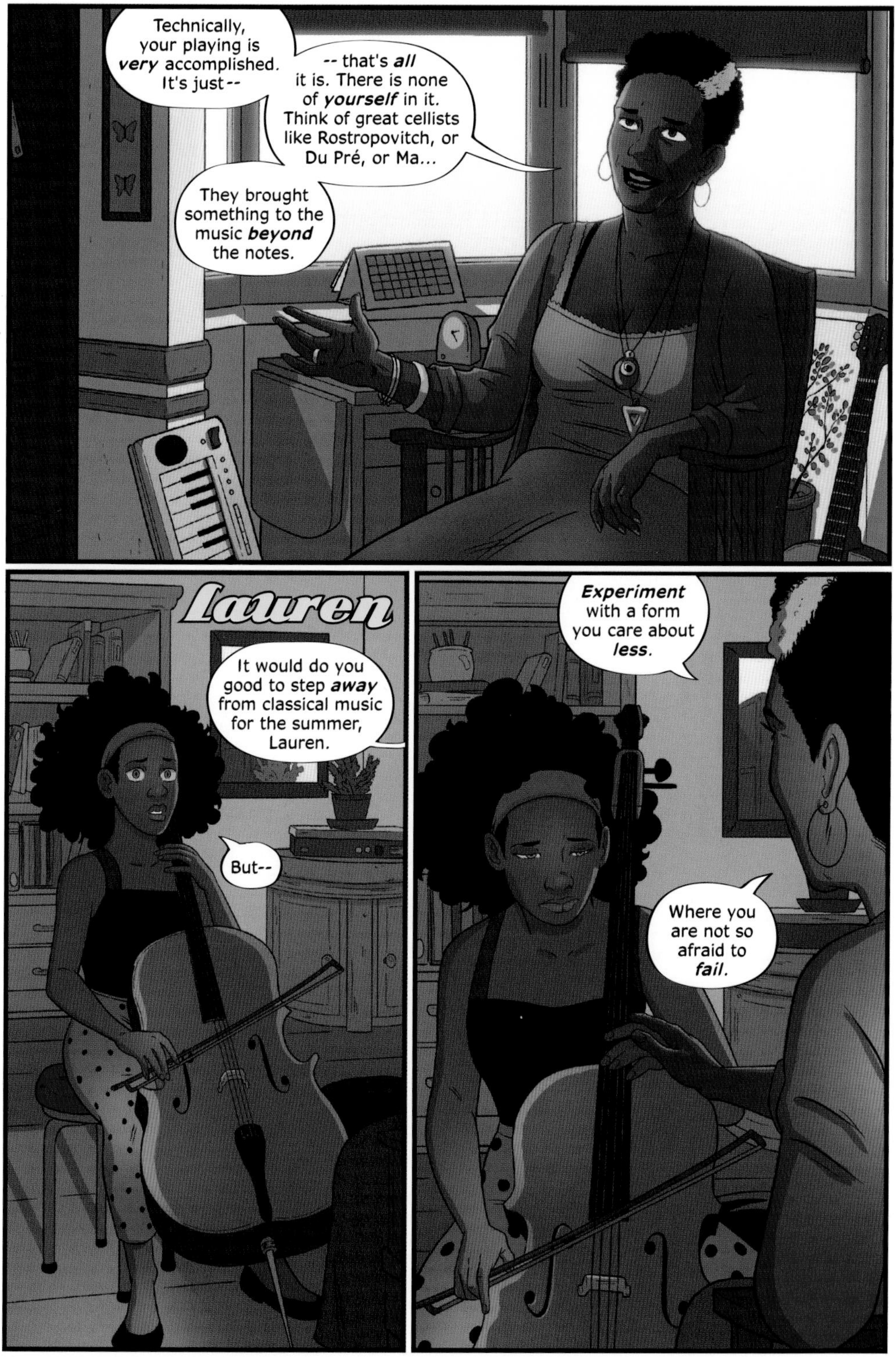
Technically, your playing is ***very*** accomplished. It's just--
-- that's ***all*** it is. There is none of ***yourself*** in it. Think of great cellists like Rostropovitch, or Du Pré, or Ma...
They brought something to the music ***beyond*** the notes.
Lauren
It would do you good to step ***away*** from classical music for the summer, Lauren.
But--
Experiment with a form you care about ***less***.
Where you are not so afraid to ***fail***.

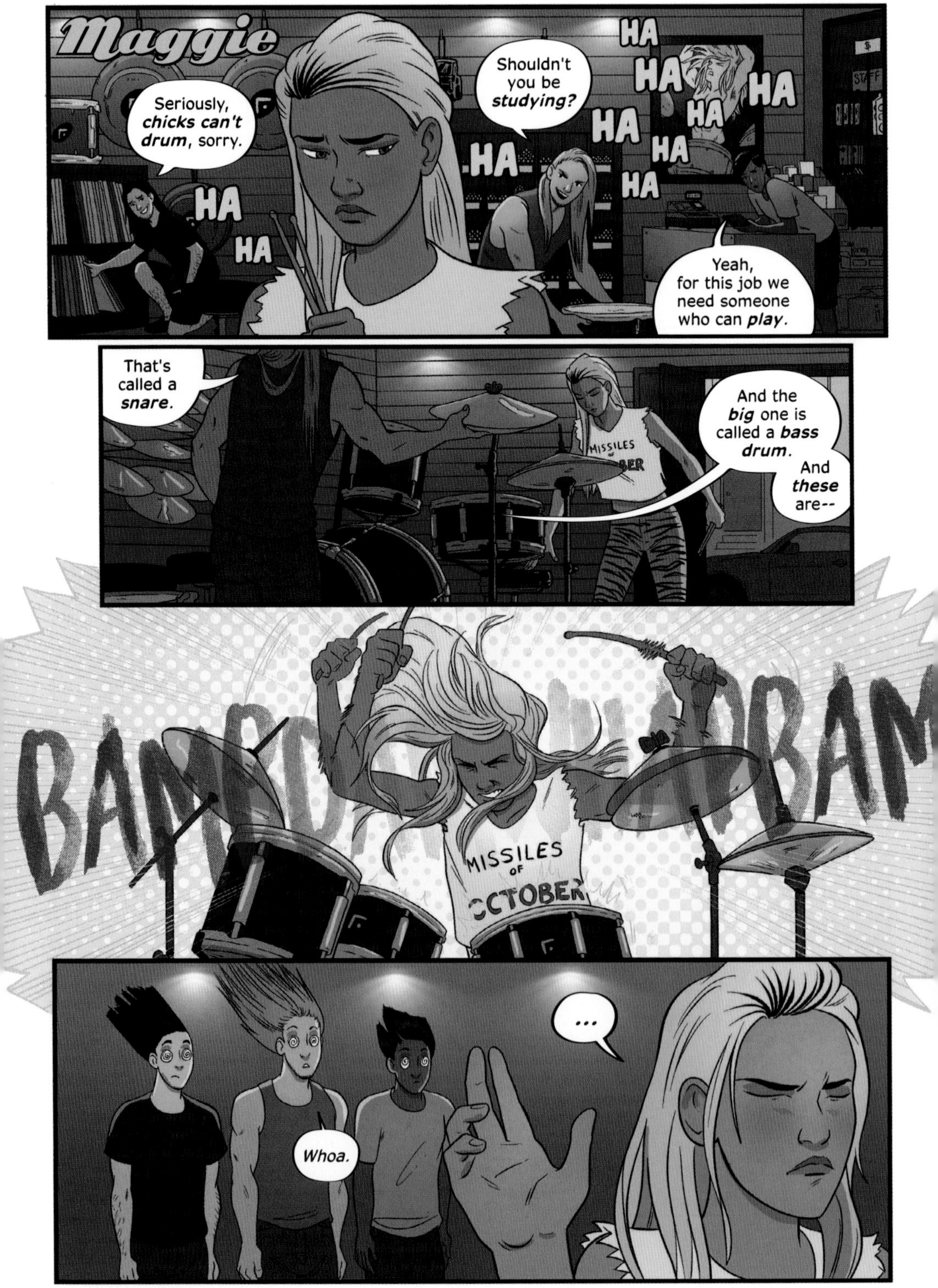
Maggie
Seriously, chicks can't drum, sorry.
Shouldn't you be studying?
HA HA HA HA HA HA HA HA HA HA
Yeah, for this job we need someone who can play.
That's called a snare.
And the big one is called a bass drum.
And these are--
MISSILES OF OCTOBER
BAMBAM
MISSILES OF OCTOBER
...
Whoa.

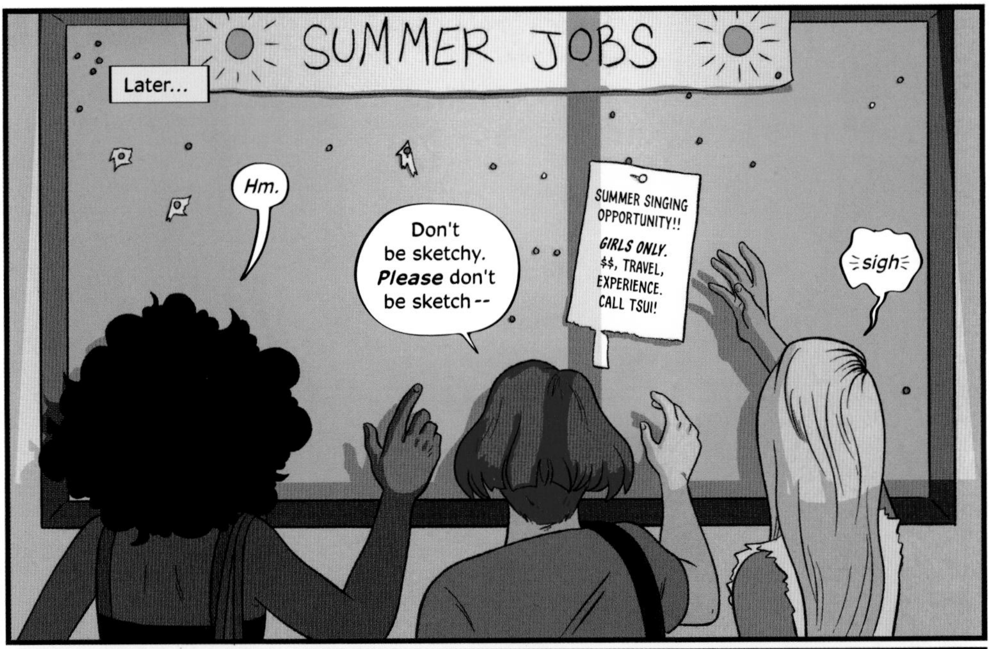
SUMMER JOBS
Later...
Hm.
Don't be sketchy. *Please* don't be sketch--
SUMMER SINGING OPPORTUNITY!! GIRLS ONLY. $$, TRAVEL, EXPERIENCE. CALL TSUI!
sigh

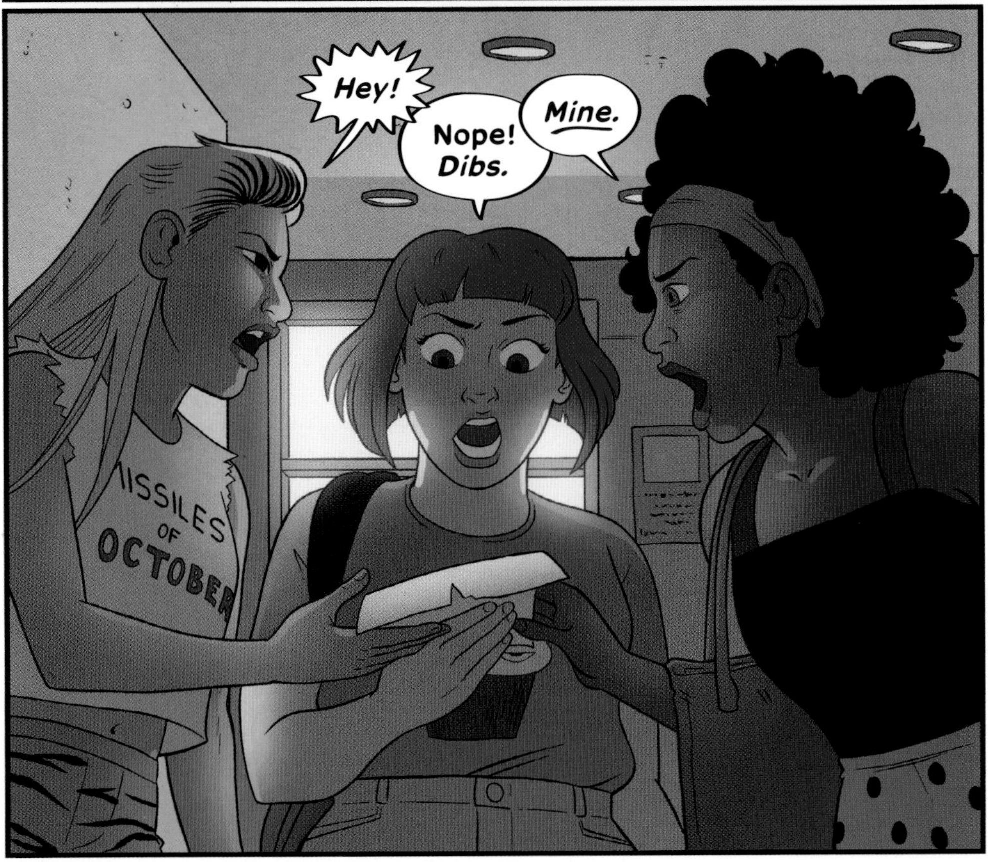
Hey!
Nope! Dibs.
Mine.
MISSILES OF OCTOBER

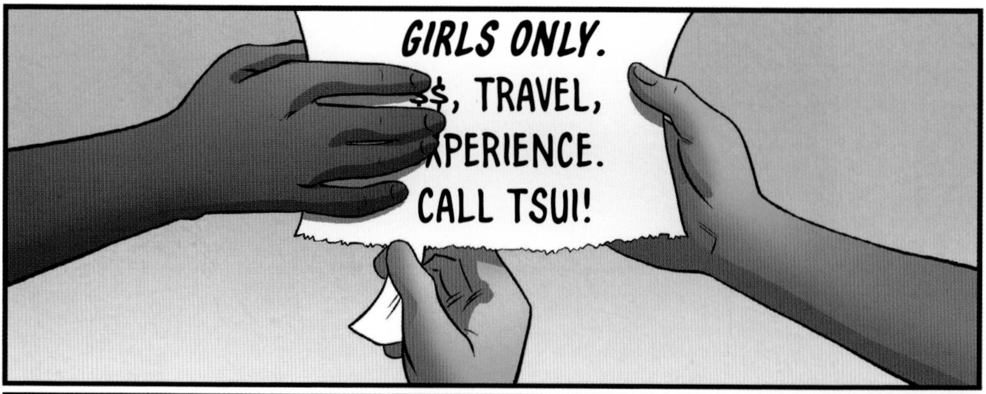
GIRLS ONLY.
$$, TRAVEL,
XPERIENCE.
CALL TSUI!

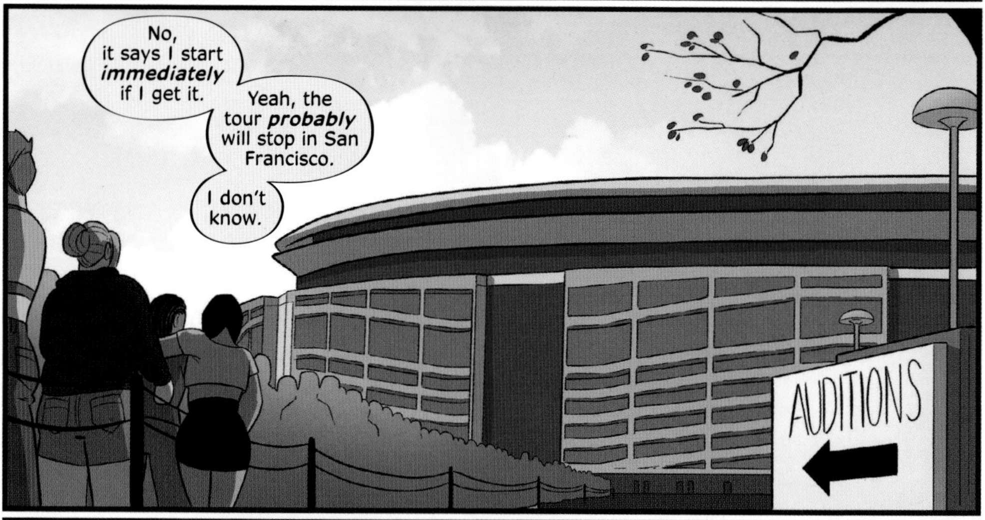
No, it says I start *immediately* if I get it.
Yeah, the tour *probably* will stop in San Francisco.
I don't know.
AUDITIONS

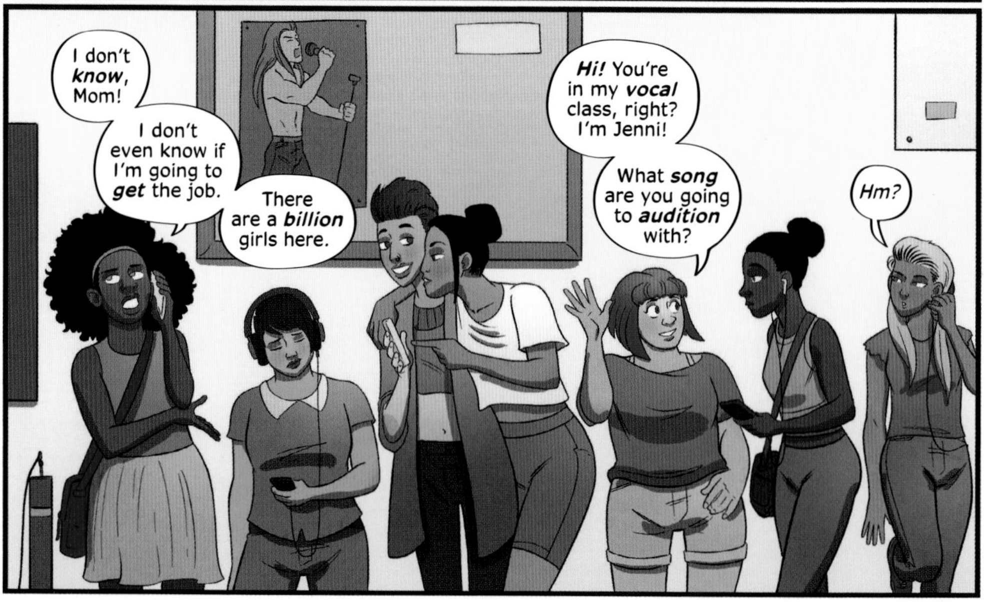
I don't *know*, Mom!
I don't even know if I'm going to *get* the job.
There are a *billion* girls here.
Hi! You're in my *vocal* class, right? I'm Jenni!
What *song* are you going to *audition* with?
Hm?

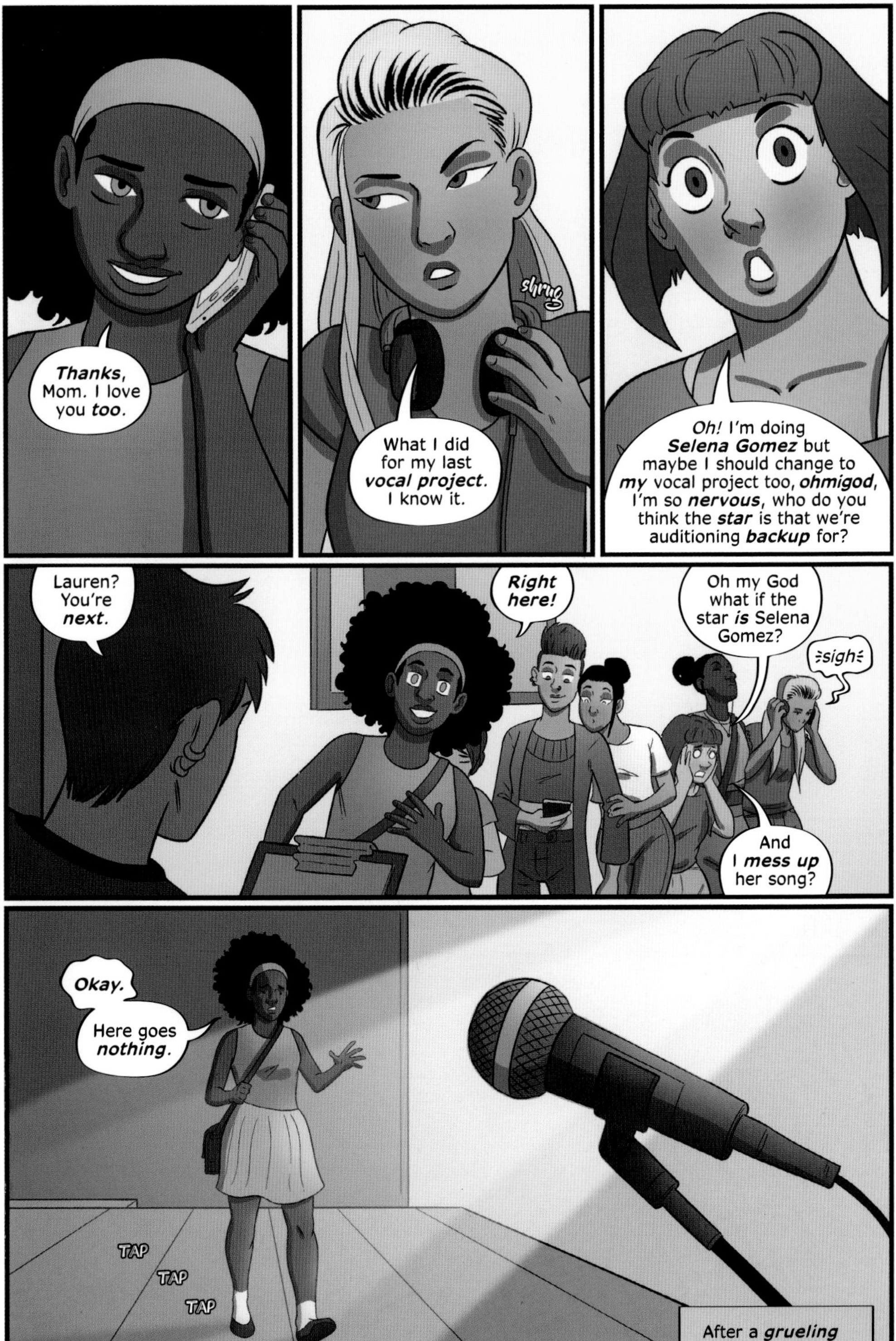
Thanks, Mom. I love you too.
What I did for my last vocal project. I know it.
shrug
Oh! I'm doing Selena Gomez but maybe I should change to my vocal project too, ohmigod, I'm so nervous, who do you think the star is that we're auditioning backup for?
Lauren? You're next.
Right here!
Oh my God what if the star is Selena Gomez?
sigh
And I mess up her song?
Okay.
Here goes nothing.
TAP
TAP
TAP
After a grueling day of callbacks...

CHAPTER
1

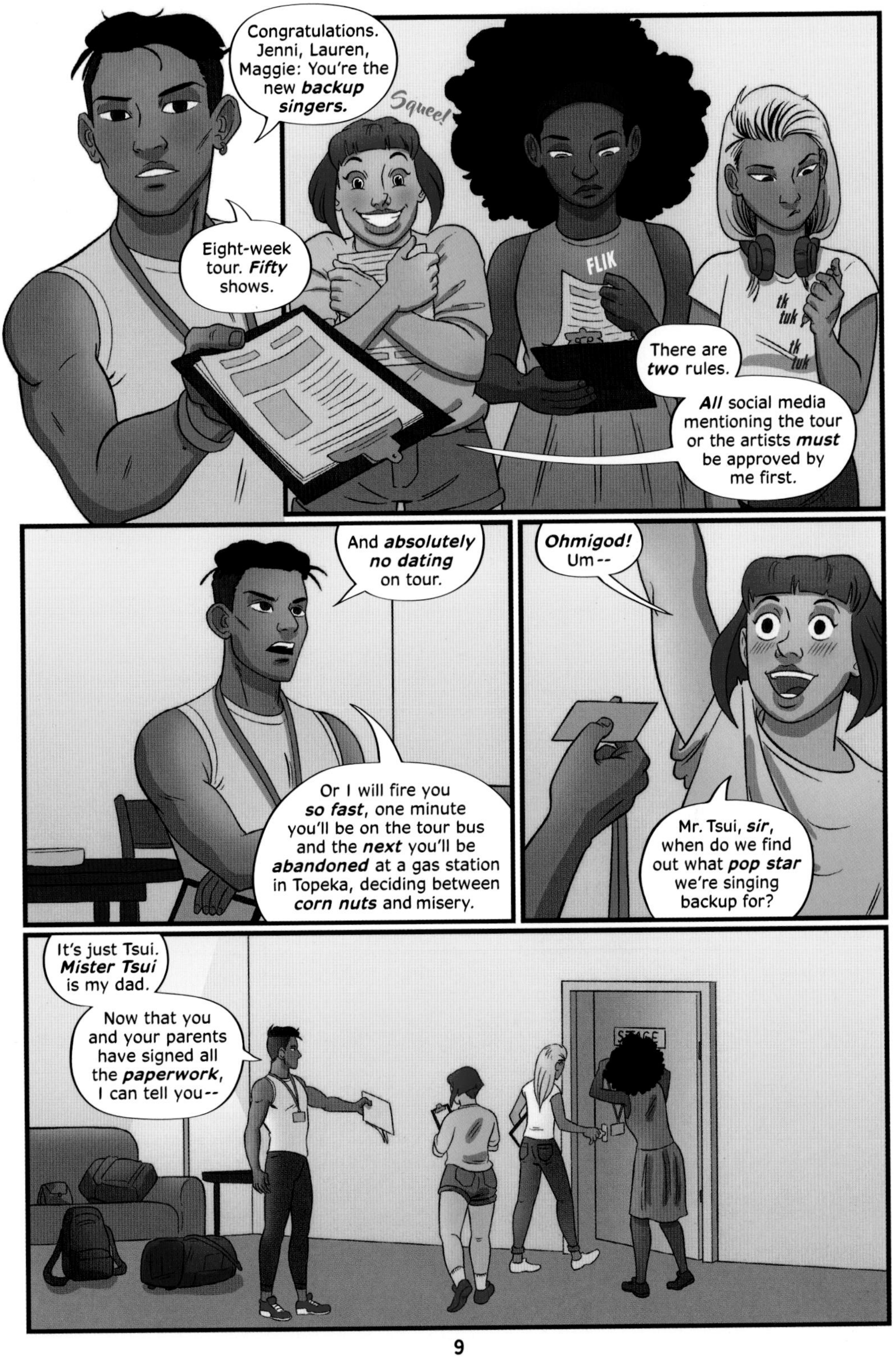
Congratulations. Jenni, Lauren, Maggie: You're the new ***backup singers.***
Squee!
Eight-week tour. ***Fifty*** shows.
FLIK
tk tuk tk tuk
There are ***two*** rules.
All social media mentioning the tour or the artists ***must*** be approved by me first.
And ***absolutely no dating*** on tour.
Or I will fire you ***so fast***, one minute you'll be on the tour bus and the ***next*** you'll be ***abandoned*** at a gas station in Topeka, deciding between ***corn nuts*** and misery.
Ohmigod! Um--
Mr. Tsui, ***sir***, when do we find out what ***pop star*** we're singing backup for?
It's just Tsui. ***Mister Tsui*** is my dad.
Now that you and your parents have signed all the ***paperwork***, I can tell you--
STAGE

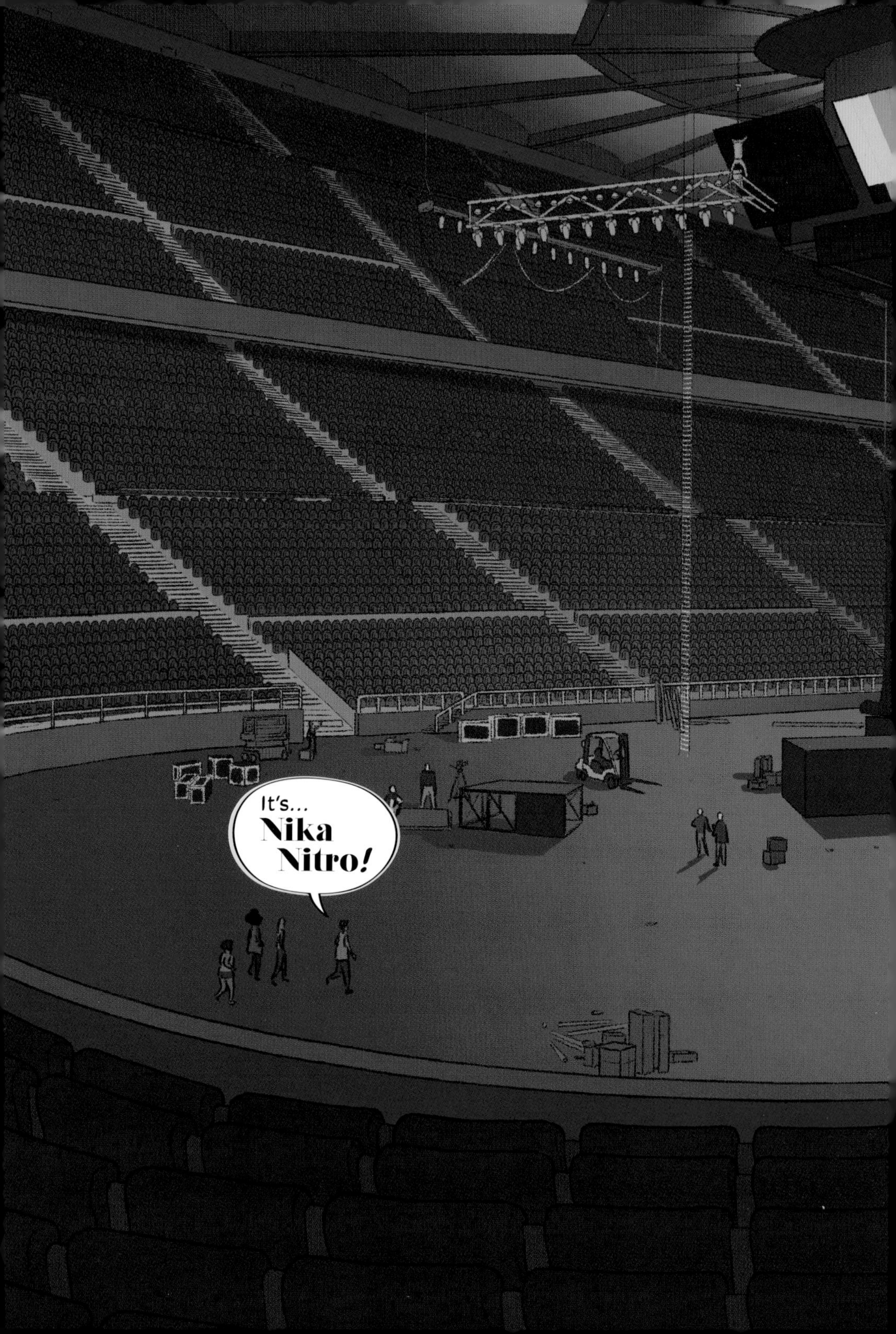
It's... Nika Nitro!

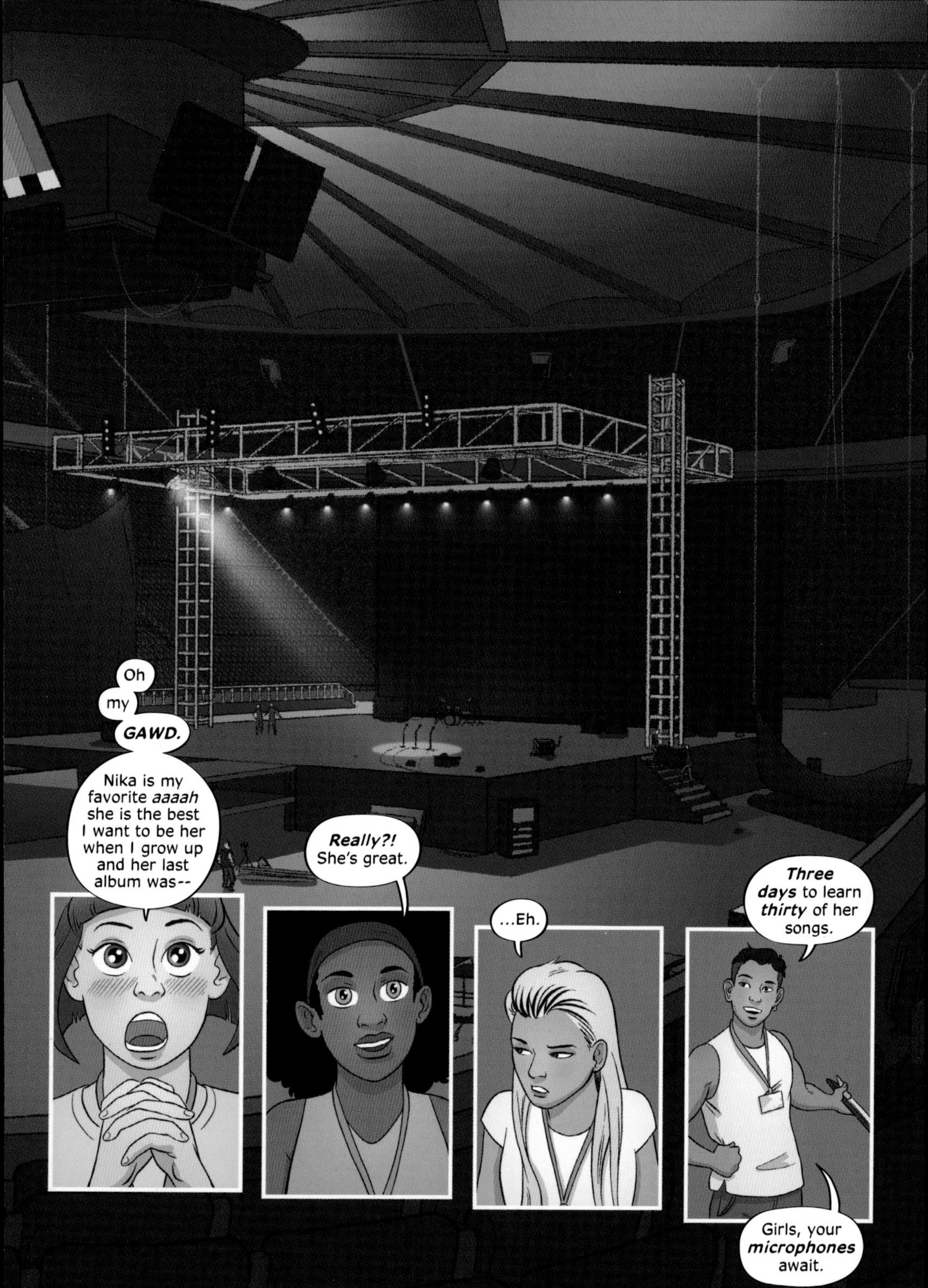
Oh
my
GAWD.
Nika is my favorite *aaaah* she is the best I want to be her when I grow up and her last album was--
Really?! She's great.
...Eh.
Three days to learn ***thirty*** of her songs.
Girls, your ***microphones*** await.

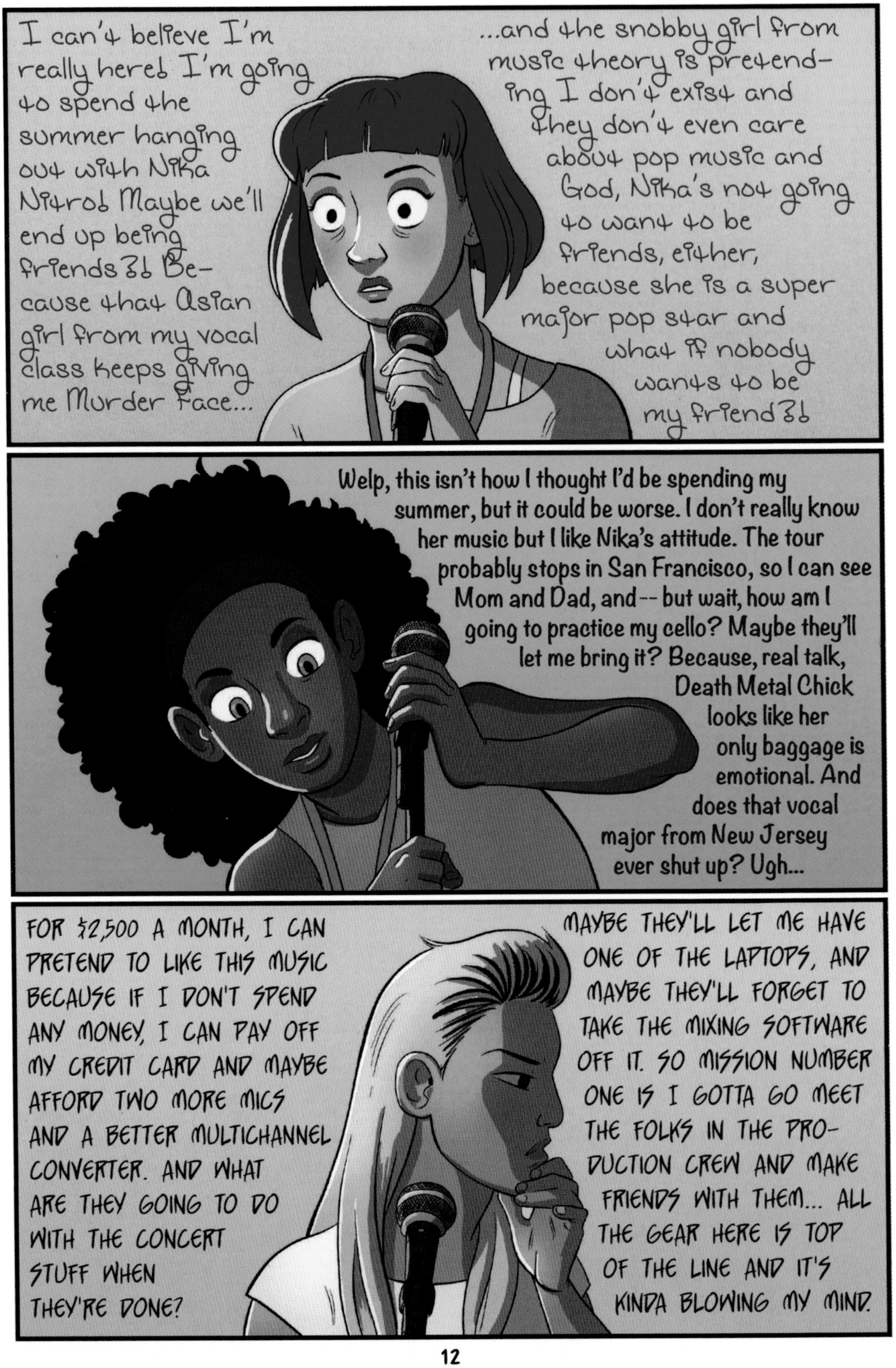
I can't believe I'm really here! I'm going to spend the summer hanging out with Nika Nitro! Maybe we'll end up being friends?! Be-cause that Asian girl from my vocal class keeps giving me Murder Face...
...and the snobby girl from music theory is pretend-ing I don't exist and they don't even care about pop music and God, Nika's not going to want to be friends, either, because she is a super major pop star and what if nobody wants to be my friend?!
Welp, this isn't how I thought I'd be spending my summer, but it could be worse. I don't really know her music but I like Nika's attitude. The tour probably stops in San Francisco, so I can see Mom and Dad, and -- but wait, how am I going to practice my cello? Maybe they'll let me bring it? Because, real talk, Death Metal Chick looks like her only baggage is emotional. And does that vocal major from New Jersey ever shut up? Ugh...
FOR $2,500 A MONTH, I CAN PRETEND TO LIKE THIS MUSIC BECAUSE IF I DON'T SPEND ANY MONEY, I CAN PAY OFF MY CREDIT CARD AND MAYBE AFFORD TWO MORE MICS AND A BETTER MULTICHANNEL CONVERTER. AND WHAT ARE THEY GOING TO DO WITH THE CONCERT STUFF WHEN THEY'RE DONE?
MAYBE THEY'LL LET ME HAVE ONE OF THE LAPTOPS, AND MAYBE THEY'LL FORGET TO TAKE THE MIXING SOFTWARE OFF IT. SO MISSION NUMBER ONE IS I GOTTA GO MEET THE FOLKS IN THE PRO-DUCTION CREW AND MAKE FRIENDS WITH THEM... ALL THE GEAR HERE IS TOP OF THE LINE AND IT'S KINDA BLOWING MY MIND.

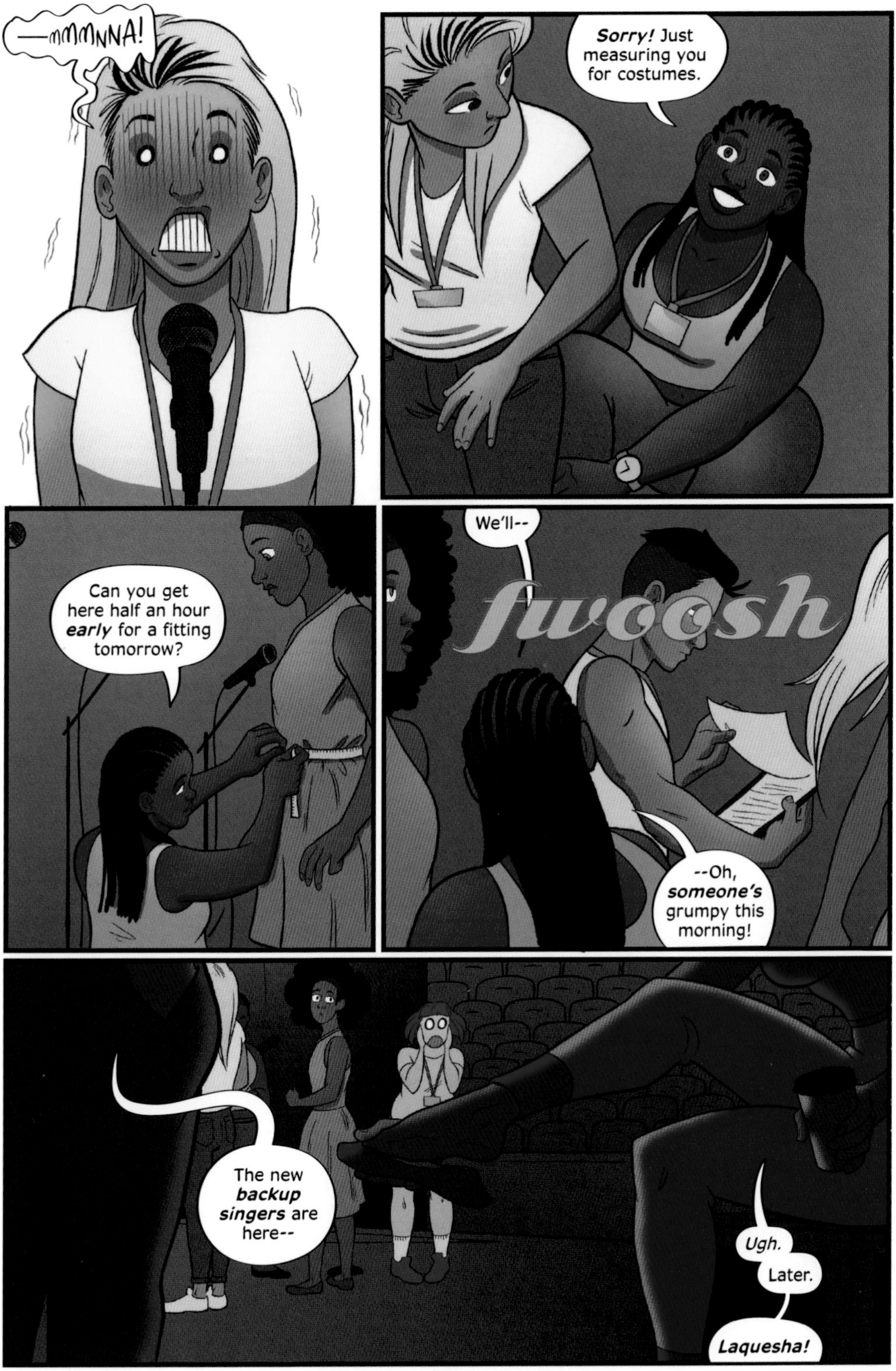
—MMMNNA!
Sorry! Just measuring you for costumes.
Can you get here half an hour *early* for a fitting tomorrow?
We'll--
fwoosh
--Oh, *someone's* grumpy this morning!
The new *backup singers* are here--
Ugh.
Later.
Laquesha!

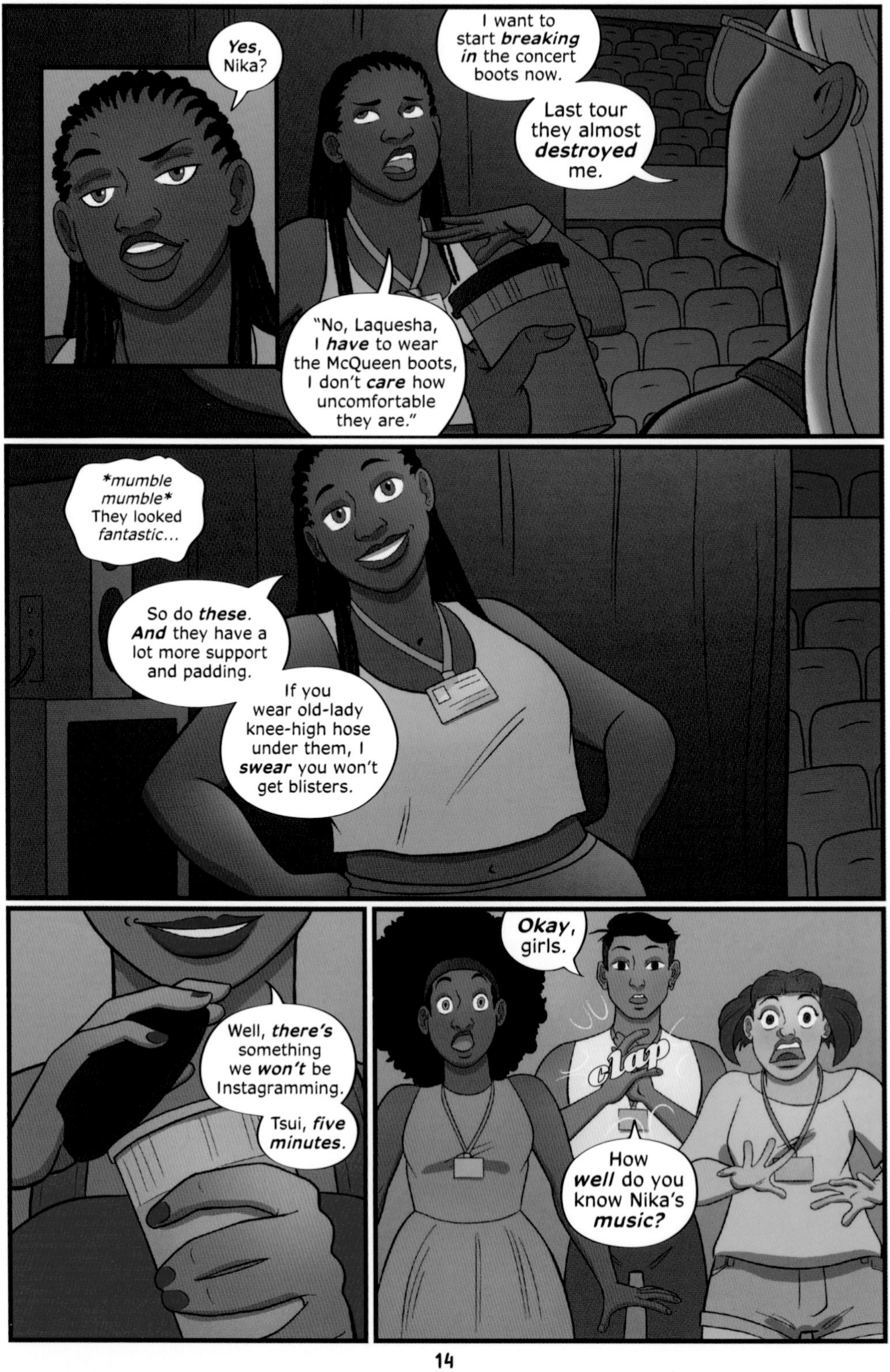
Yes, Nika?
I want to start breaking in the concert boots now.
Last tour they almost destroyed me.
"No, Laquesha, I have to wear the McQueen boots, I don't care how uncomfortable they are."
mumble mumble They looked fantastic...
So do these. And they have a lot more support and padding.
If you wear old-lady knee-high hose under them, I swear you won't get blisters.
Well, there's something we won't be Instagramming.
Tsui, five minutes.
Okay, girls.
clap
How well do you know Nika's music?

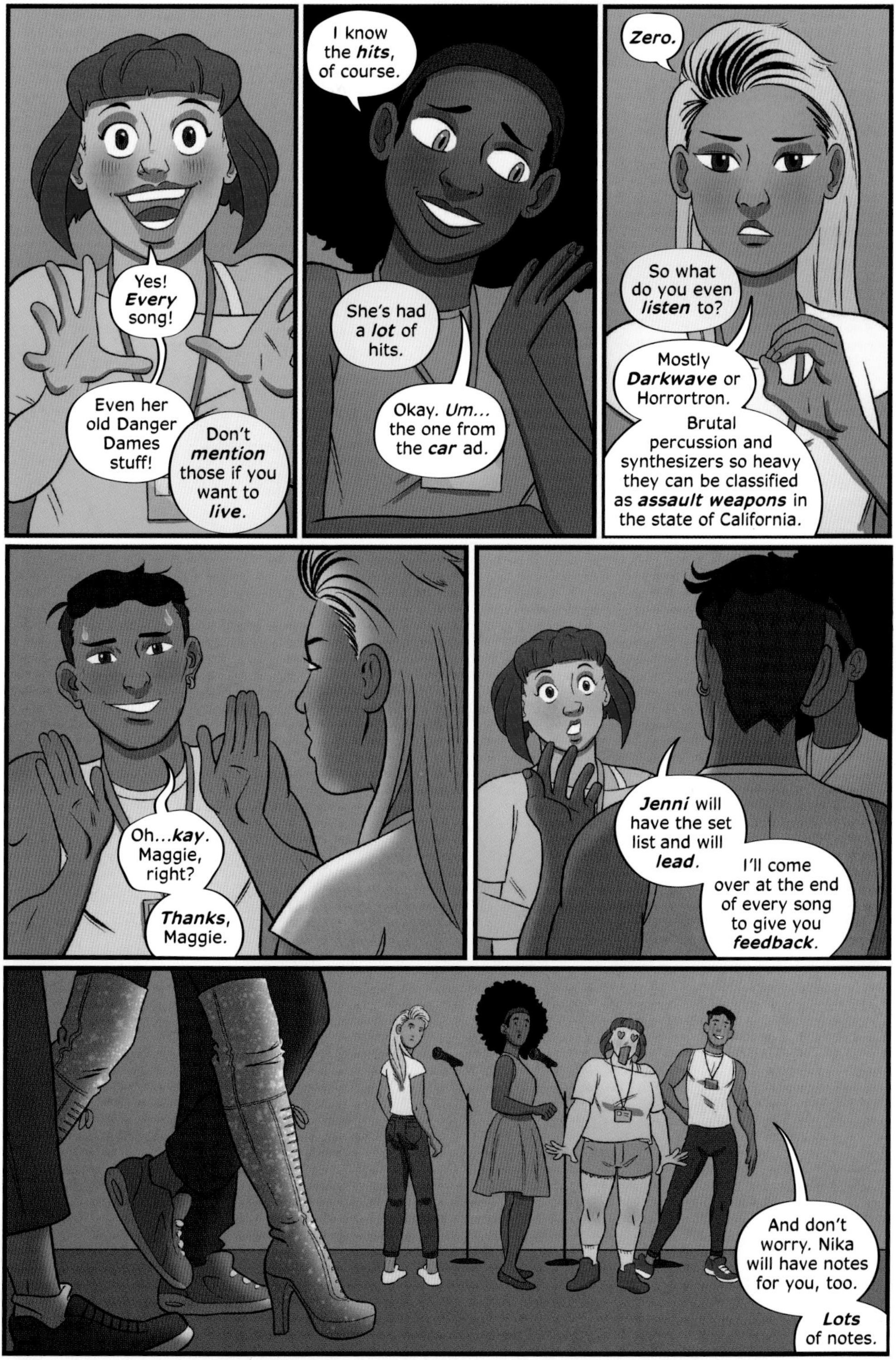
Yes! *Every* song!
Even her old Danger Dames stuff!
Don't *mention* those if you want to *live*.
I know the *hits*, of course.
She's had a *lot* of hits.
Okay. *Um...* the one from the *car* ad.
Zero.
So what do you even *listen* to?
Mostly *Darkwave* or Horrortron.
Brutal percussion and synthesizers so heavy they can be classified as *assault weapons* in the state of California.
Oh...*kay*. Maggie, right?
Thanks, Maggie.
Jenni will have the set list and will *lead*.
I'll come over at the end of every song to give you *feedback*.
And don't worry. Nika will have notes for you, too.
Lots of notes.

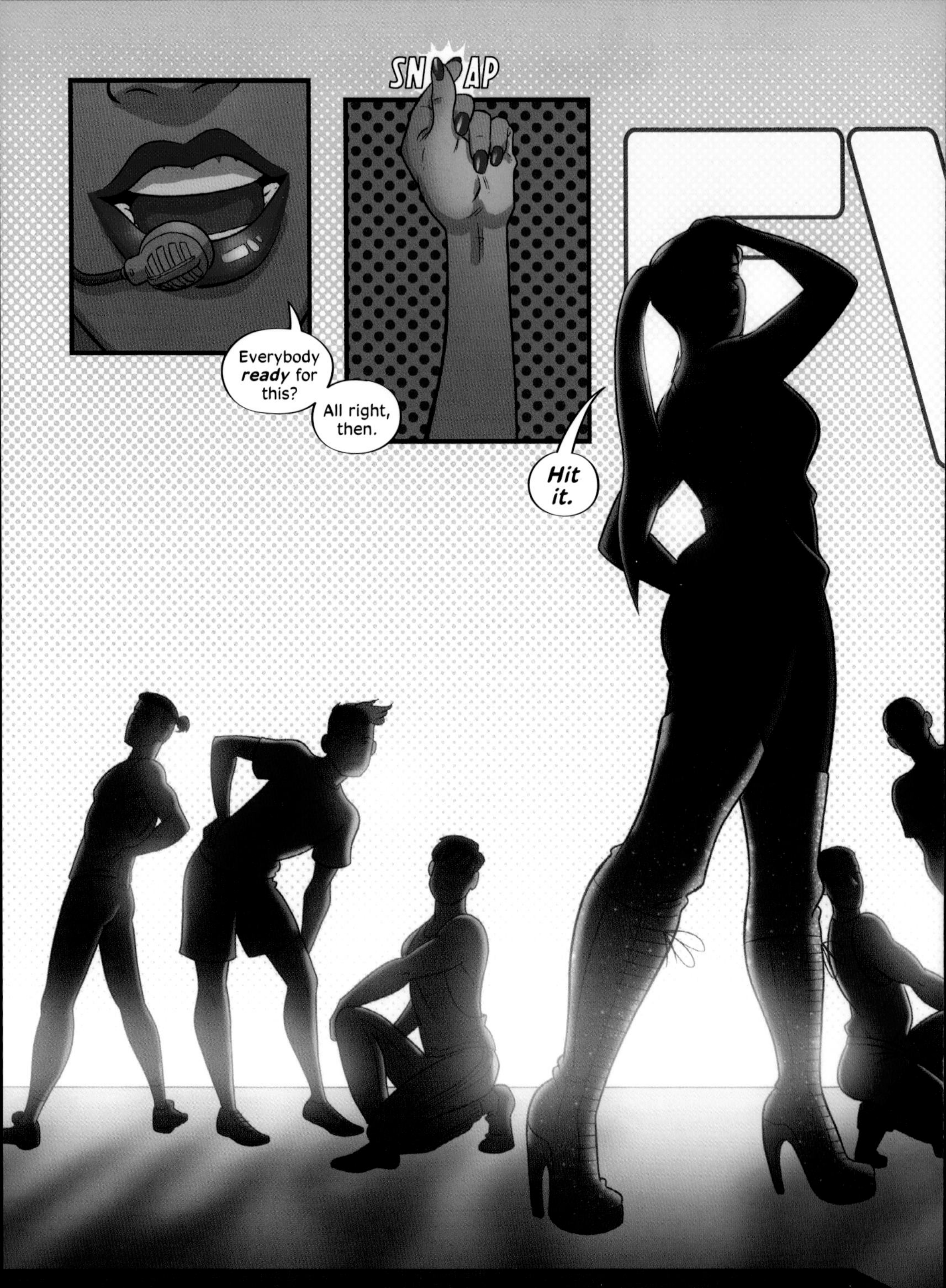
SNAP
Everybody *ready* for this?
All right, then.
Hit it.

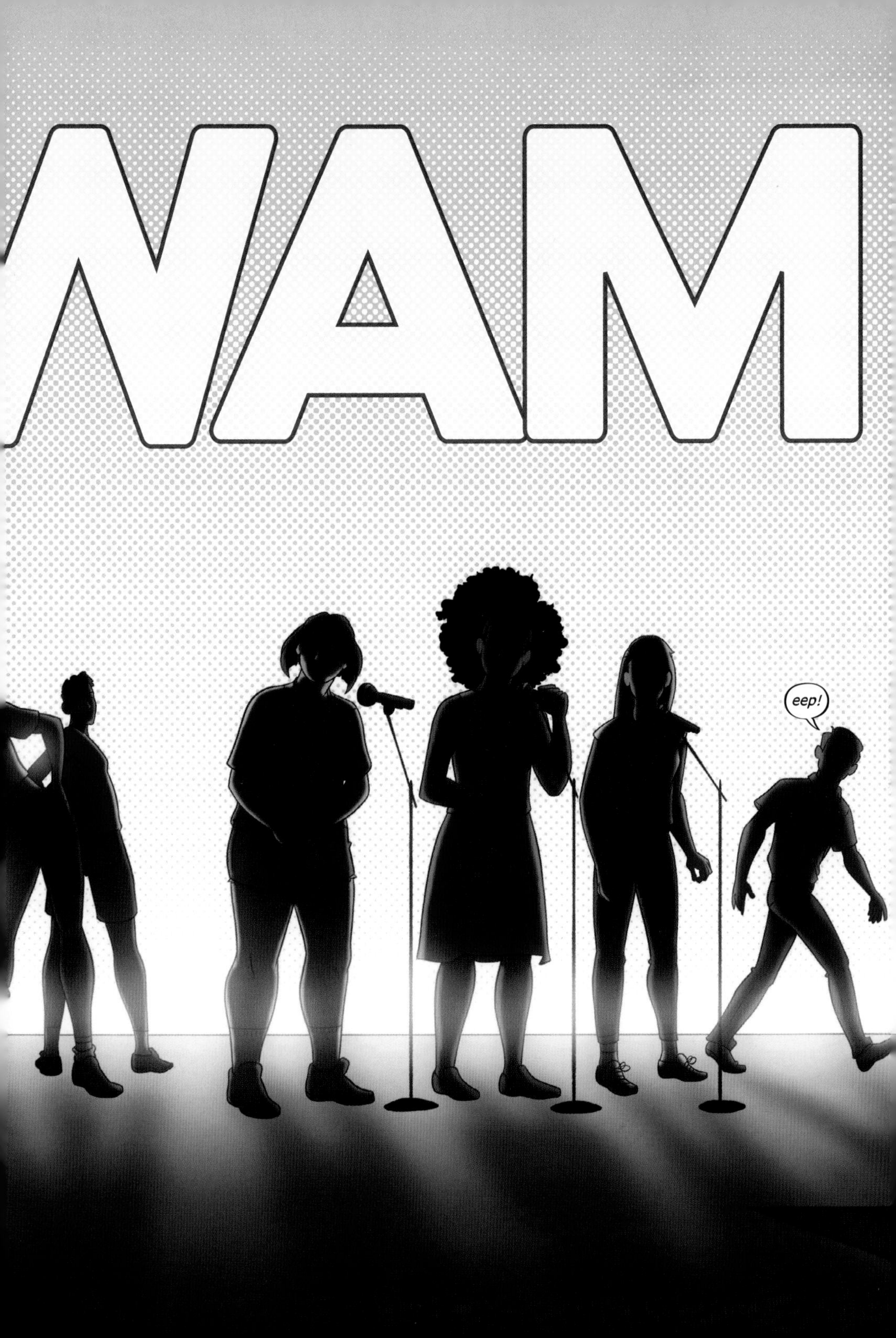
WAM
eep!

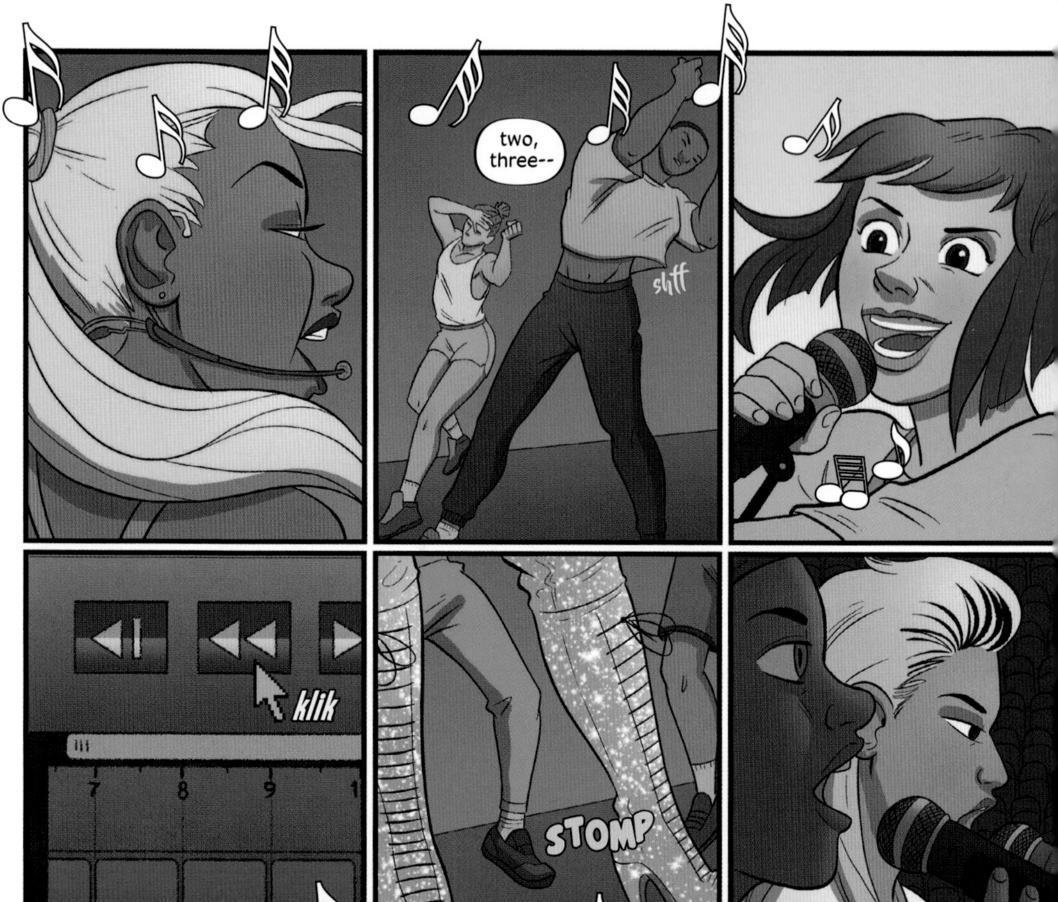
two, three--
shff
klik
STOMP
Down.
Now.
Sorry...
They're *high schoolers*, Nika.
It's their *first day.*
Gonna be their *last*, too.

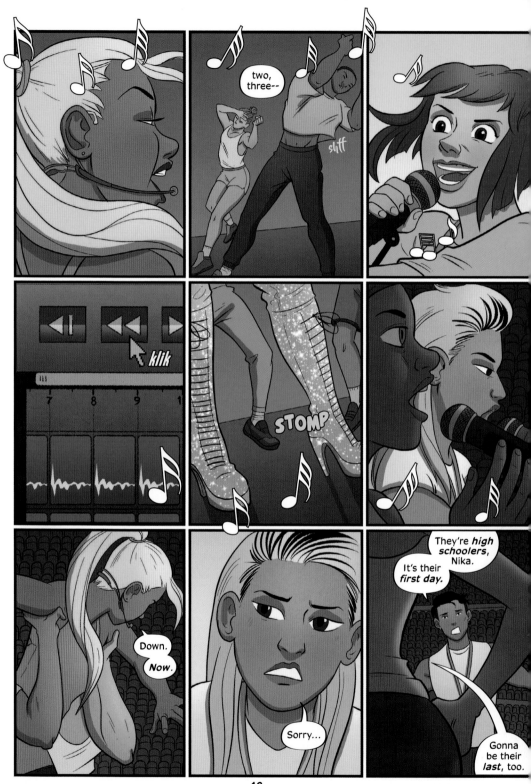

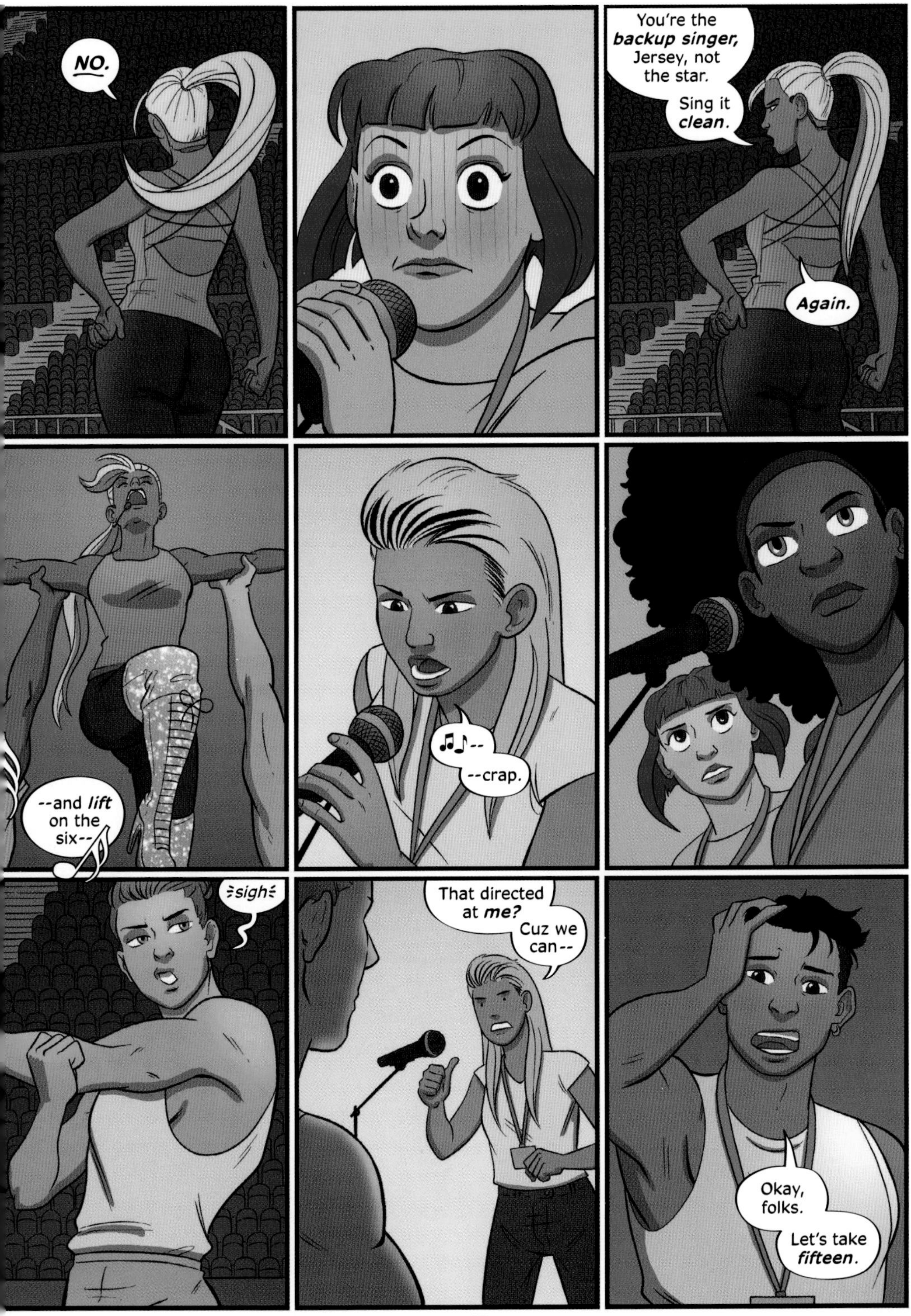
NO.
You're the backup singer, Jersey, not the star.
Sing it clean.
Again.
--and lift on the six--
--
--crap.
sigh
That directed at me?
Cuz we can--
Okay, folks.
Let's take fifteen.

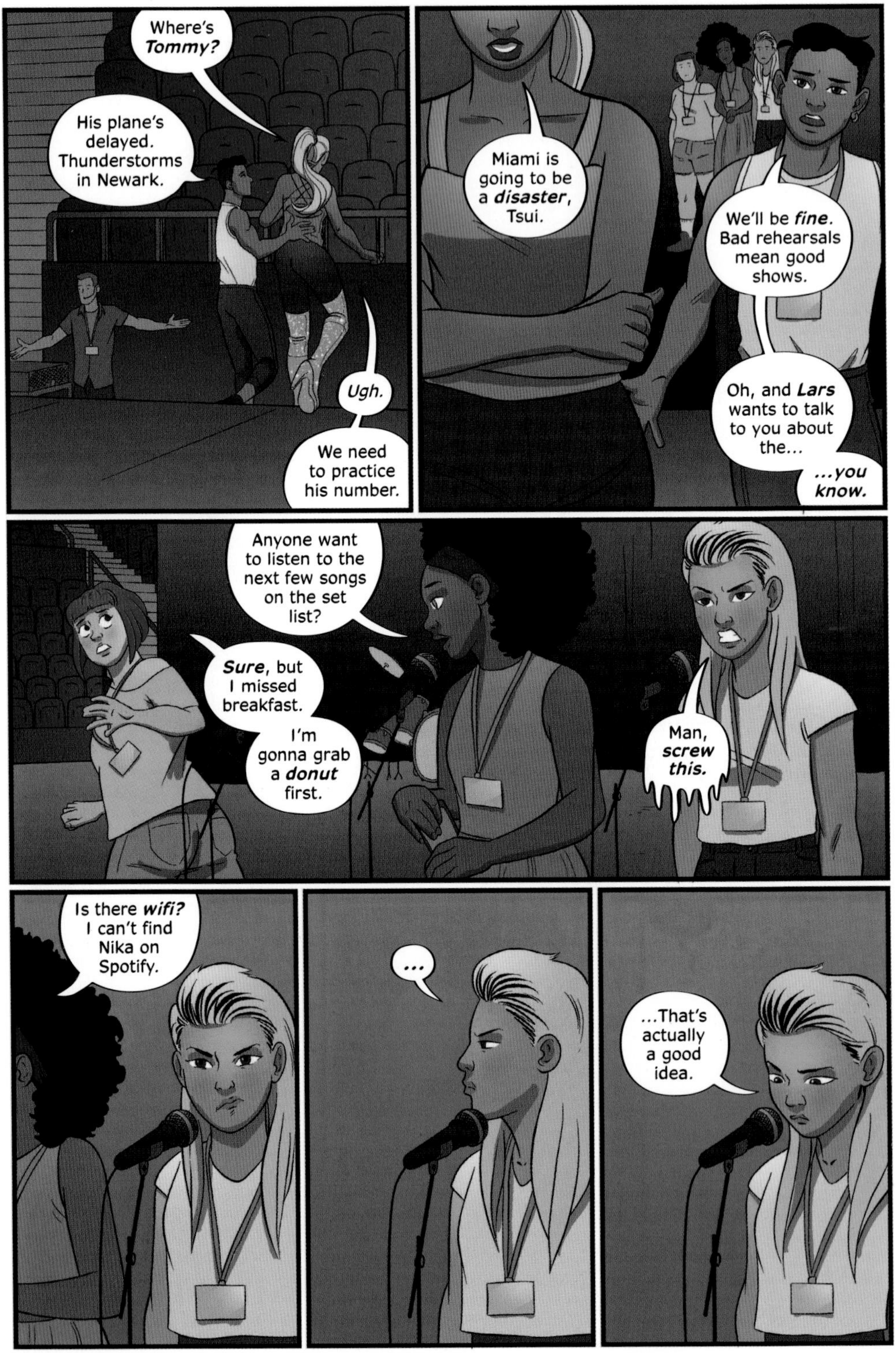
Where's *Tommy?*
His plane's delayed. Thunderstorms in Newark.
Ugh.
We need to practice his number.
Miami is going to be a ***disaster***, Tsui.
We'll be ***fine.*** Bad rehearsals mean good shows.
Oh, and ***Lars*** wants to talk to you about the...
...you know.
Anyone want to listen to the next few songs on the set list?
Sure, but I missed breakfast.
I'm gonna grab a ***donut*** first.
Man, ***screw this.***
Is there ***wifi?*** I can't find Nika on Spotify.
...
...That's actually a good idea.

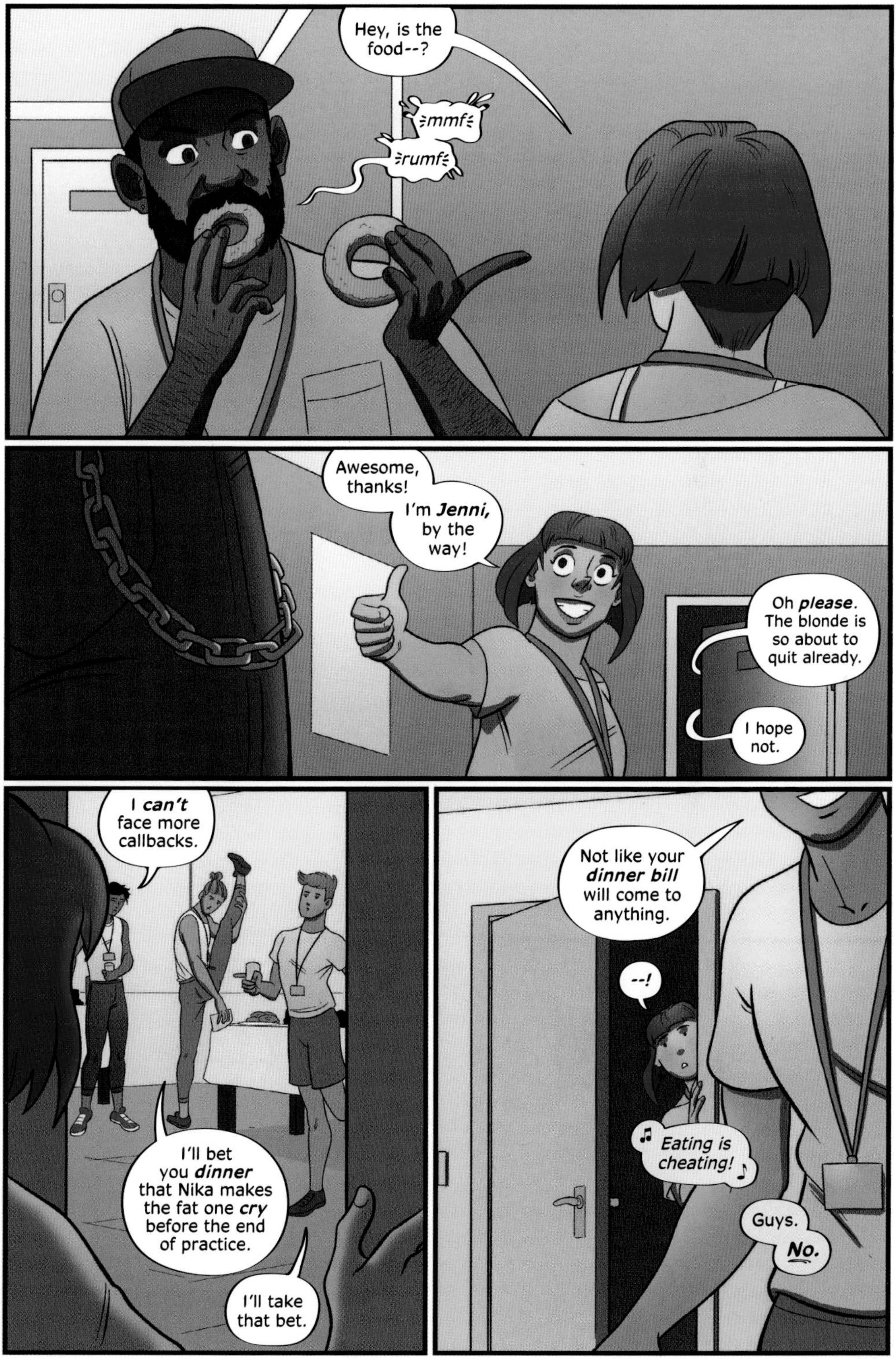
Hey, is the food--?
mmf
rumf
Awesome, thanks!
I'm *Jenni,* by the way!
Oh *please*. The blonde is so about to quit already.
I hope not.
I *can't* face more callbacks.
I'll bet you *dinner* that Nika makes the fat one *cry* before the end of practice.
I'll take that bet.
Not like your *dinner bill* will come to anything.
--!
Eating is cheating!
Guys. No.

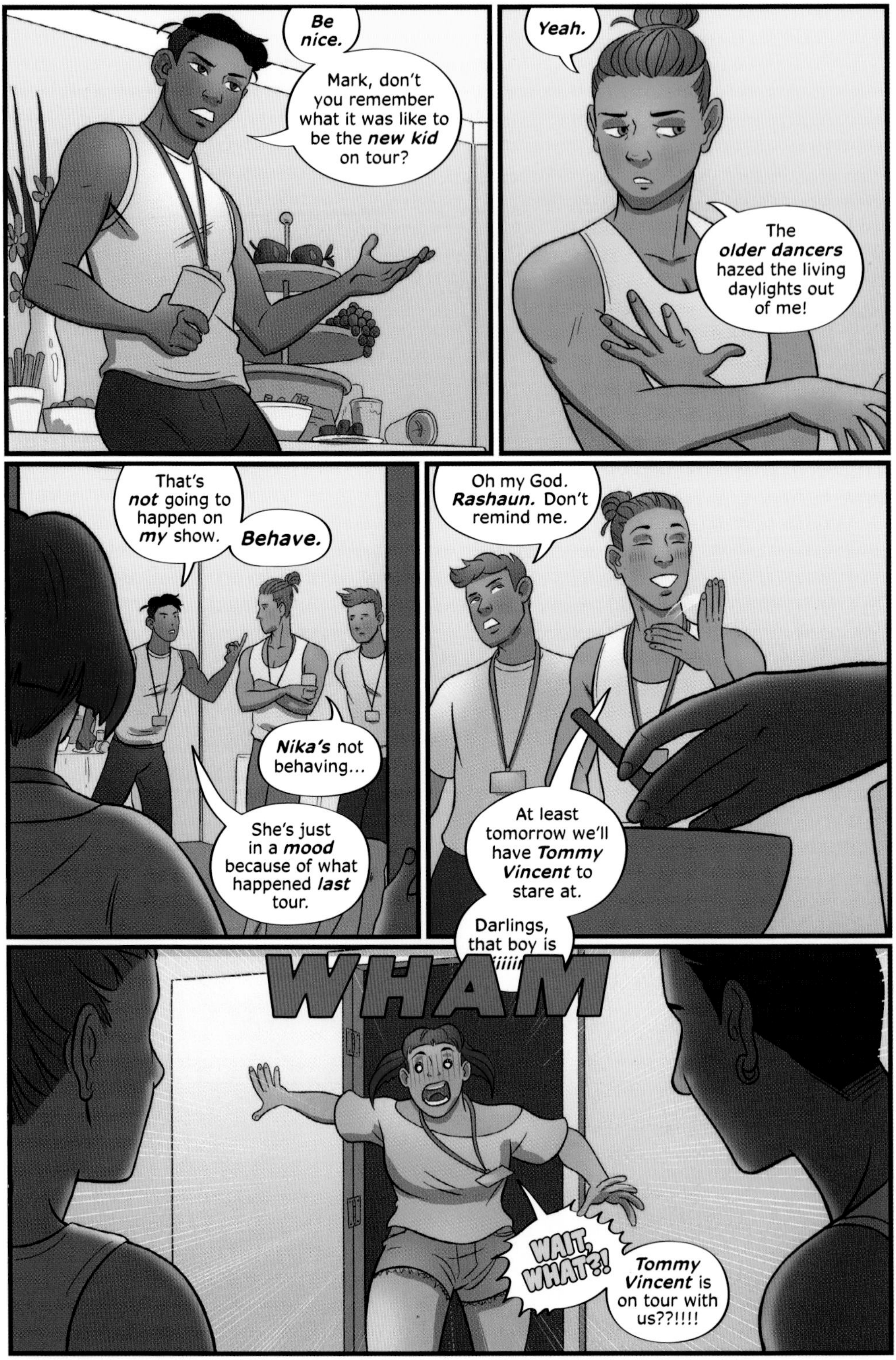
Be nice.
Mark, don't you remember what it was like to be the *new kid* on tour?
Yeah.
The *older dancers* hazed the living daylights out of me!
That's *not* going to happen on *my* show.
Behave.
Nika's not behaving...
She's just in a *mood* because of what happened *last* tour.
Oh my God. *Rashaun.* Don't remind me.
At least tomorrow we'll have *Tommy Vincent* to stare at.
Darlings, that boy is
WHAM
WAIT, WHAT?!
Tommy Vincent is on tour with us??!!!!

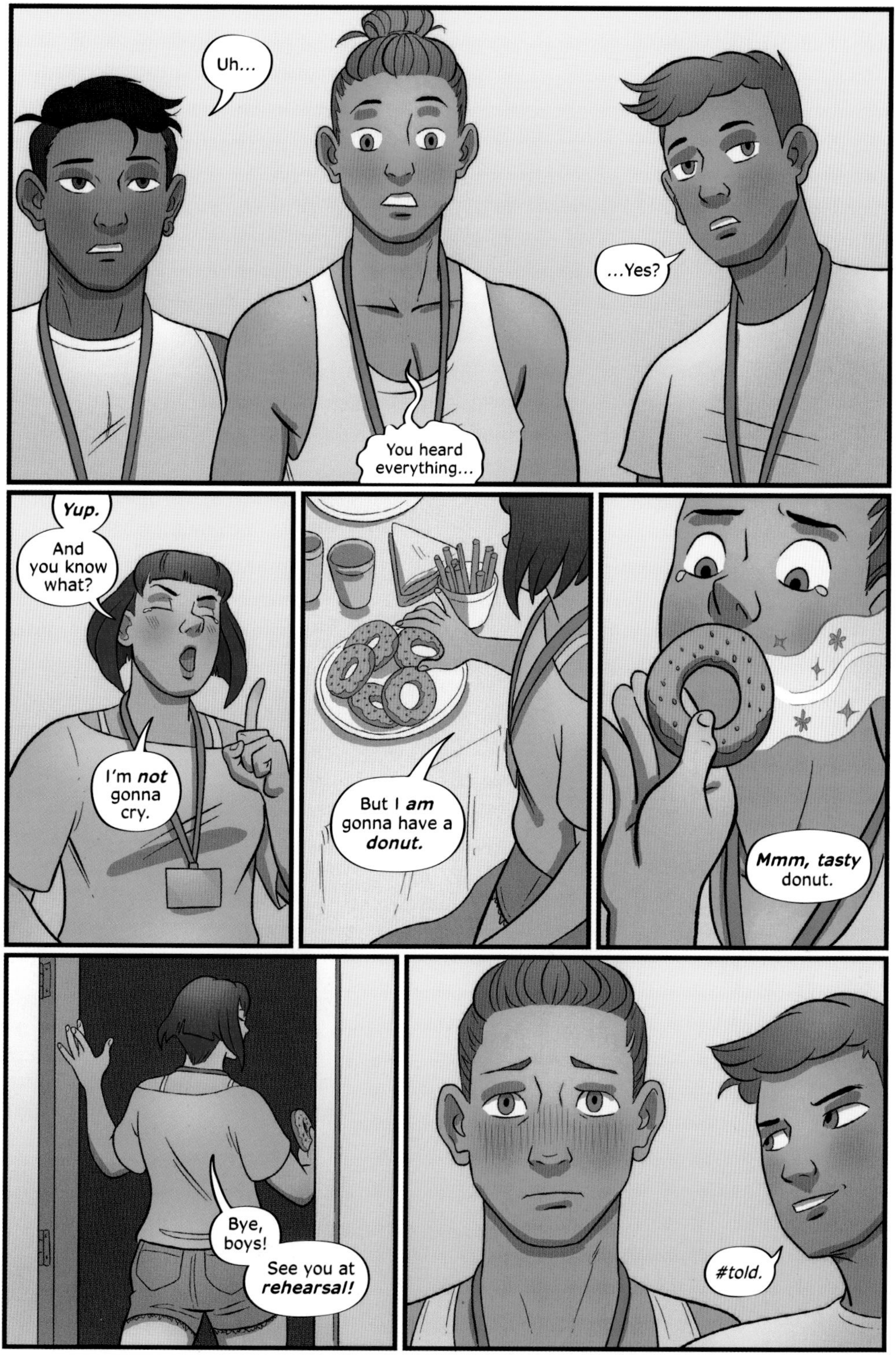
Uh...
...Yes?
You heard everything...
Yup.
And you know what?
I'm not gonna cry.
But I am gonna have a donut.
Mmm, tasty donut.
Bye, boys!
See you at rehearsal!
#told.

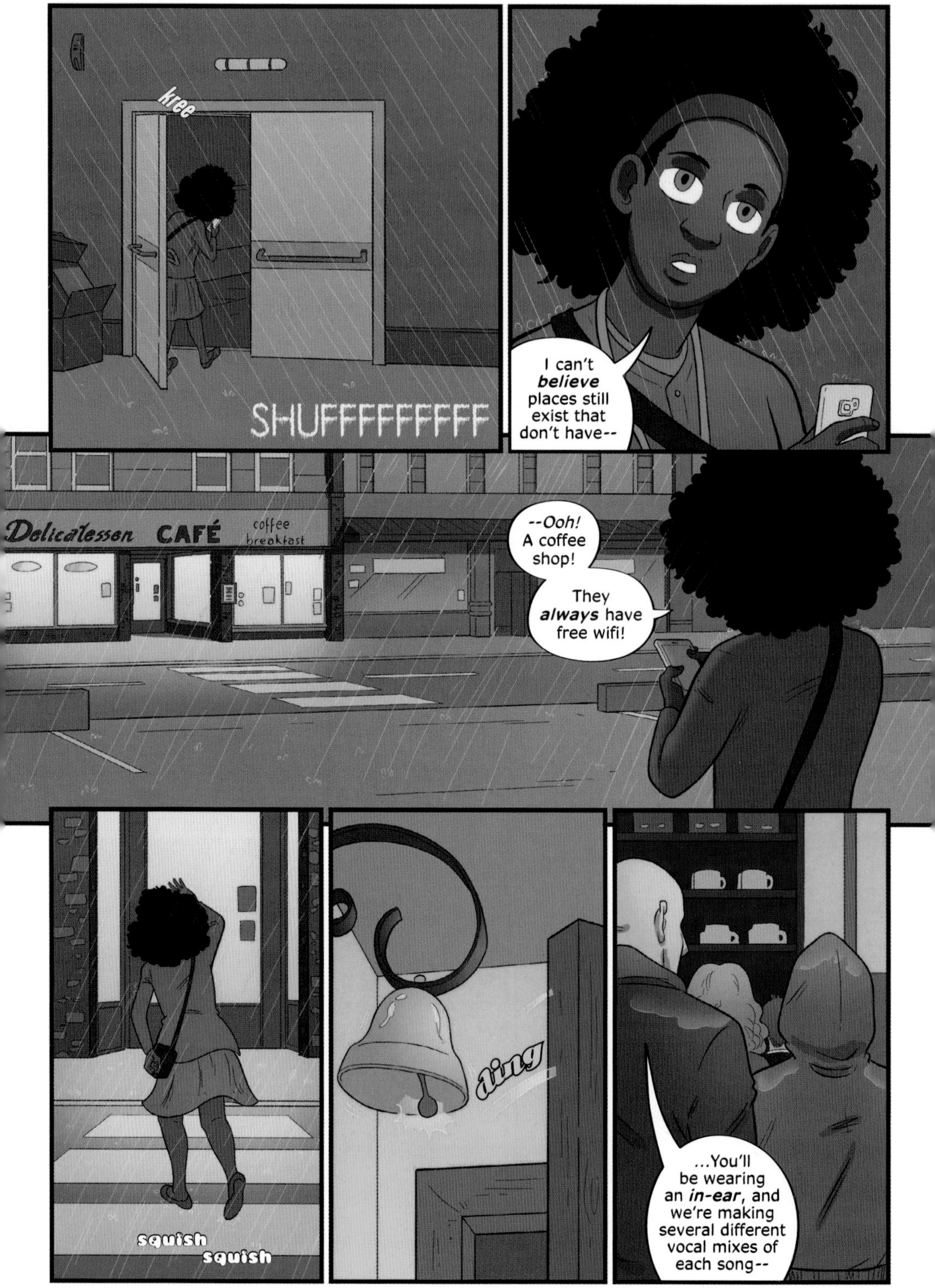
kree
SHUFFFFFFFFF
I can't *believe* places still exist that don't have--
Delicatessen CAFÉ coffee breakfast
--*Ooh!* A coffee shop!
They *always* have free wifi!
squish squish
ding
...You'll be wearing an *in-ear*, and we're making several different vocal mixes of each song--

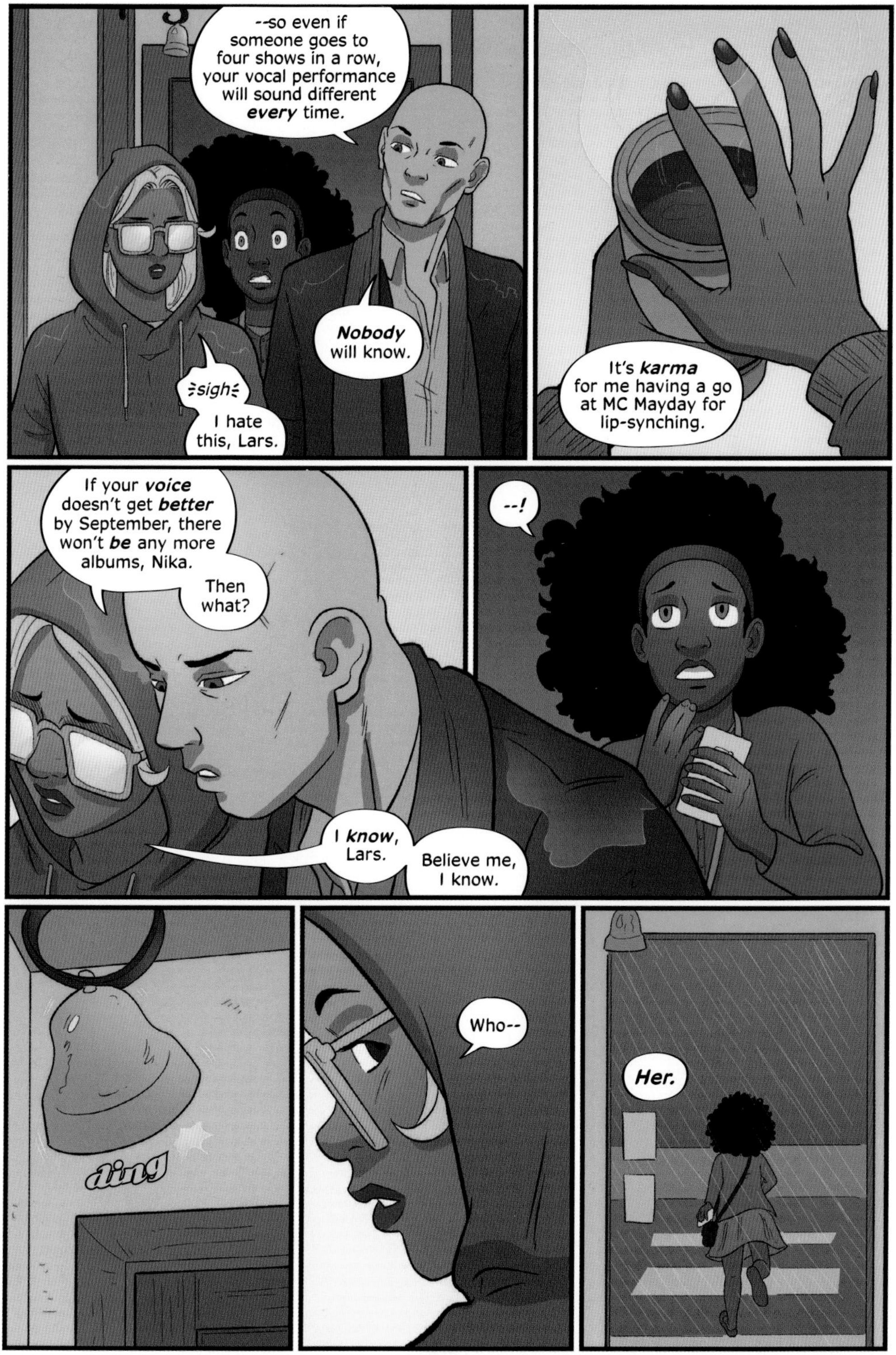
--so even if someone goes to four shows in a row, your vocal performance will sound different *every* time.
Nobody will know.
sigh
I hate this, Lars.
It's *karma* for me having a go at MC Mayday for lip-synching.
If your *voice* doesn't get *better* by September, there won't *be* any more albums, Nika.
Then what?
--!
I *know*, Lars.
Believe me, I know.
ding
Who--
Her.

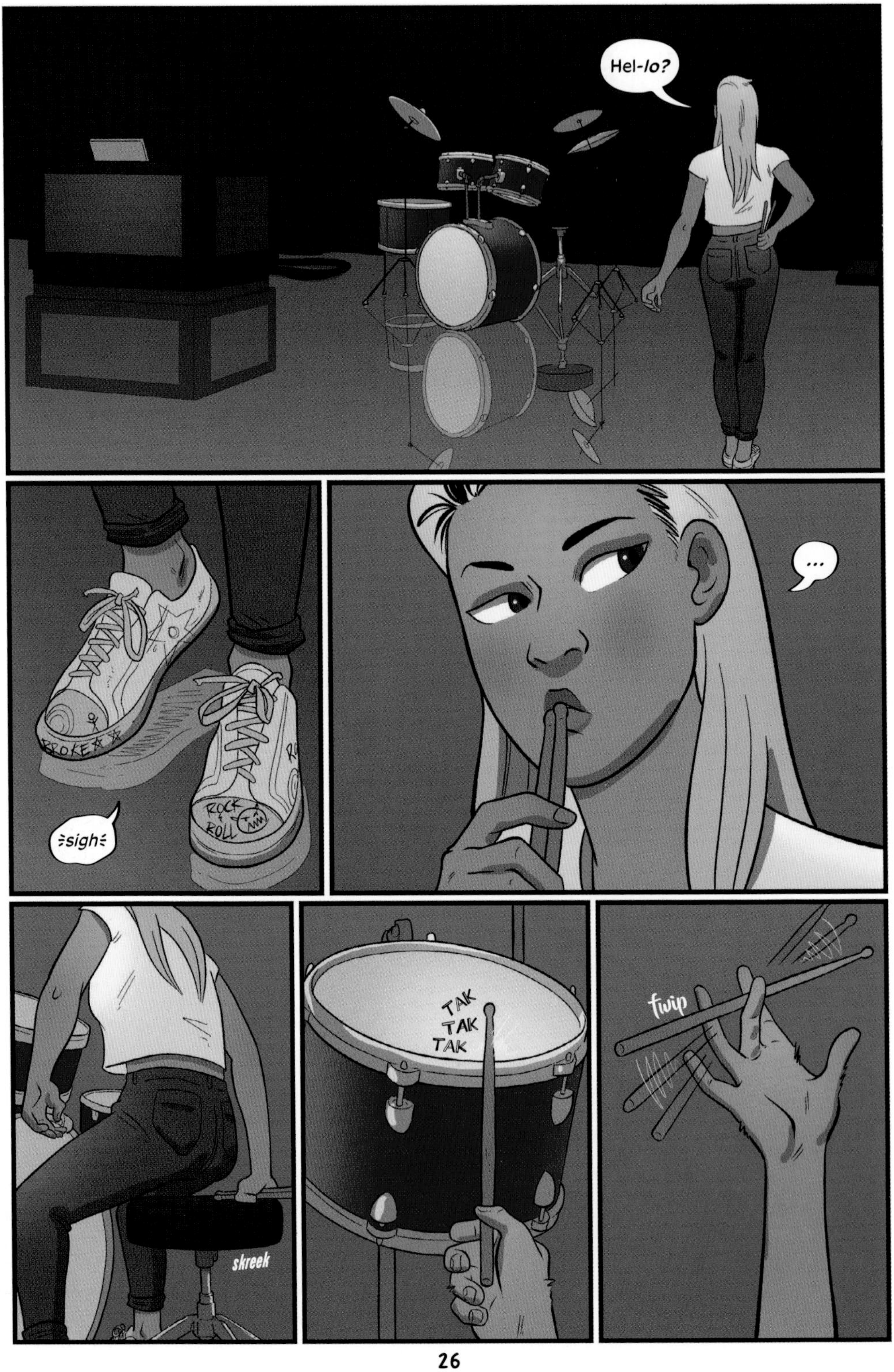
Hel-lo?
BROKE
ROCK & ROLL
sigh
...
skreek
TAK
TAK
TAK
twip

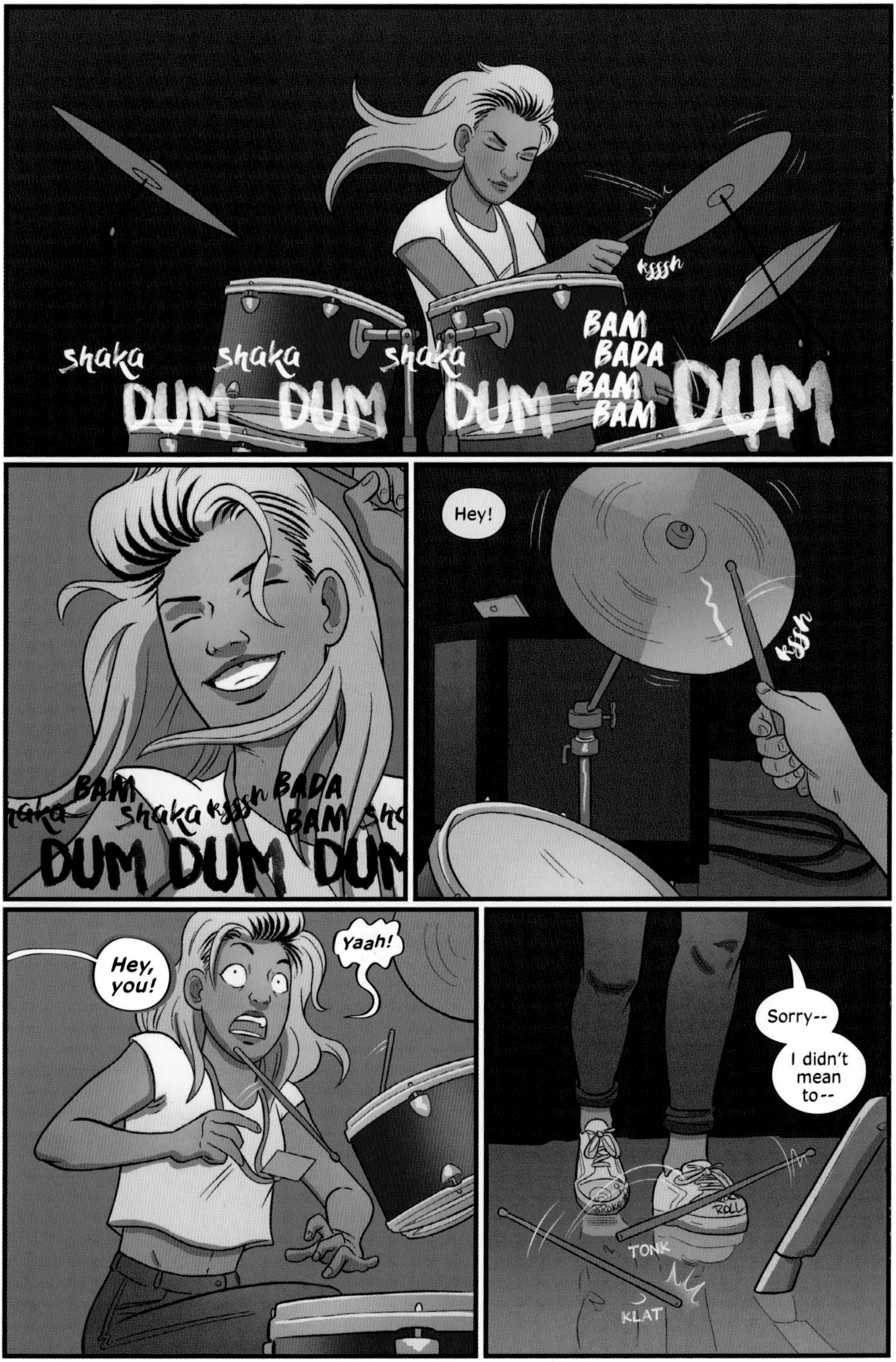
ksssh
shaka
DUM
shaka
DUM
shaka
DUM
BAM
BADA
BAM
BAM
DUM
BAM
shaka
ksssh
BADA
BAM
DUM
DUM
Hey!
ksssh
Hey, you!
Yaah!
Sorry--
I didn't mean to--
TONK
KLAT

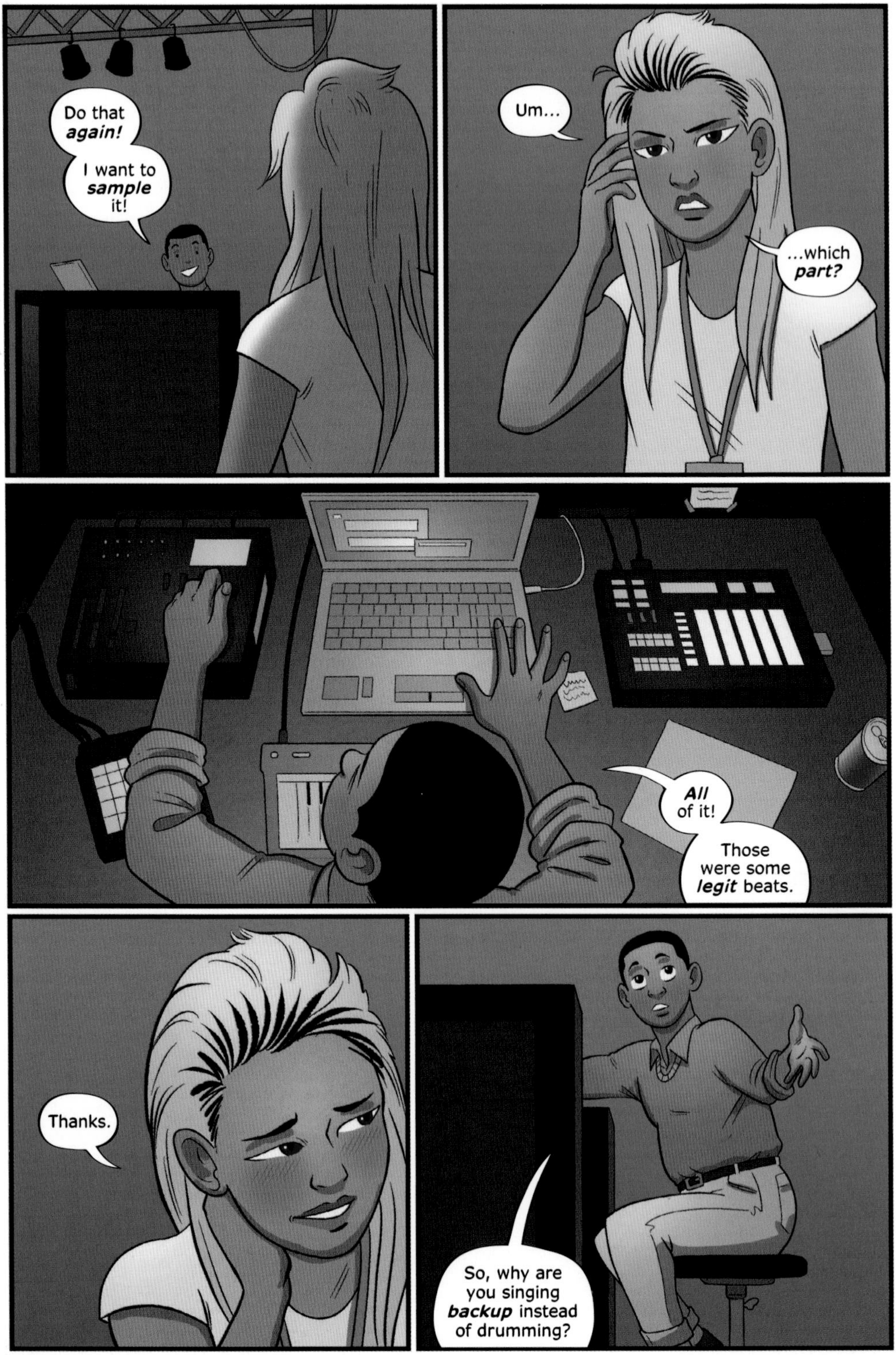
Do that *again!*
I want to *sample* it!
Um...
...which *part?*
All of it!
Those were some *legit* beats.
Thanks.
So, why are you singing *backup* instead of drumming?

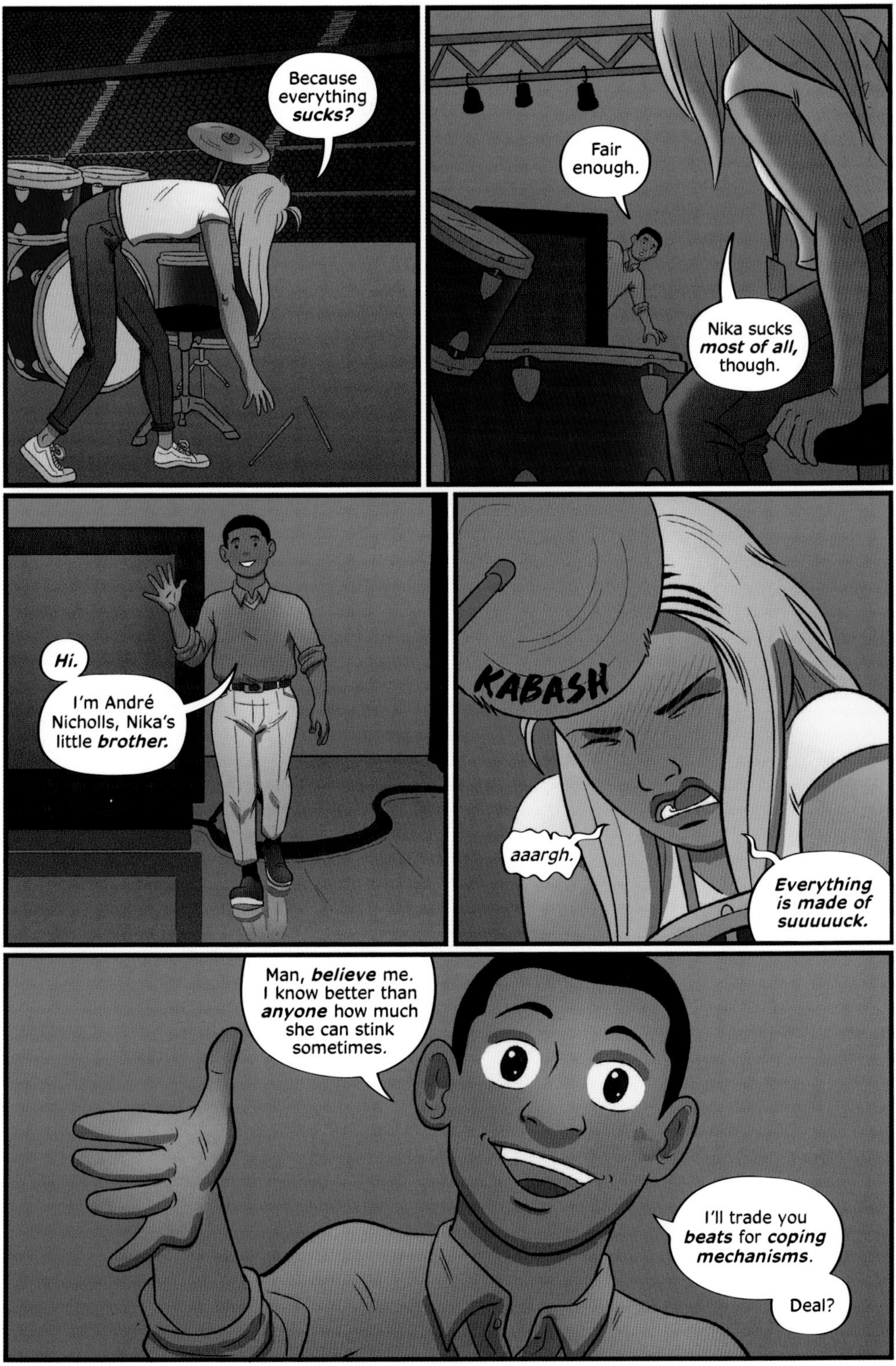
Because everything *sucks?*
Fair enough.
Nika sucks *most of all,* though.
Hi.
I'm André Nicholls, Nika's little *brother.*
KABASH
aaargh.
Everything is made of suuuuuck.
Man, *believe* me. I know better than *anyone* how much she can stink sometimes.
I'll trade you *beats* for *coping mechanisms*.
Deal?

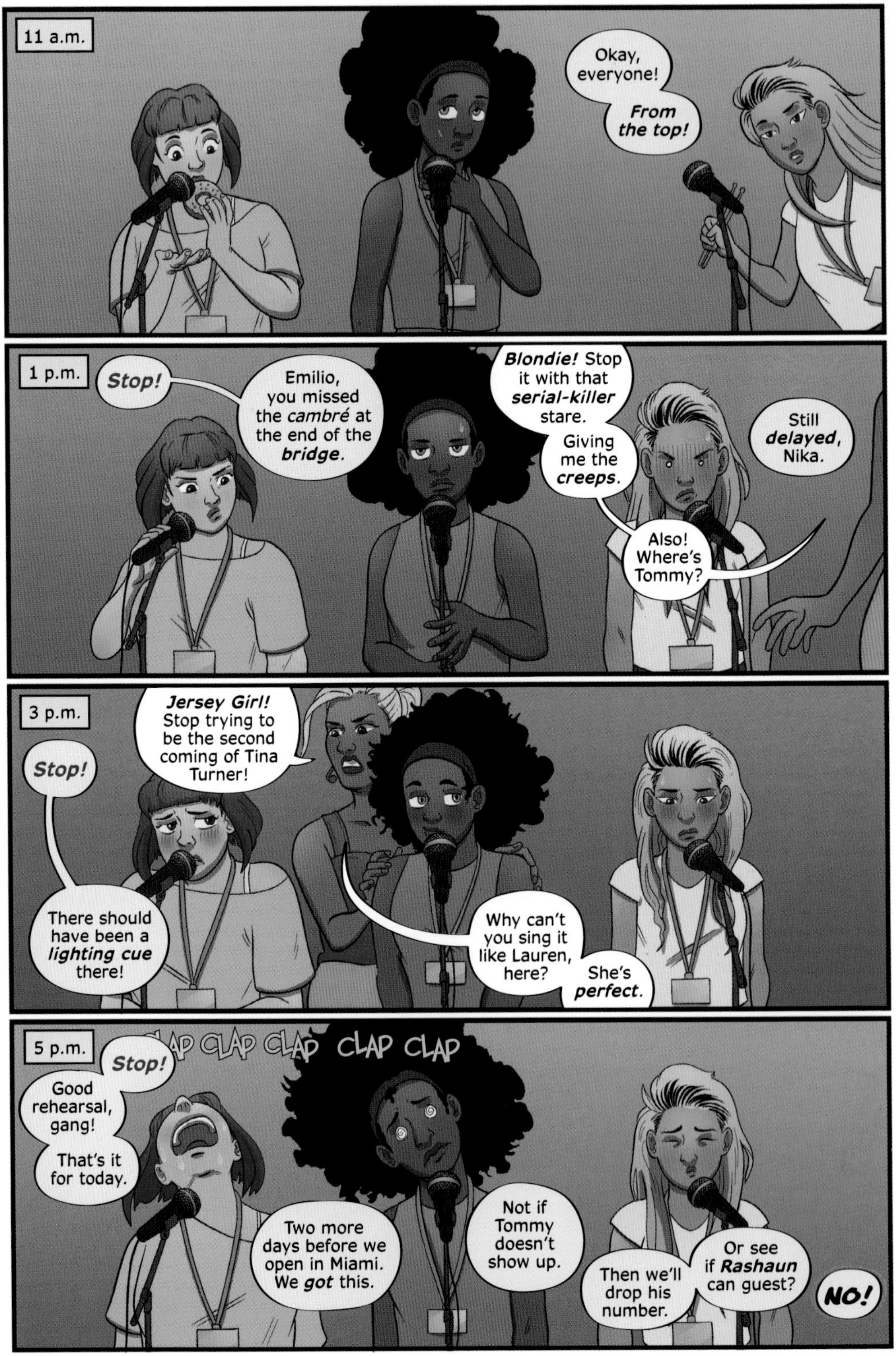

11 a.m.
Okay, everyone!
From the top!
1 p.m.
Stop!
Emilio, you missed the cambré at the end of the bridge.
Blondie! Stop it with that serial-killer stare.
Giving me the creeps.
Also! Where's Tommy?
Still delayed, Nika.
3 p.m.
Stop!
Jersey Girl! Stop trying to be the second coming of Tina Turner!
There should have been a lighting cue there!
Why can't you sing it like Lauren, here?
She's perfect.
5 p.m.
CLAP CLAP CLAP CLAP CLAP
Stop!
Good rehearsal, gang!
That's it for today.
Two more days before we open in Miami. We got this.
Not if Tommy doesn't show up.
Then we'll drop his number.
Or see if Rashaun can guest?
NO!

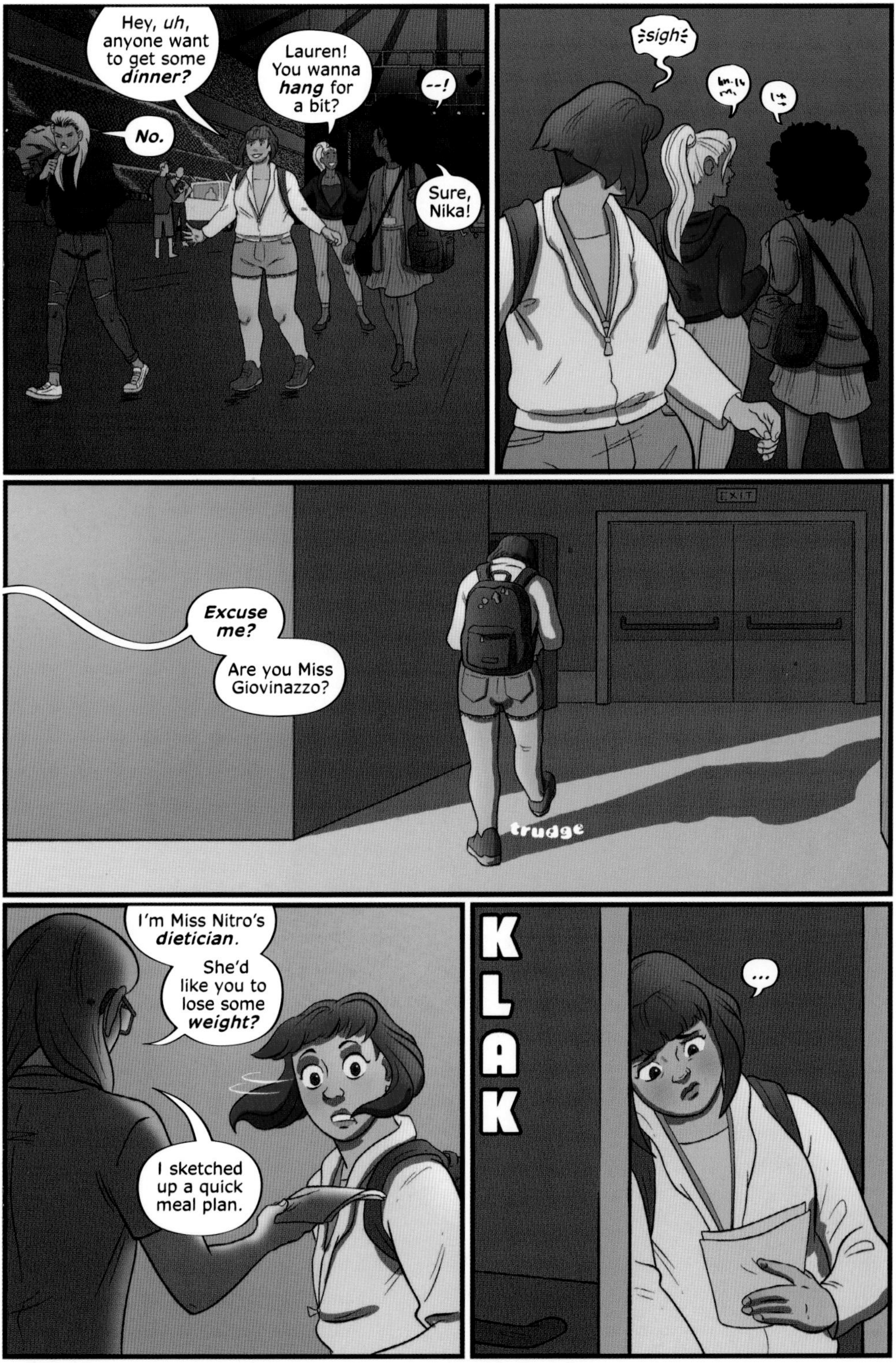

Hey, *uh*, anyone want to get some ***dinner?***
No.
Lauren! You wanna ***hang*** for a bit?
--!
Sure, Nika!
sigh
Excuse me?
Are you Miss Giovinazzo?
trudge
I'm Miss Nitro's ***dietician***.
She'd like you to lose some ***weight?***
I sketched up a quick meal plan.
KLAK
...

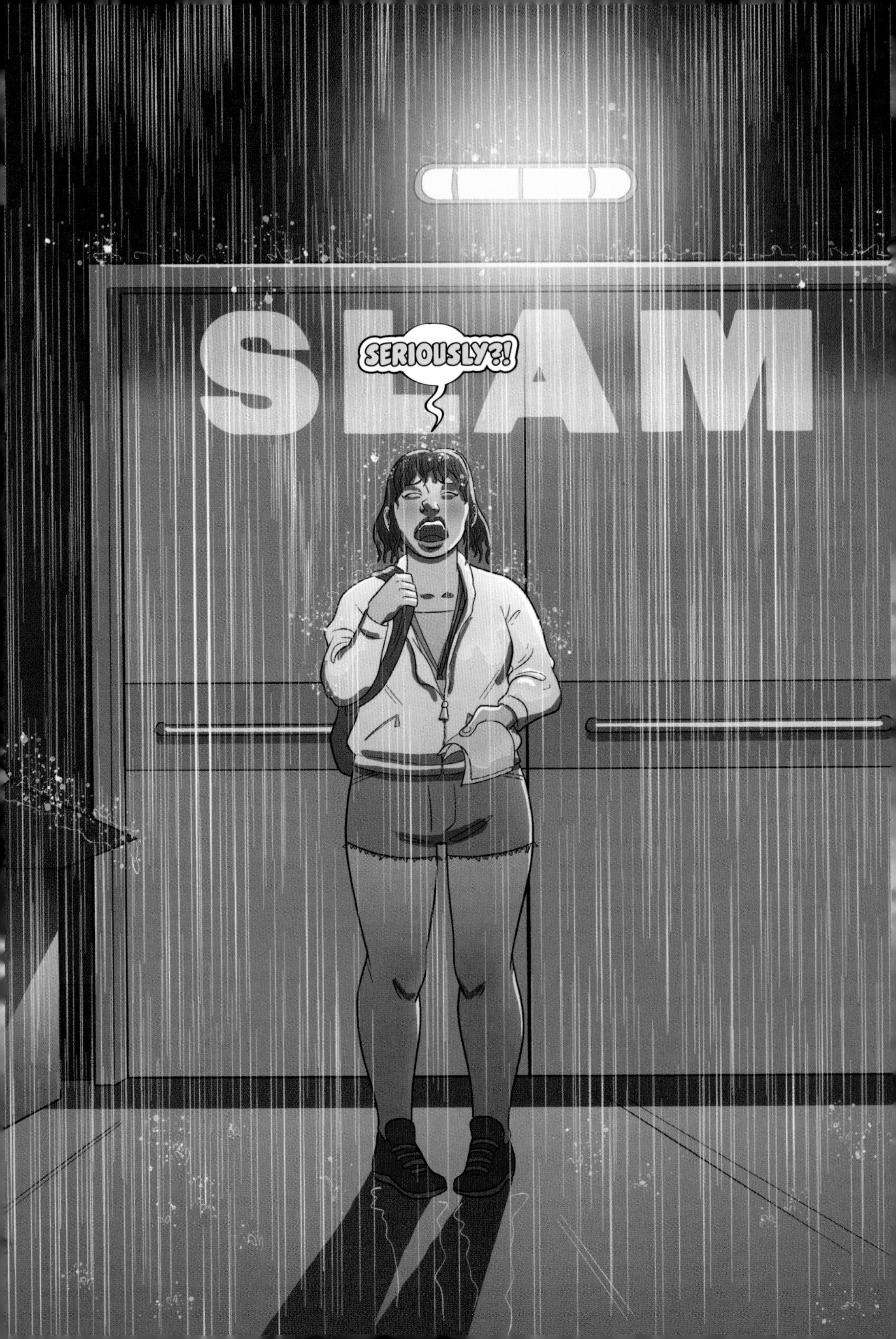
SLAM
SERIOUSLY?!

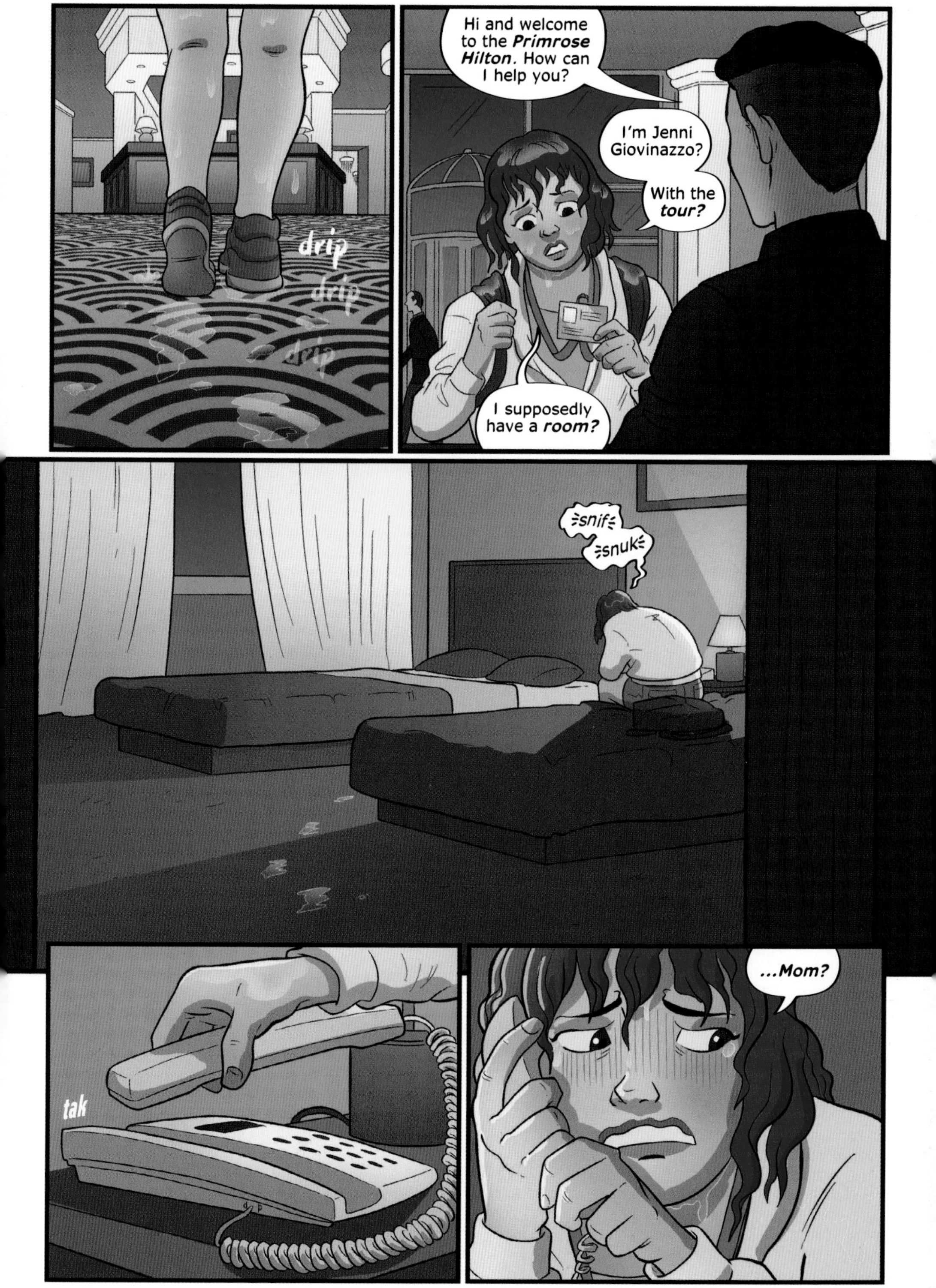
drip
drip
drip
Hi and welcome to the *Primrose Hilton*. How can I help you?
I'm Jenni Giovinazzo?
With the *tour?*
I supposedly have a *room?*
snif
snuk
tak
...Mom?

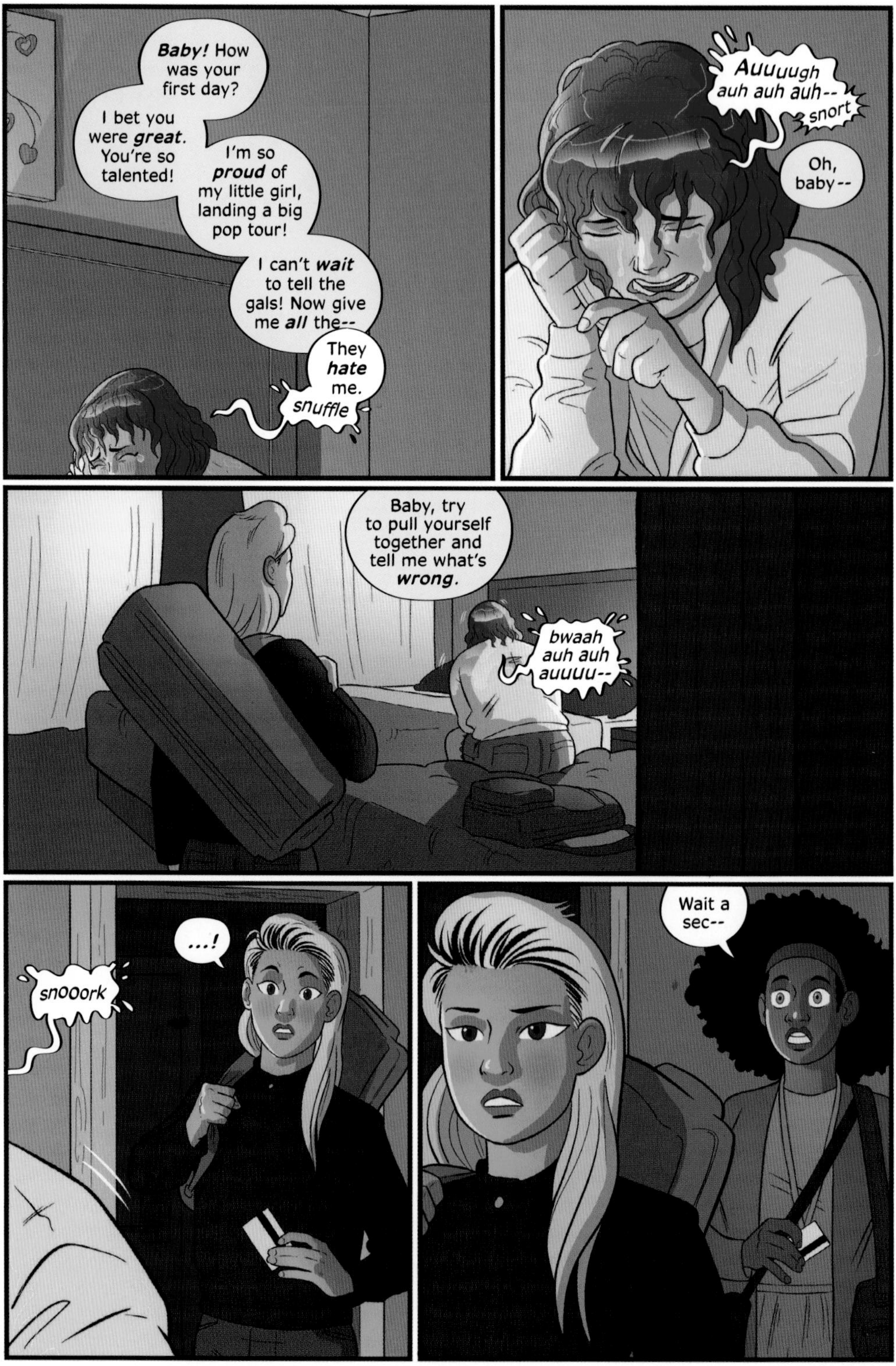
Baby! How was your first day?
I bet you were great. You're so talented!
I'm so proud of my little girl, landing a big pop tour!
I can't wait to tell the gals! Now give me all the--
They hate me.
snuffle
Auuuugh auh auh auh--
snort
Oh, baby--
Baby, try to pull yourself together and tell me what's wrong.
bwaah auh auh auuuu--
snOoork
...!
Wait a sec--

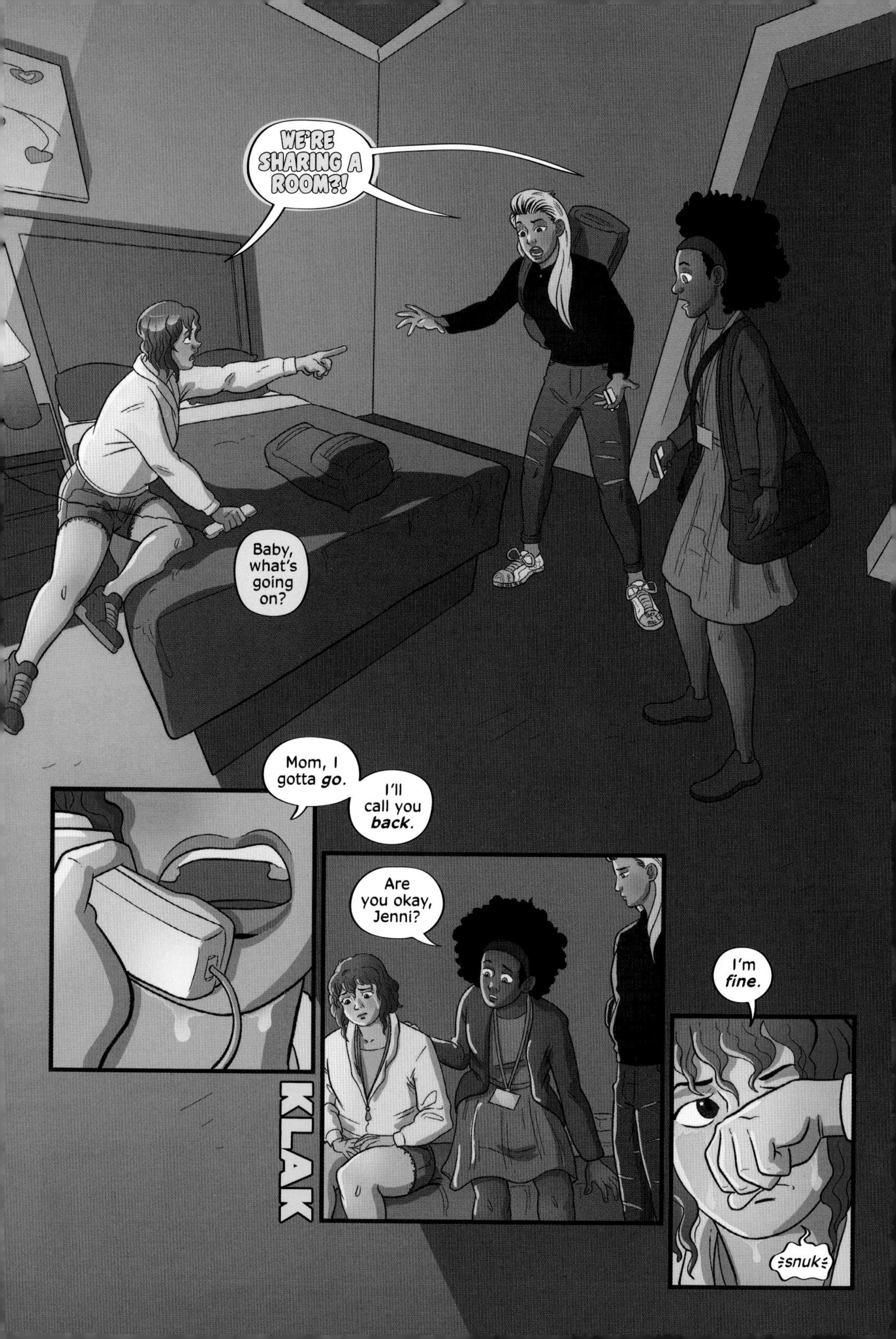
WE'RE SHARING A ROOM?!
Baby, what's going on?
Mom, I gotta *go*.
I'll call you ***back***.
KLAK
Are you okay, Jenni?
I'm *fine*.
snuk

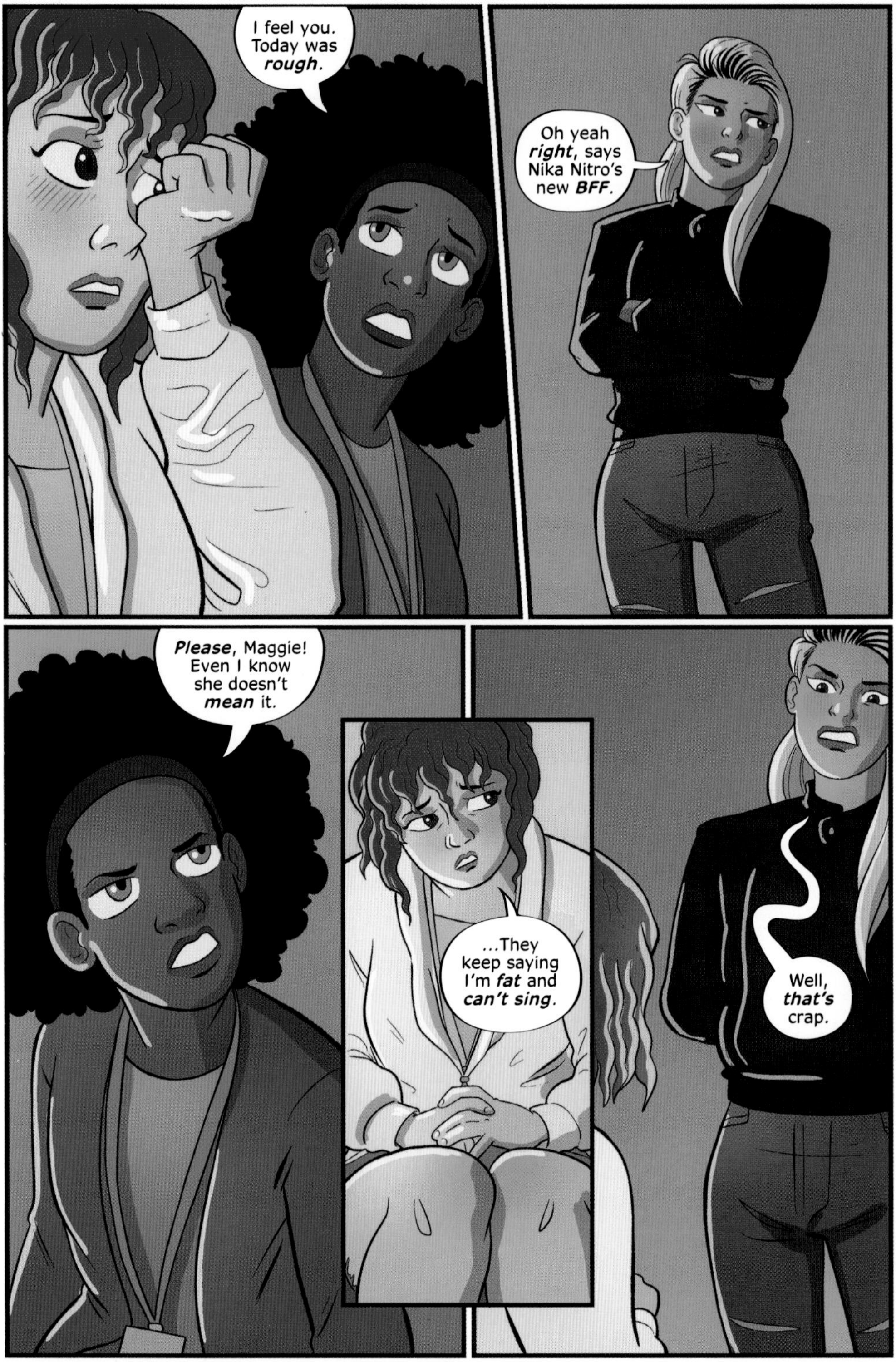
I feel you. Today was *rough*.
Oh yeah *right*, says Nika Nitro's new *BFF*.
Please, Maggie! Even I know she doesn't *mean* it.
...They keep saying I'm *fat* and *can't sing*.
Well, *that's* crap.

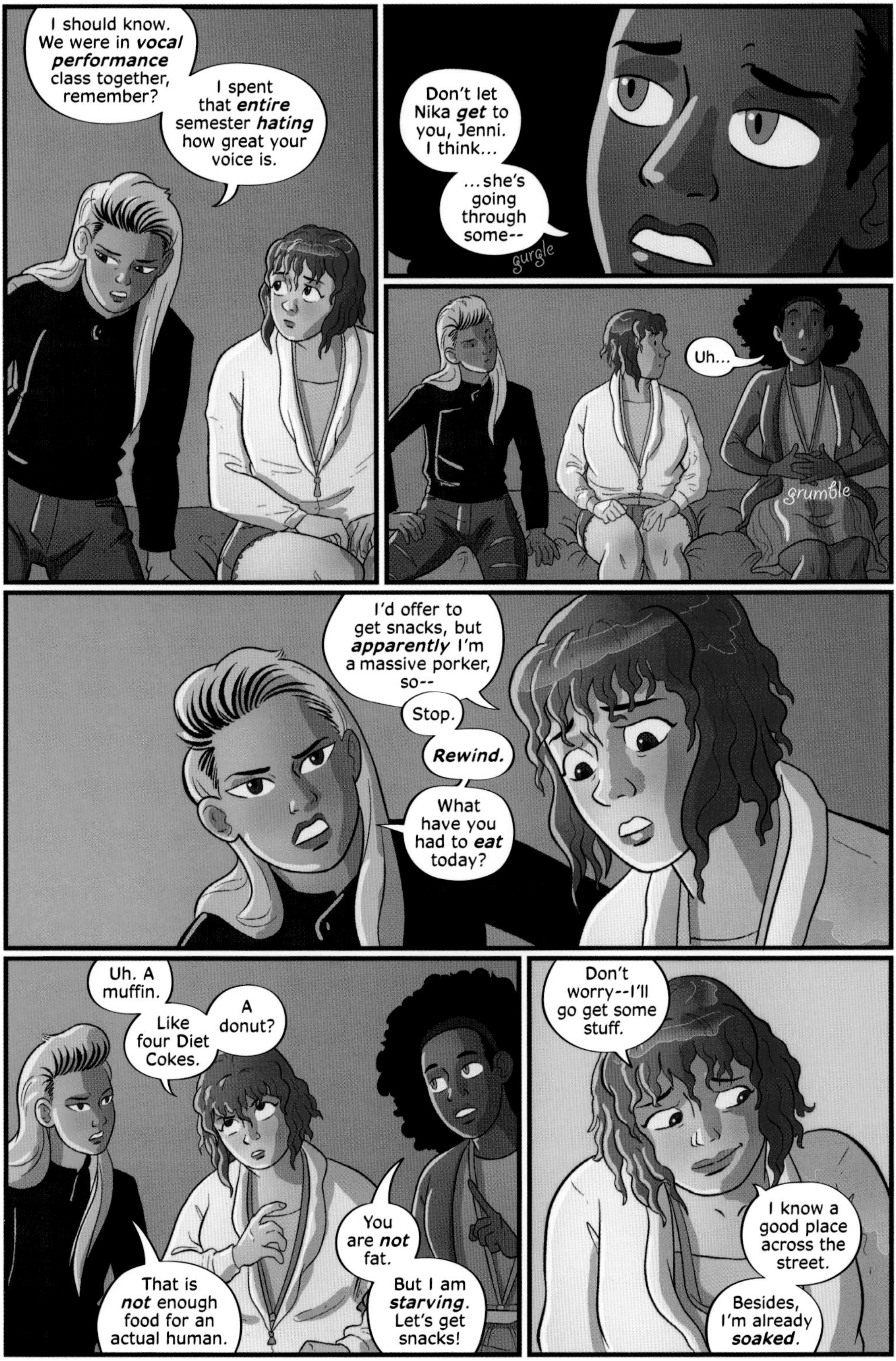
I should know. We were in vocal performance class together, remember?
I spent that entire semester hating how great your voice is.
Don't let Nika get to you, Jenni. I think...
...she's going through some--
gurgle
Uh...
grumble
I'd offer to get snacks, but apparently I'm a massive porker, so--
Stop.
Rewind.
What have you had to eat today?
Uh. A muffin.
A donut?
Like four Diet Cokes.
That is not enough food for an actual human.
You are not fat.
But I am starving. Let's get snacks!
Don't worry--I'll go get some stuff.
I know a good place across the street.
Besides, I'm already soaked.

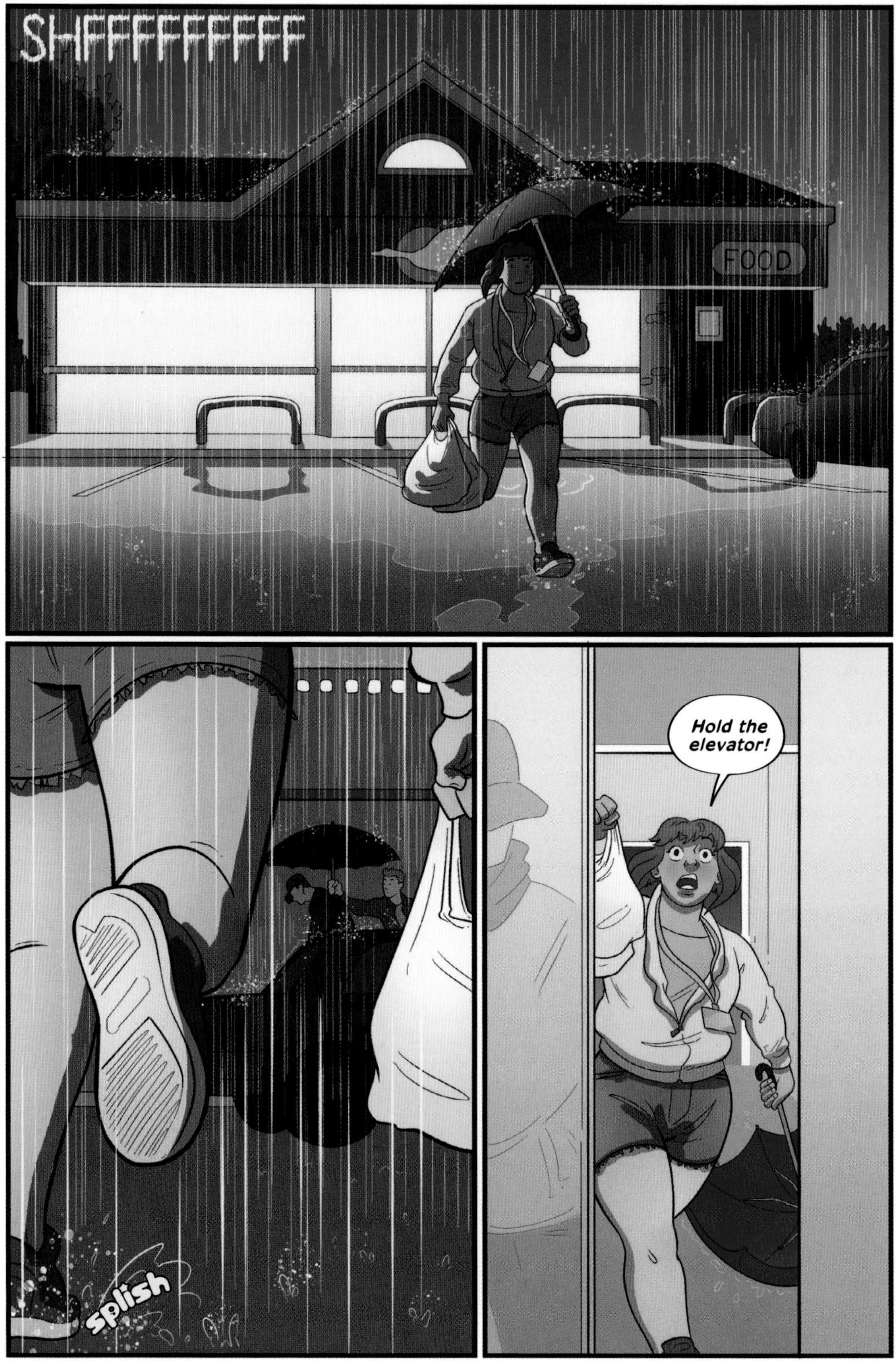
SHFFFFFFFFF
FOOD
splish
Hold the elevator!

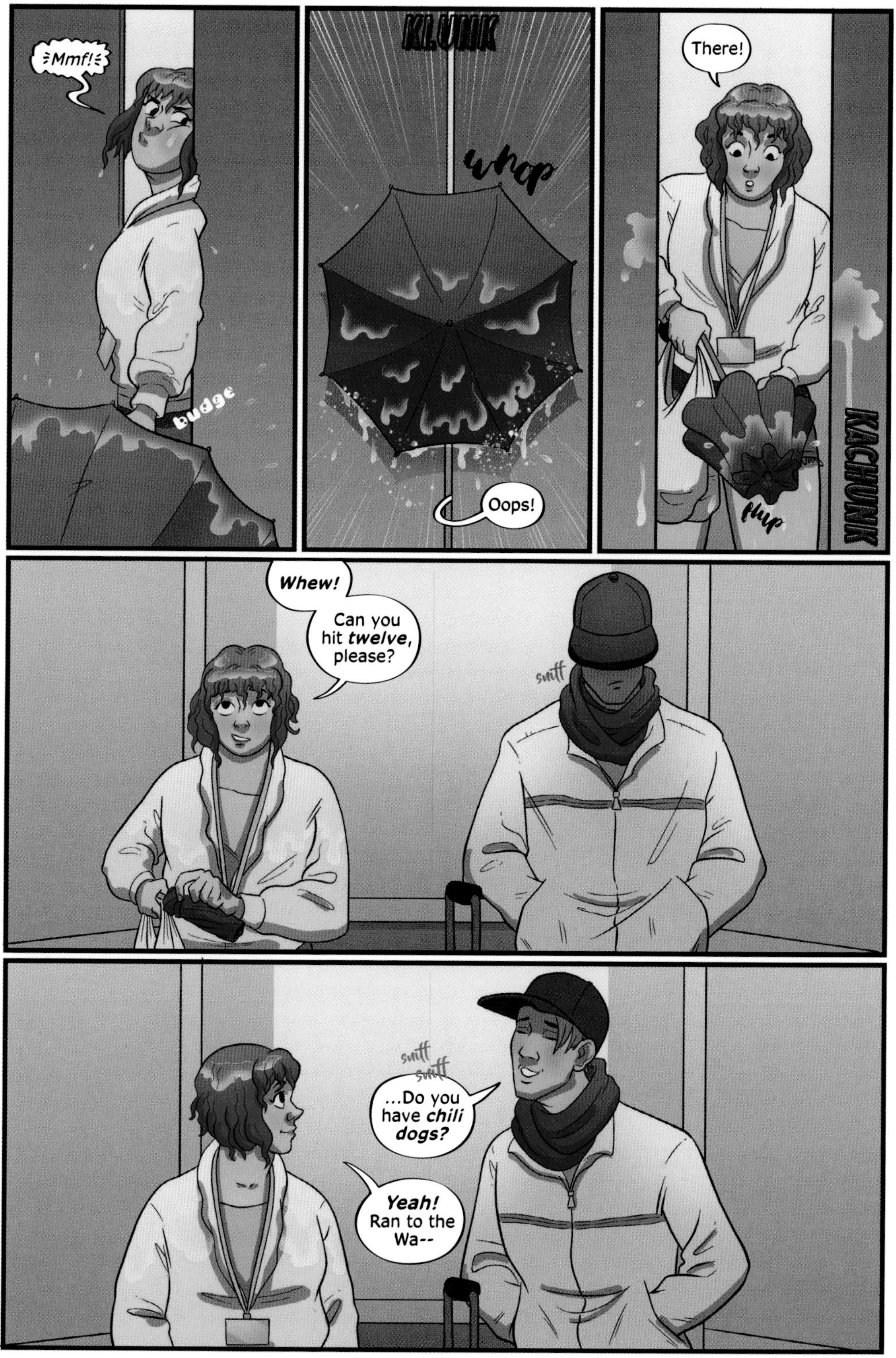
Mmf!
budge
KLUNK
whap
Oops!
There!
KACHUNK
flup
Whew!
Can you hit *twelve*, please?
sniff
sniff
sniff
...Do you have *chili dogs?*
Yeah! Ran to the Wa--

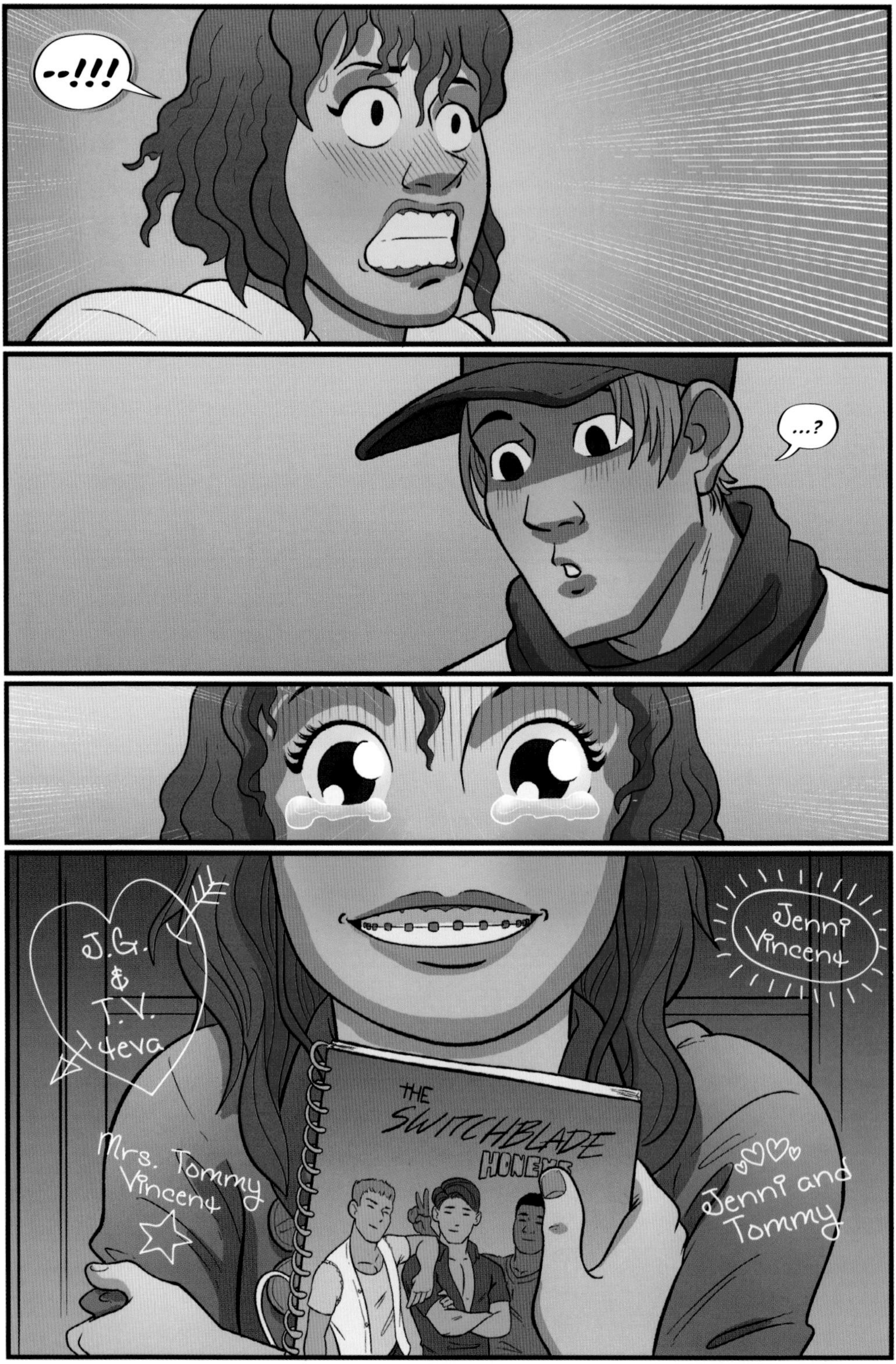
--!!!
...?
J.G. & T.V. 4eva
Jenni Vincent
THE SWITCHBLADE
Mrs. Tommy Vincent
Jenni and Tommy

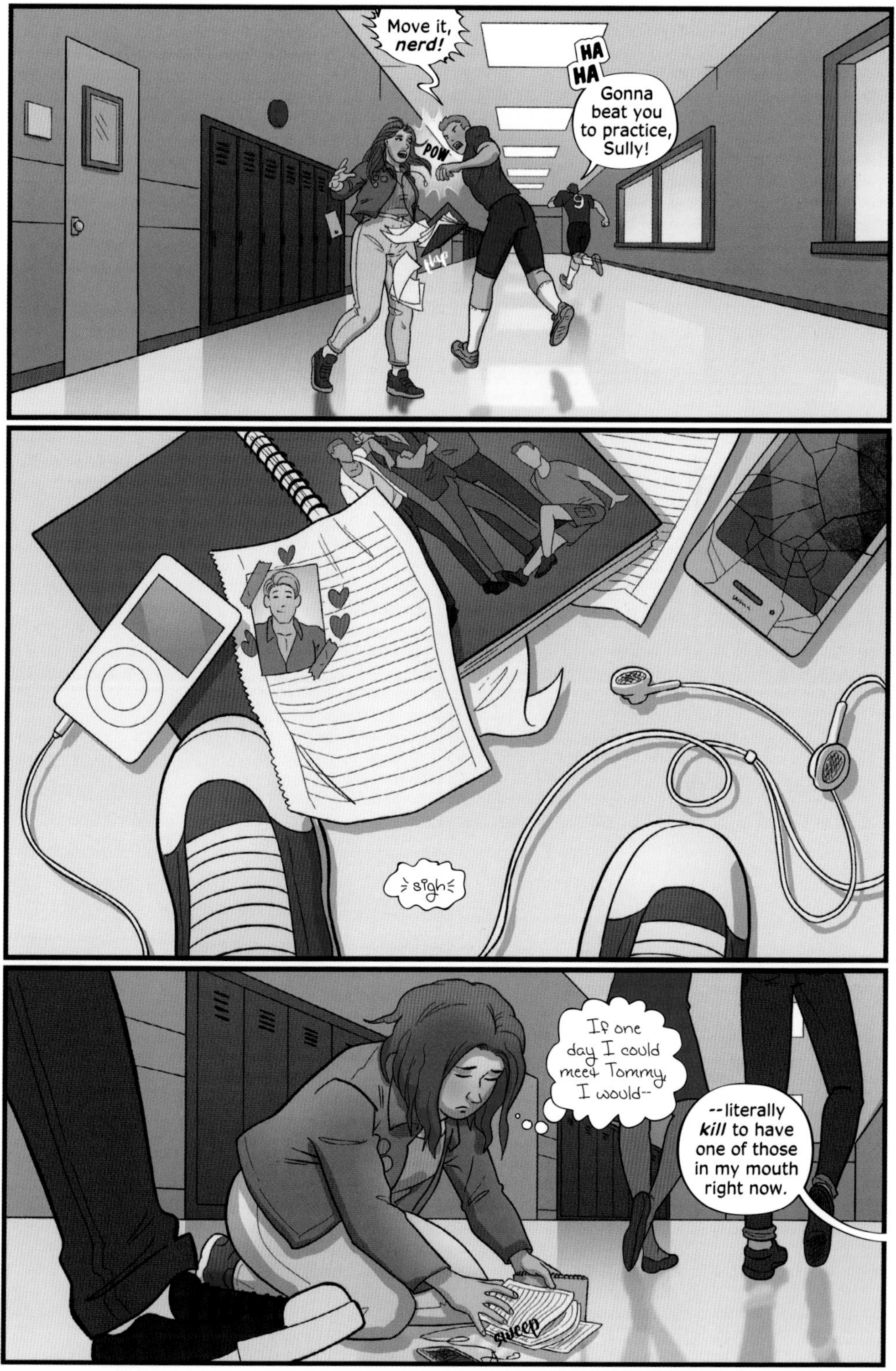
Move it, *nerd!*
POW
flap
HA
HA
Gonna beat you to practice, Sully!
sigh
If one day I could meet Tommy, I would--
--literally *kill* to have one of those in my mouth right now.
sweep

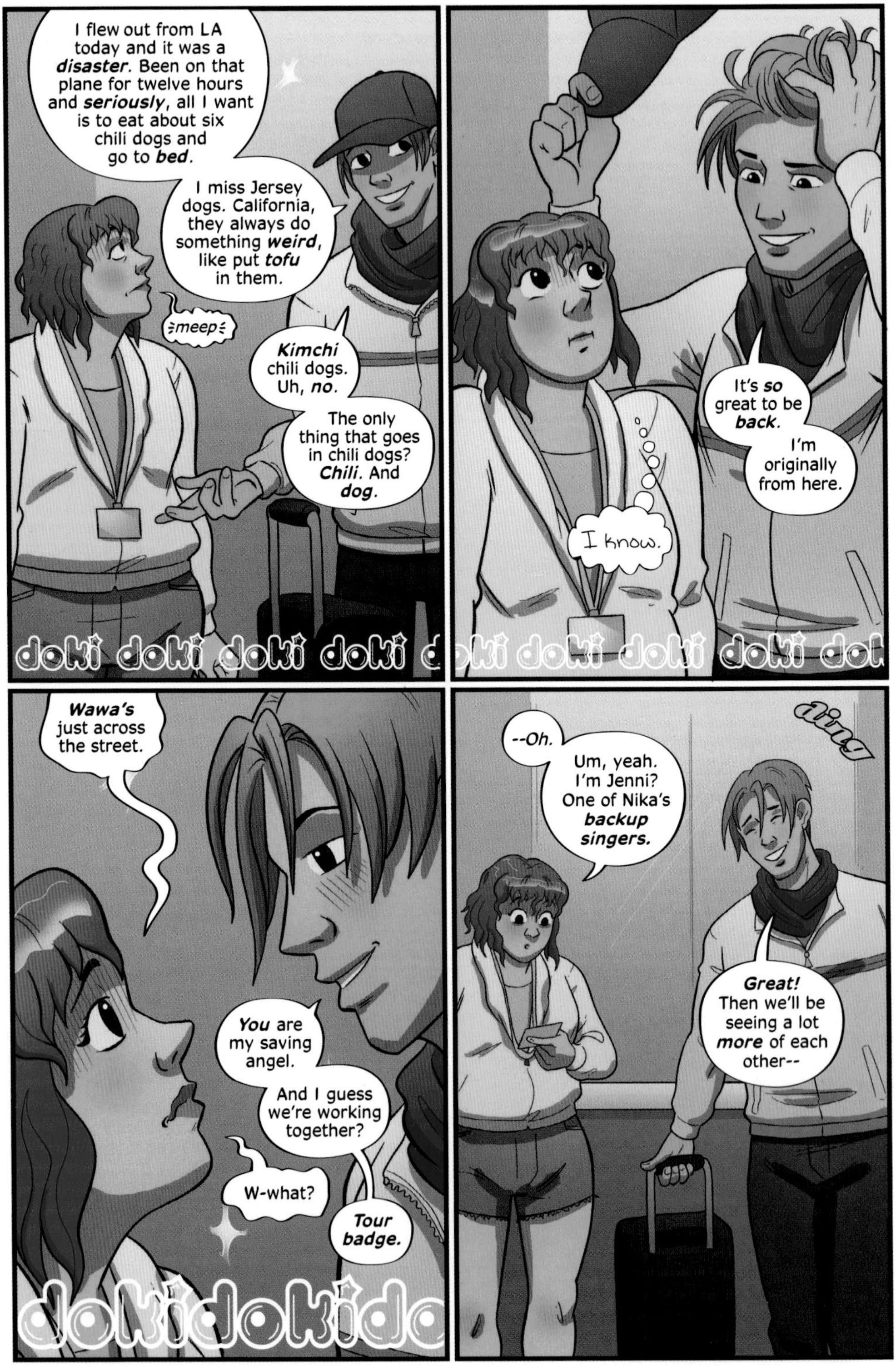
I flew out from LA today and it was a *disaster*. Been on that plane for twelve hours and *seriously*, all I want is to eat about six chili dogs and go to *bed*.
I miss Jersey dogs. California, they always do something *weird*, like put *tofu* in them.
meep
Kimchi chili dogs. Uh, *no*.
The only thing that goes in chili dogs? *Chili*. And *dog*.
doki doki doki doki doki doki doki doki doki
It's *so* great to be *back*.
I'm originally from here.
I know.
Wawa's just across the street.
You are my saving angel.
And I guess we're working together?
W-what?
Tour badge.
dokidokido
--Oh.
Um, yeah. I'm Jenni? One of Nika's *backup singers.*
ding
Great! Then we'll be seeing a lot *more* of each other--

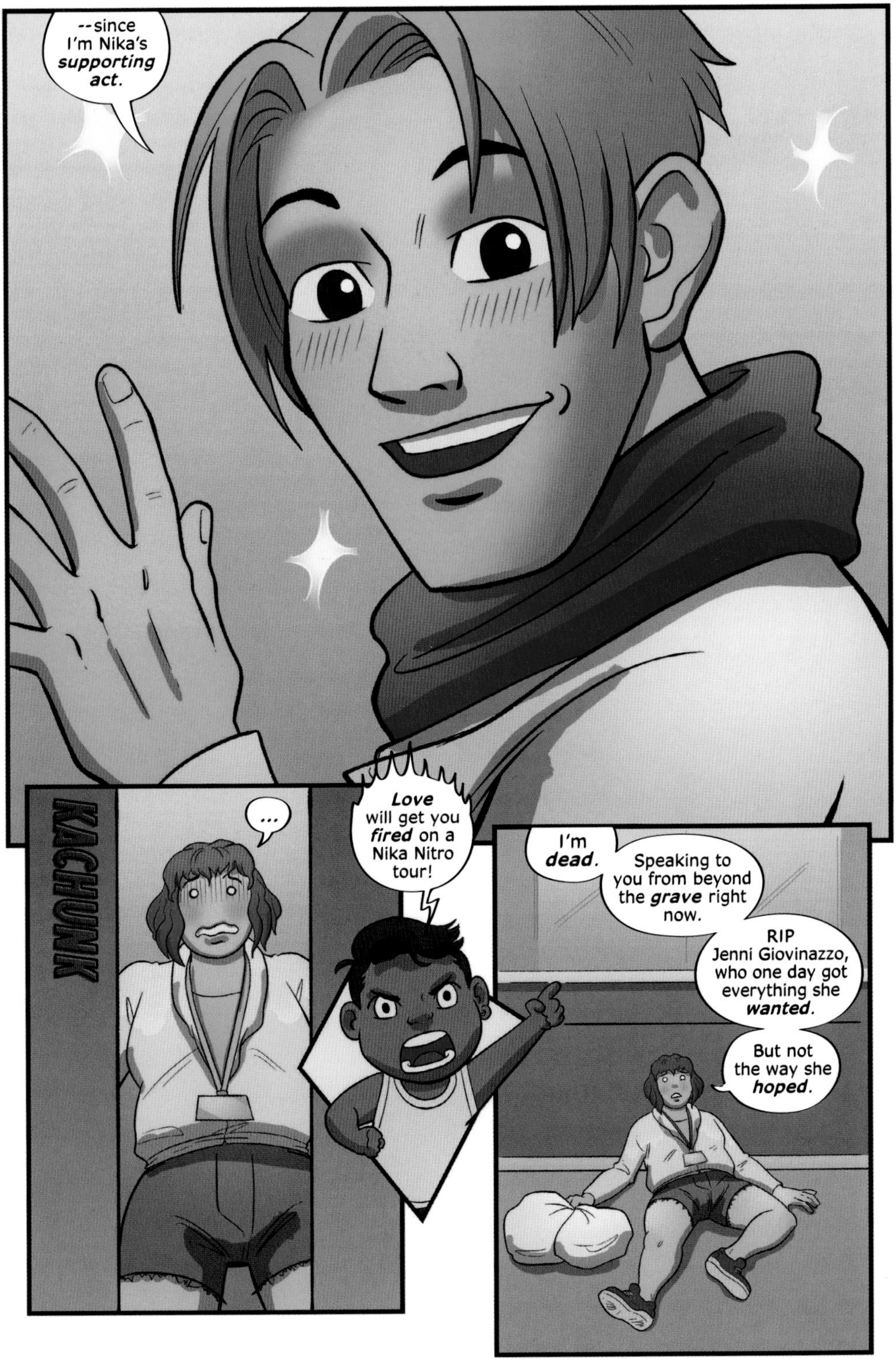
--since I'm Nika's *supporting act*.
KACHUNK
...
Love will get you *fired* on a Nika Nitro tour!
I'm *dead*.
Speaking to you from beyond the *grave* right now.
RIP Jenni Giovinazzo, who one day got everything she *wanted*.
But not the way she *hoped*.

CHAPTER
2

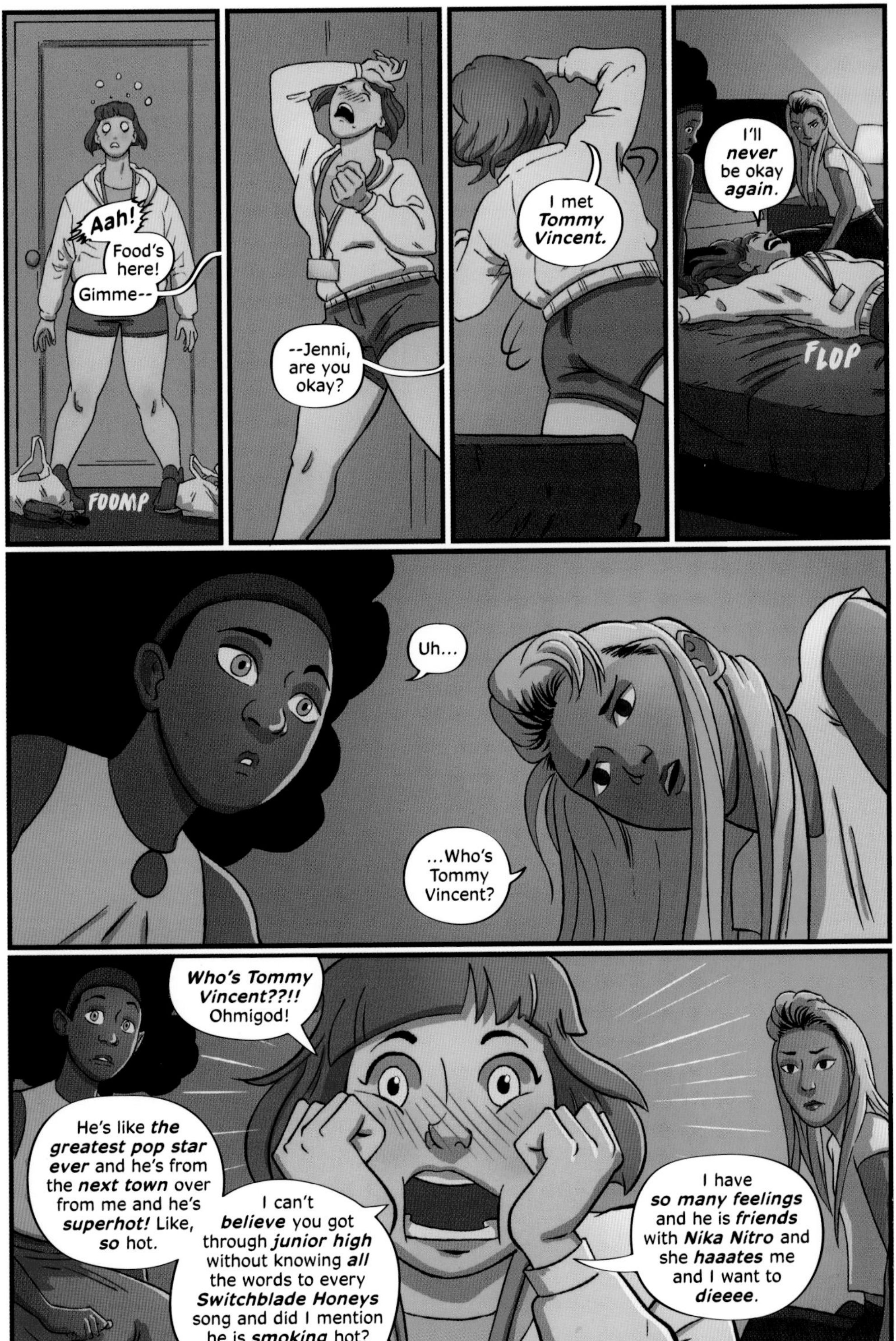
Aah!
Food's here! Gimme--
--Jenni, are you okay?
I met *Tommy Vincent.*
I'll *never* be okay *again*.
FLOP
FOOMP
Uh...
...Who's Tommy Vincent?
Who's Tommy Vincent??!! Ohmigod!
He's like ***the greatest pop star ever*** and he's from the ***next town*** over from me and he's ***superhot!*** Like, ***so*** hot.
I can't ***believe*** you got through ***junior high*** without knowing ***all*** the words to every ***Switchblade Honeys*** song and did I mention he is ***smoking*** hot?
I have ***so many feelings*** and he is ***friends*** with ***Nika Nitro*** and she ***haaates*** me and I want to ***dieeee***.

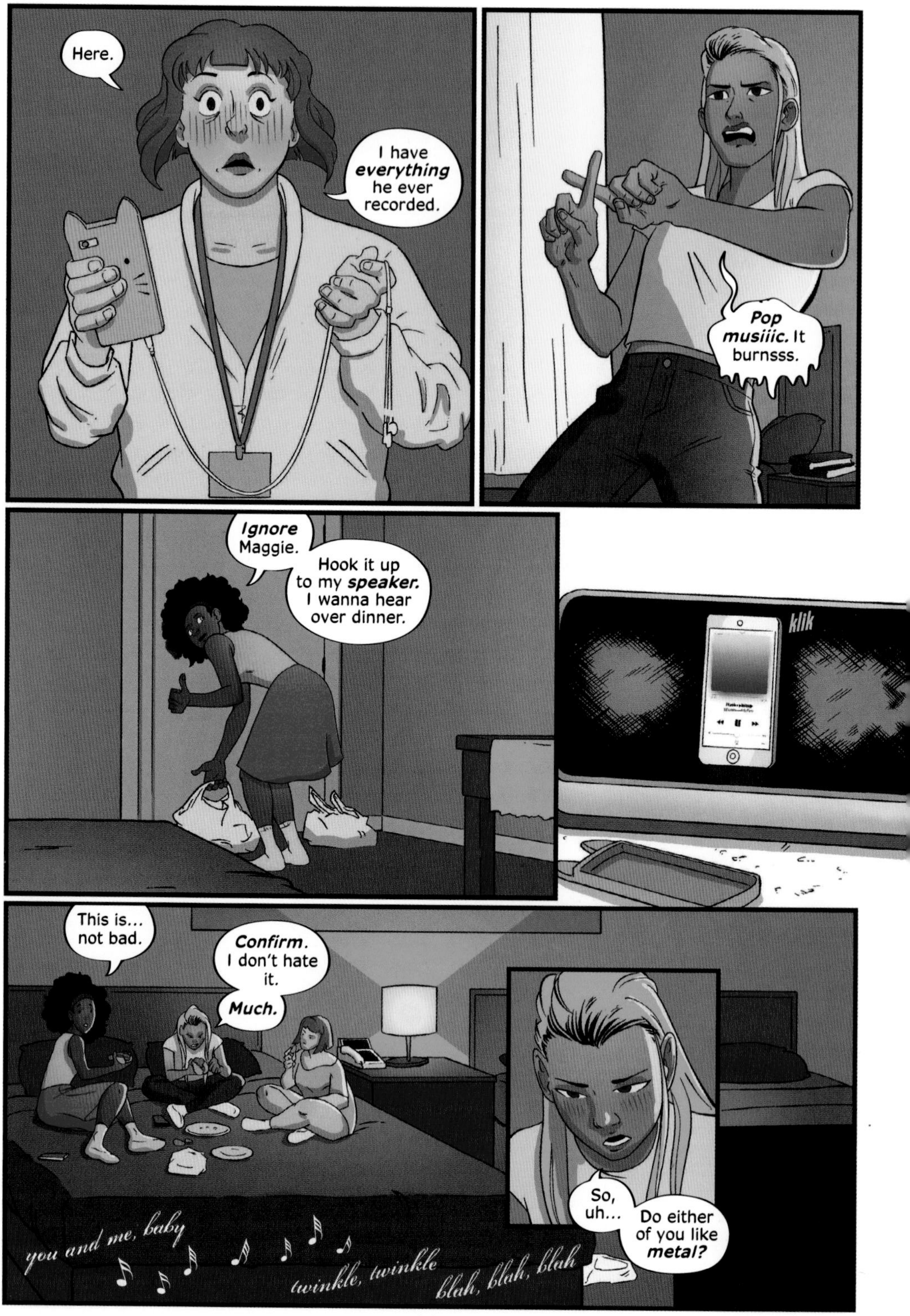
Here.
I have *everything* he ever recorded.
Pop musiiic. It burnsss.
Ignore Maggie.
Hook it up to my ***speaker.*** I wanna hear over dinner.
klik
This is... not bad.
Confirm. I don't hate it.
Much.
So, uh...
Do either of you like ***metal?***
you and me, baby
twinkle, twinkle
blah, blah, blah

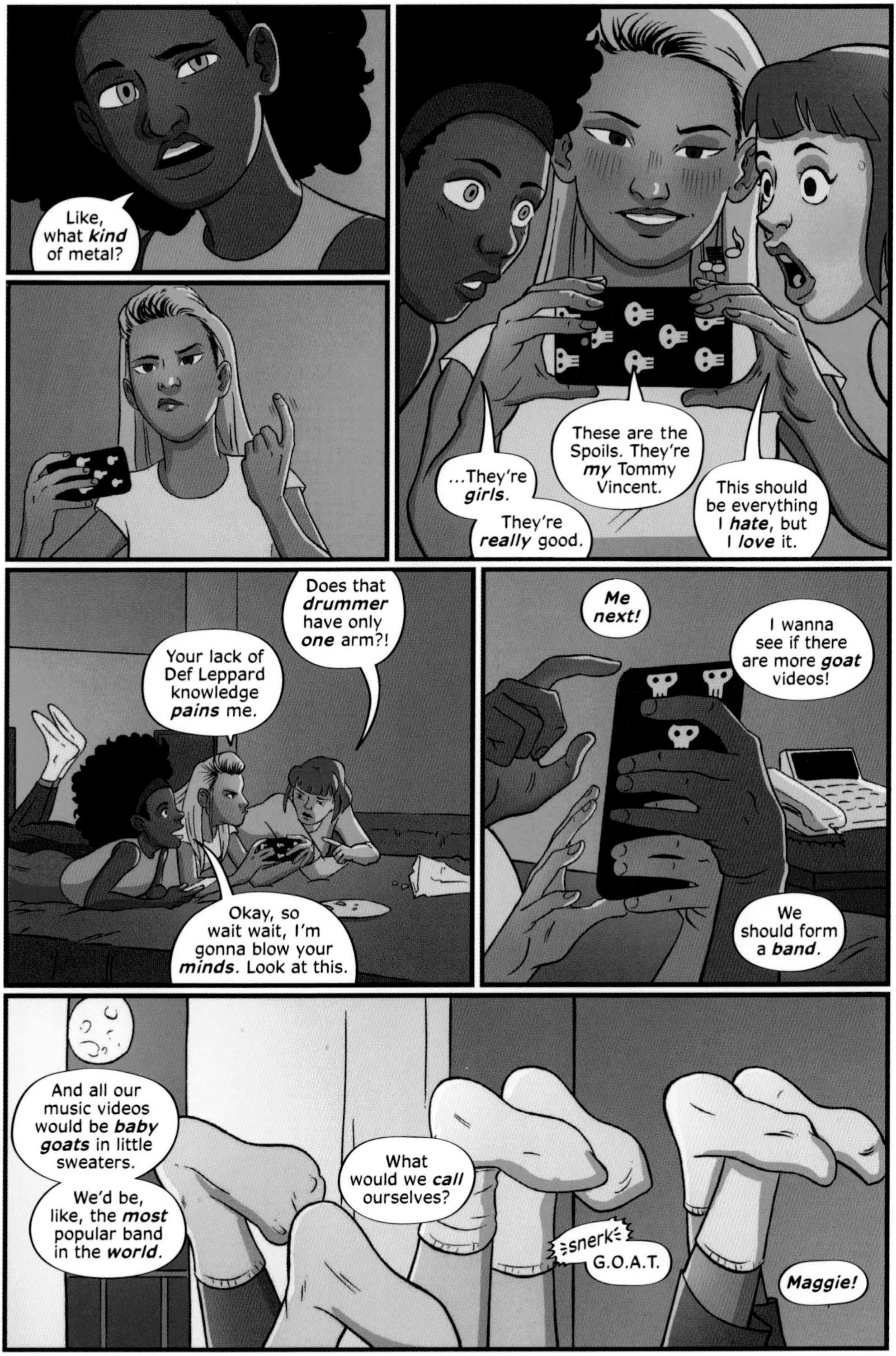
Like, what *kind* of metal?
These are the Spoils. They're *my* Tommy Vincent.
...They're *girls*.
They're *really* good.
This should be everything I *hate*, but I *love* it.
Okay, so wait wait, I'm gonna blow your *minds*. Look at this.
Your lack of Def Leppard knowledge *pains* me.
Does that *drummer* have only *one* arm?!
Me next!
I wanna see if there are more *goat* videos!
We should form a *band*.
And all our music videos would be *baby goats* in little sweaters.
We'd be, like, the *most* popular band in the *world*.
What would we *call* ourselves?
snerk
G.O.A.T.
Maggie!

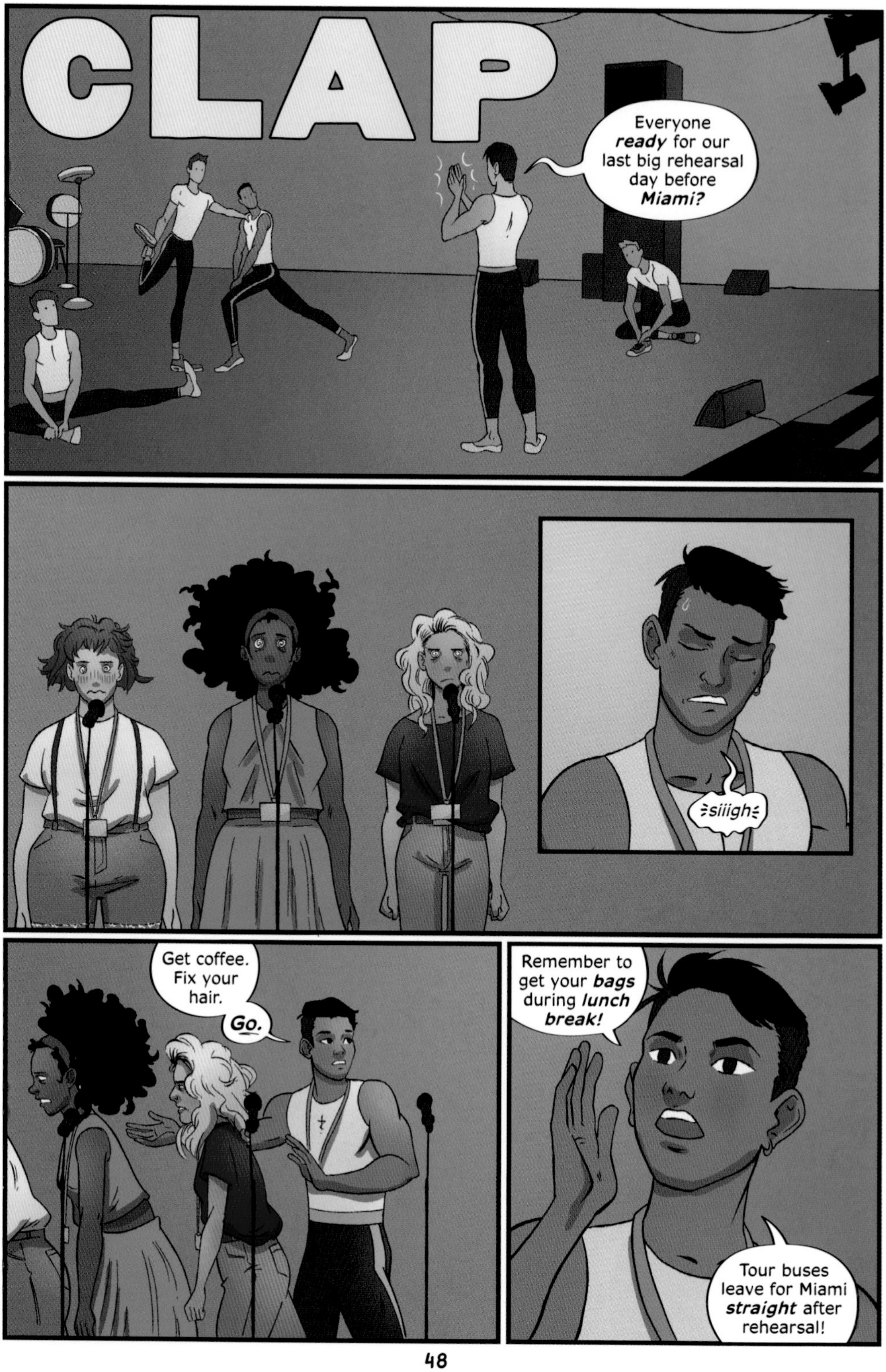
CLAP
Everyone ready for our last big rehearsal day before Miami?
siiigh
Get coffee. Fix your hair.
Go.
Remember to get your bags during lunch break!
Tour buses leave for Miami straight after rehearsal!

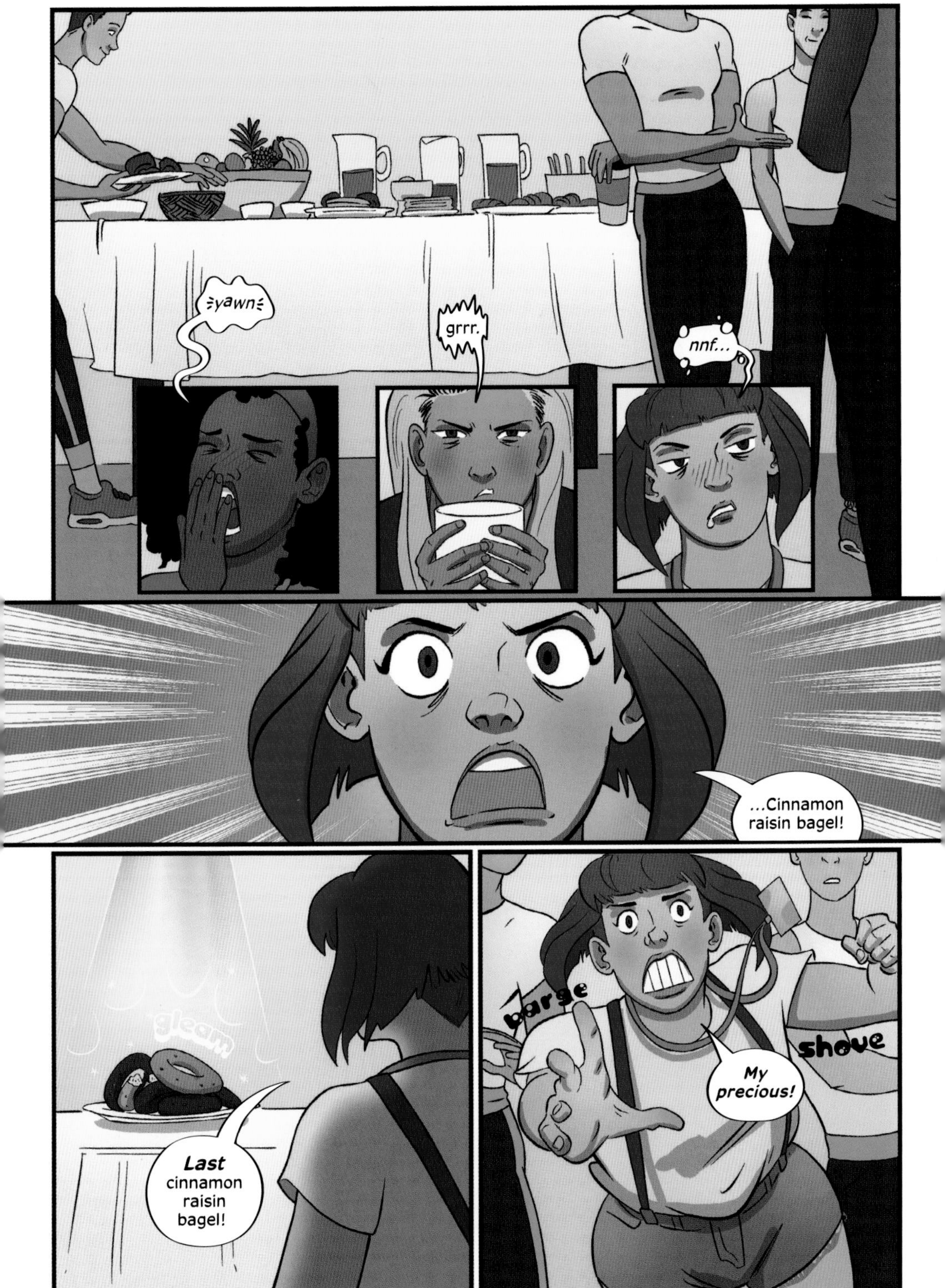
yawn
grrr.
nnf...
...Cinnamon raisin bagel!
gleam
Last cinnamon raisin bagel!
barge
shove
My precious!

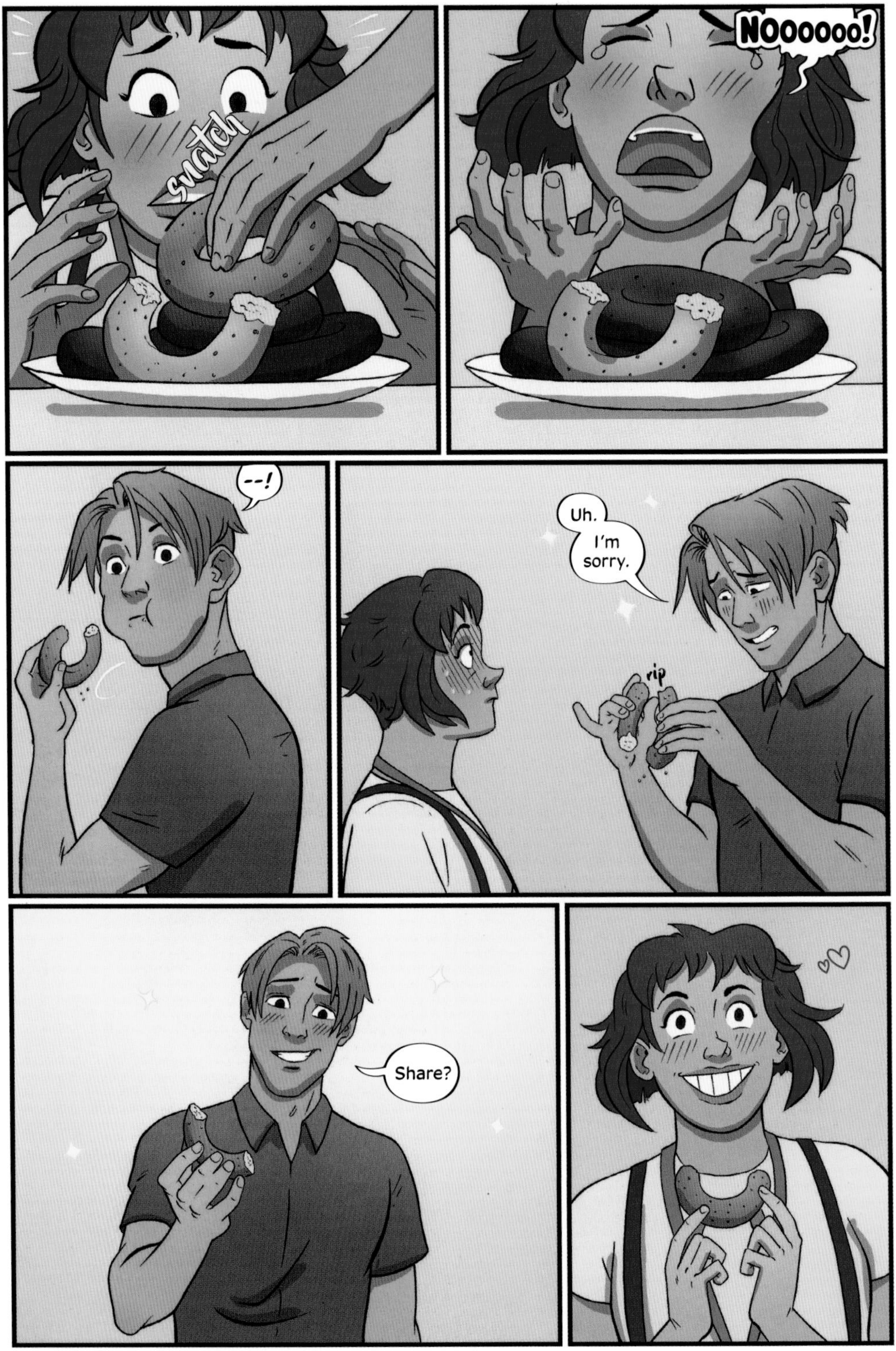
snatch
NOOOOOO!
--!
Uh.
I'm sorry.
rip
Share?

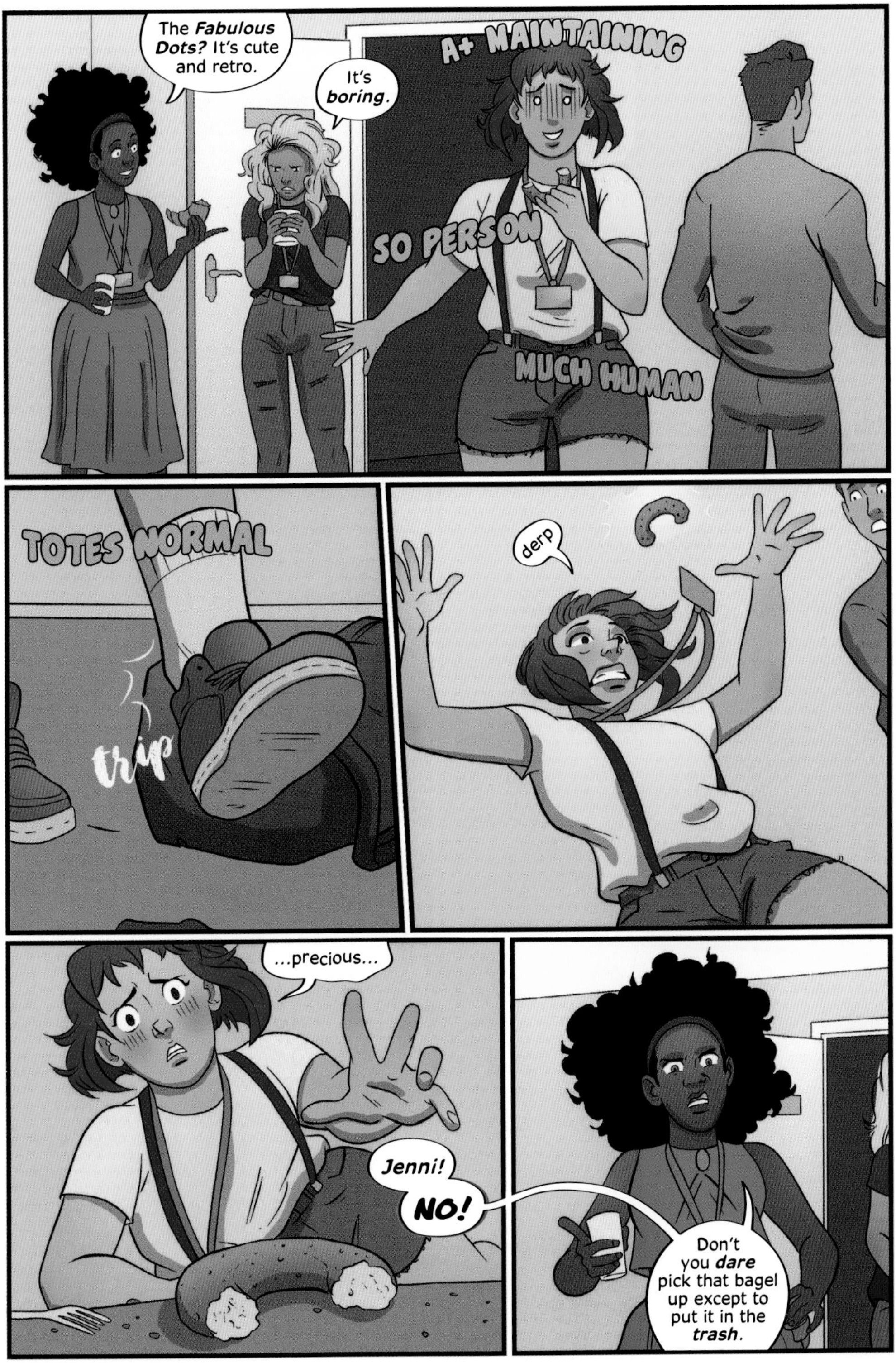
The Fabulous Dots? It's cute and retro.
It's boring.
A+ MAINTAINING
SO PERSON
MUCH HUMAN
TOTES NORMAL
trip
derp
...precious...
Jenni! NO!
Don't you dare pick that bagel up except to put it in the trash.

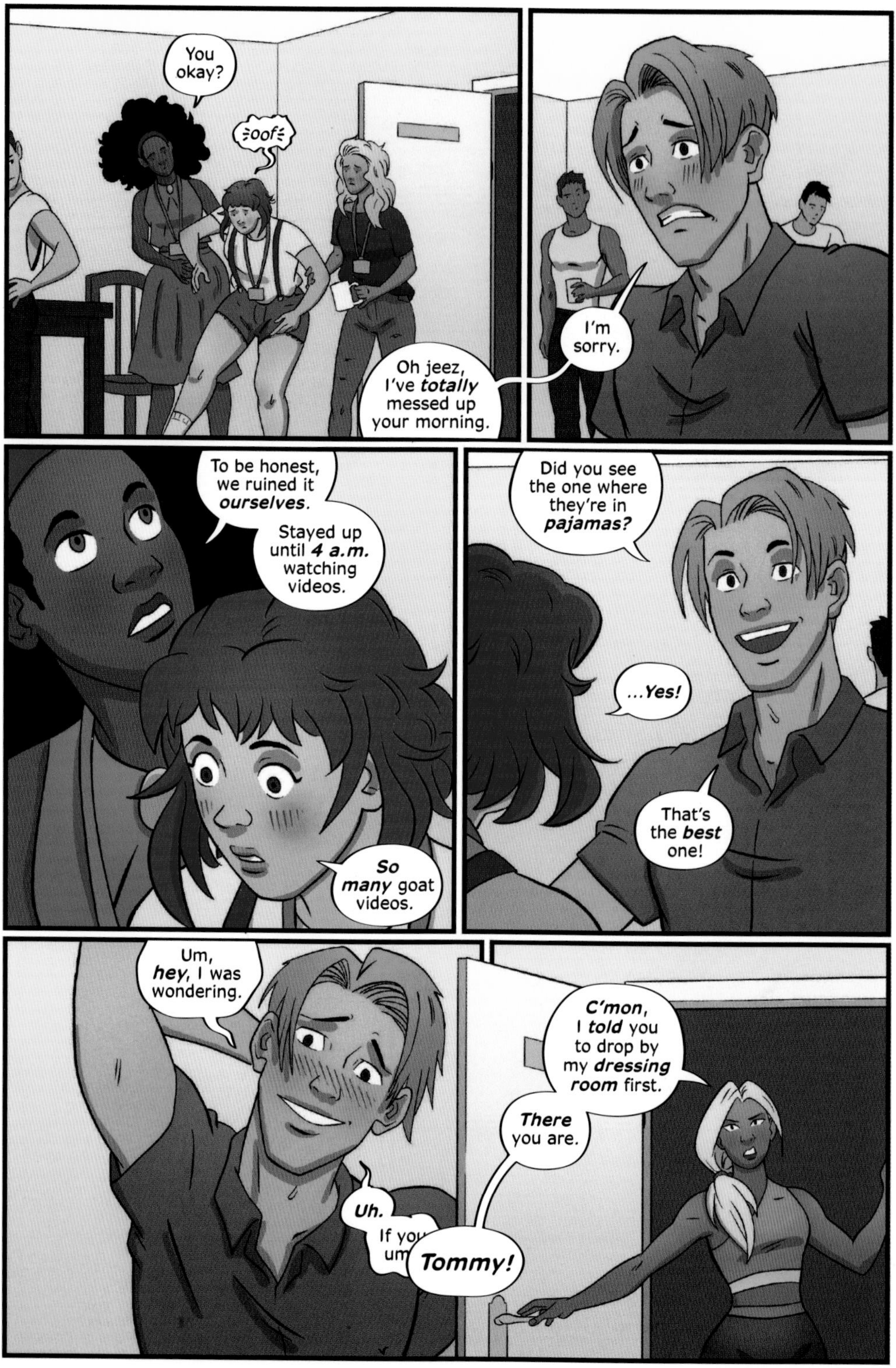
You okay?
oof
Oh jeez, I've *totally* messed up your morning.
I'm sorry.
To be honest, we ruined it *ourselves*.
Stayed up until *4 a.m.* watching videos.
So many goat videos.
Did you see the one where they're in *pajamas?*
...*Yes!*
That's the *best* one!
Um, *hey*, I was wondering.
Uh.
If you um
C'mon, I *told* you to drop by my *dressing room* first.
There you are.
Tommy!

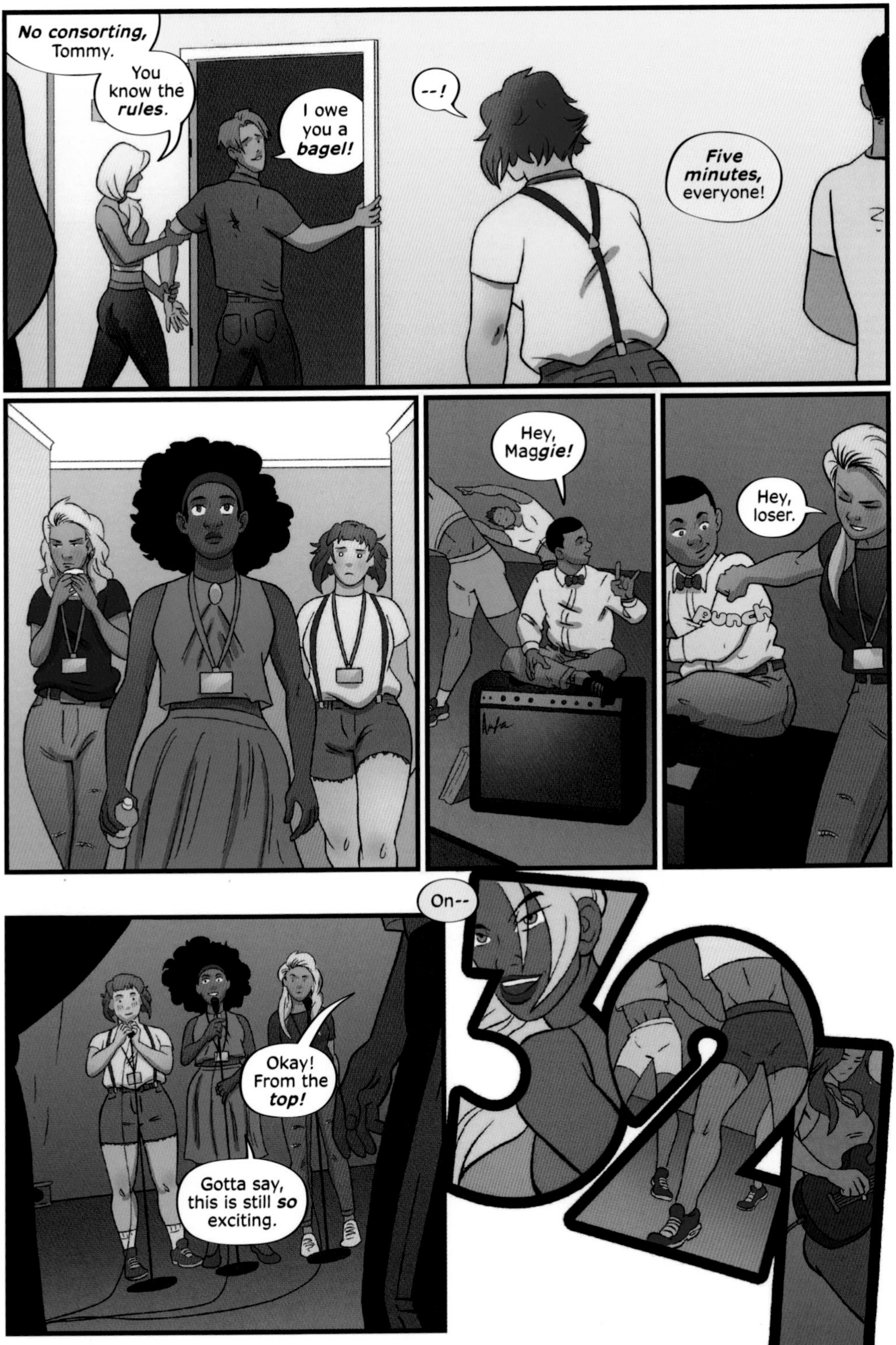
No consorting, Tommy.
You know the rules.
I owe you a bagel!
--!
Five minutes, everyone!
Hey, Maggie!
Hey, loser.
Punch
Okay! From the top!
Gotta say, this is still so exciting.
On--

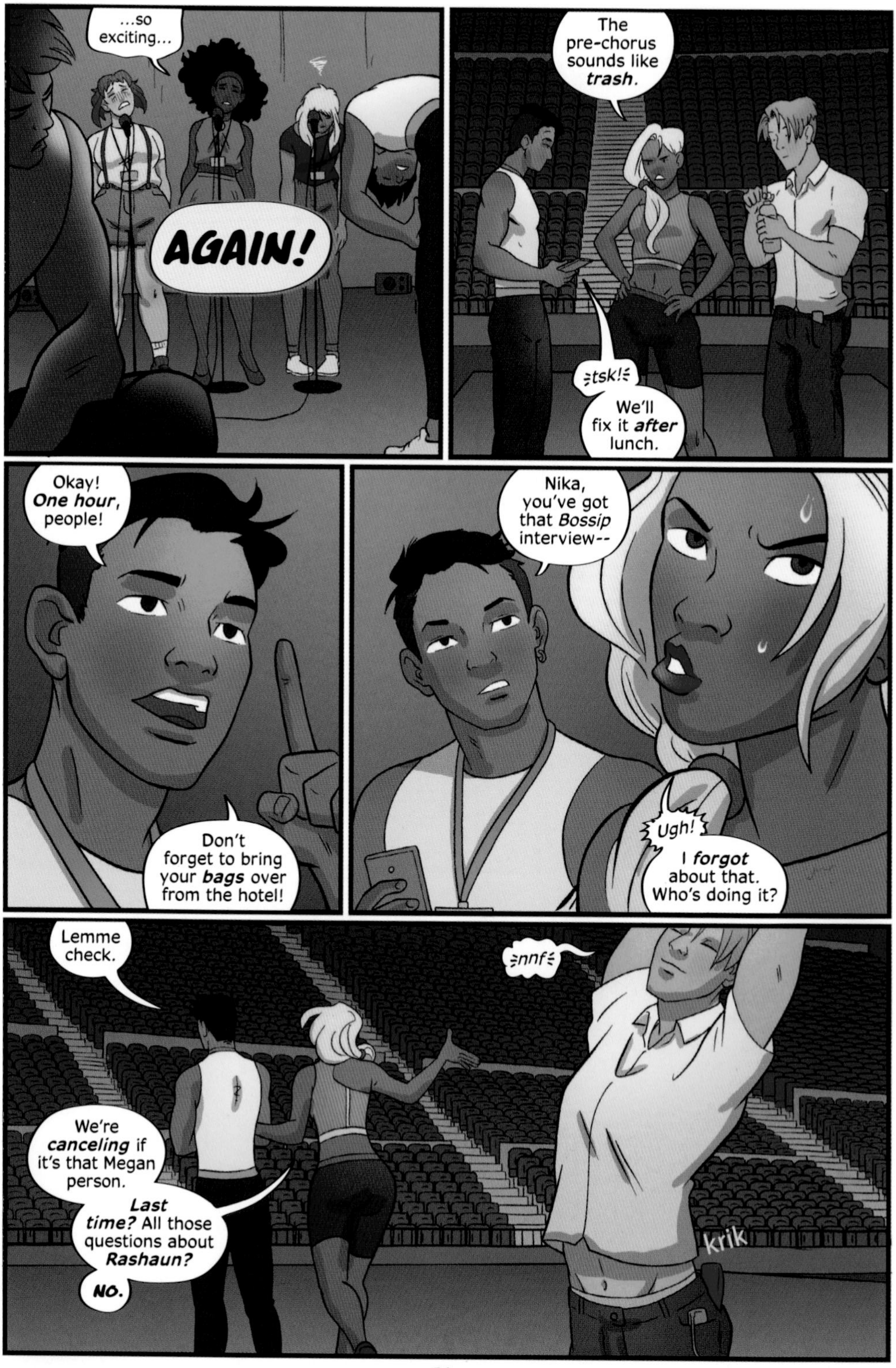
...so exciting...
AGAIN!
The pre-chorus sounds like *trash*.
tsk!
We'll fix it *after* lunch.
Okay! *One hour*, people!
Don't forget to bring your *bags* over from the hotel!
Nika, you've got that *Bossip* interview--
Ugh!
I *forgot* about that. Who's doing it?
Lemme check.
nnf
We're *canceling* if it's that Megan person.
Last time? All those questions about *Rashaun?*
NO.
krik

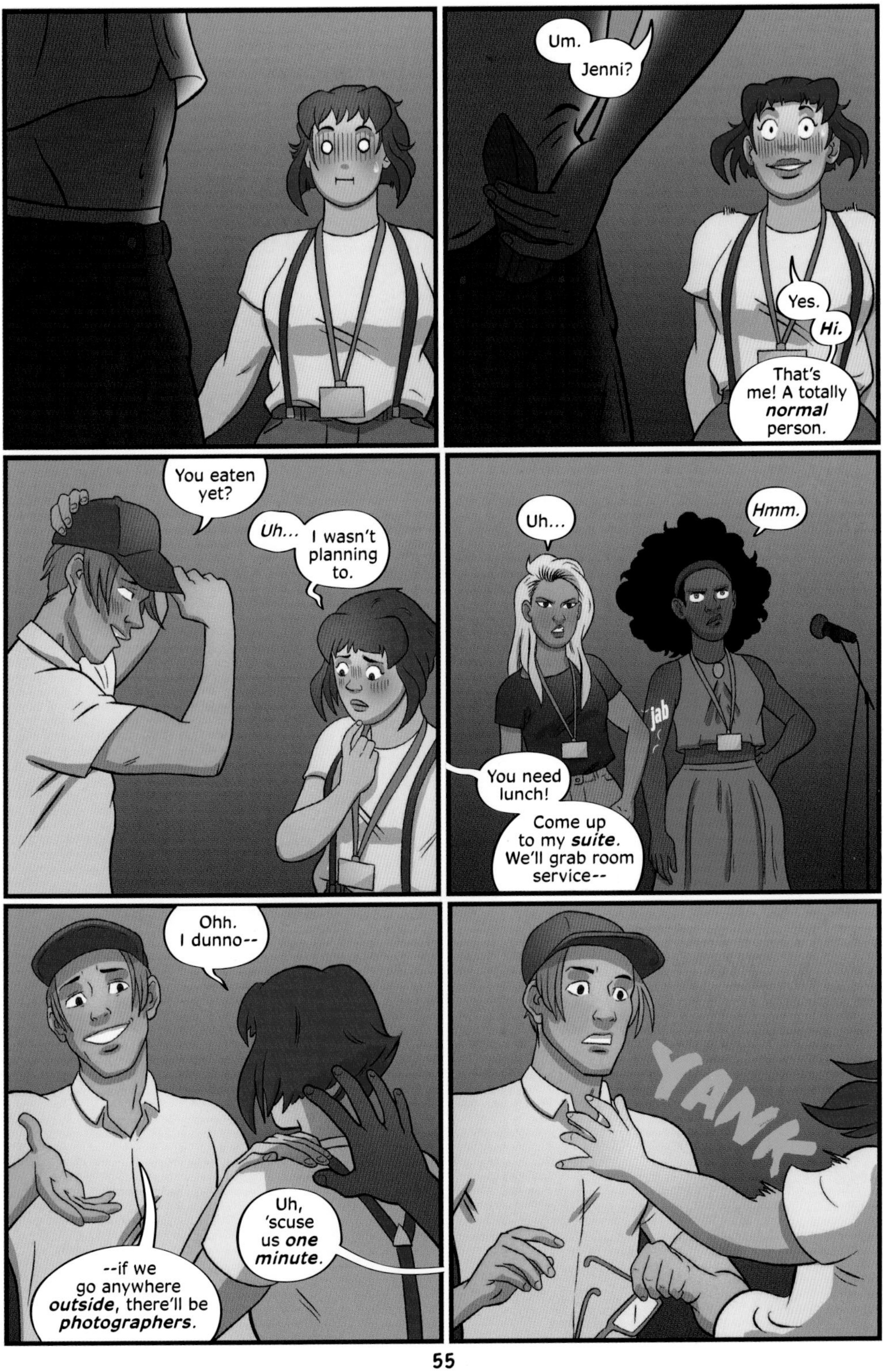

Um.
Jenni?
Yes.
Hi.
That's me! A totally ***normal*** person.
You eaten yet?
Uh...
I wasn't planning to.
Uh...
Hmm.
jab
You need lunch!
Come up to my ***suite***. We'll grab room service--
Ohh. I dunno--
--if we go anywhere ***outside***, there'll be ***photographers***.
Uh, 'scuse us ***one minute***.
YANK

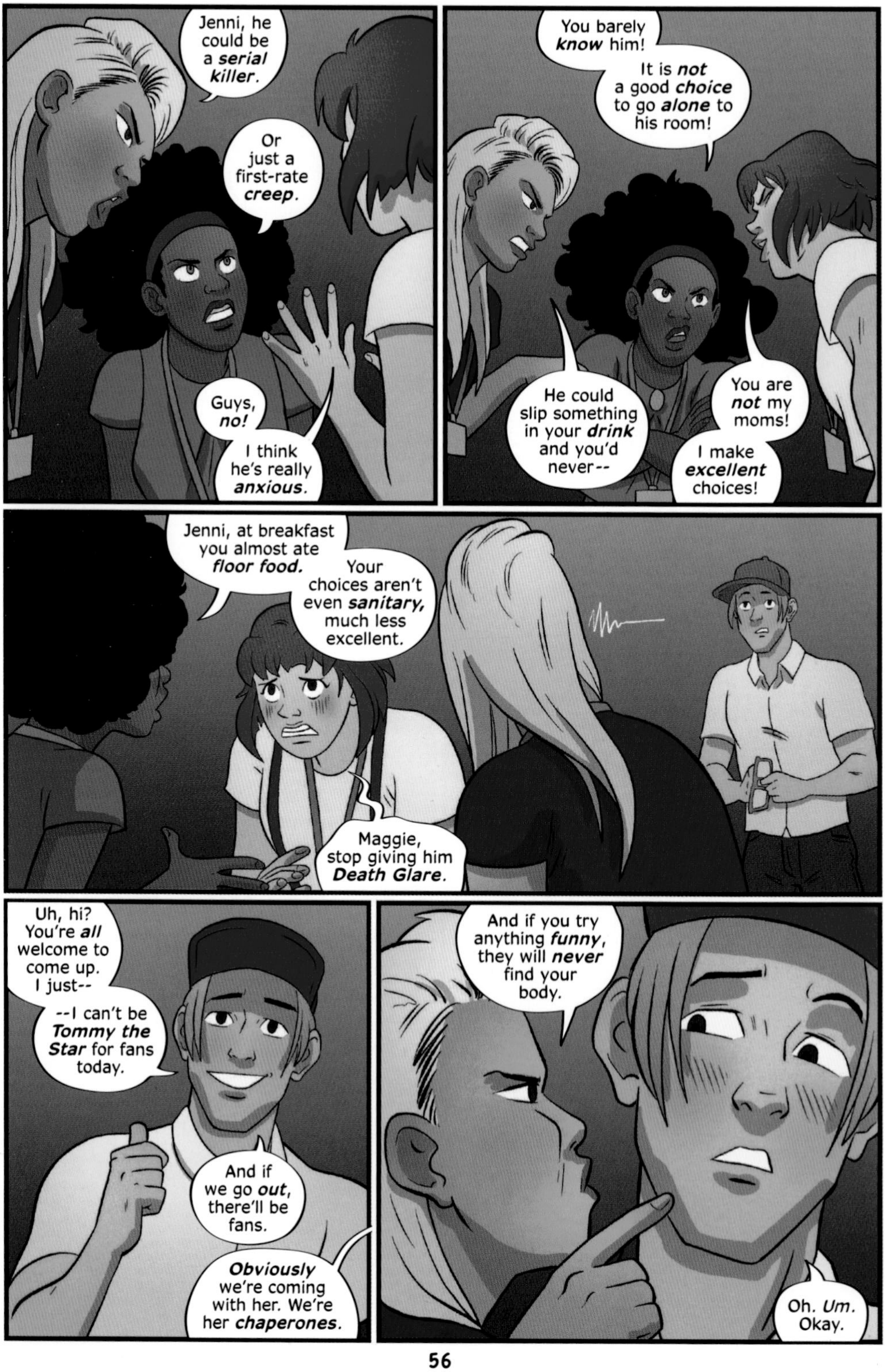

Jenni, he could be a *serial killer*.
Or just a first-rate *creep*.
Guys, *no!*
I think he's really *anxious*.
You barely *know* him!
It is *not* a good *choice* to go *alone* to his room!
He could slip something in your *drink* and you'd never--
You are *not* my moms!
I make *excellent* choices!
Jenni, at breakfast you almost ate *floor food.*
Your choices aren't even *sanitary,* much less excellent.
Maggie, stop giving him *Death Glare*.
Uh, hi? You're *all* welcome to come up. I just--
--I can't be *Tommy the Star* for fans today.
And if we go *out*, there'll be fans.
Obviously we're coming with her. We're her *chaperones*.
And if you try anything *funny*, they will *never* find your body.
Oh. *Um*. Okay.

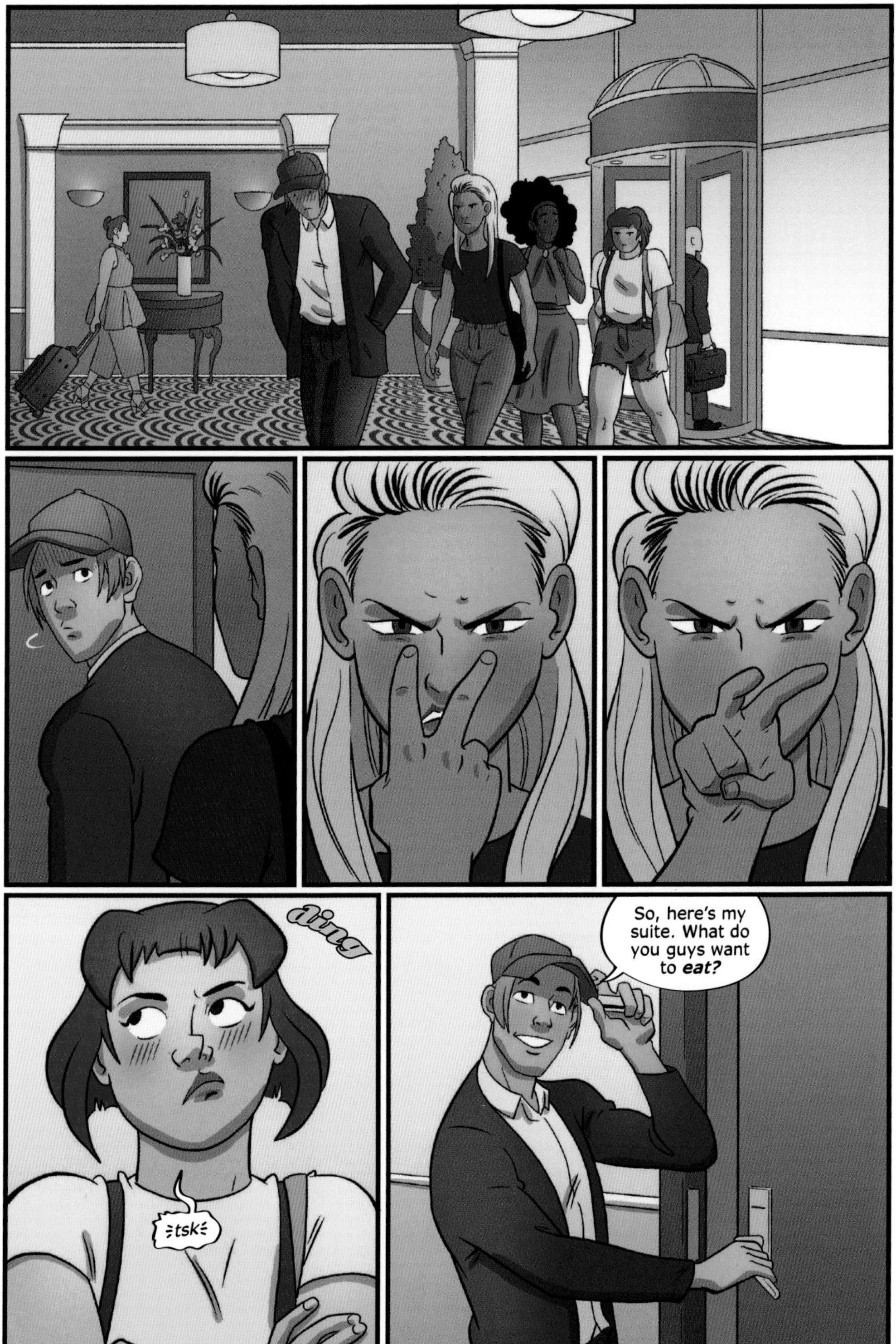
ding
tsk
So, here's my suite. What do you guys want to *eat?*

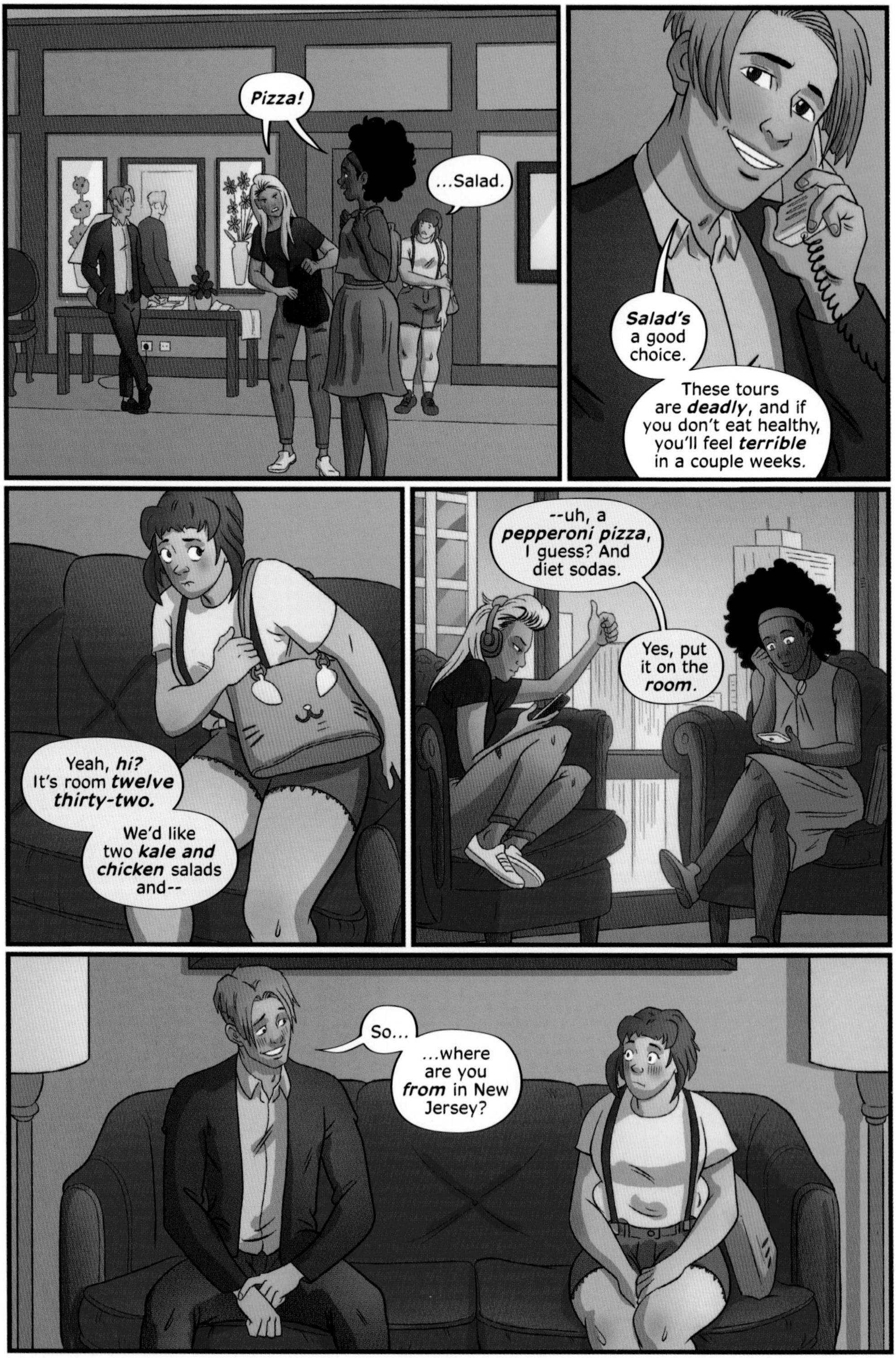
Pizza!
...Salad.
Salad's a good choice.
These tours are deadly, and if you don't eat healthy, you'll feel terrible in a couple weeks.
Yeah, hi? It's room twelve thirty-two.
We'd like two kale and chicken salads and--
--uh, a pepperoni pizza, I guess? And diet sodas.
Yes, put it on the room.
So...
...where are you from in New Jersey?

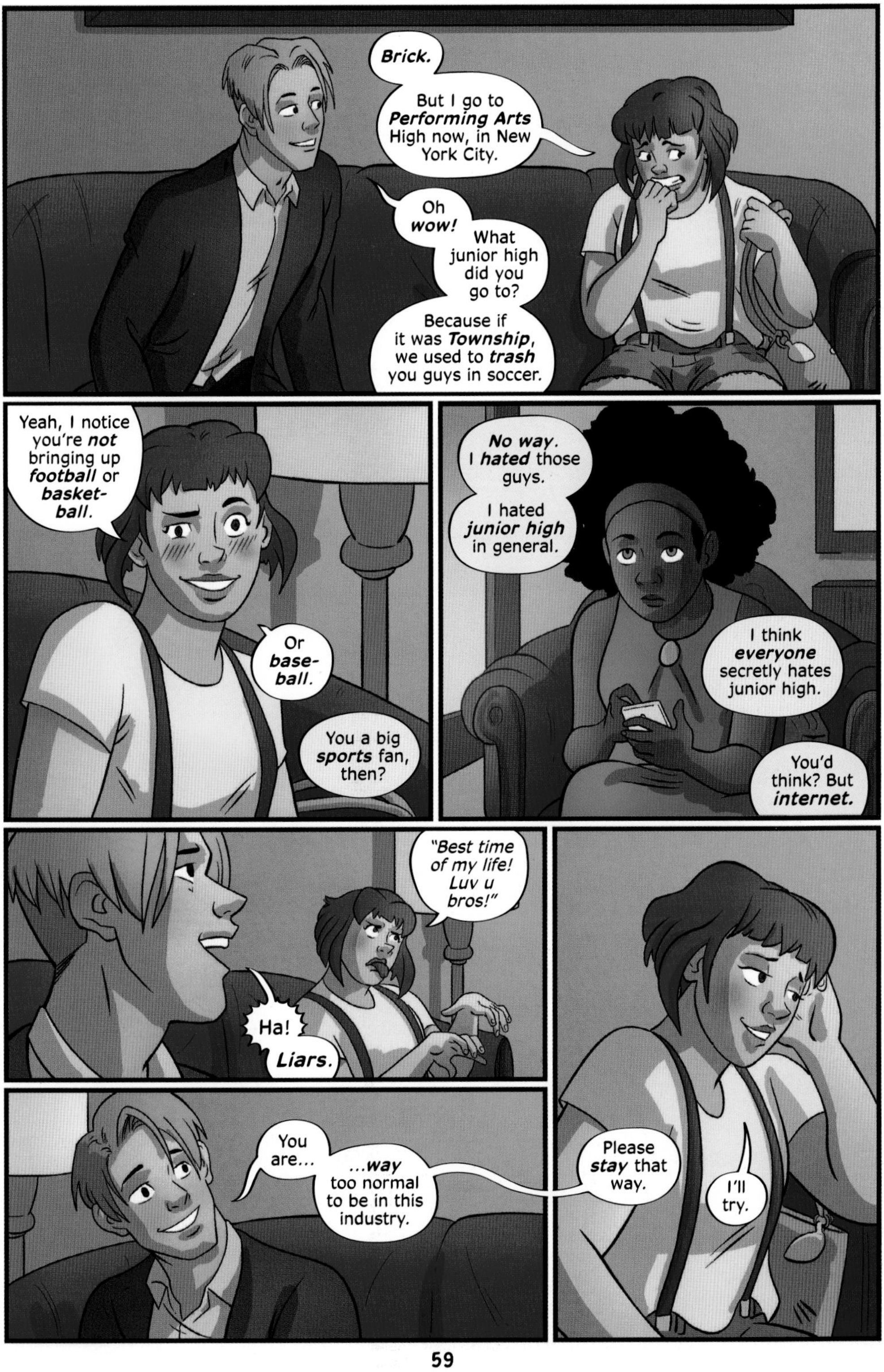

Brick.
But I go to Performing Arts High now, in New York City.
Oh wow!
What junior high did you go to?
Because if it was Township, we used to trash you guys in soccer.
Yeah, I notice you're not bringing up football or basket-ball.
Or base-ball.
You a big sports fan, then?
No way. I hated those guys.
I hated junior high in general.
I think everyone secretly hates junior high.
You'd think? But internet.
"Best time of my life! Luv u bros!"
Ha!
Liars.
You are...
...way too normal to be in this industry.
Please stay that way.
I'll try.

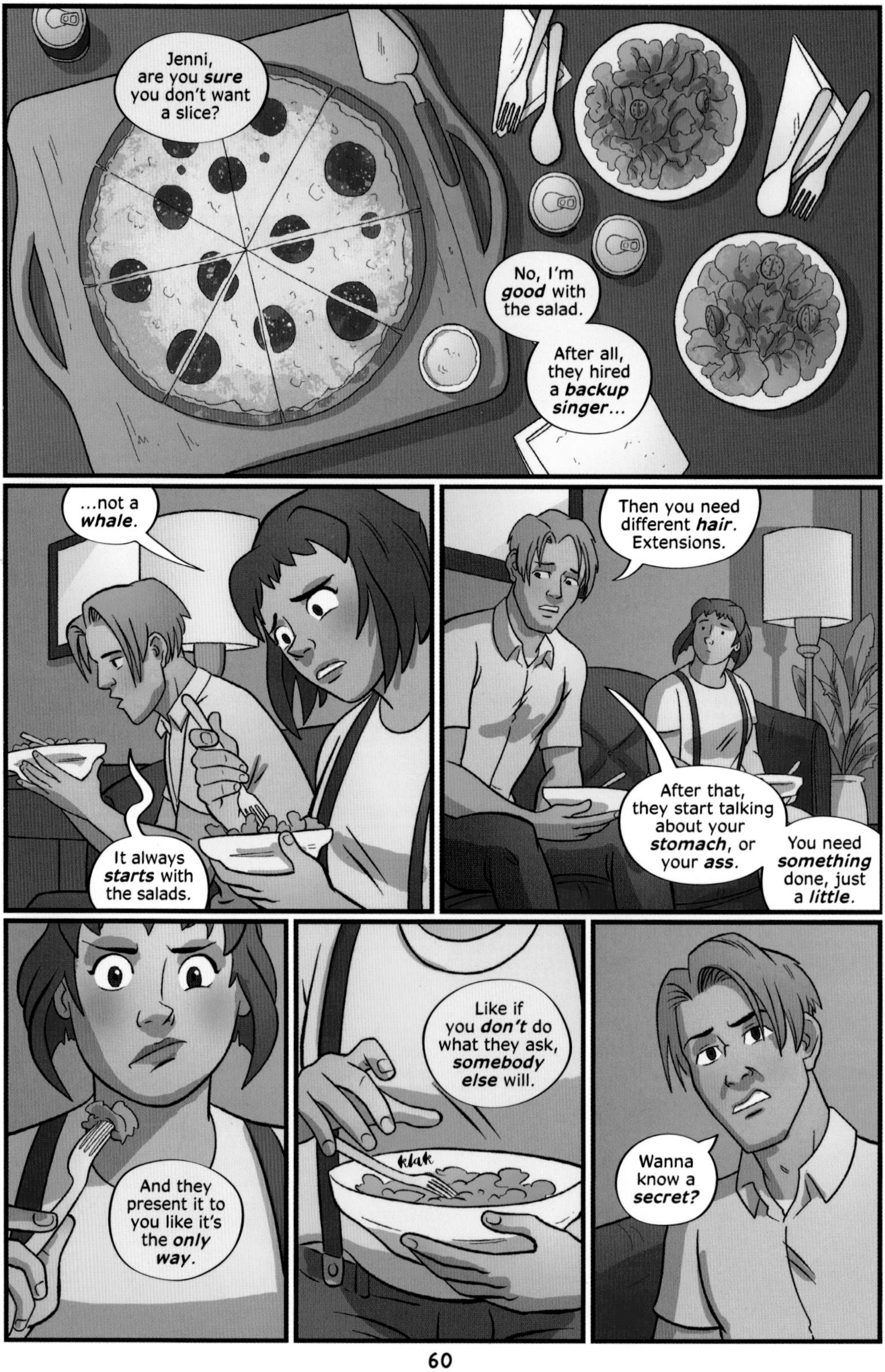
Jenni, are you *sure* you don't want a slice?
No, I'm *good* with the salad.
After all, they hired a *backup singer*...
...not a *whale*.
It always *starts* with the salads.
Then you need different *hair*. Extensions.
After that, they start talking about your *stomach*, or your *ass*.
You need *something* done, just a *little*.
And they present it to you like it's the *only way*.
Like if you *don't* do what they ask, *somebody else* will.
klak
Wanna know a *secret?*

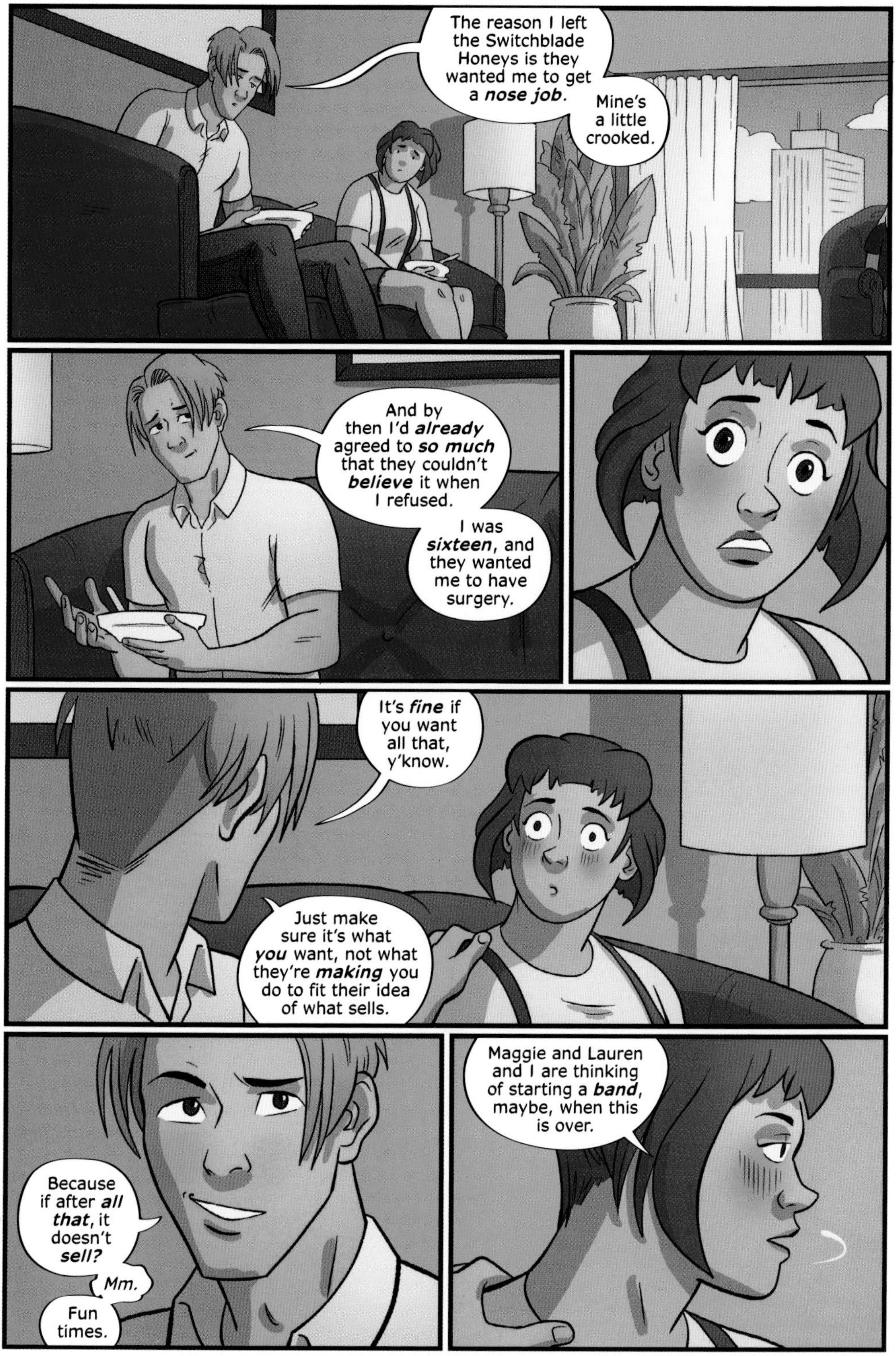
The reason I left the Switchblade Honeys is they wanted me to get a ***nose job***.
Mine's a little crooked.
And by then I'd ***already*** agreed to ***so much*** that they couldn't ***believe*** it when I refused.
I was ***sixteen***, and they wanted me to have surgery.
It's ***fine*** if you want all that, y'know.
Just make sure it's what ***you*** want, not what they're ***making*** you do to fit their idea of what sells.
Because if after ***all that***, it doesn't ***sell?***
Mm.
Fun times.
Maggie and Lauren and I are thinking of starting a ***band***, maybe, when this is over.

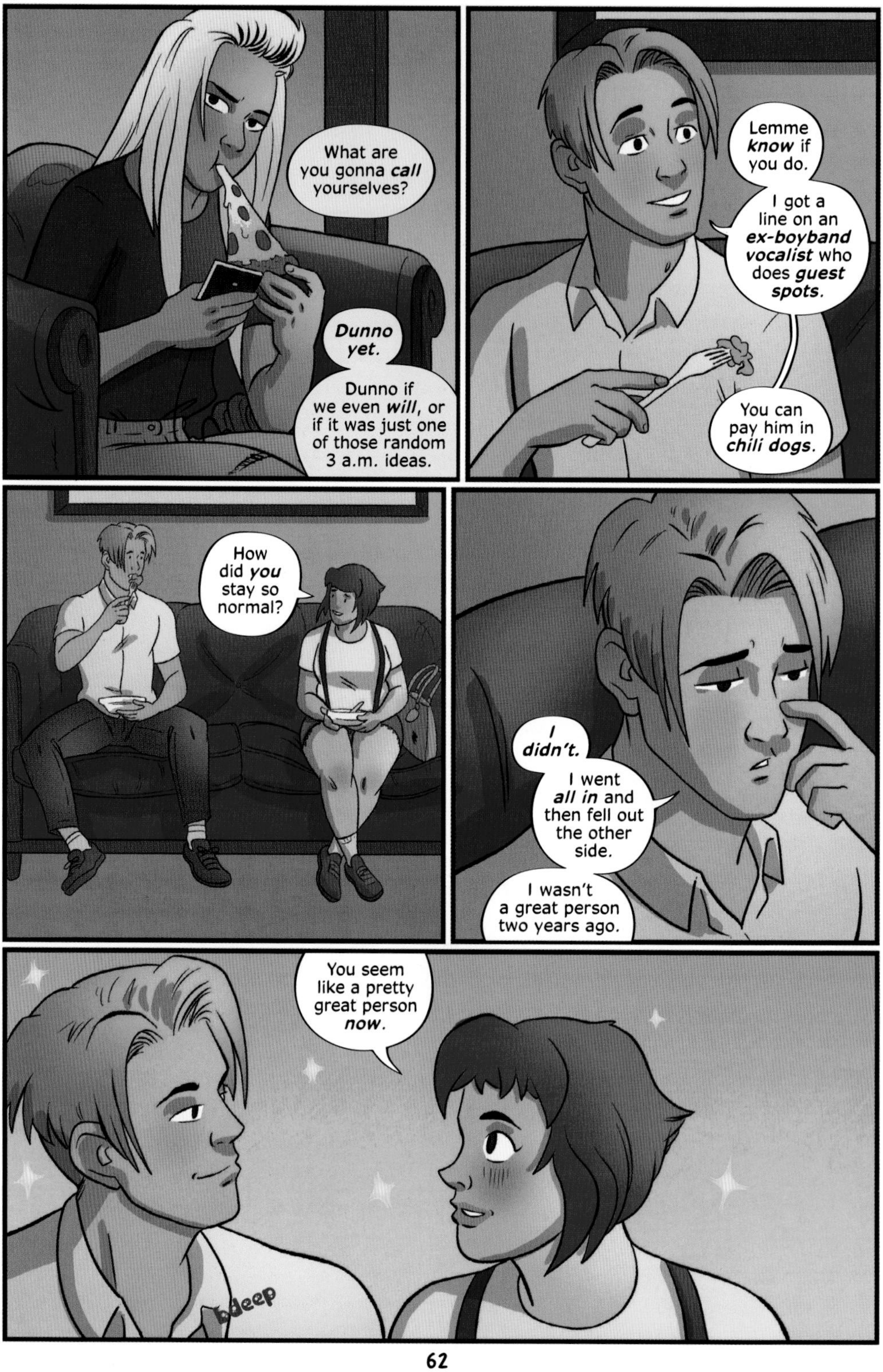
What are you gonna *call* yourselves?
Dunno yet.
Dunno if we even *will*, or if it was just one of those random 3 a.m. ideas.
Lemme *know* if you do.
I got a line on an ***ex-boyband vocalist*** who does ***guest spots.***
You can pay him in ***chili dogs.***
How did *you* stay so normal?
I didn't.
I went *all in* and then fell out the other side.
I wasn't a great person two years ago.
You seem like a pretty great person *now*.
bdeep

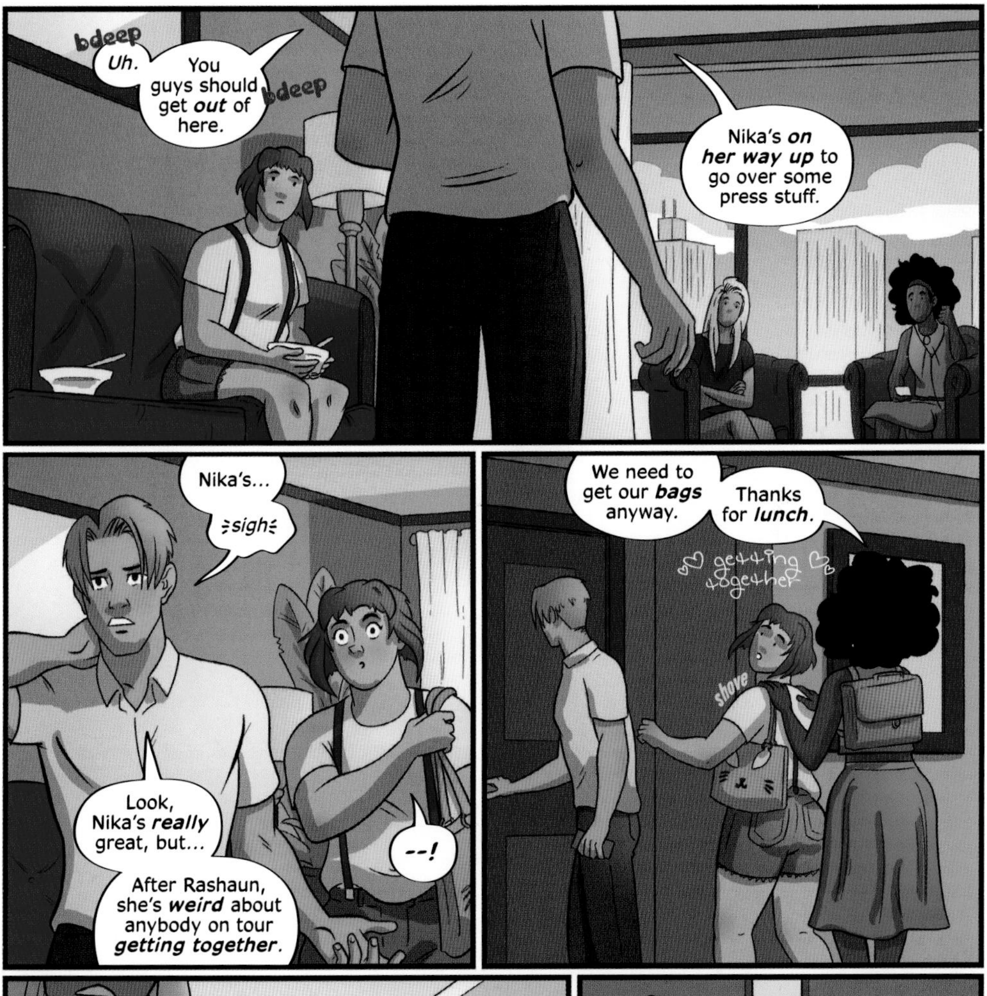
bdeep
Uh.
You guys should get *out* of here.
bdeep
Nika's ***on her way up*** to go over some press stuff.
Nika's...
sigh
Look, Nika's ***really*** great, but...
After Rashaun, she's ***weird*** about anybody on tour ***getting together***.
--!
We need to get our ***bags*** anyway.
Thanks for ***lunch***.
getting together
shove
Who's ***Rashaun?***
See you back at rehearsal!
Maggie, ***how*** do you ***not know*** who ***Rashaun Reed*** is?
ding

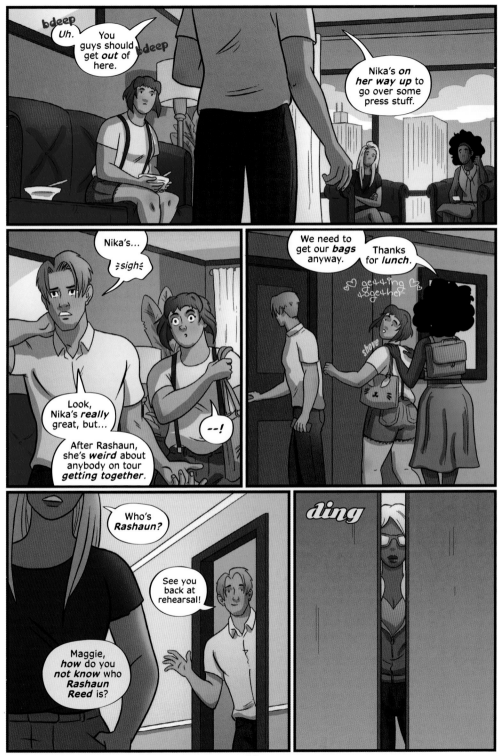

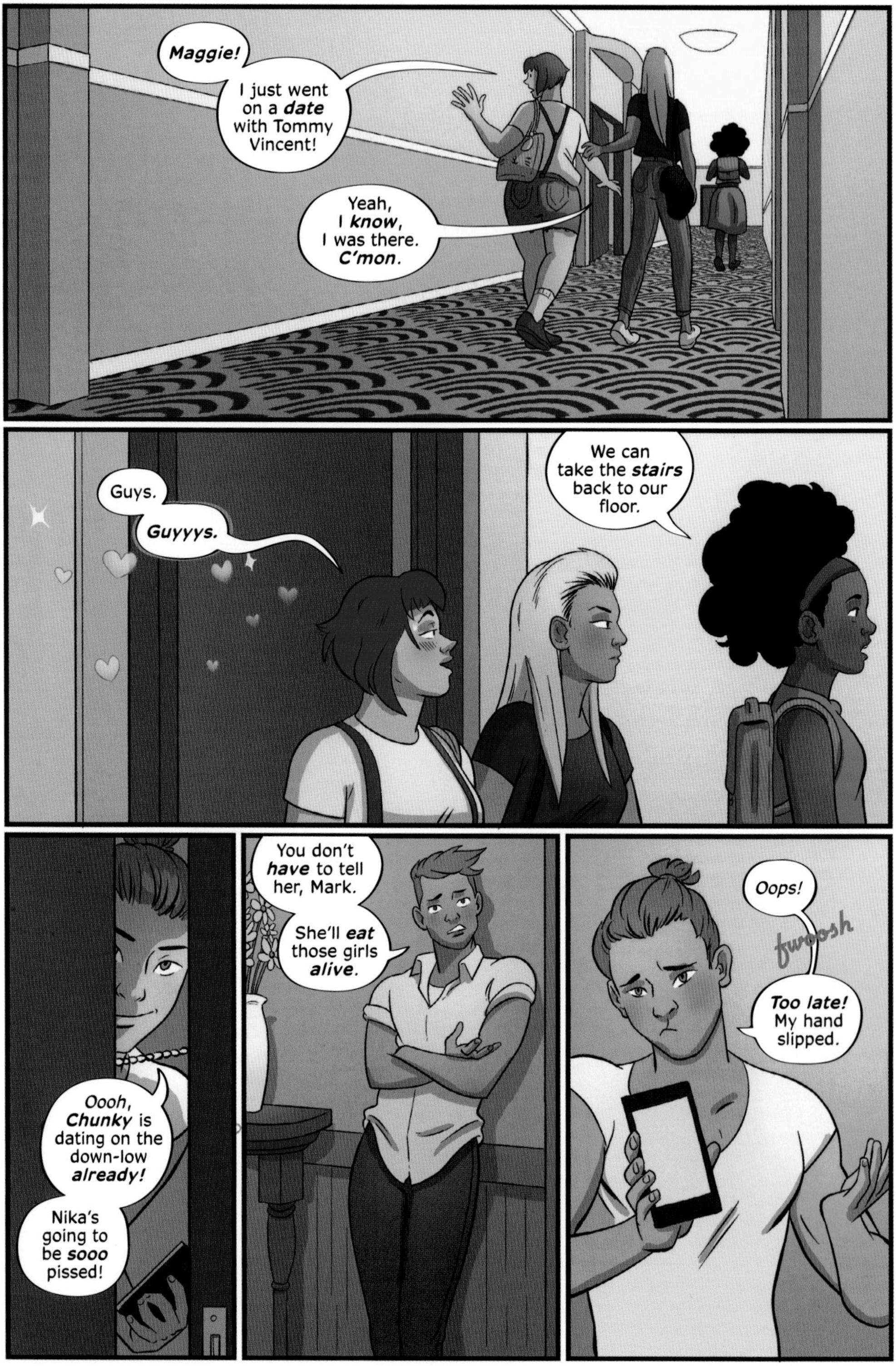
Maggie!
I just went on a date with Tommy Vincent!
Yeah, I know, I was there. C'mon.
Guys.
Guyyys.
We can take the stairs back to our floor.
Oooh, Chunky is dating on the down-low already!
Nika's going to be sooo pissed!
You don't have to tell her, Mark.
She'll eat those girls alive.
Oops!
fwoosh
Too late! My hand slipped.

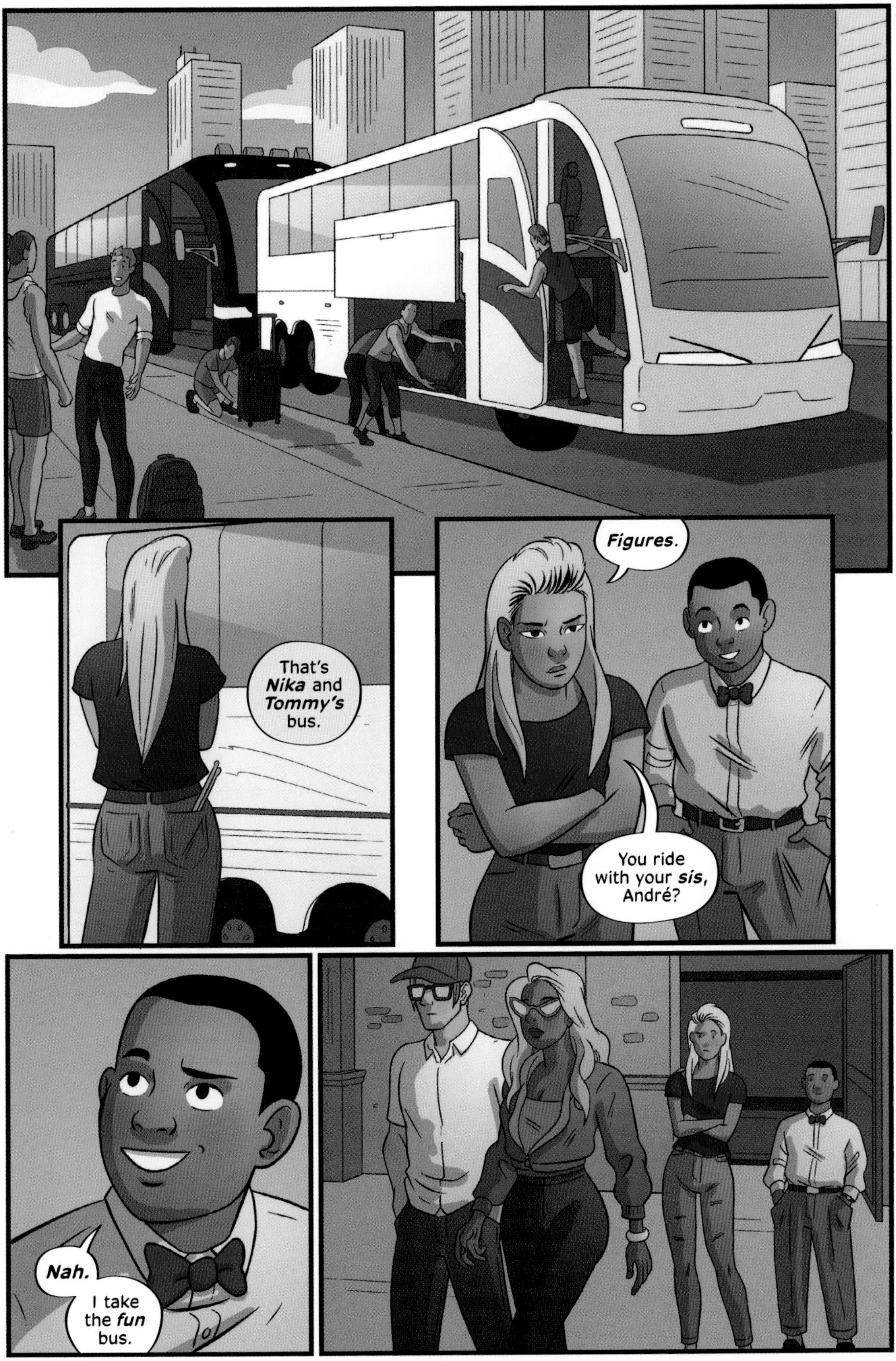
That's *Nika* and *Tommy's* bus.
Figures.
You ride with your *sis*, André?
Nah.
I take the *fun* bus.

66

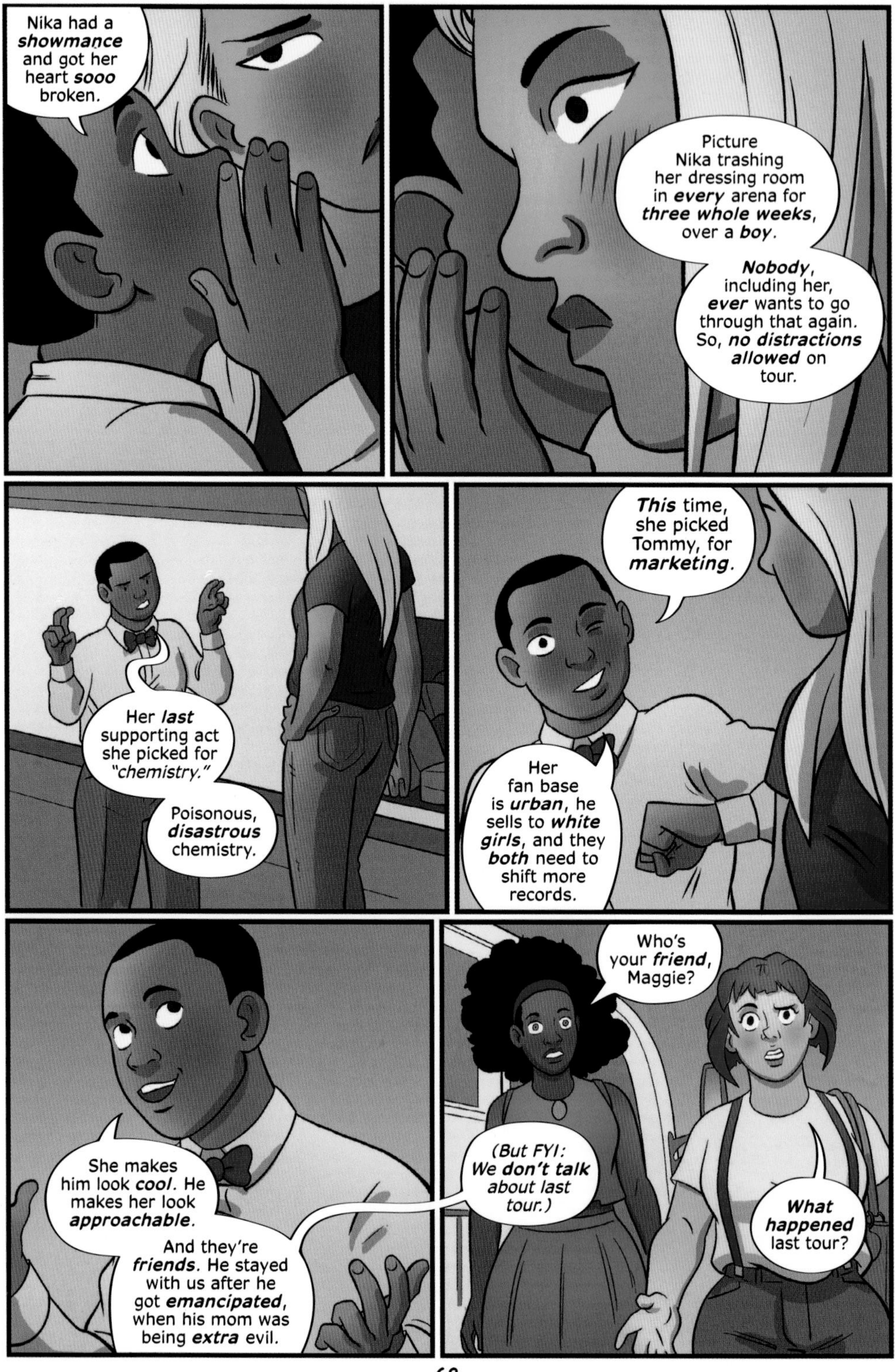

Nika had a *showmance* and got her heart *sooo* broken.
Picture Nika trashing her dressing room in *every* arena for *three whole weeks*, over a *boy*.
Nobody, including her, *ever* wants to go through that again. So, *no distractions allowed* on tour.
Her *last* supporting act she picked for *"chemistry."*
Poisonous, *disastrous* chemistry.
This time, she picked Tommy, for *marketing*.
Her fan base is *urban*, he sells to *white girls*, and they *both* need to shift more records.
She makes him look *cool*. He makes her look *approachable*.
And they're *friends*. He stayed with us after he got *emancipated*, when his mom was being *extra* evil.
Who's your *friend*, Maggie?
*(But FYI: We **don't talk** about last tour.)*
What happened last tour?

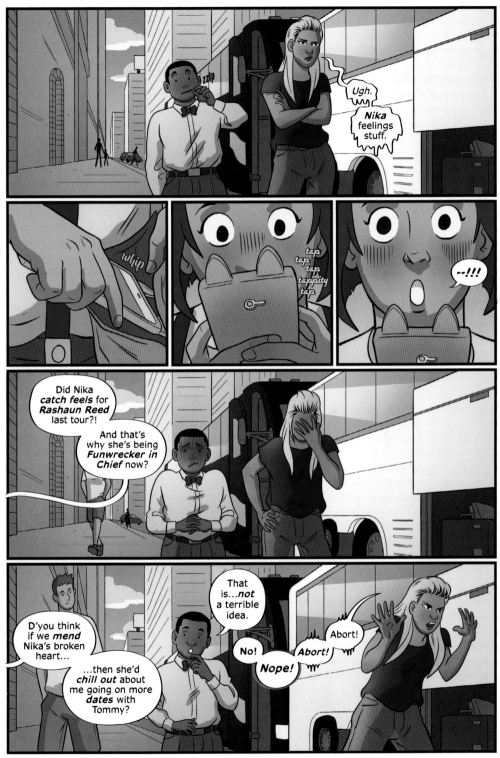

Panel 1:

Ugh.

Nika feelings stuff.

Panel 2:

zzip

whip

tap tap tap tappity tap

--!!!

Panel 3:

Did Nika *catch feels* for *Rashaun Reed* last tour?!

And that's why she's being *Funwrecker in Chief* now?

Panel 4:

D'you think if we *mend* Nika's broken heart...

...then she'd *chill out* about me going on more *dates* with Tommy?

That is...*not* a terrible idea.

No!

Abort!

Nope!

Abort!

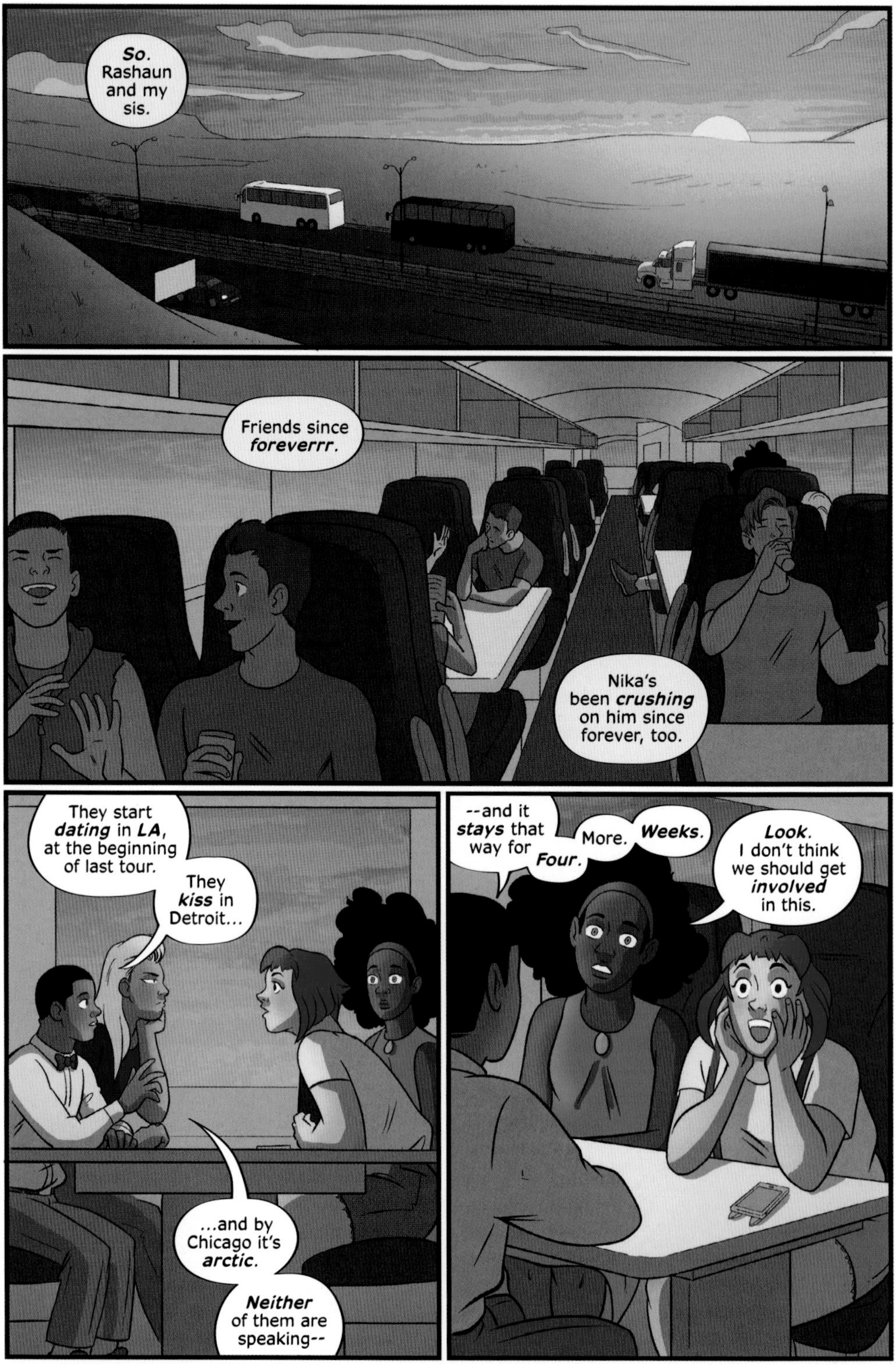
So. Rashaun and my sis.
Friends since foreverrr.
Nika's been crushing on him since forever, too.
They start dating in LA, at the beginning of last tour.
They kiss in Detroit...
...and by Chicago it's arctic.
Neither of them are speaking--
--and it stays that way for
Four.
More.
Weeks.
Look. I don't think we should get involved in this.

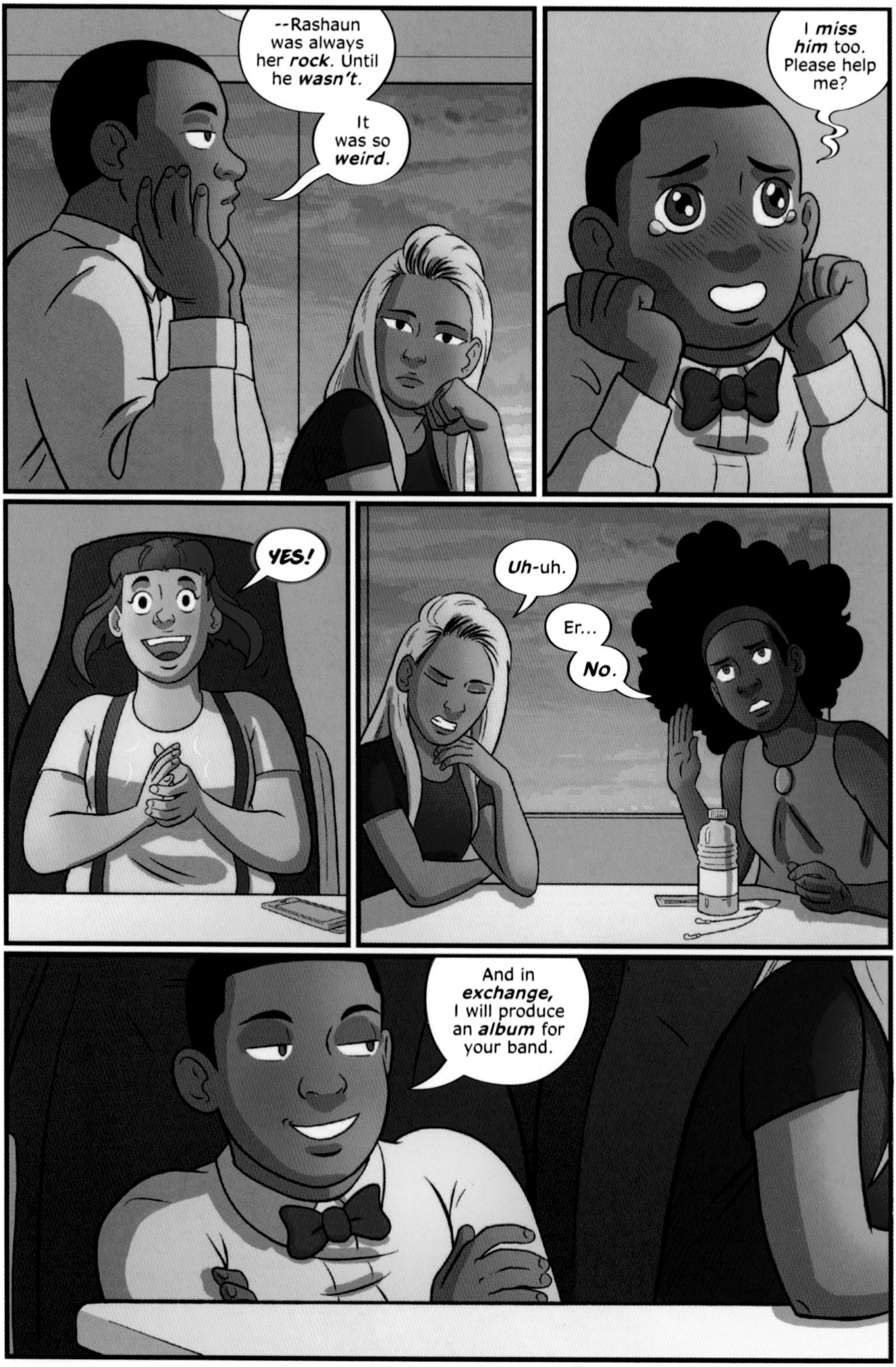
--Rashaun was always her *rock*. Until he *wasn't*.
It was so *weird*.
I *miss him* too. Please help me?
YES!
Uh-uh.
Er...
No.
And in *exchange,* I will produce an *album* for your band.

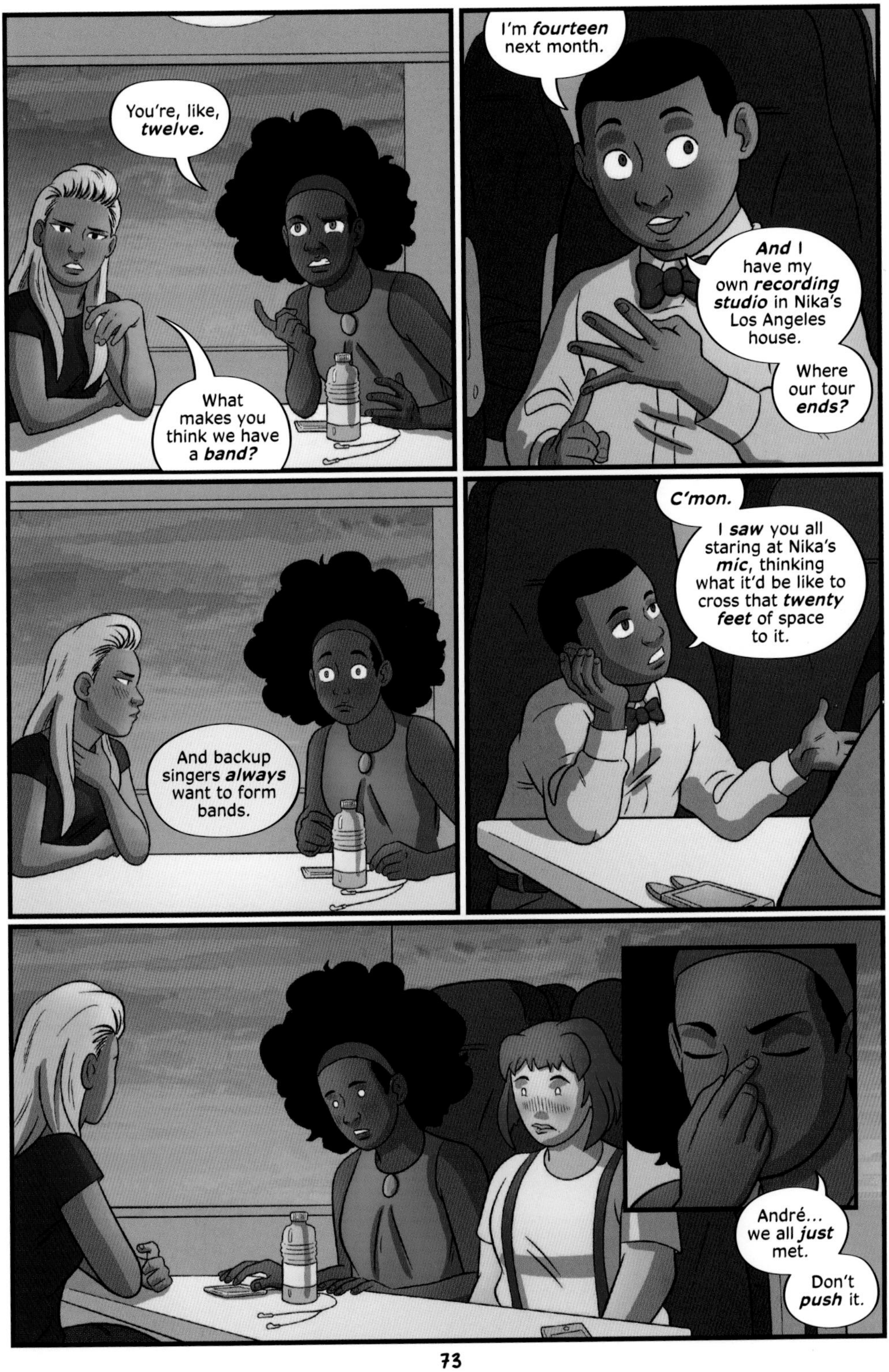
You're, like, *twelve.*
What makes you think we have a *band?*
I'm *fourteen* next month.
And I have my own *recording studio* in Nika's Los Angeles house.
Where our tour *ends?*
And backup singers *always* want to form bands.
C'mon.
I *saw* you all staring at Nika's *mic*, thinking what it'd be like to cross that *twenty feet* of space to it.
André... we all *just* met.
Don't *push* it.

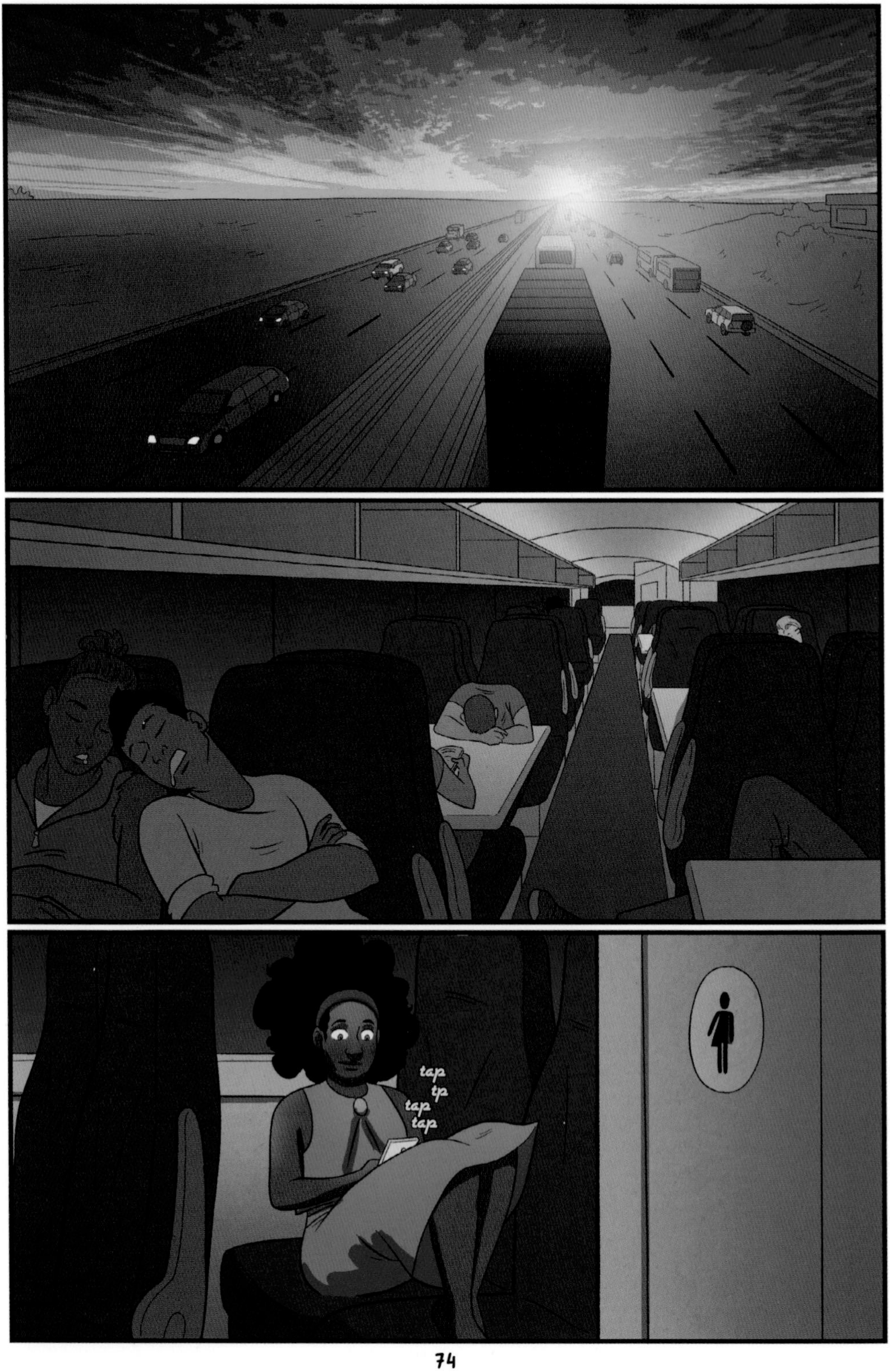
tap
tp
tap
tap

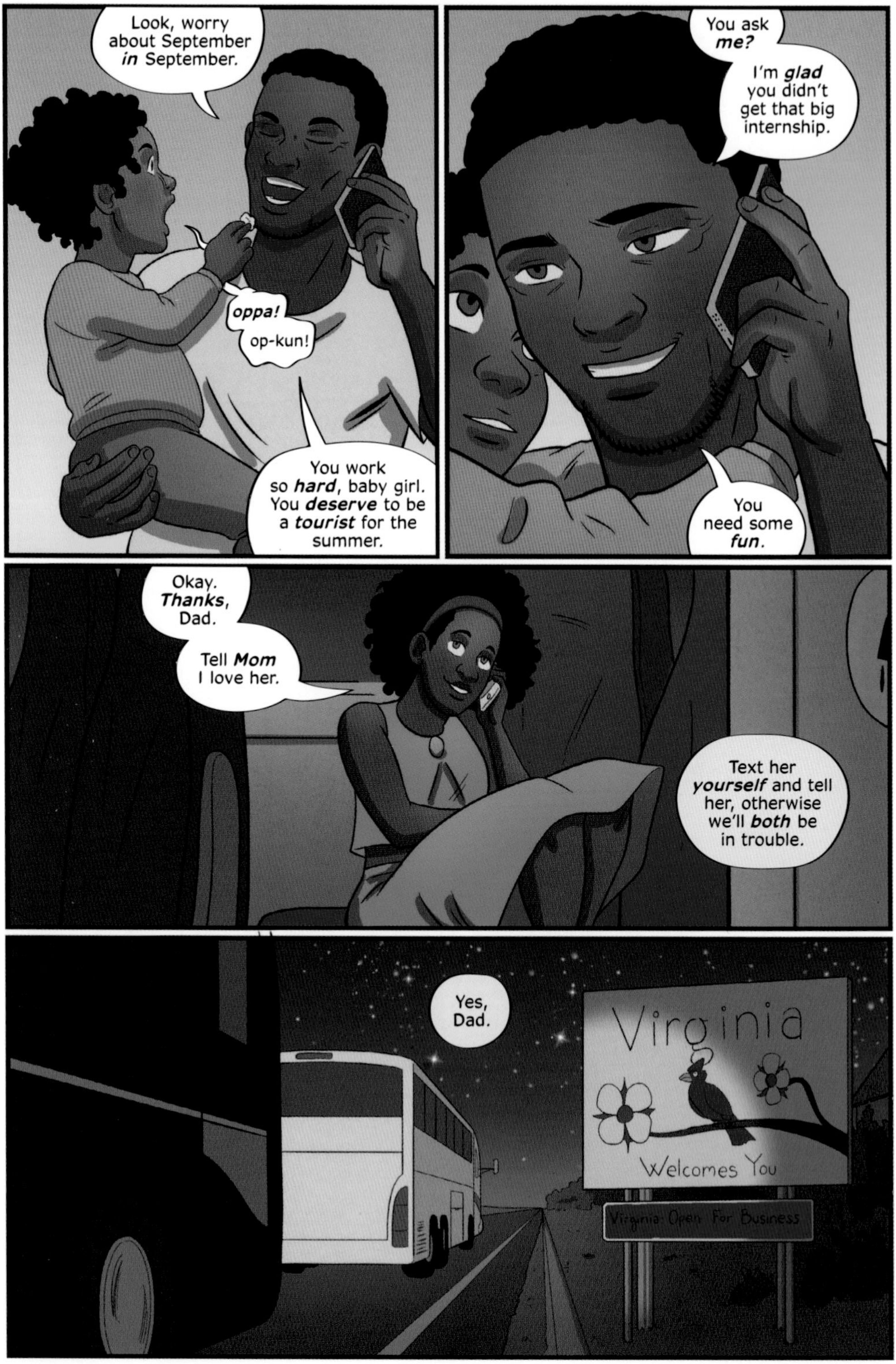
Look, worry about September *in* September.
oppa!
op-kun!
You work so ***hard***, baby girl. You ***deserve*** to be a ***tourist*** for the summer.
You ask ***me?***
I'm ***glad*** you didn't get that big internship.
You need some ***fun***.
Okay. ***Thanks***, Dad.
Tell ***Mom*** I love her.
Text her ***yourself*** and tell her, otherwise we'll ***both*** be in trouble.
Yes, Dad.
Virginia
Welcomes You
Virginia: Open For Business

CHAPTER 3

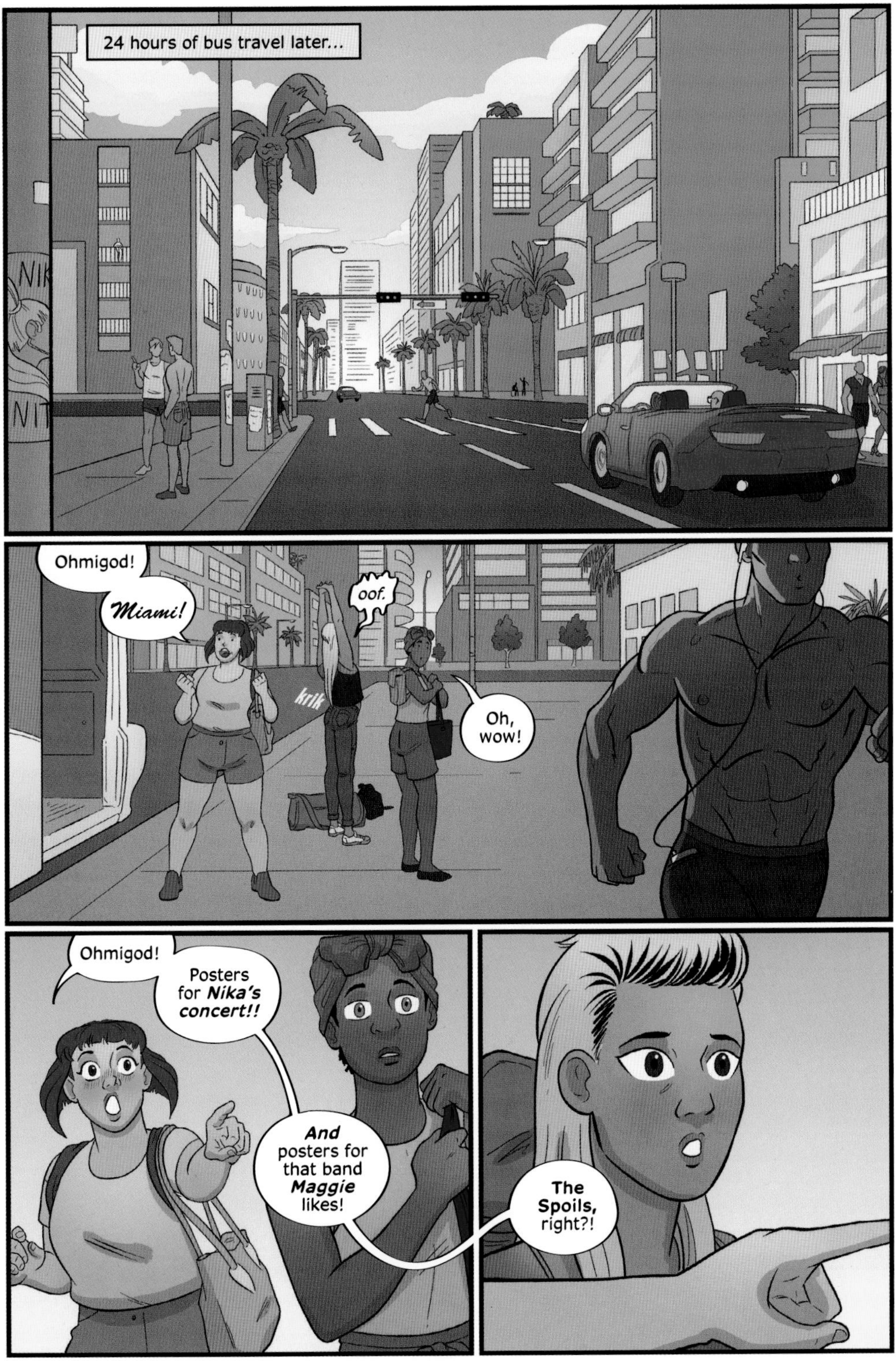
24 hours of bus travel later...
NIK
NIT
Ohmigod!
Miami!
oof.
krik
Oh, wow!
Ohmigod!
Posters for Nika's concert!!
And posters for that band Maggie likes!
The Spoils, right?!

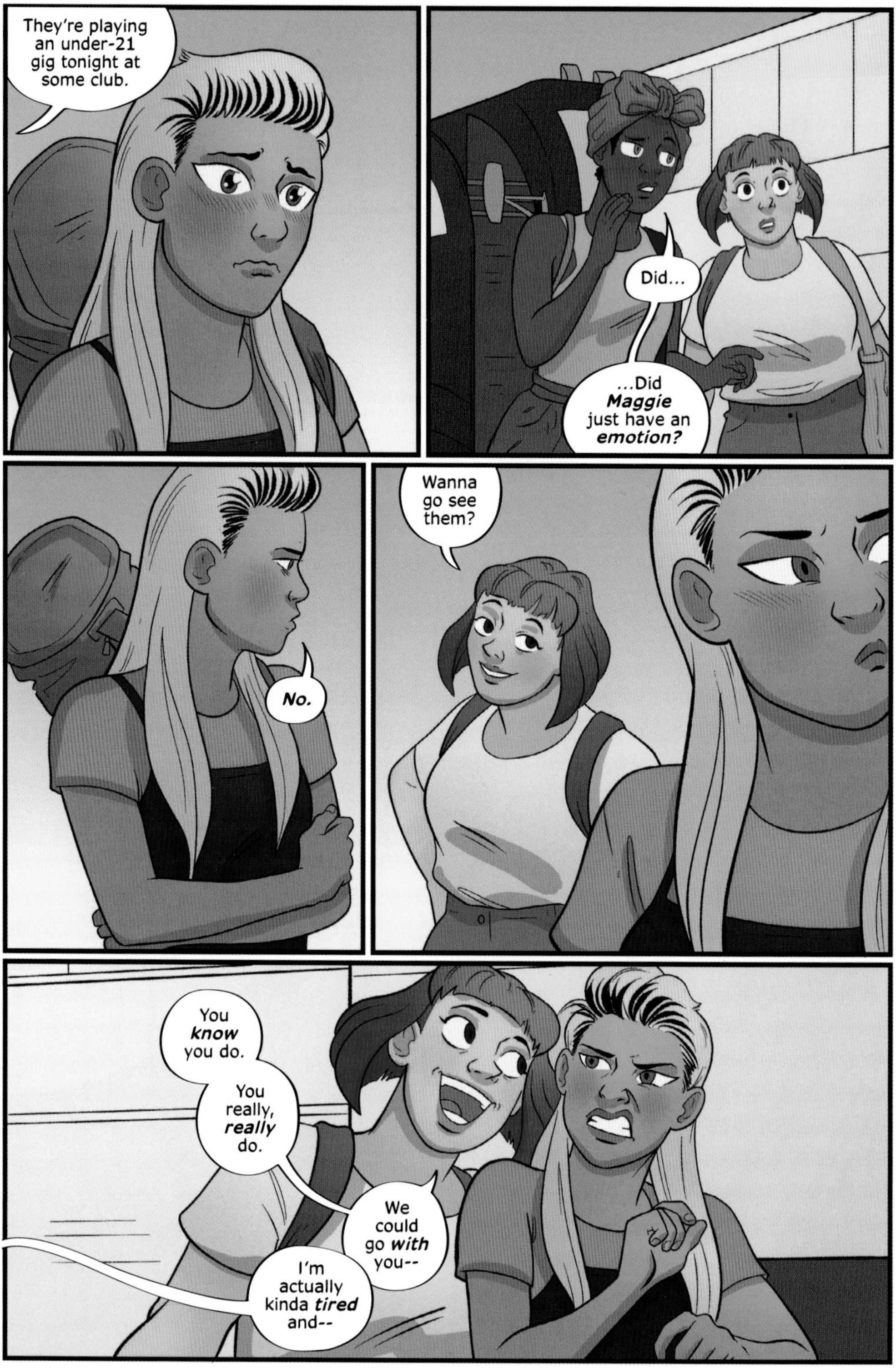
They're playing an under-21 gig tonight at some club.
Did...
...Did *Maggie* just have an *emotion?*
No.
Wanna go see them?
You *know* you do.
You really, *really* do.
We could go *with* you--
I'm actually kinda *tired* and--

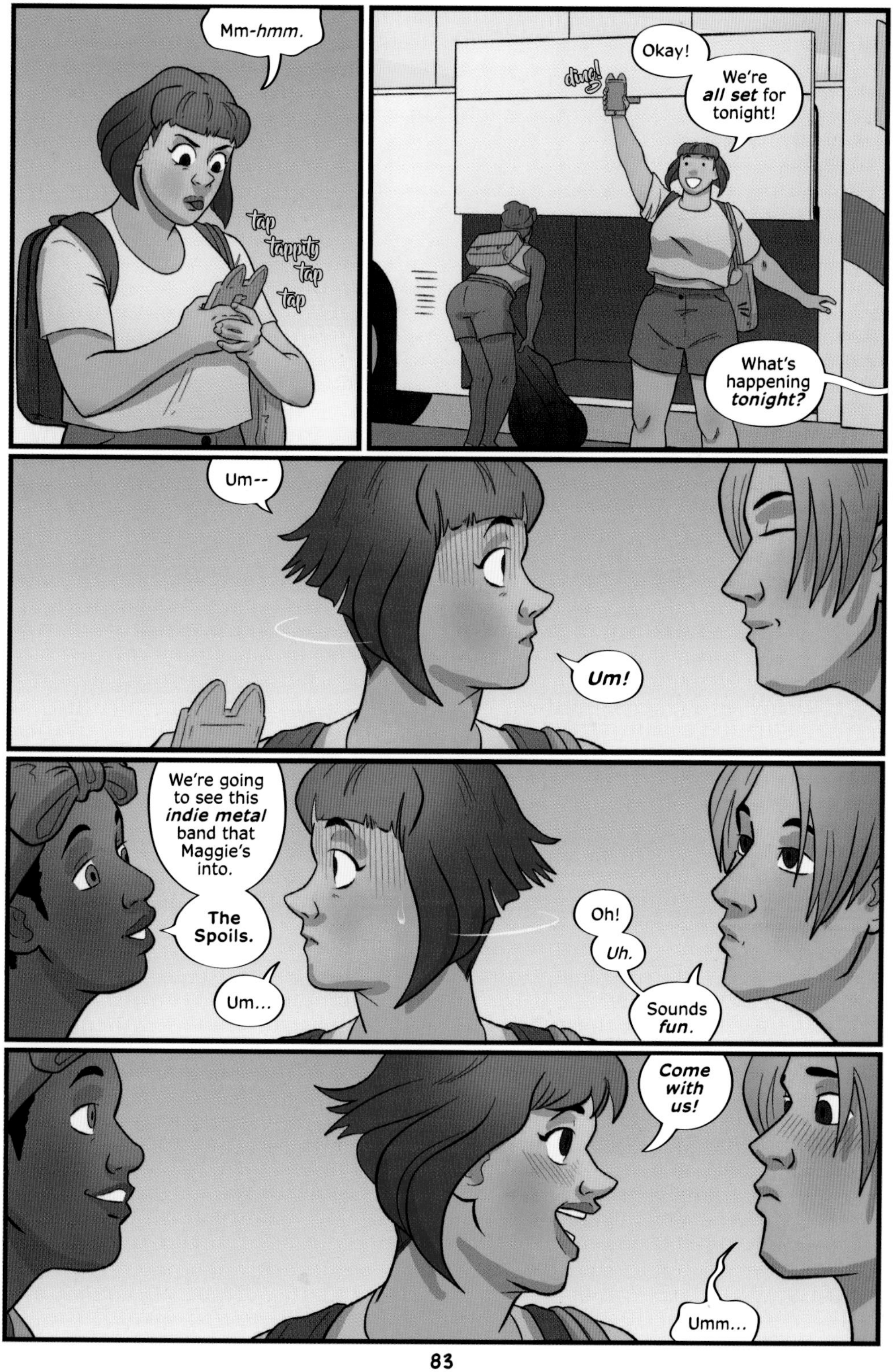
Mm-*hmm*.
tap
tappity
tap
tap
Okay!
ding!
We're **all set** for tonight!
What's happening ***tonight?***
Um--
Um!
We're going to see this ***indie metal*** band that Maggie's into.
The Spoils.
Um...
Oh!
Uh.
Sounds ***fun***.
Come with us!
Umm...

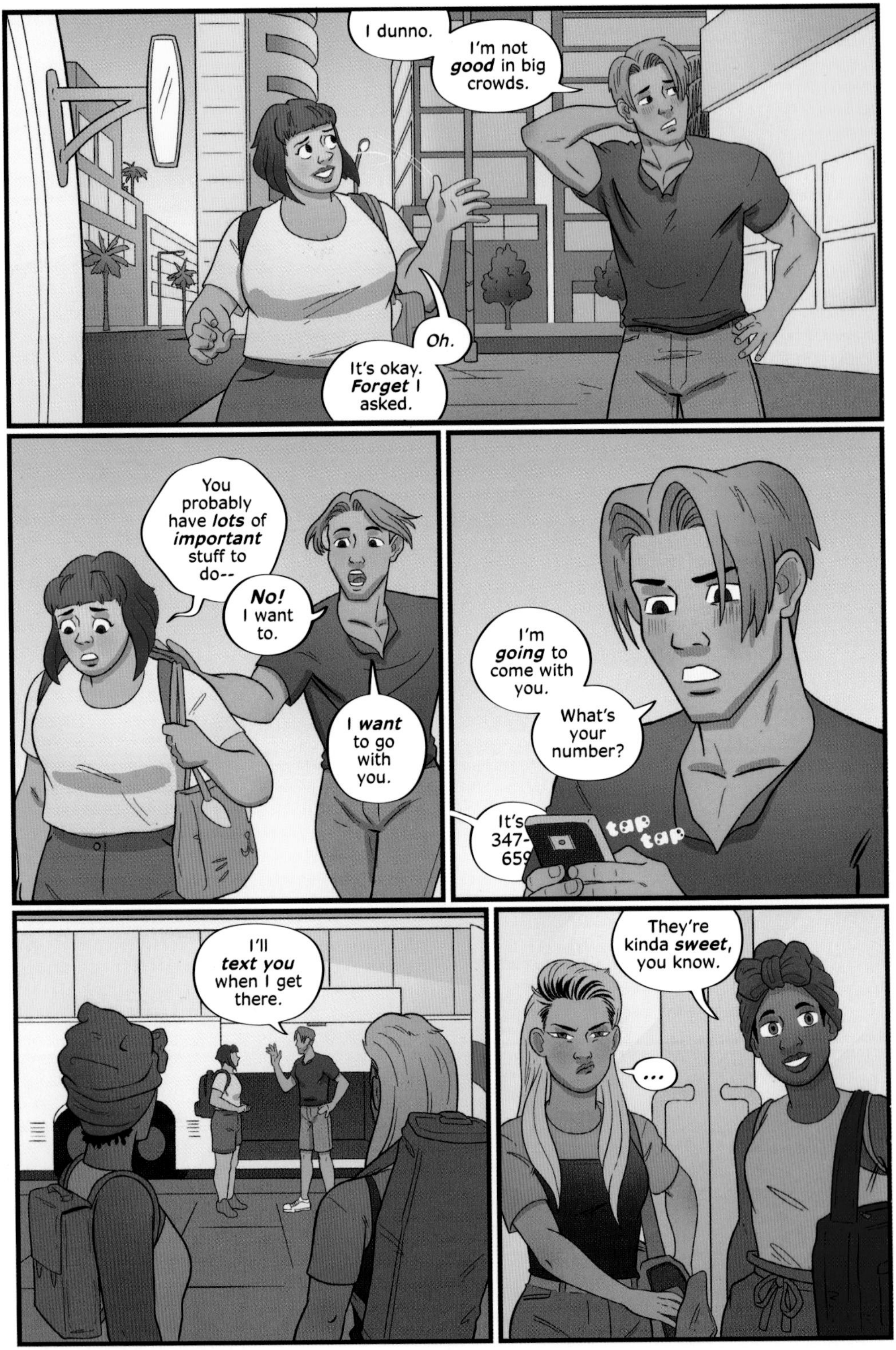
I dunno.
I'm not *good* in big crowds.
Oh.
It's okay. ***Forget*** I asked.
You probably have ***lots*** of ***important*** stuff to do--
No! I want to.
I ***want*** to go with you.
I'm ***going*** to come with you.
What's your number?
It's 347-659
tap tap
I'll ***text you*** when I get there.
They're kinda ***sweet,*** you know.
...

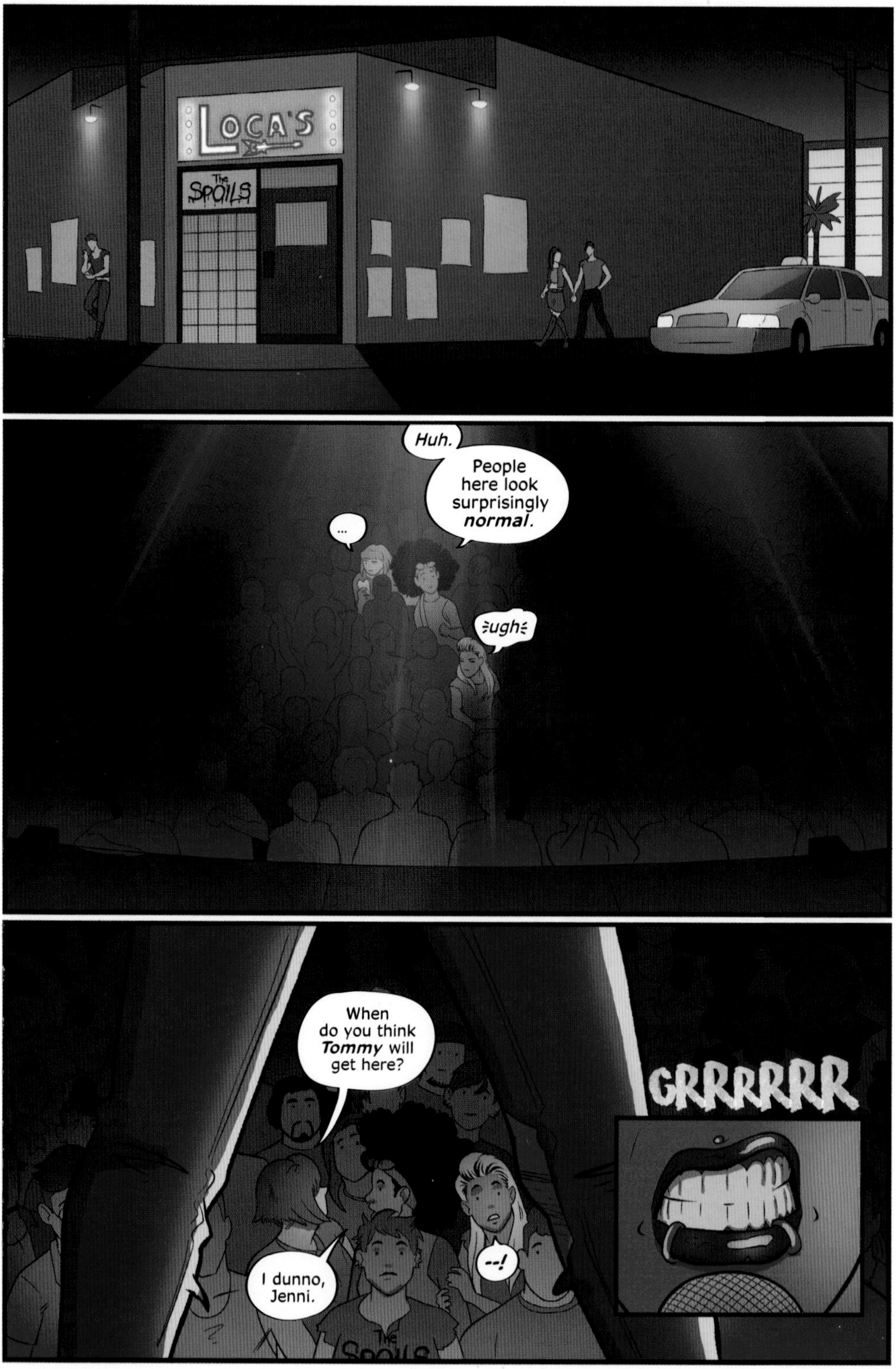
LOCA'S
The SPOILS
Huh.
People here look surprisingly *normal*.
...
ugh
When do you think *Tommy* will get here?
I dunno, Jenni.
--!
GRRRRRR
The SPOILS

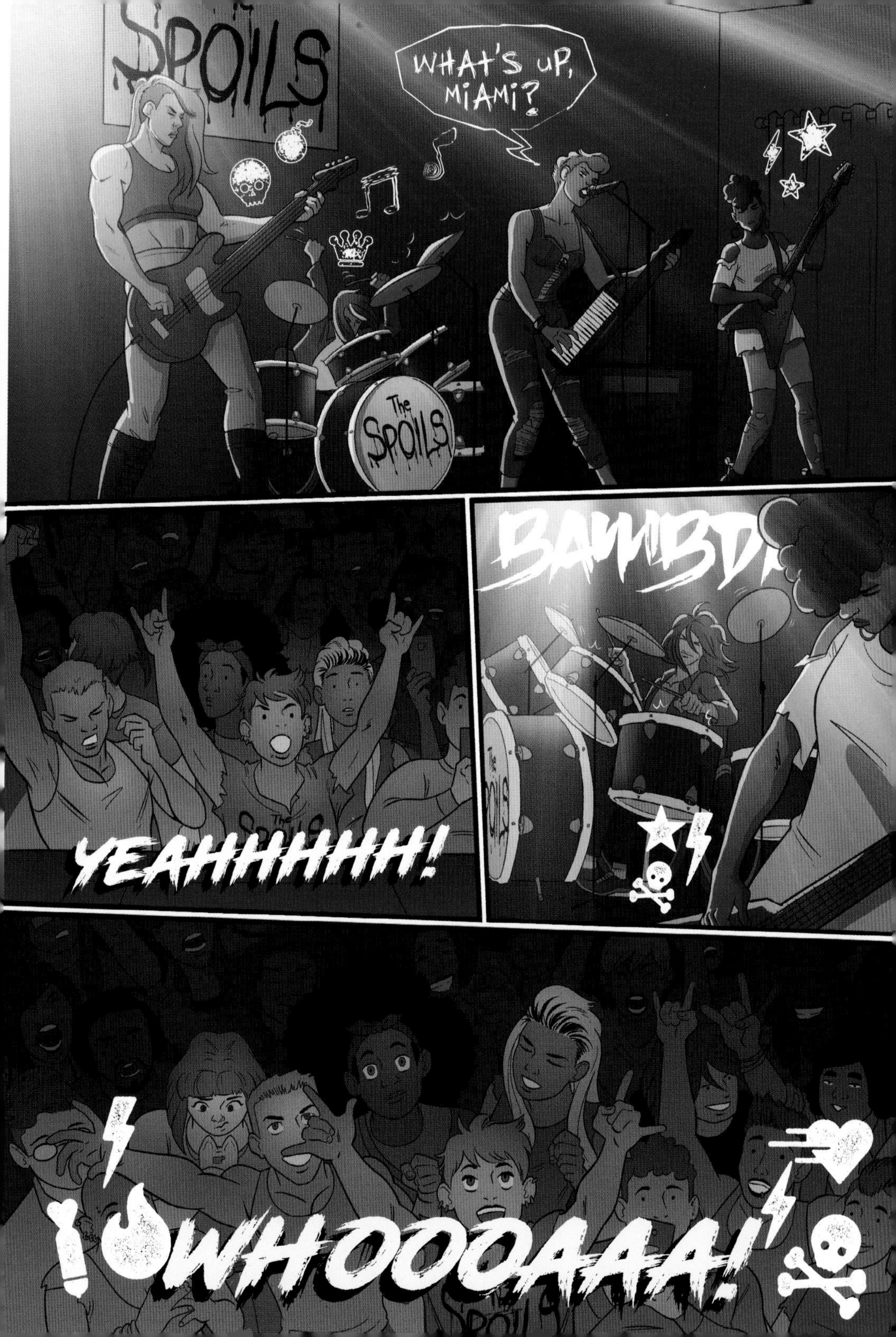
SPOILS
WHAT'S UP, MIAMI?
The SPOILS
YEAHHHHHH!
BAMBDA
The SPOILS
WHOOOOAAA!

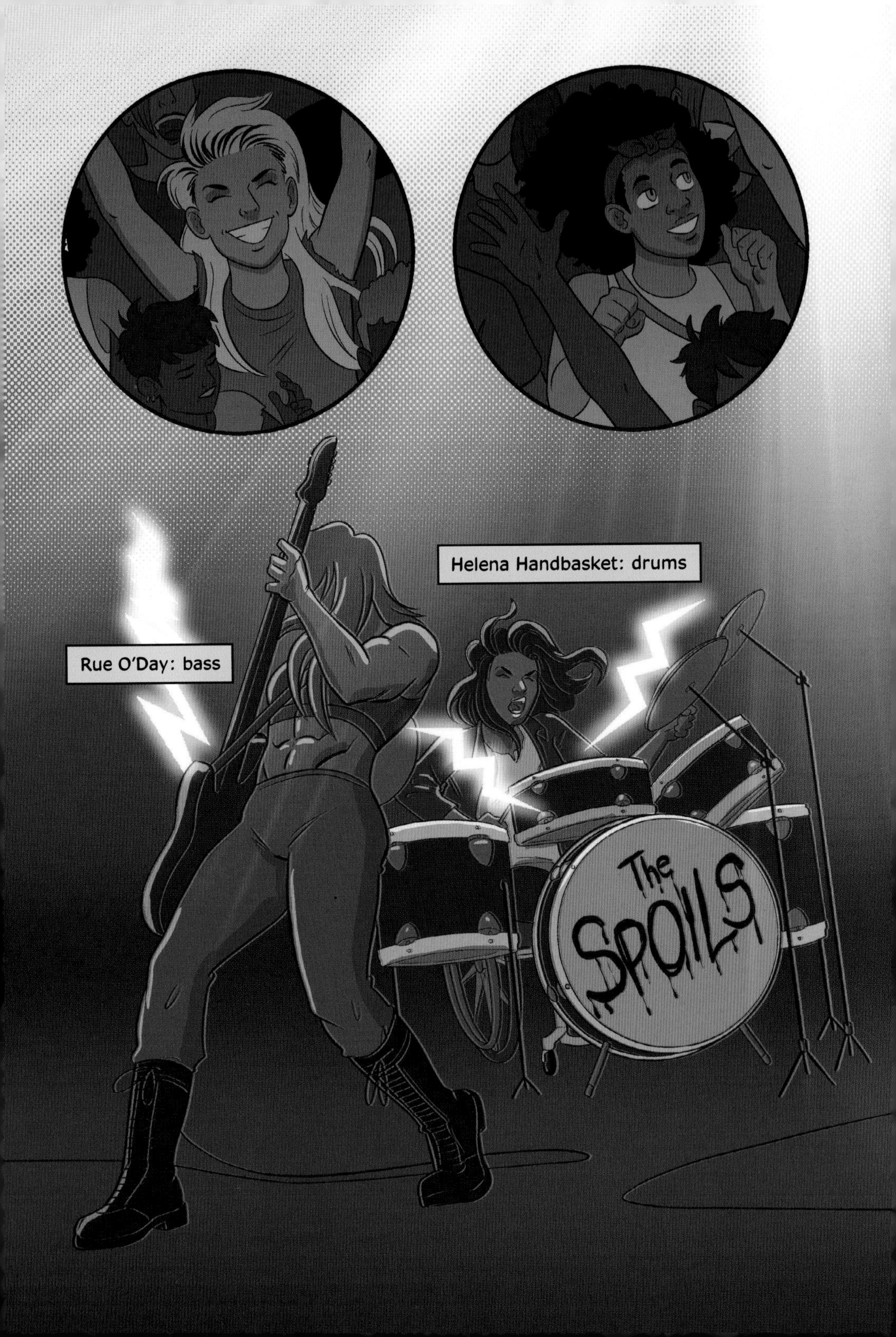
Helena Handbasket: drums
Rue O'Day: bass
The SPOILS

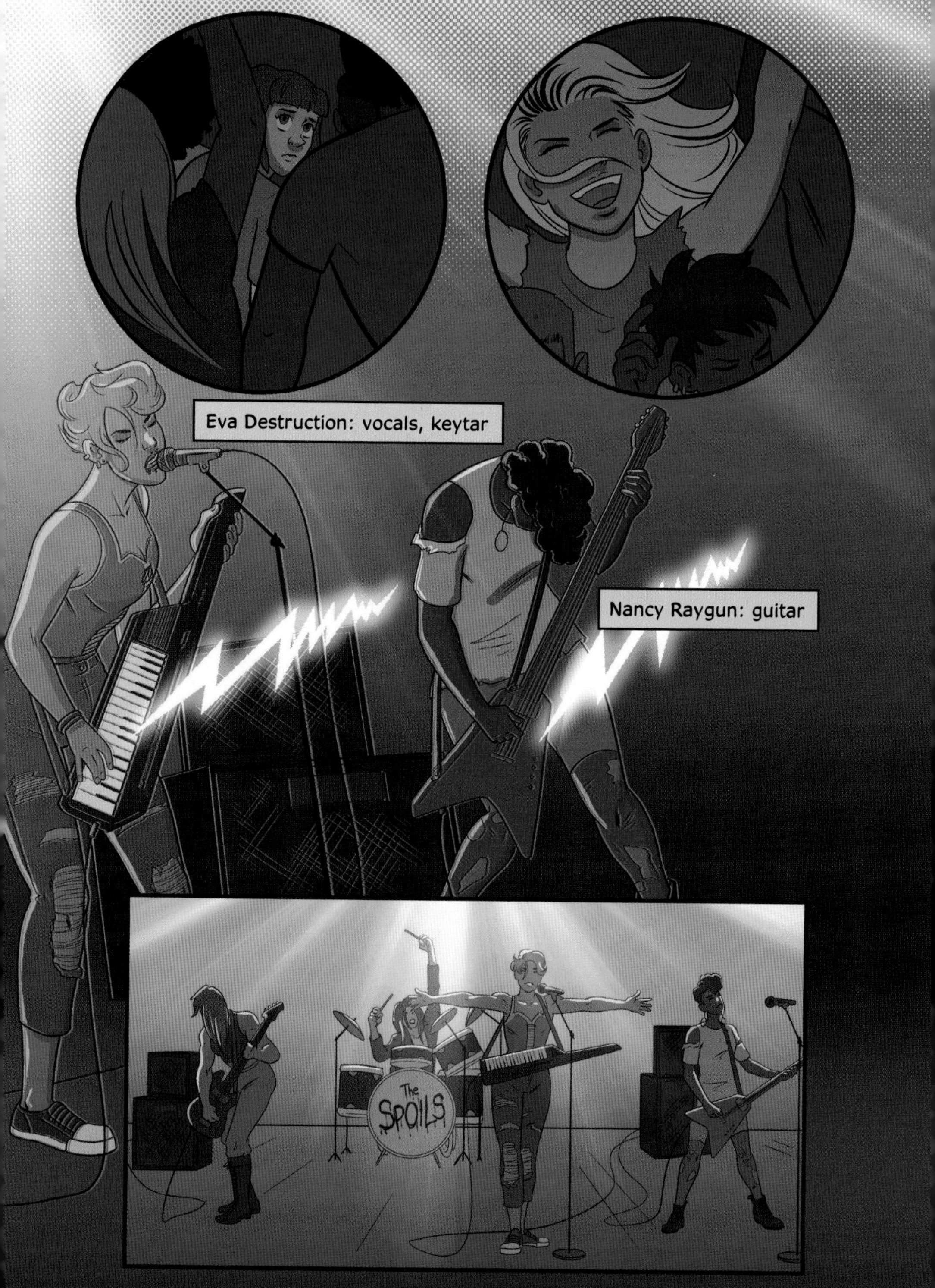
Eva Destruction: vocals, keytar
Nancy Raygun: guitar
The SPOILS

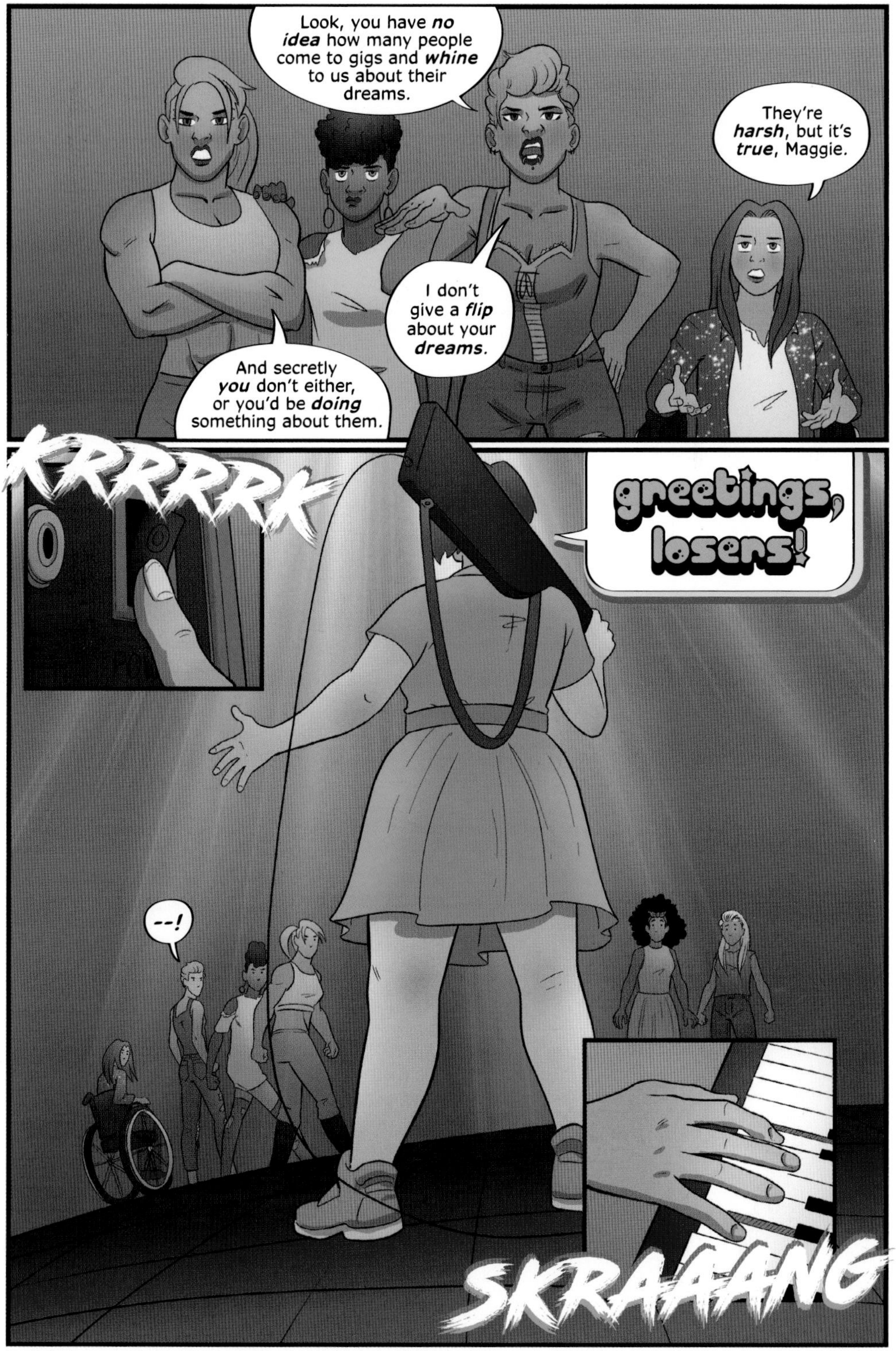
Look, you have *no idea* how many people come to gigs and *whine* to us about their dreams.
I don't give a *flip* about your *dreams*.
And secretly *you* don't either, or you'd be *doing* something about them.
They're *harsh*, but it's *true*, Maggie.
KRRRRK
greetings, losers!
--!
SKRAAANG

94

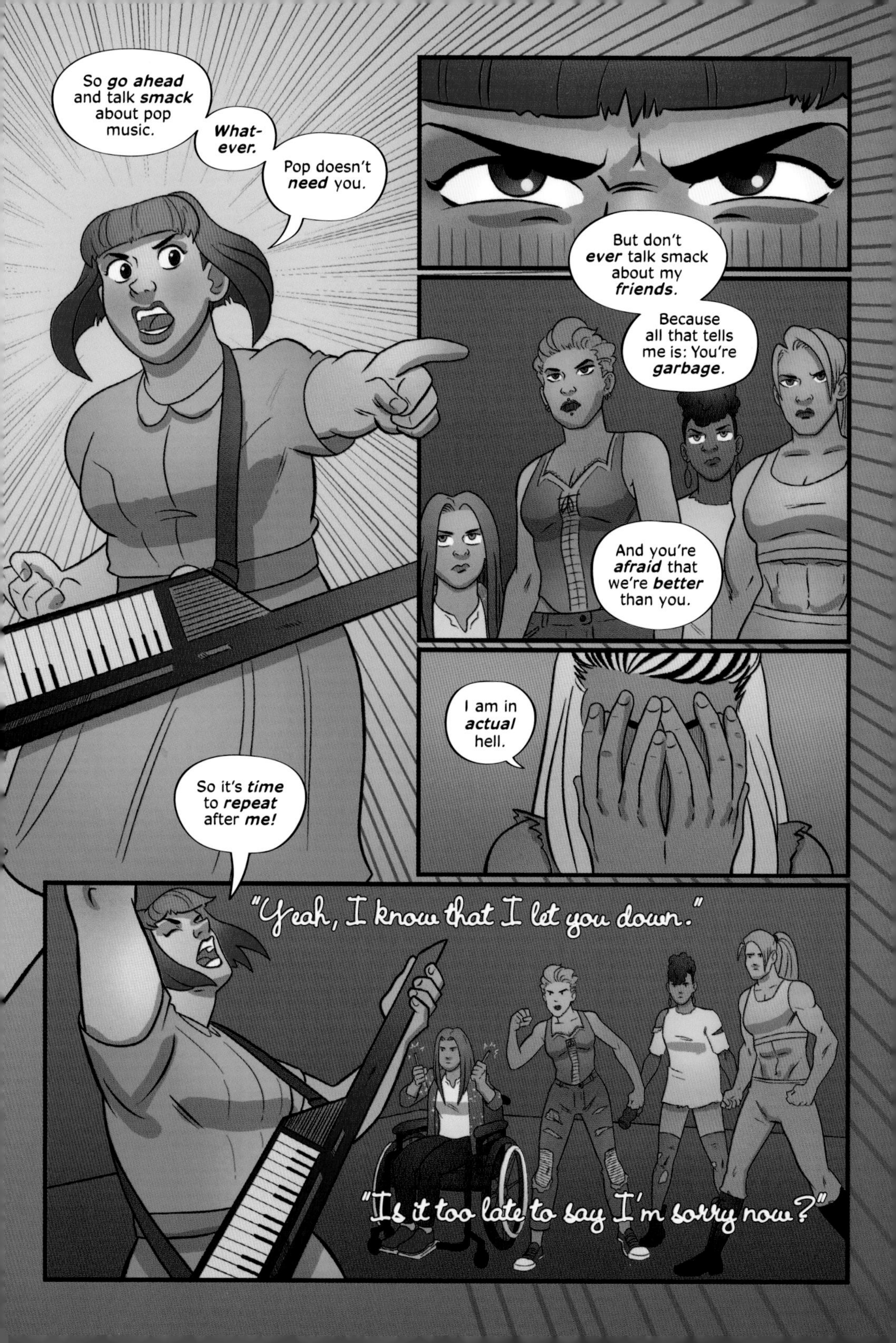

So *go ahead* and talk *smack* about pop music.
What-ever.
Pop doesn't *need* you.
But don't *ever* talk smack about my *friends*.
Because all that tells me is: You're *garbage*.
And you're *afraid* that we're *better* than you.
I am in *actual* hell.
So it's *time* to *repeat* after *me!*
"Yeah, I know that I let you down."
"Is it too late to say I'm sorry now?"

96

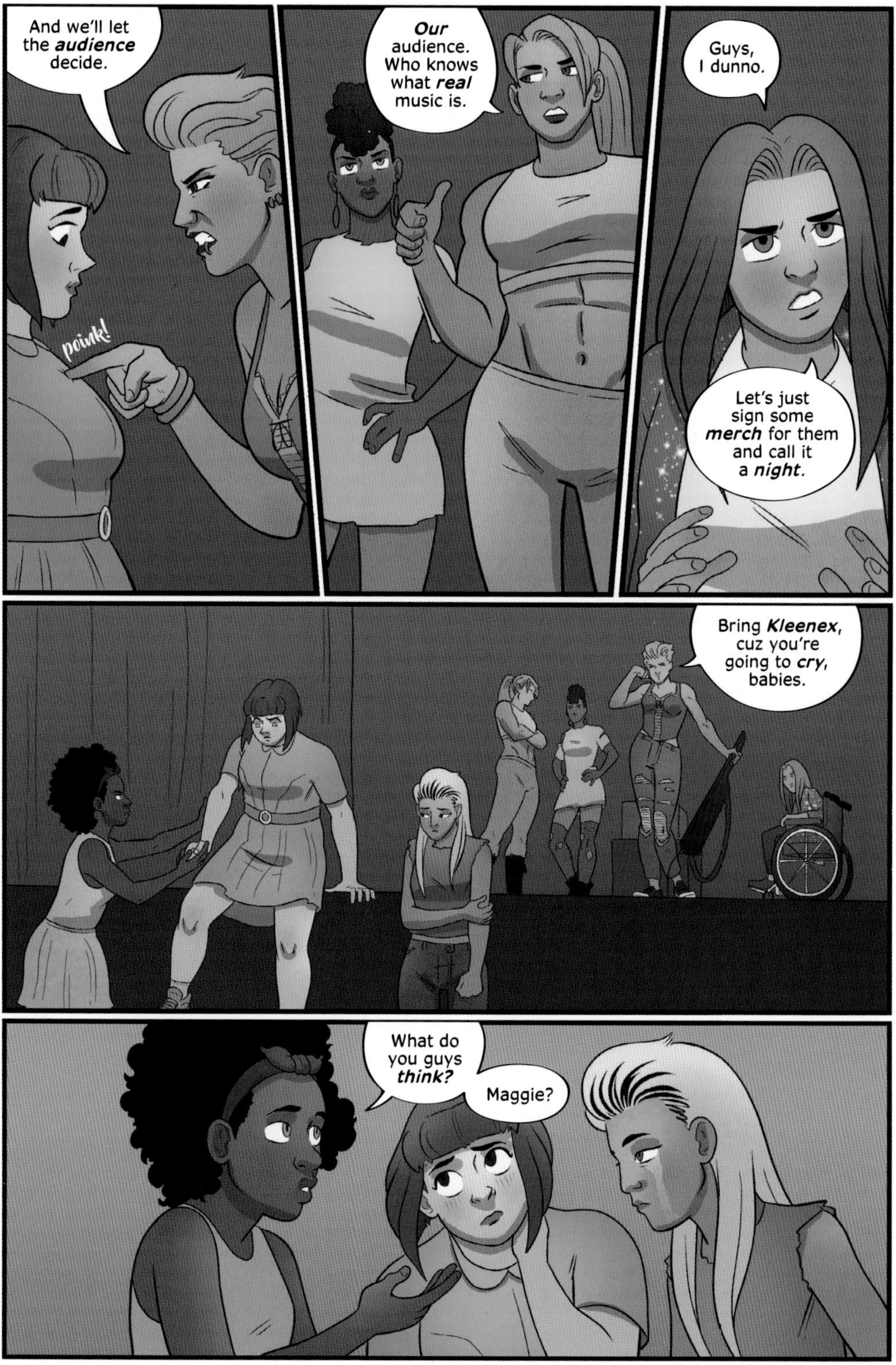
And we'll let the *audience* decide.
poink!
Our audience. Who knows what *real* music is.
Guys, I dunno.
Let's just sign some *merch* for them and call it a *night*.
Bring *Kleenex*, cuz you're going to *cry*, babies.
What do you guys *think?*
Maggie?

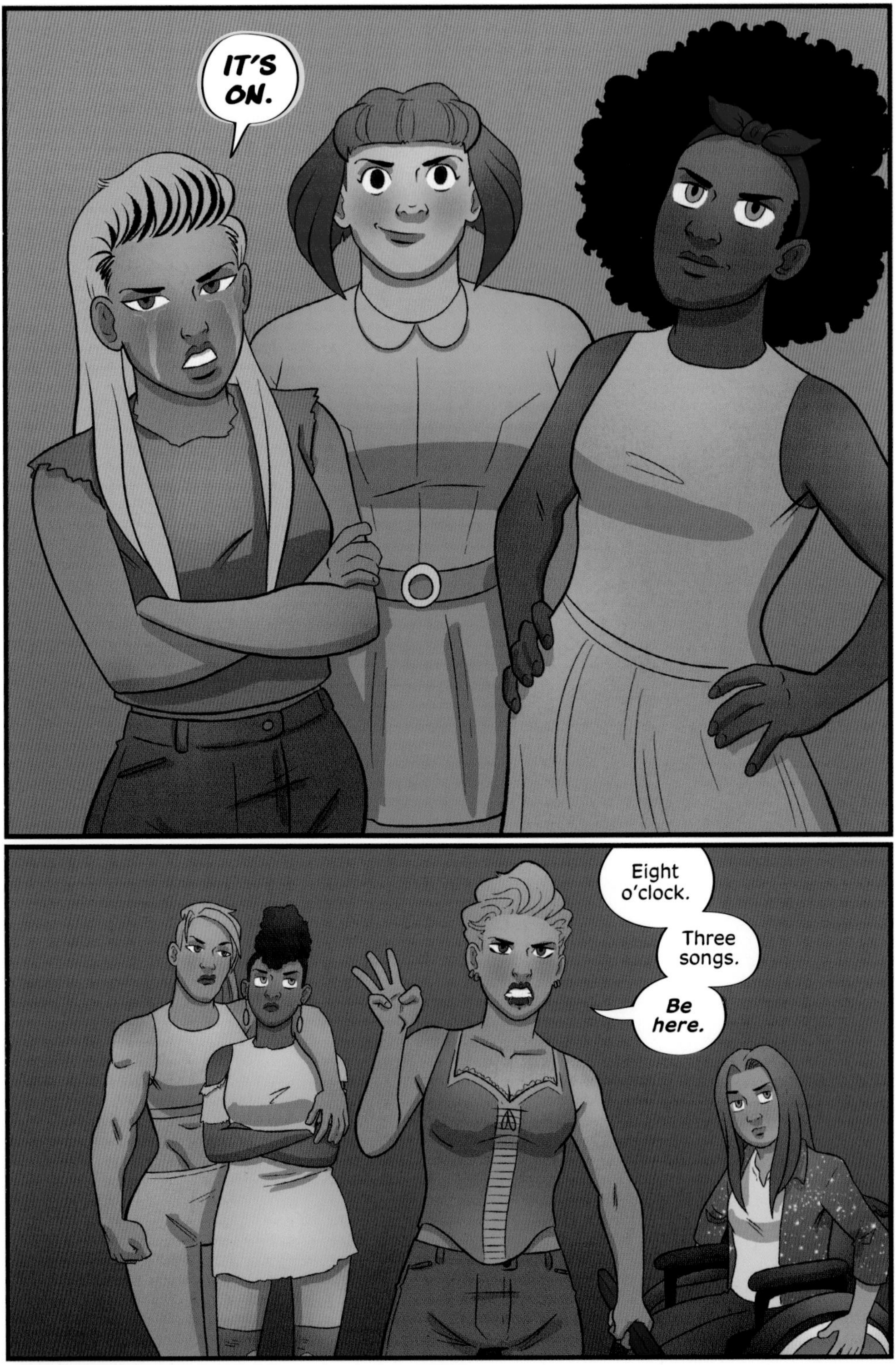
IT'S ON.
Eight o'clock.
Three songs.
Be here.

100

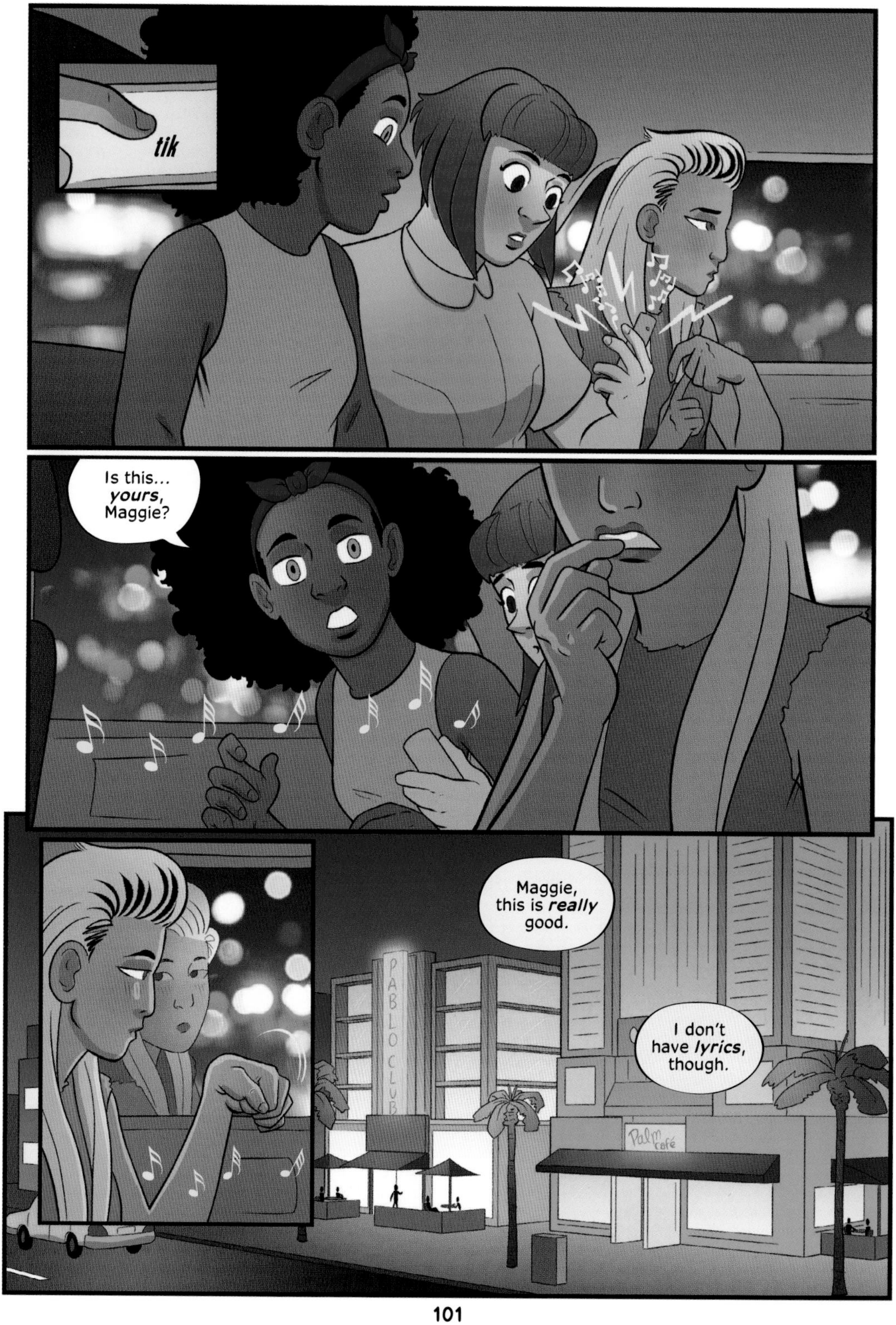
tik
Is this... ***yours***, Maggie?
Maggie, this is ***really*** good.
I don't have ***lyrics***, though.
PABLO CLUB
Palm café

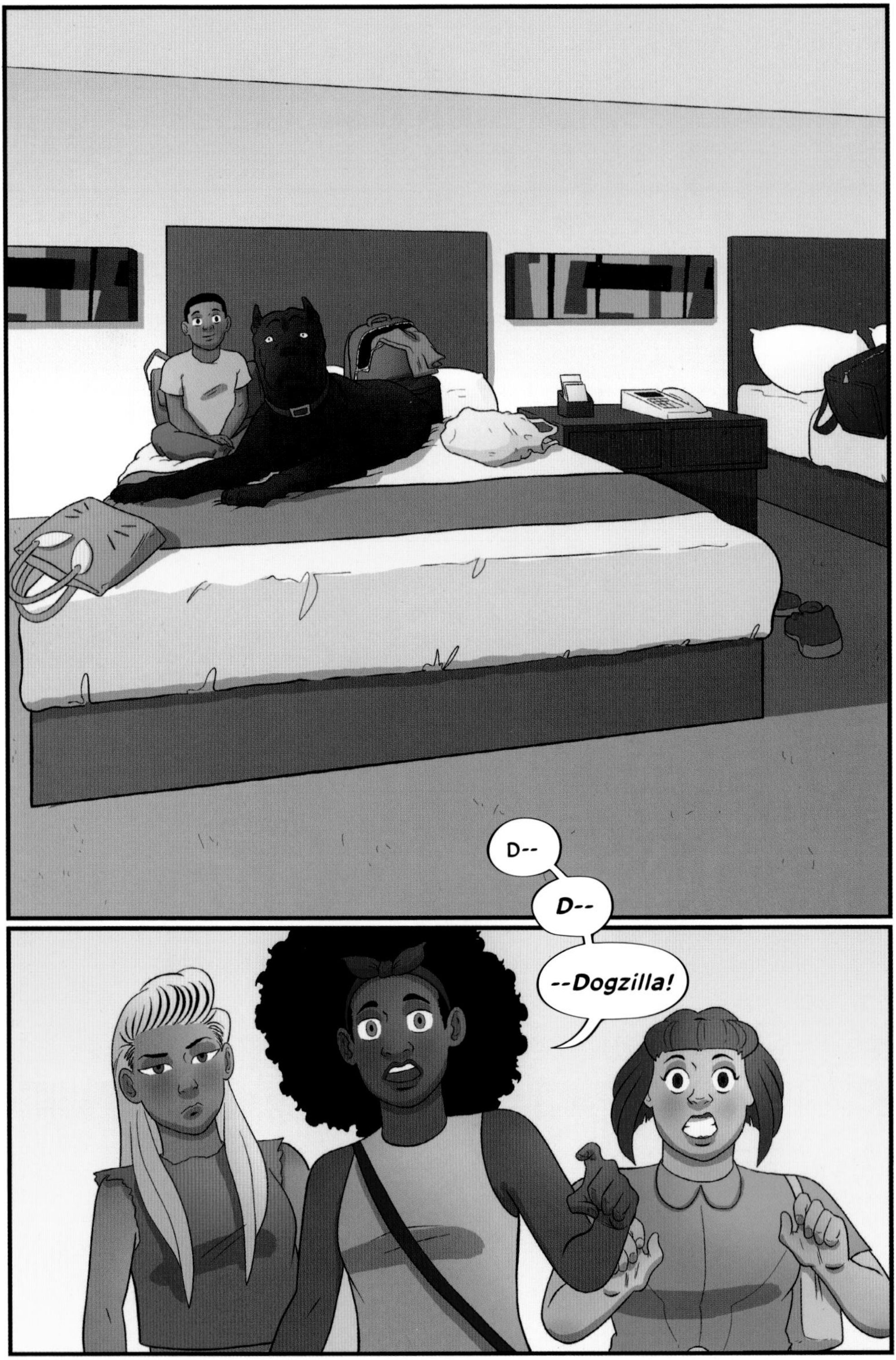
D--
D--
--Dogzilla!

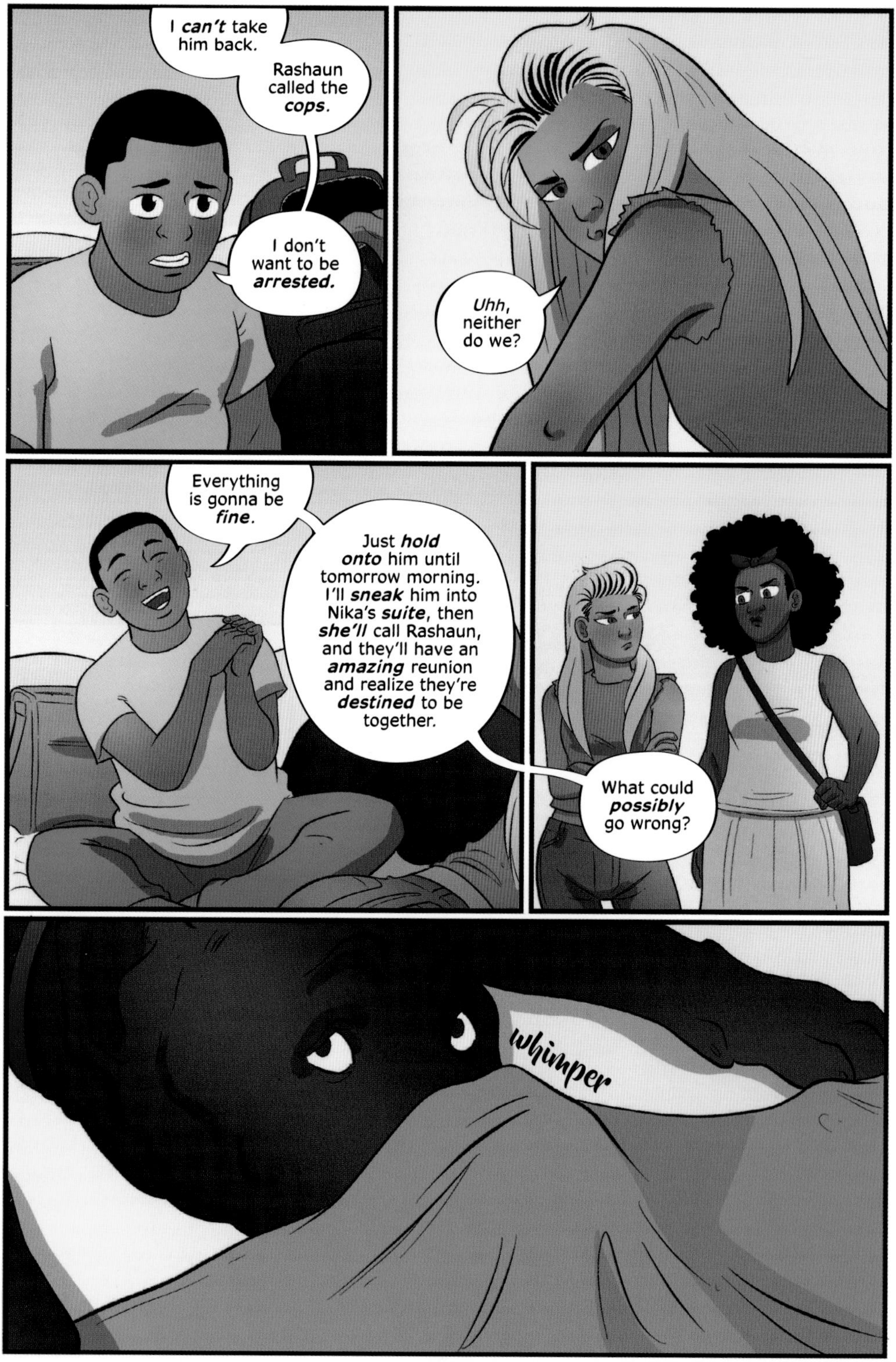
I *can't* take him back.
Rashaun called the *cops*.
I don't want to be *arrested.*
Uhh, neither do we?
Everything is gonna be *fine*.
Just *hold onto* him until tomorrow morning. I'll *sneak* him into Nika's *suite*, then *she'll* call Rashaun, and they'll have an *amazing* reunion and realize they're *destined* to be together.
What could *possibly* go wrong?
whimper

CHAPTER
4

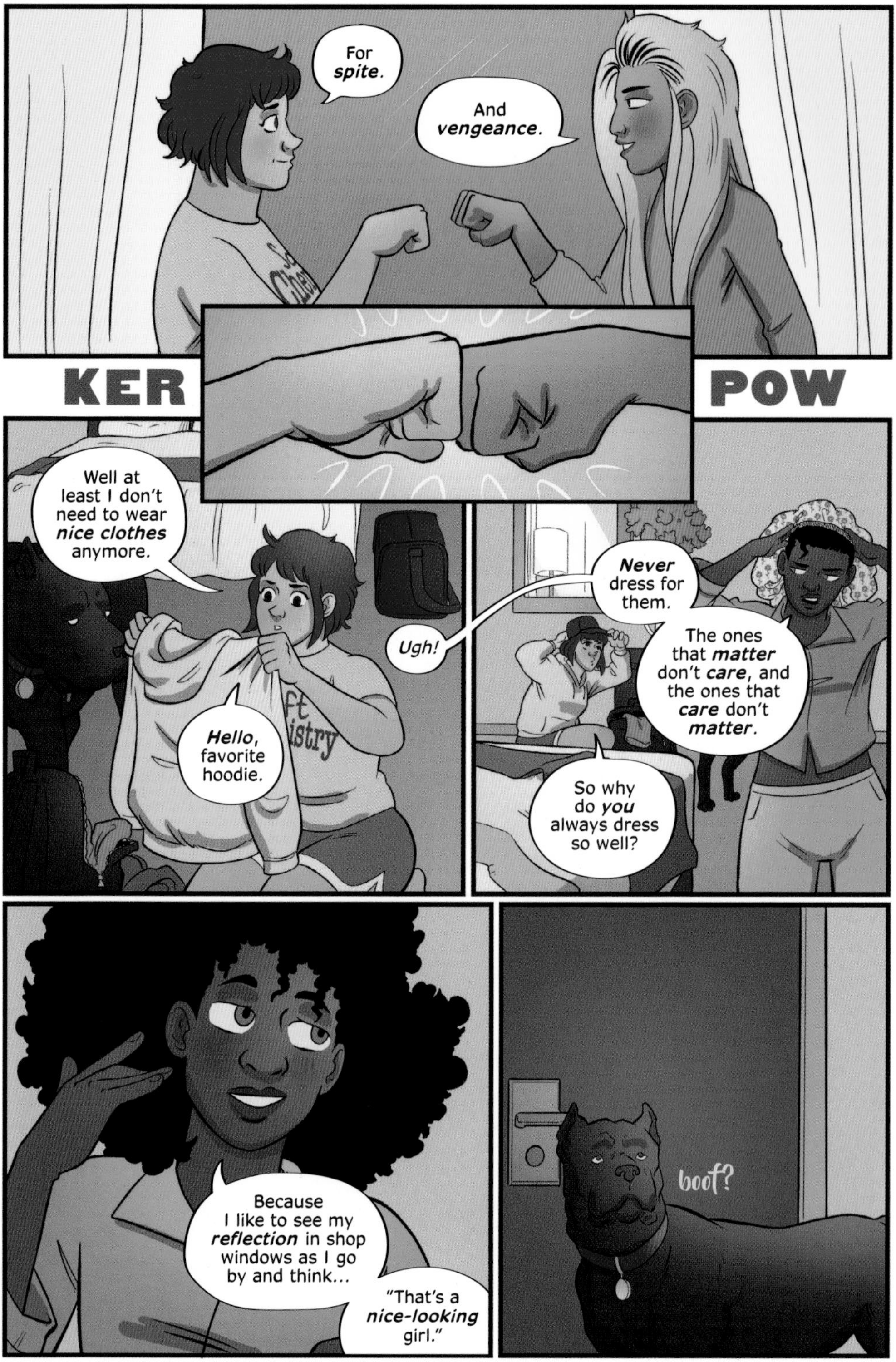
For *spite*.
And *vengeance*.
KER
POW
Well at least I don't need to wear *nice clothes* anymore.
Hello, favorite hoodie.
Ugh!
Never dress for them.
The ones that *matter* don't *care*, and the ones that *care* don't *matter*.
So why do *you* always dress so well?
Because I like to see my *reflection* in shop windows as I go by and think...
"That's a *nice-looking* girl."
boof?

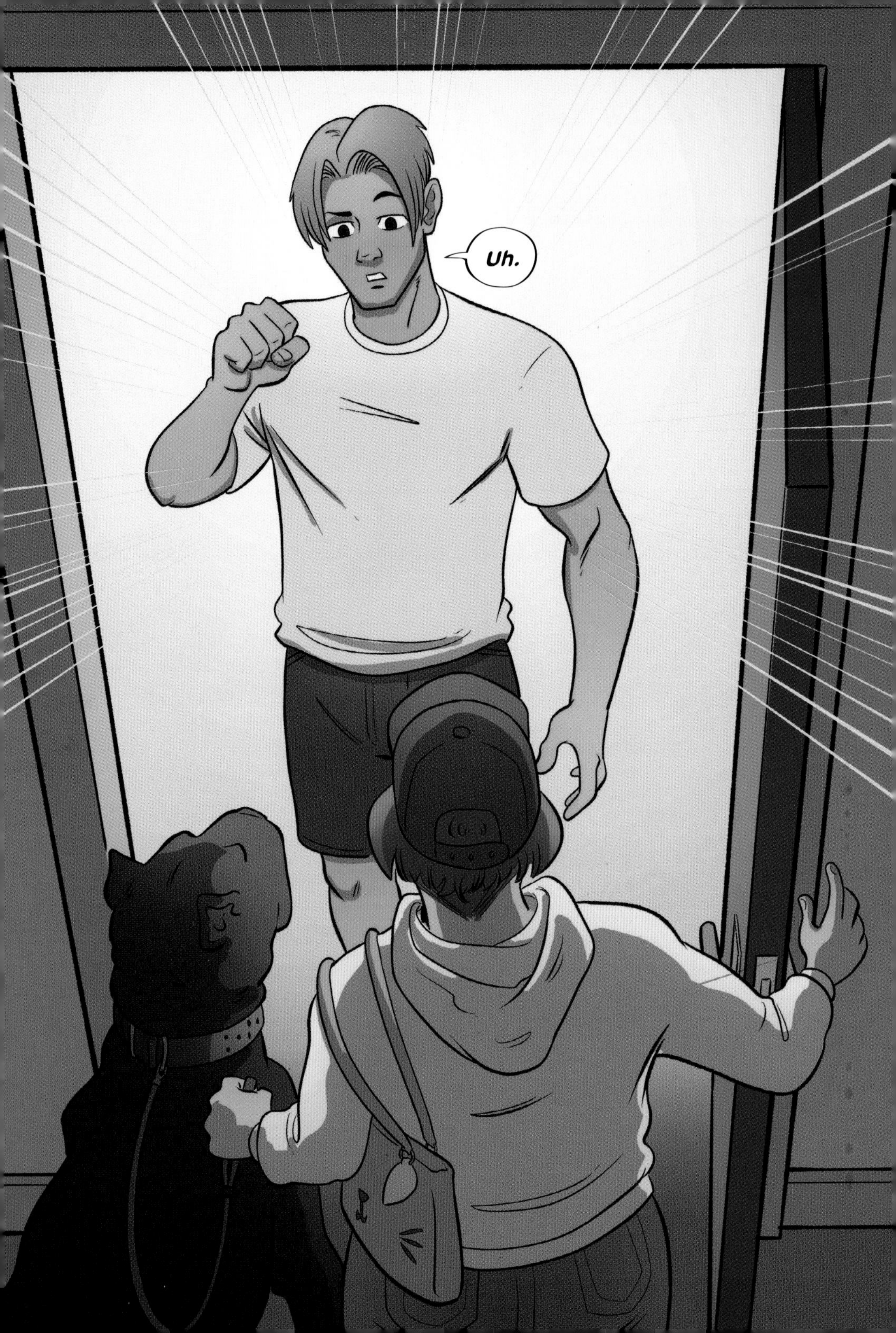
Uh.

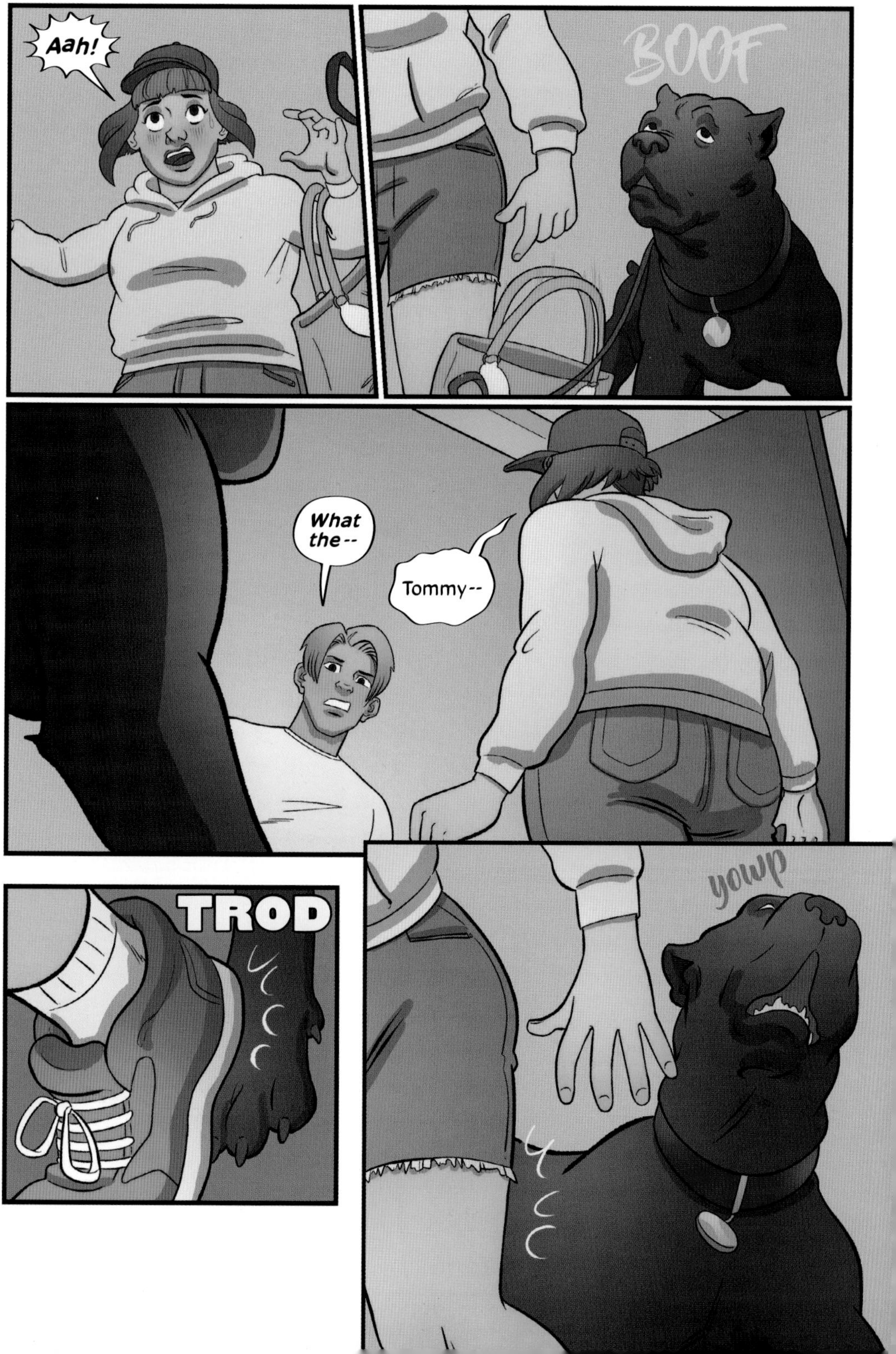
Aah!
BOOF
What the--
Tommy--
TROD
yowp

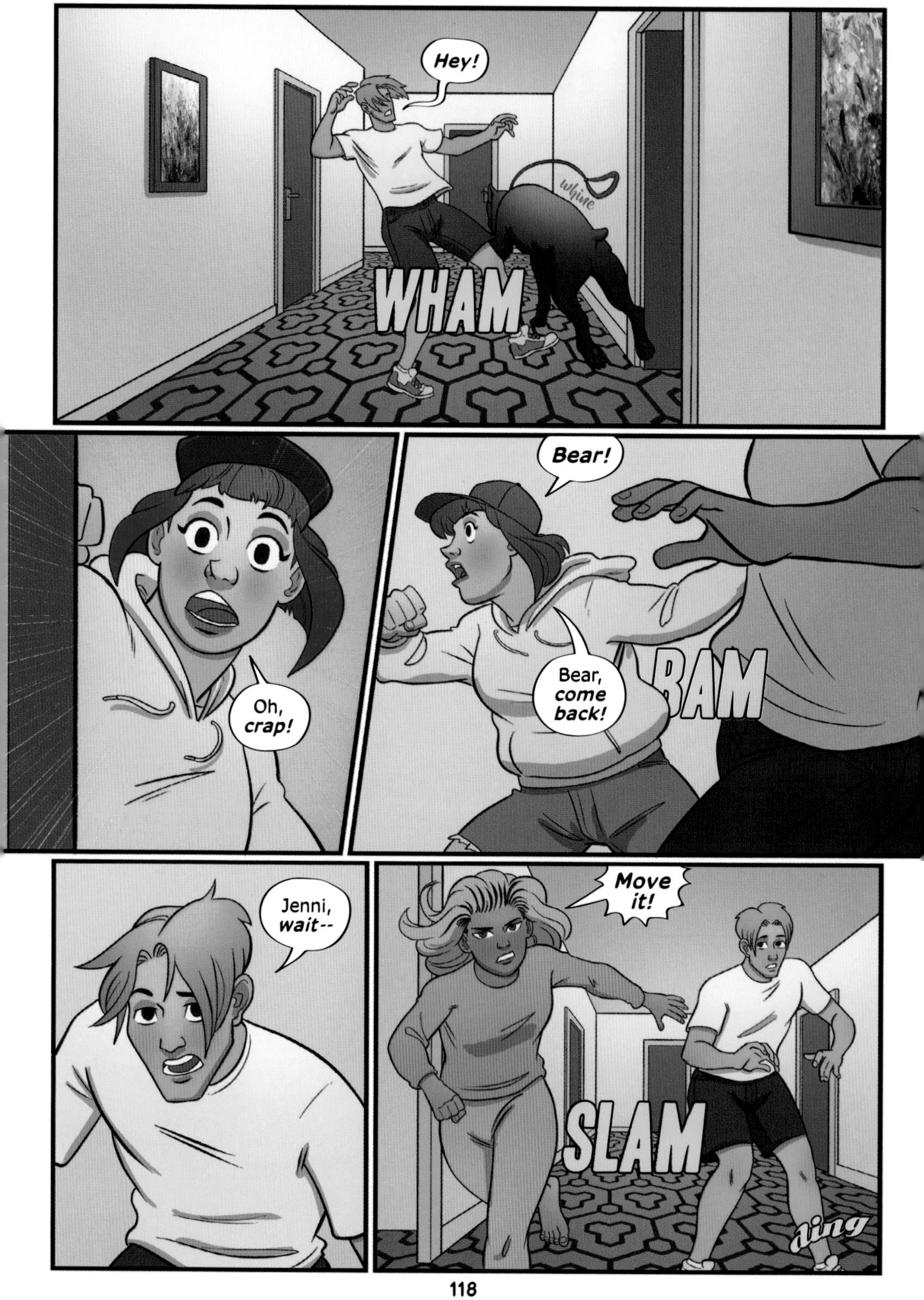

Hey!
whine
WHAM
Oh, crap!
Bear!
Bear, come back!
BAM
Jenni, wait--
Move it!
SLAM
ding

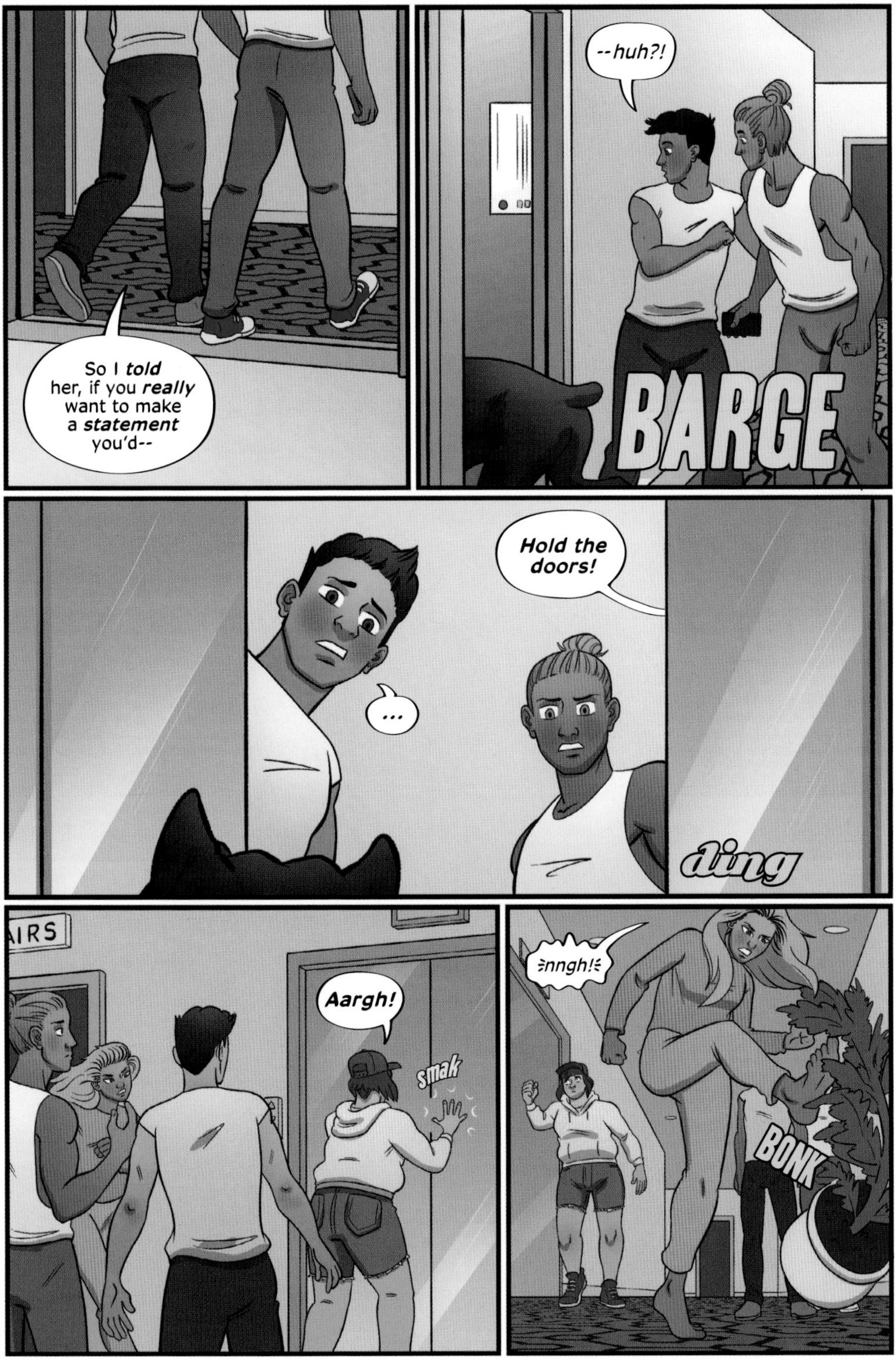
So I told her, if you really want to make a statement you'd--
--huh?!
BARGE
Hold the doors!
...
ding
AIRS
Aargh!
smak
nngh!
BONK

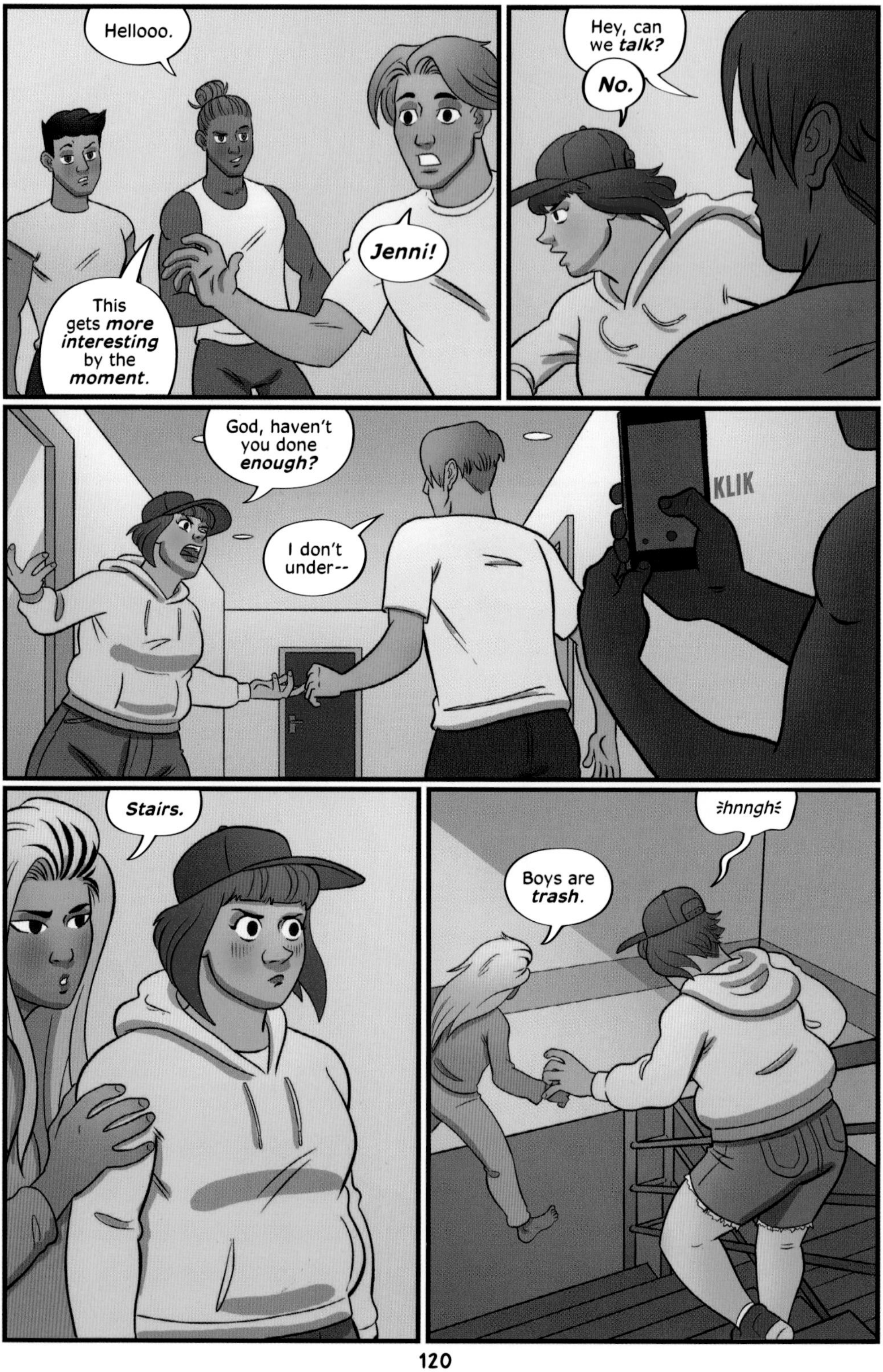
Hellooo.
Jenni!
This gets *more interesting* by the *moment*.
Hey, can we *talk?*
No.
God, haven't you done *enough?*
I don't under--
KLIK
Stairs.
hnngh
Boys are *trash*.

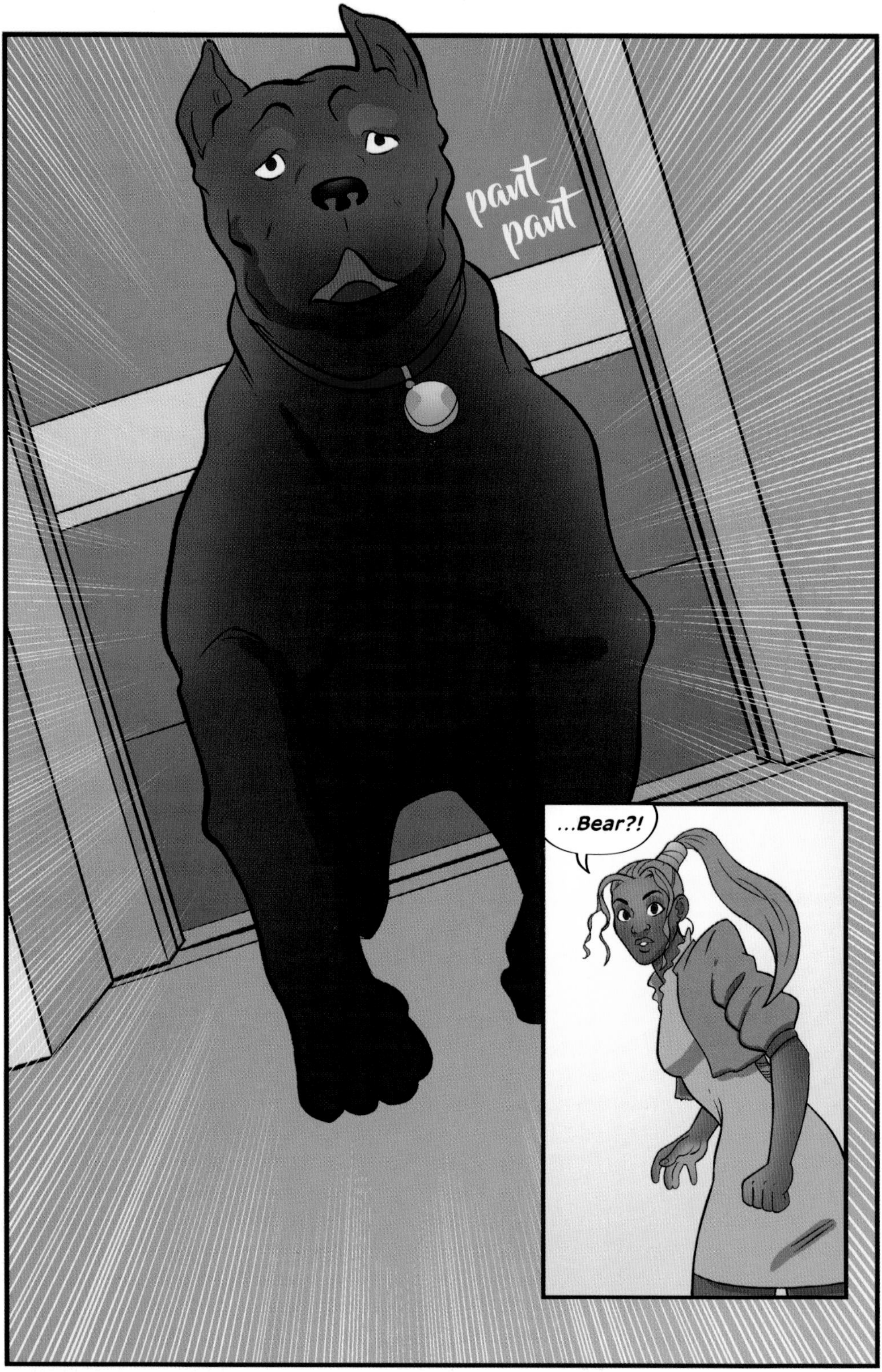
pant
pant
...Bear?!

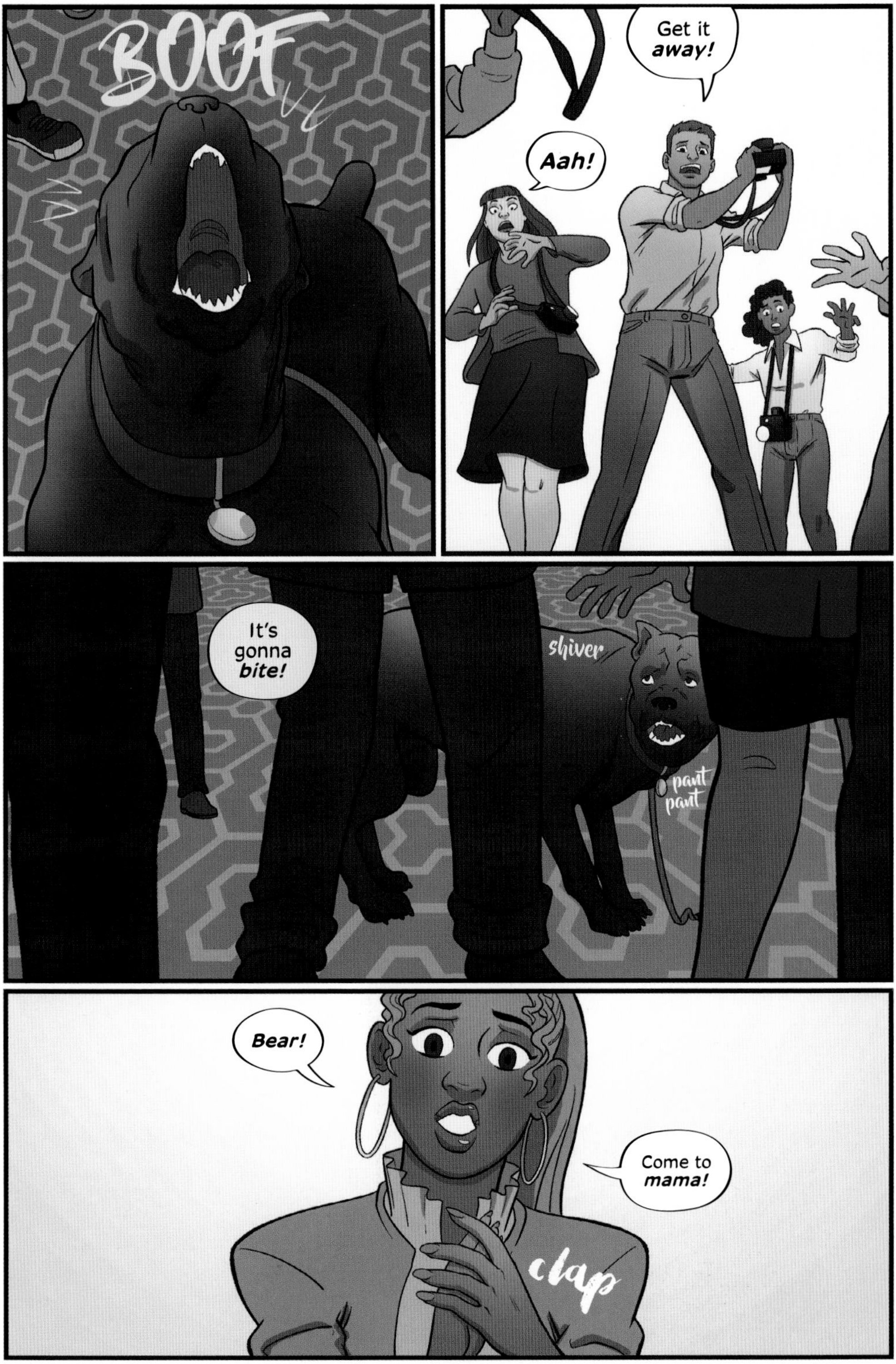
BOOF
Get it *away!*
Aah!
It's gonna *bite!*
shiver
pant pant
Bear!
Come to *mama!*
clap

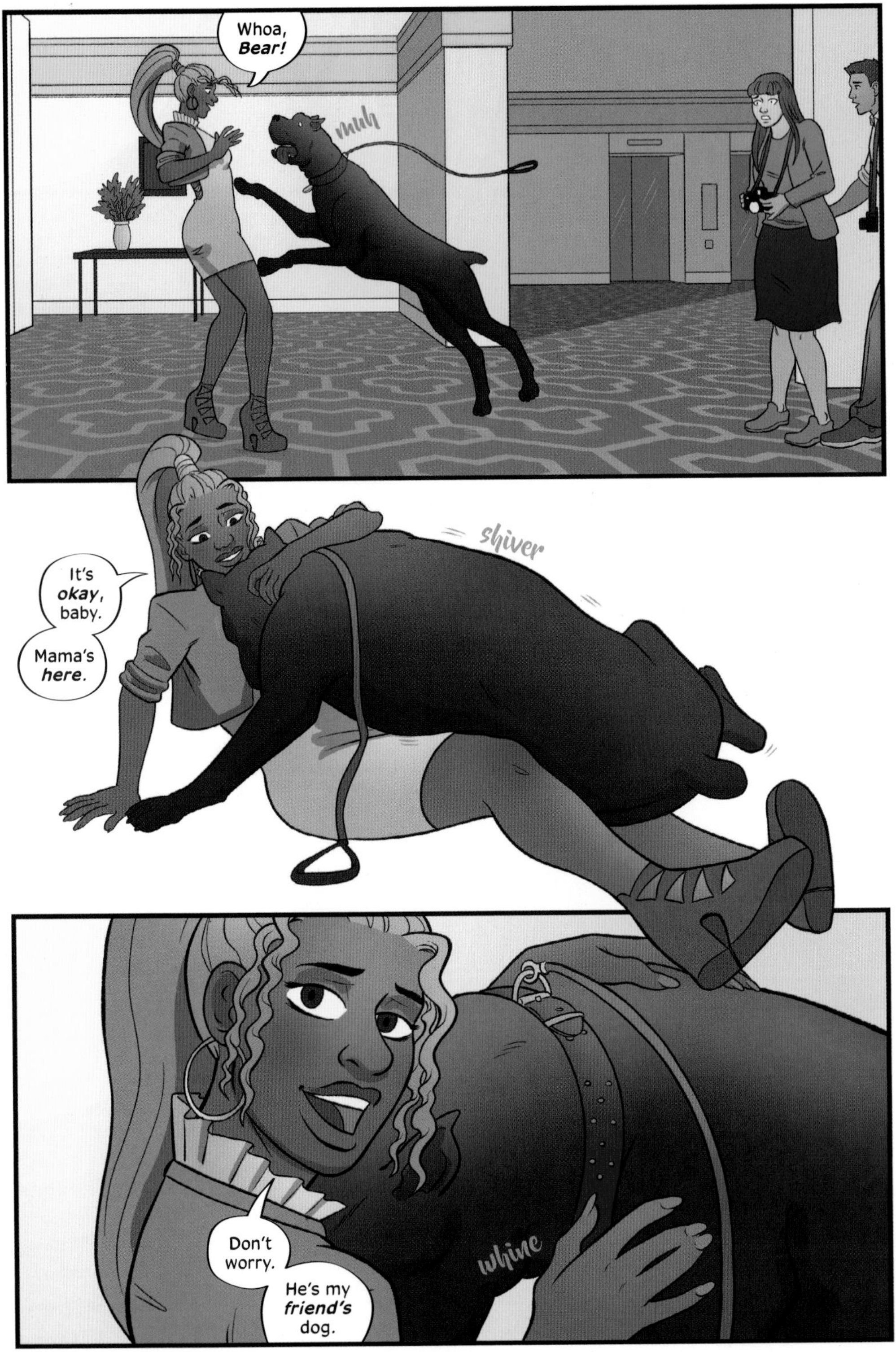
Whoa, Bear!
muh
shiver
It's okay, baby.
Mama's here.
Don't worry.
He's my friend's dog.
whine

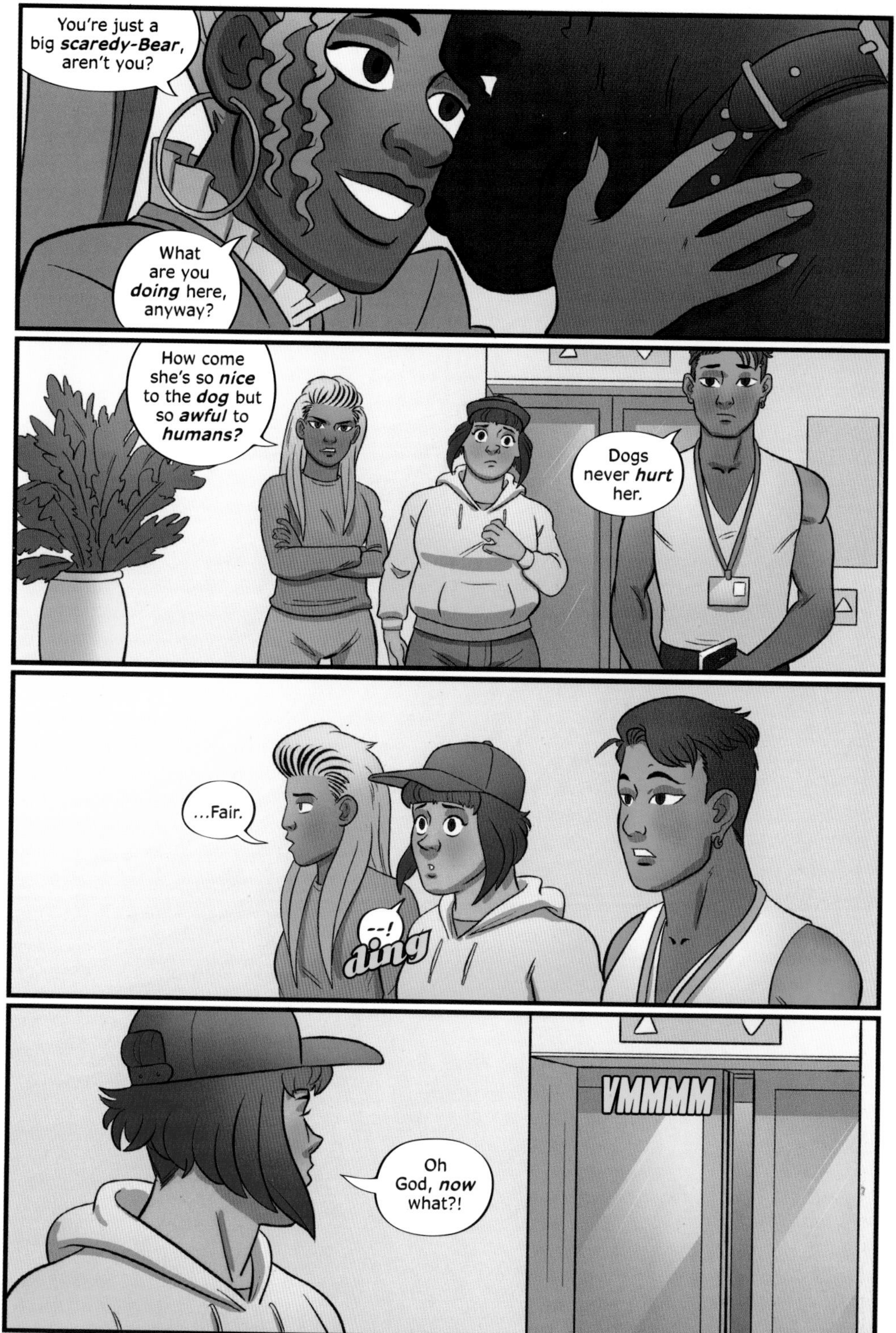
You're just a big ***scaredy-Bear***, aren't you?
What are you ***doing*** here, anyway?
How come she's so ***nice*** to the ***dog*** but so ***awful*** to ***humans?***
Dogs never ***hurt*** her.
...Fair.
--!
ding
VMMMM
Oh God, ***now*** what?!

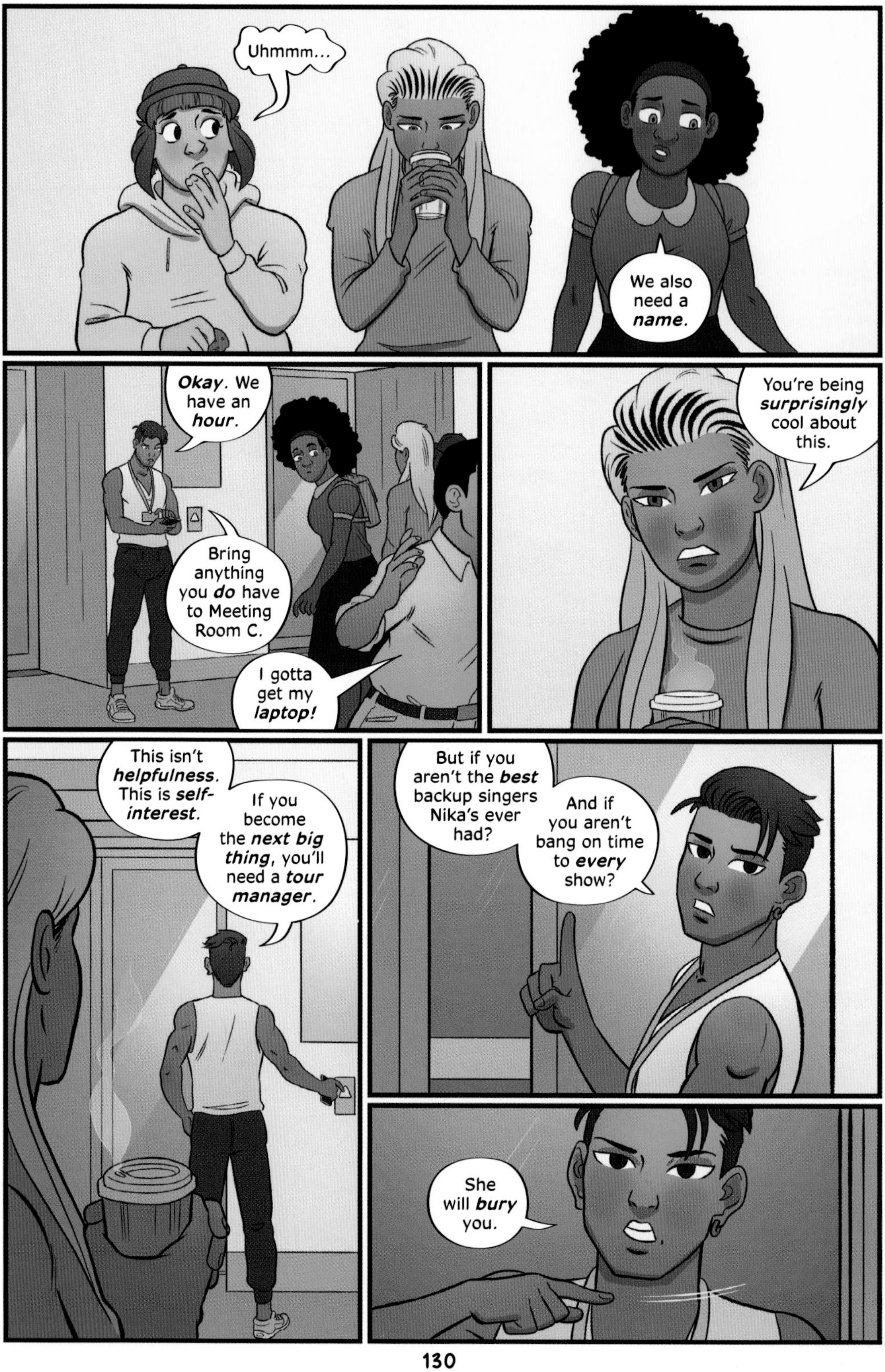
Uhmmm...
We also need a *name*.
Okay. We have an *hour*.
Bring anything you *do* have to Meeting Room C.
I gotta get my *laptop!*
You're being *surprisingly* cool about this.
This isn't *helpfulness*. This is *self-interest*.
If you become the *next big thing*, you'll need a *tour manager*.
But if you aren't the *best* backup singers Nika's ever had?
And if you aren't bang on time to *every* show?
She will *bury* you.

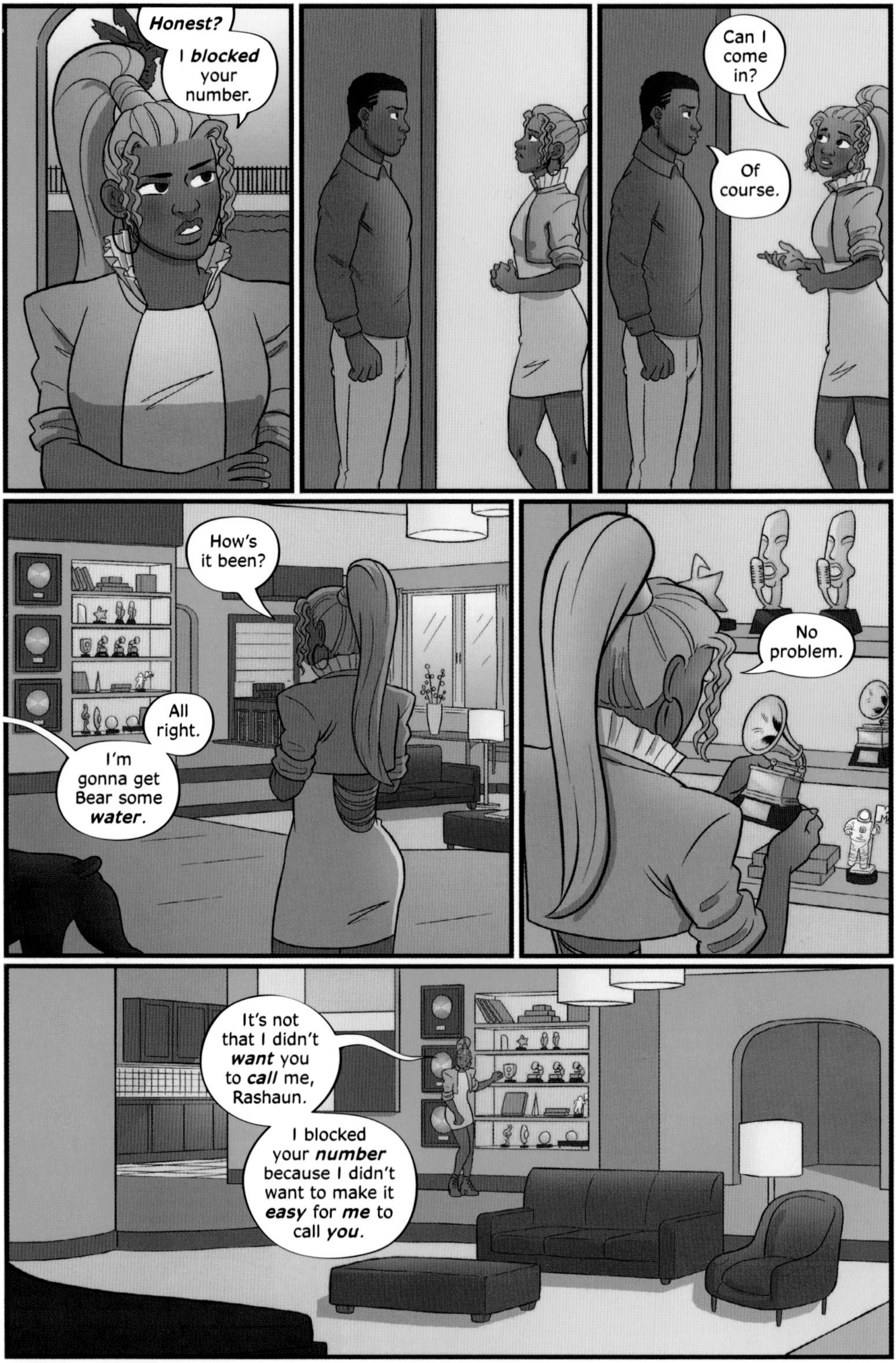
Honest?
I ***blocked*** your number.
Can I come in?
Of course.
How's it been?
All right.
I'm gonna get Bear some ***water***.
No problem.
It's not that I didn't ***want*** you to ***call*** me, Rashaun.
I blocked your ***number*** because I didn't want to make it ***easy*** for ***me*** to call ***you***.

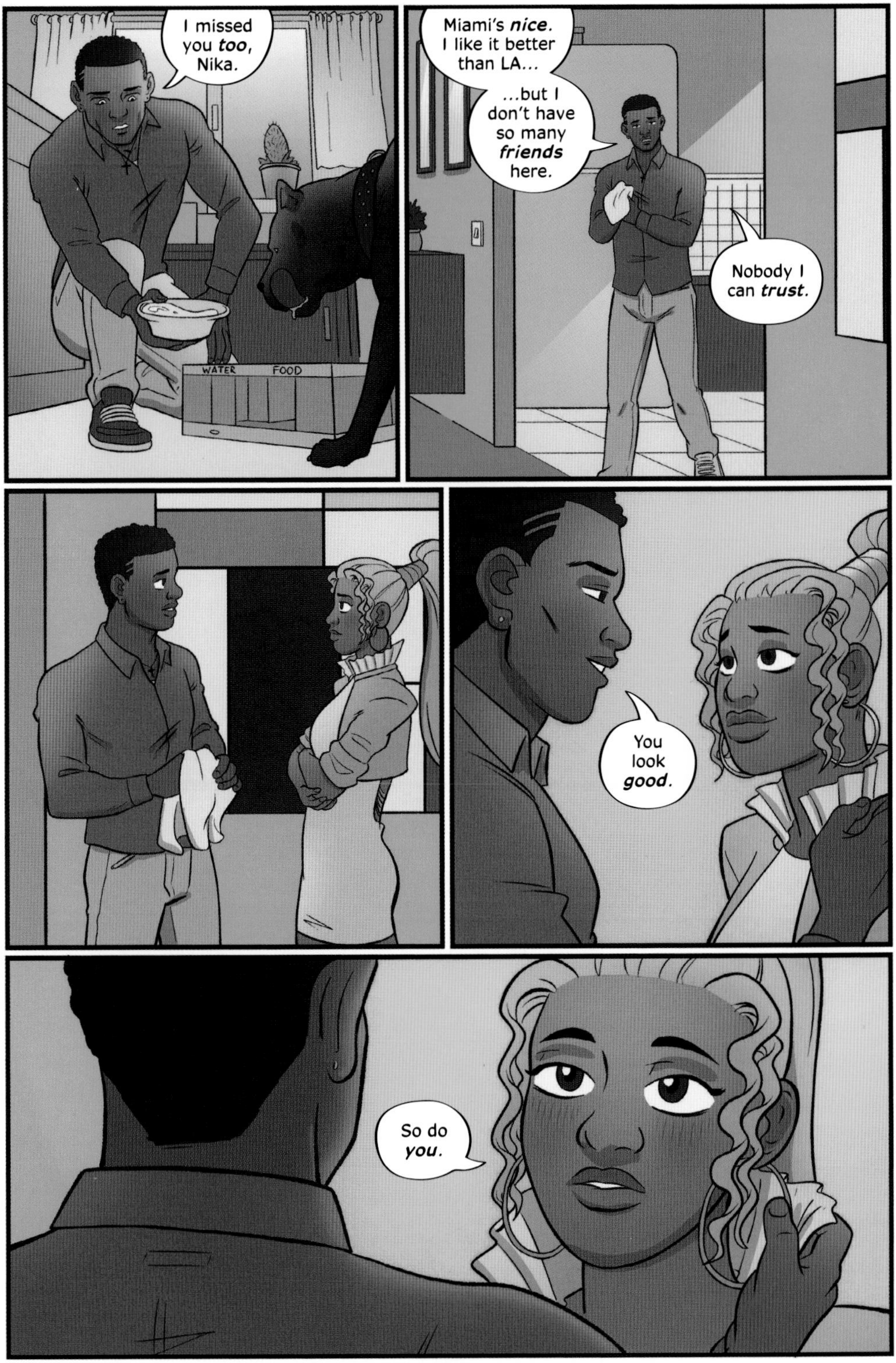
I missed you *too*, Nika.
Miami's *nice*. I like it better than LA...
...but I don't have so many *friends* here.
Nobody I can *trust*.
WATER
FOOD
You look *good*.
So do *you*.

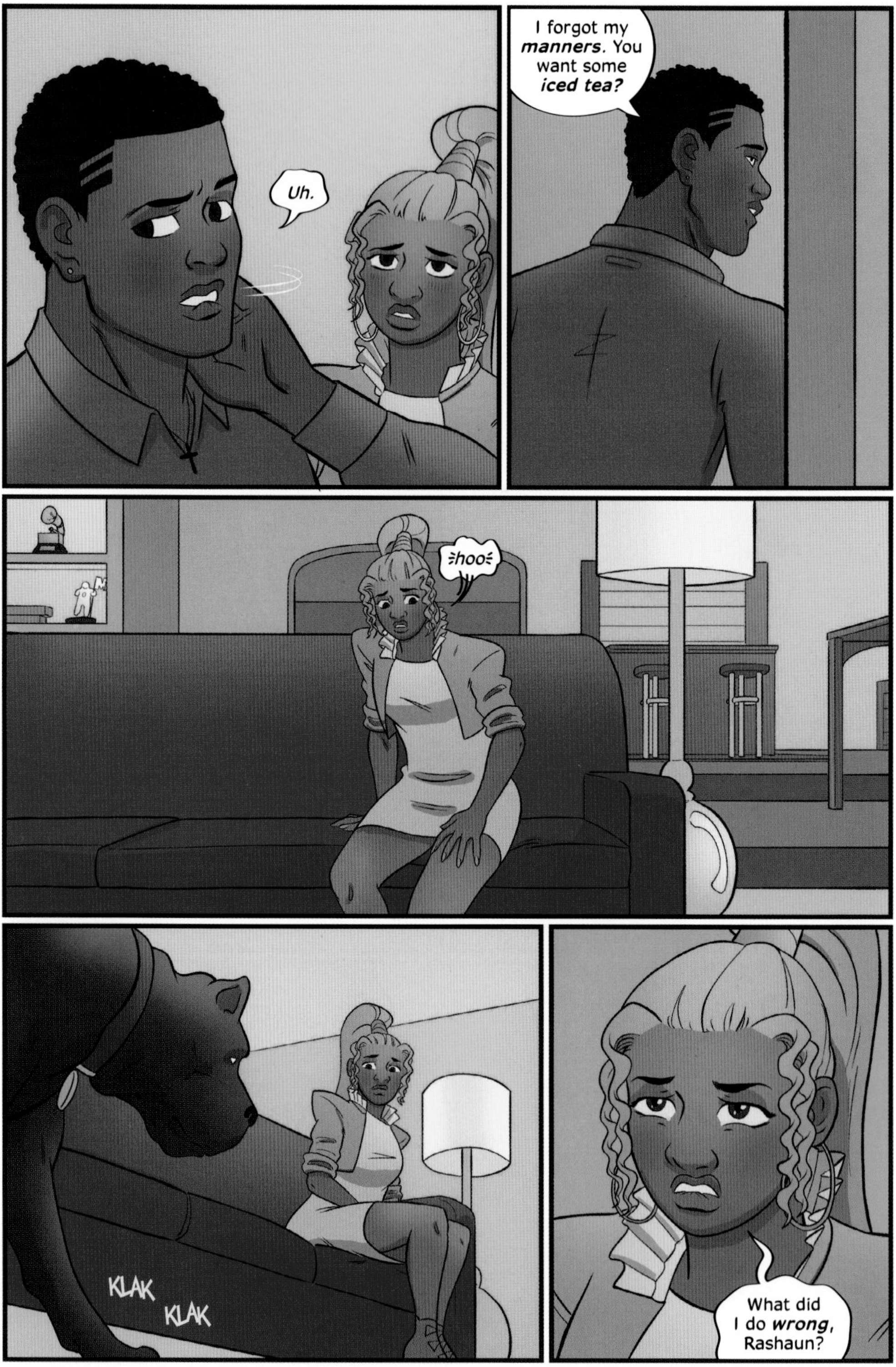
Uh.
I forgot my manners. You want some iced tea?
hoo
KLAK KLAK
What did I do wrong, Rashaun?

135

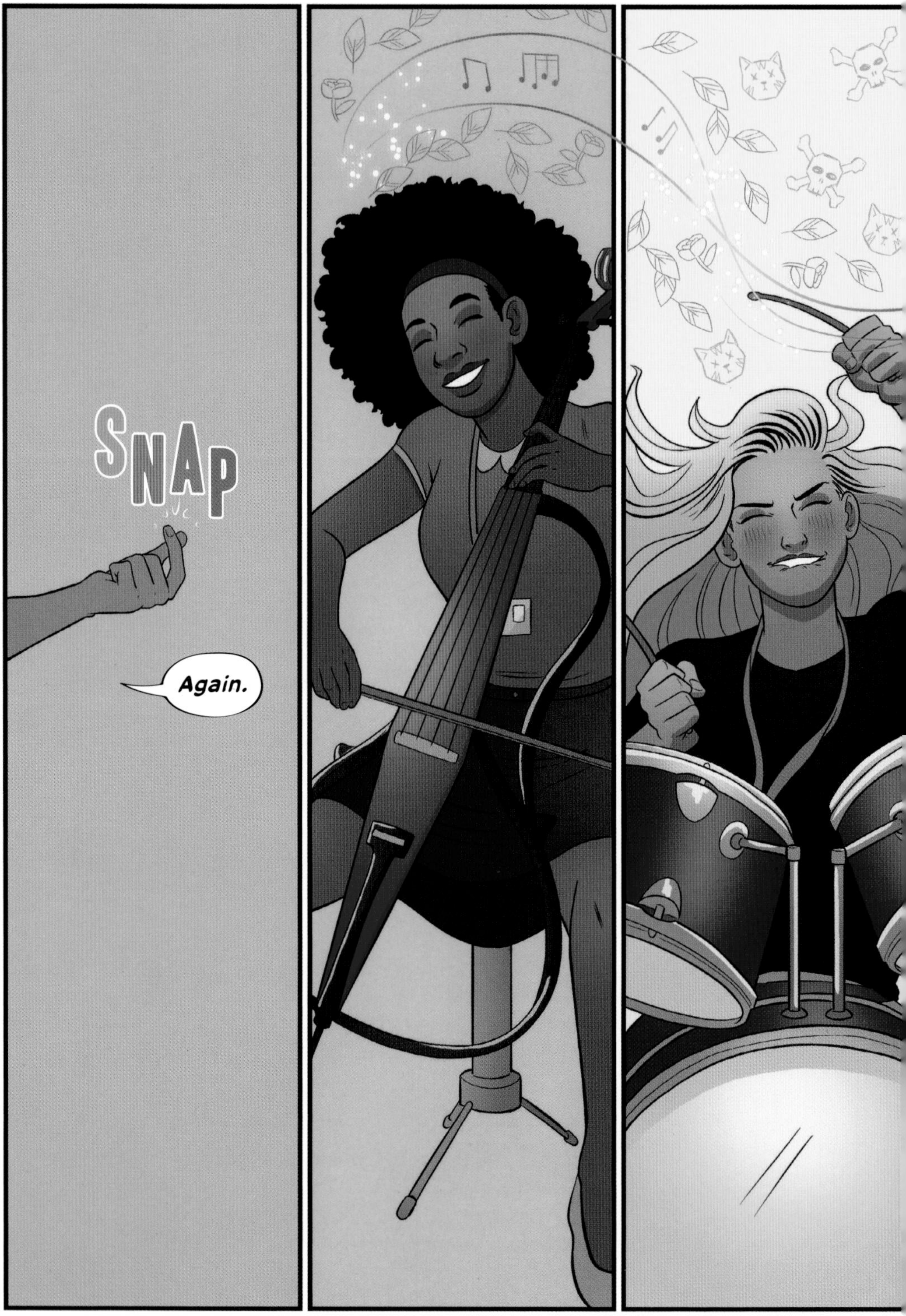
SNAP
Again.

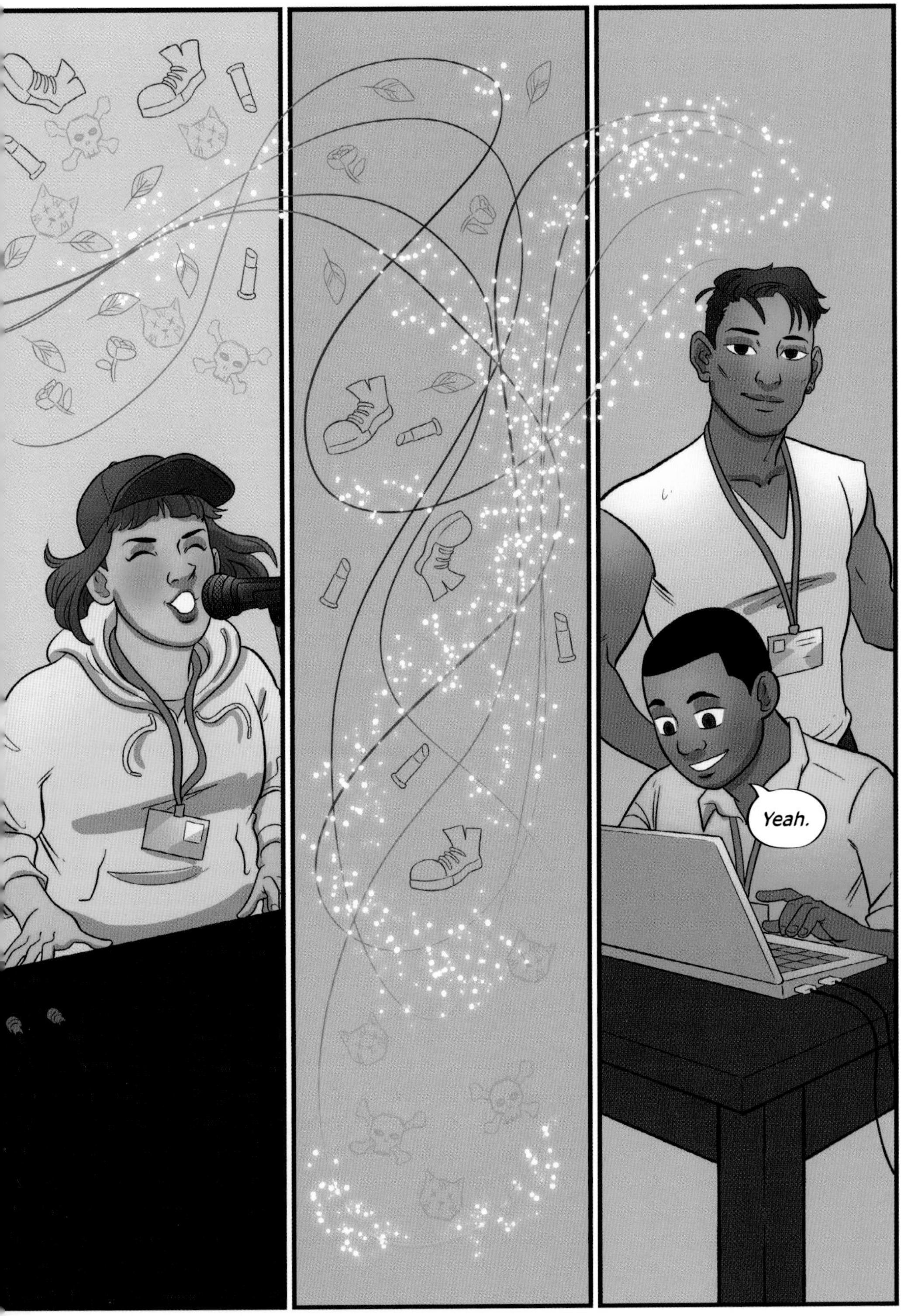
Yeah.

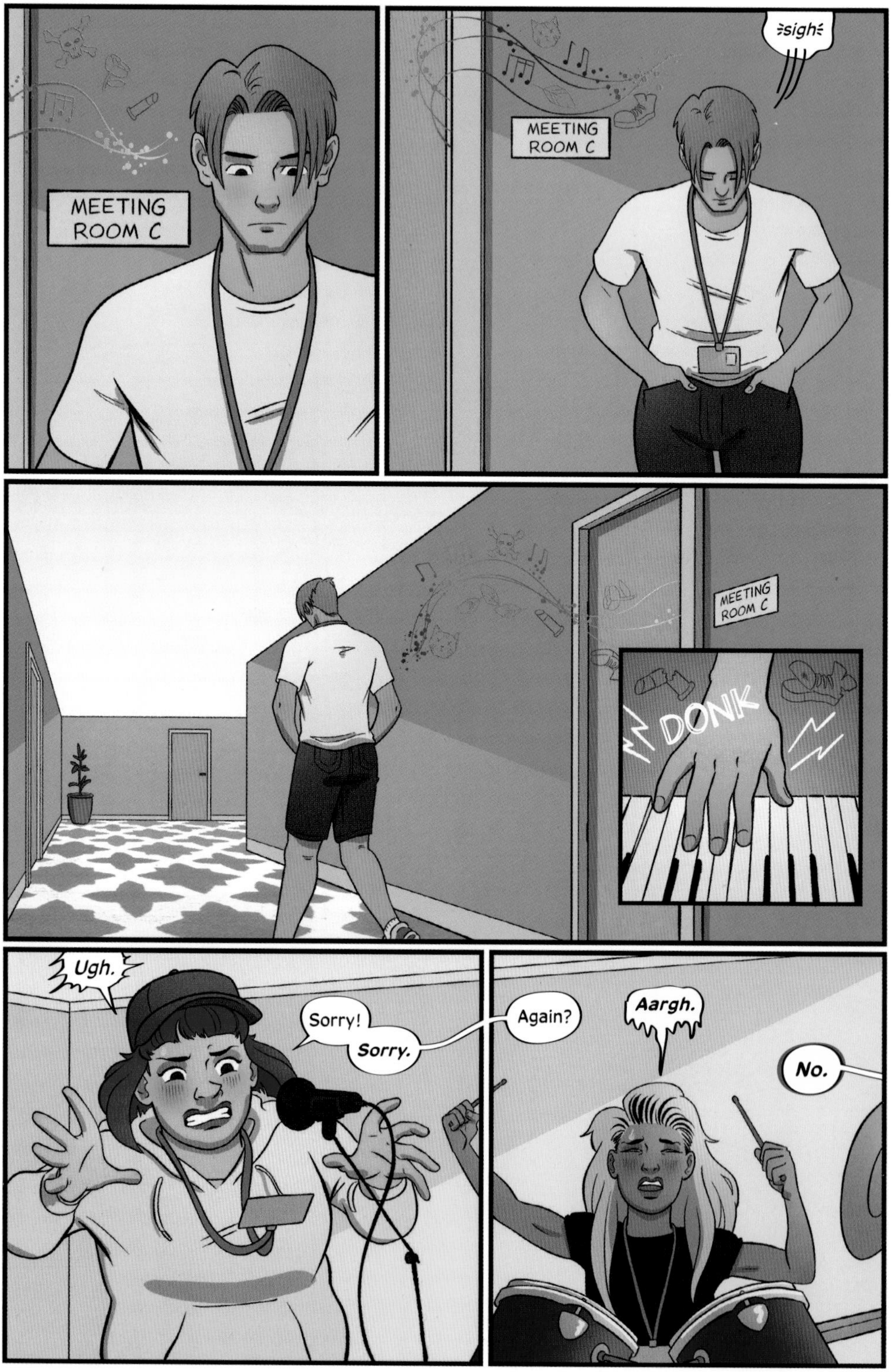
MEETING ROOM C
MEETING ROOM C
sigh
MEETING ROOM C
DONK
Ugh.
Sorry!
Sorry.
Again?
Aargh.
No.

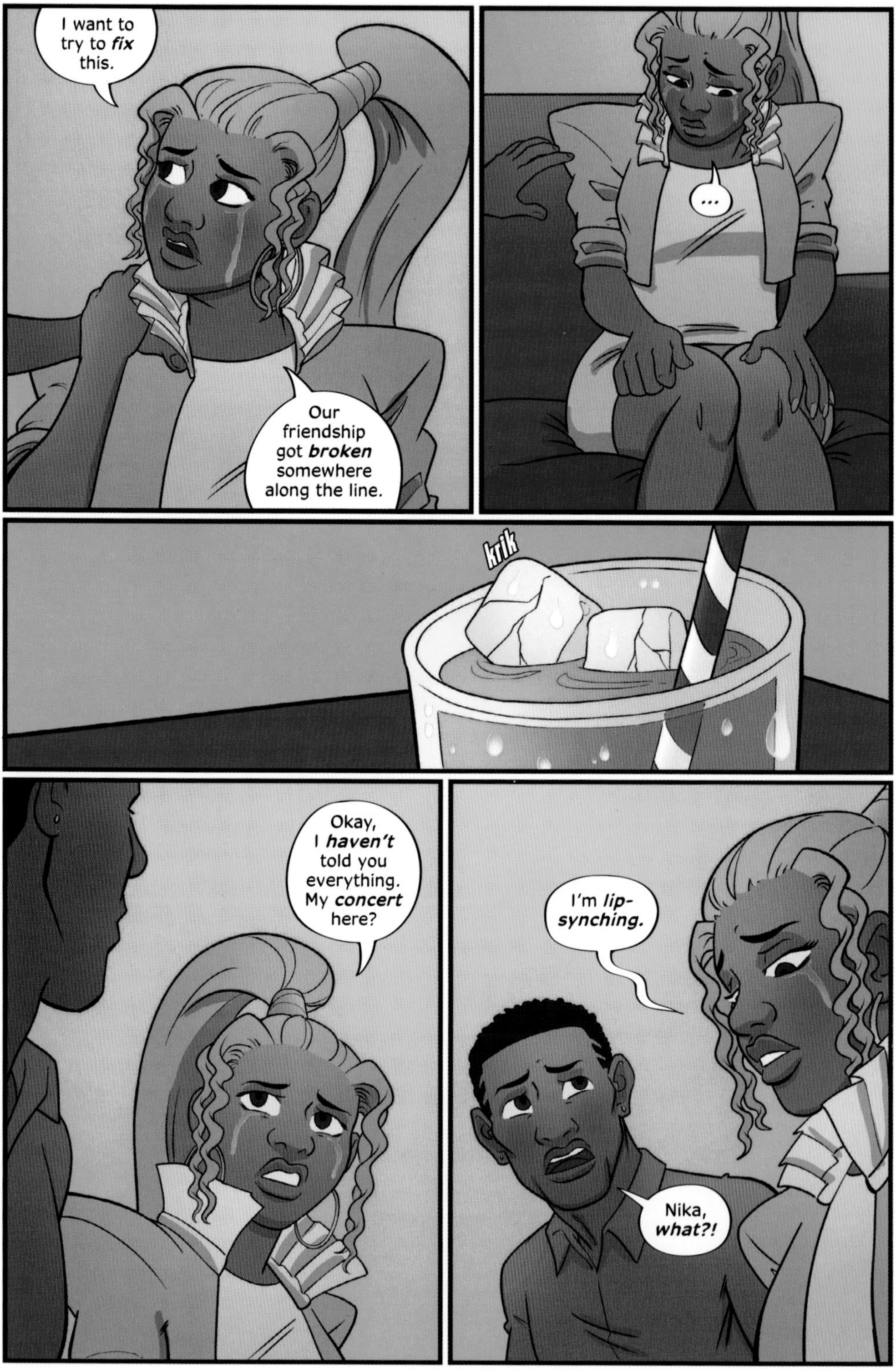
I want to try to *fix* this.
Our friendship got ***broken*** somewhere along the line.
...
krik
Okay, I ***haven't*** told you everything. My ***concert*** here?
I'm *lip-synching.*
Nika, ***what?!***

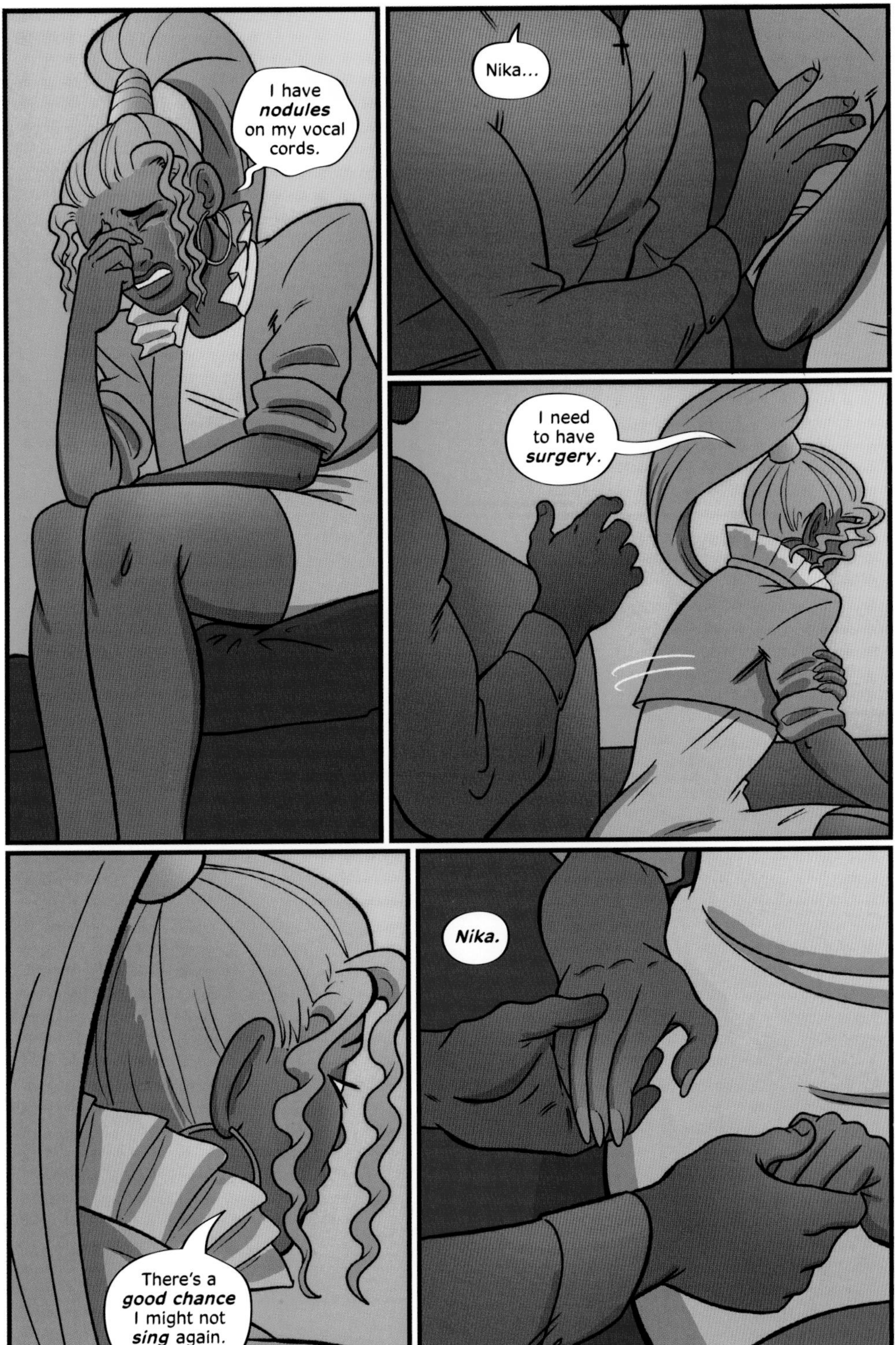
I have *nodules* on my vocal cords.
Nika...
I need to have *surgery*.
There's a *good chance* I might not *sing* again.
Nika.

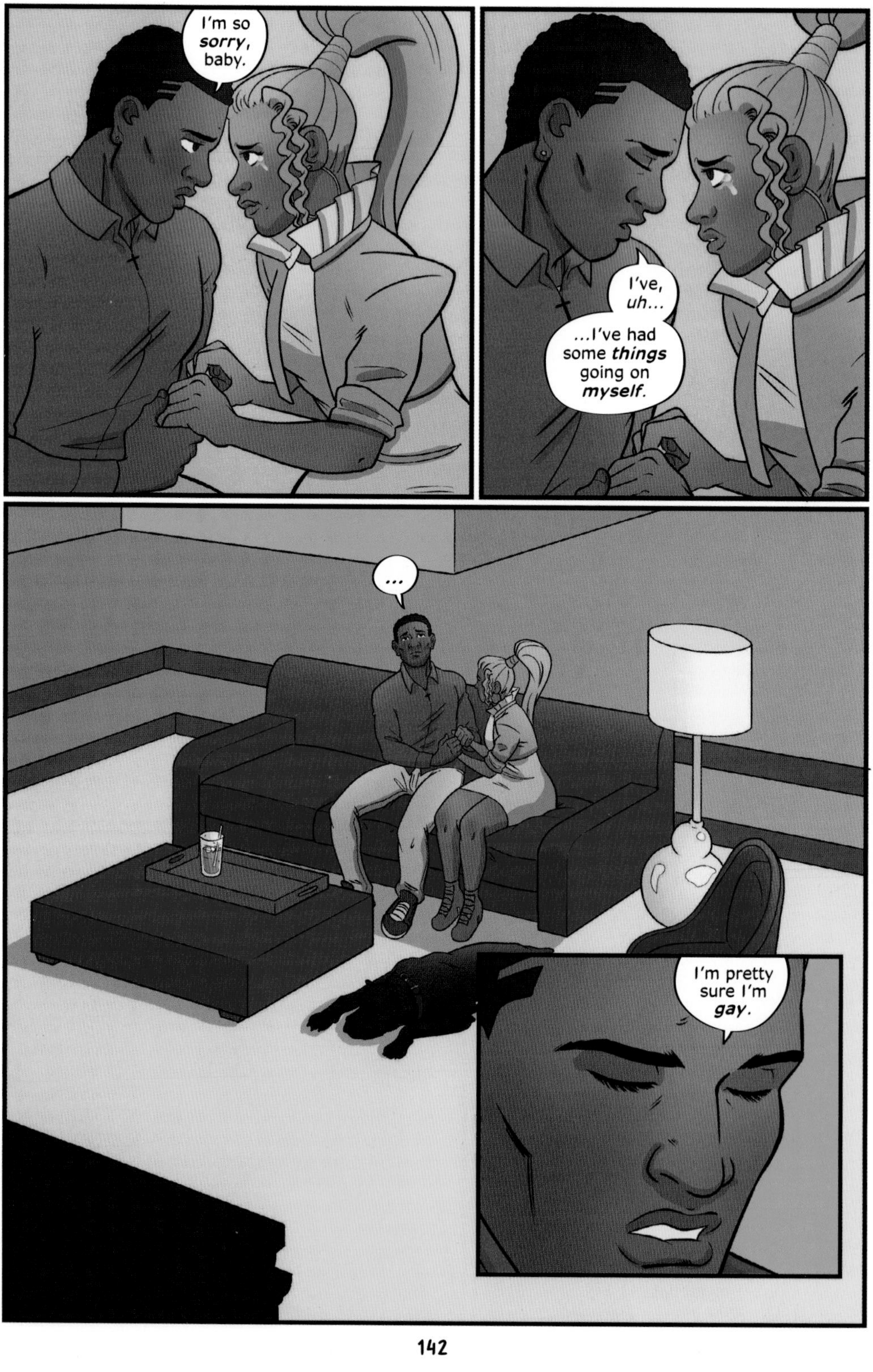
I'm so *sorry*, baby.
I've, *uh*...
...I've had some *things* going on *myself*.
...
I'm pretty sure I'm *gay*.

CHAPTER
5

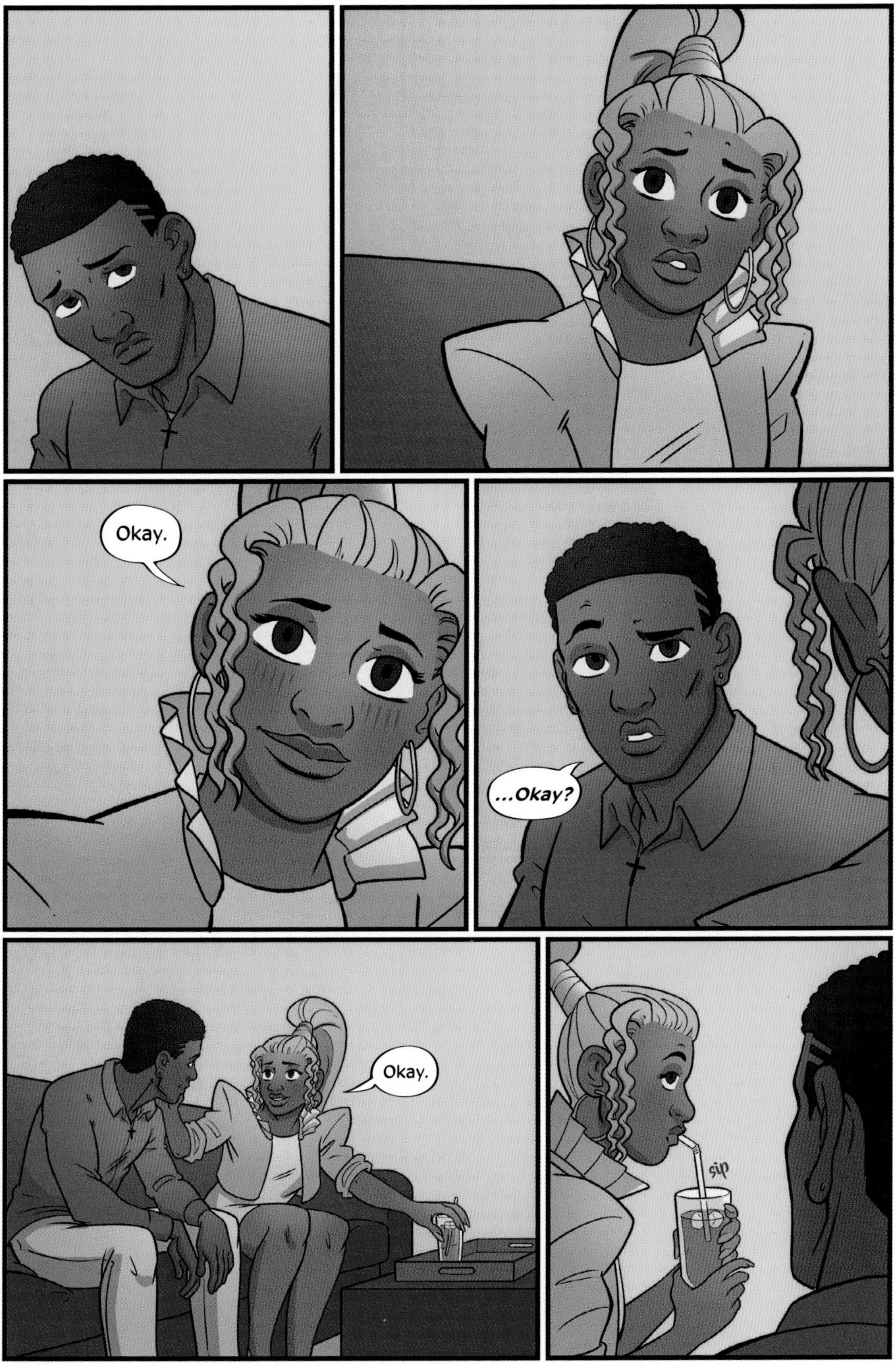
Okay.
...Okay?
Okay.
sip

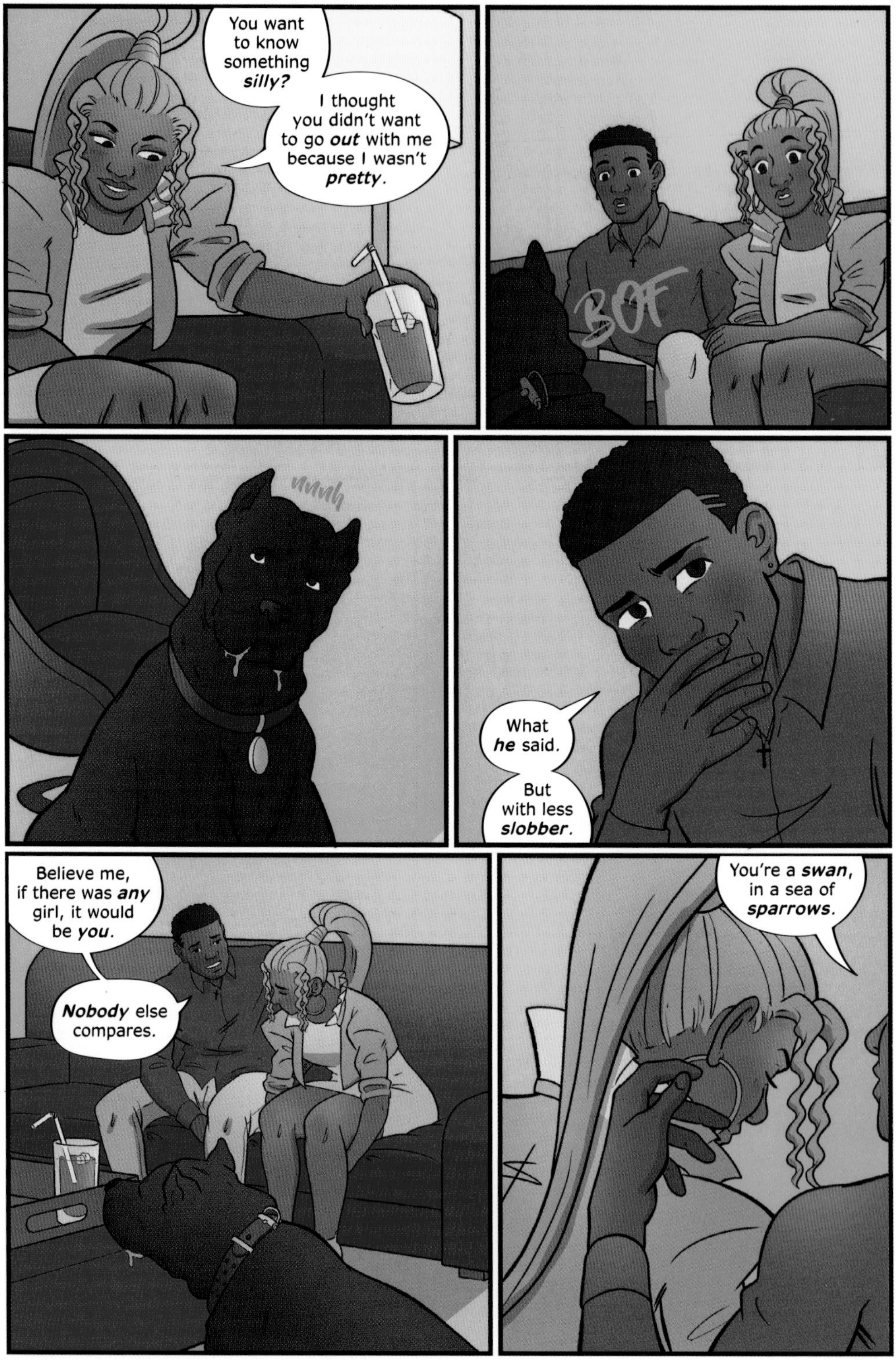
You want to know something *silly?*
I thought you didn't want to go *out* with me because I wasn't *pretty*.
BOF
What *he* said.
But with less *slobber*.
Believe me, if there was *any* girl, it would be *you*.
Nobody else compares.
You're a *swan*, in a sea of *sparrows*.

148

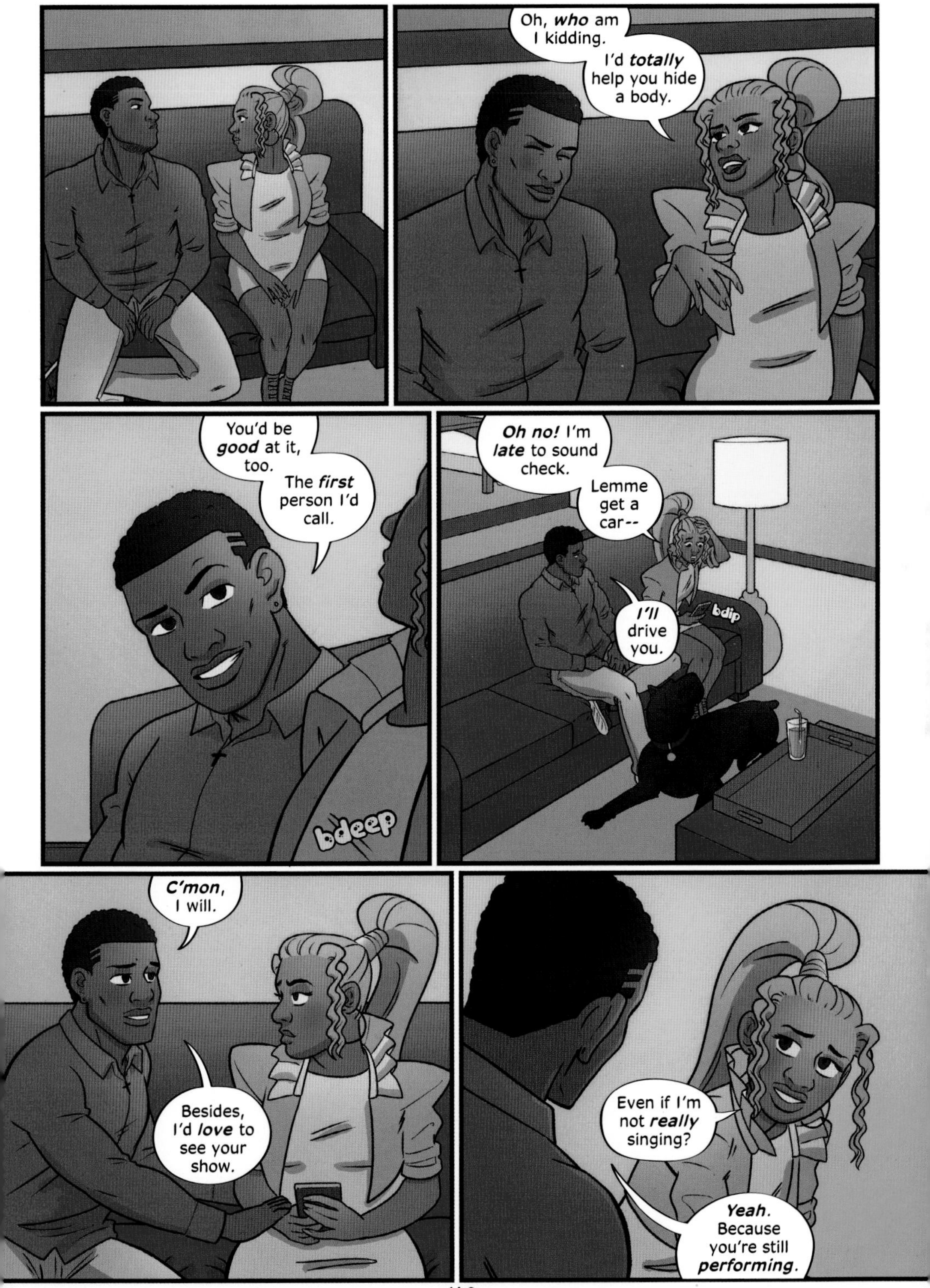

Oh, *who* am I kidding.
I'd *totally* help you hide a body.
You'd be *good* at it, too.
The *first* person I'd call.
bdeep
Oh no! I'm *late* to sound check.
Lemme get a car--
bdip
I'll drive you.
C'mon, I will.
Besides, I'd *love* to see your show.
Even if I'm not *really* singing?
Yeah. Because you're still *performing*.

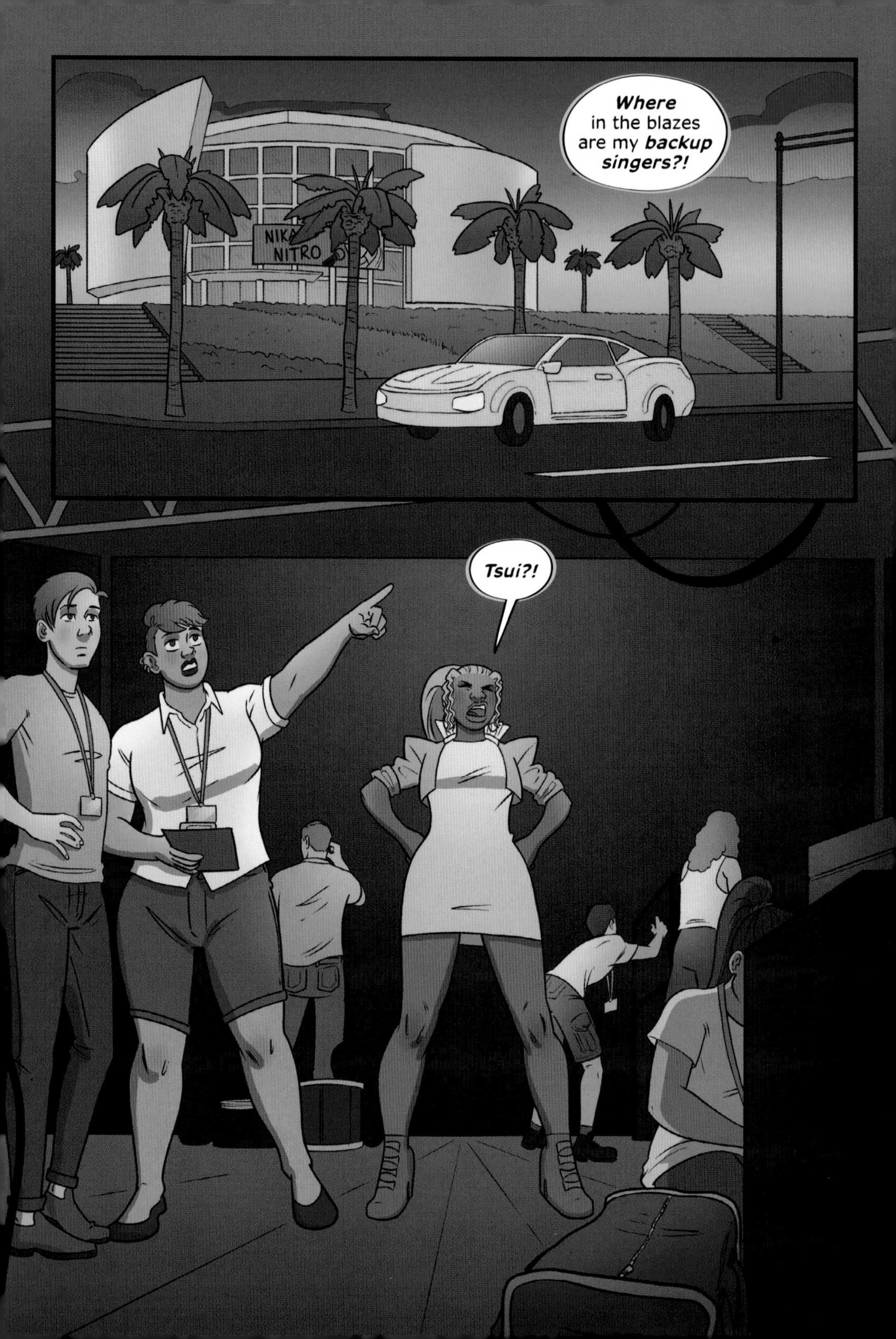

NIKA NITRO
Where in the blazes are my backup singers?!
Tsui?!

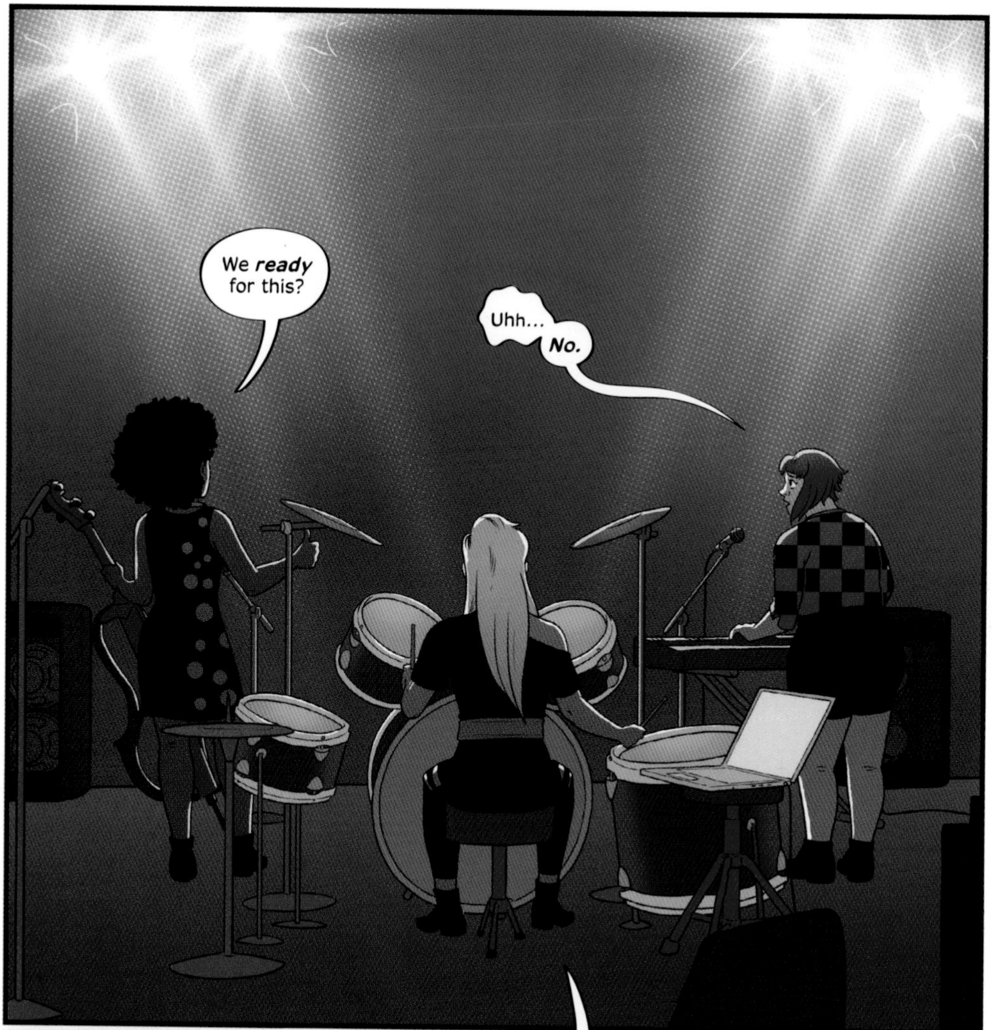
We *ready* for this?
Uhh... ***No.***

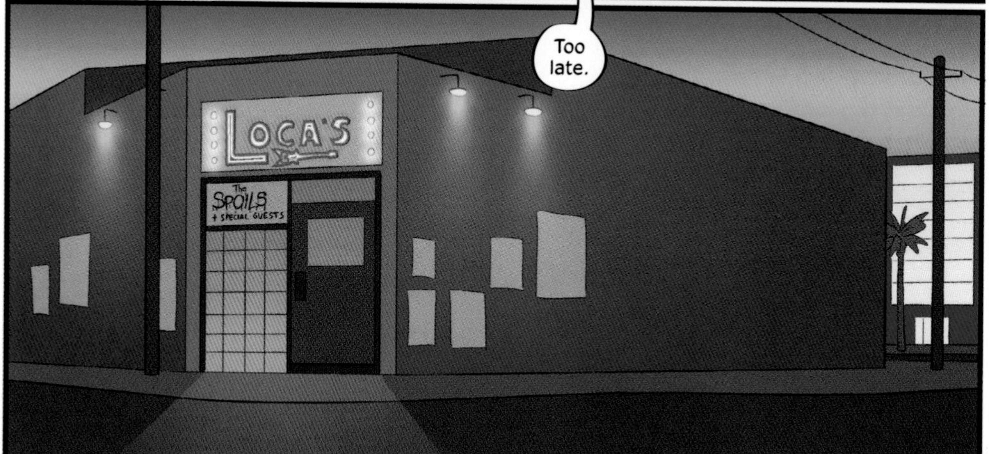
Too late.
LOCA'S
The SPOILS + SPECIAL GUESTS

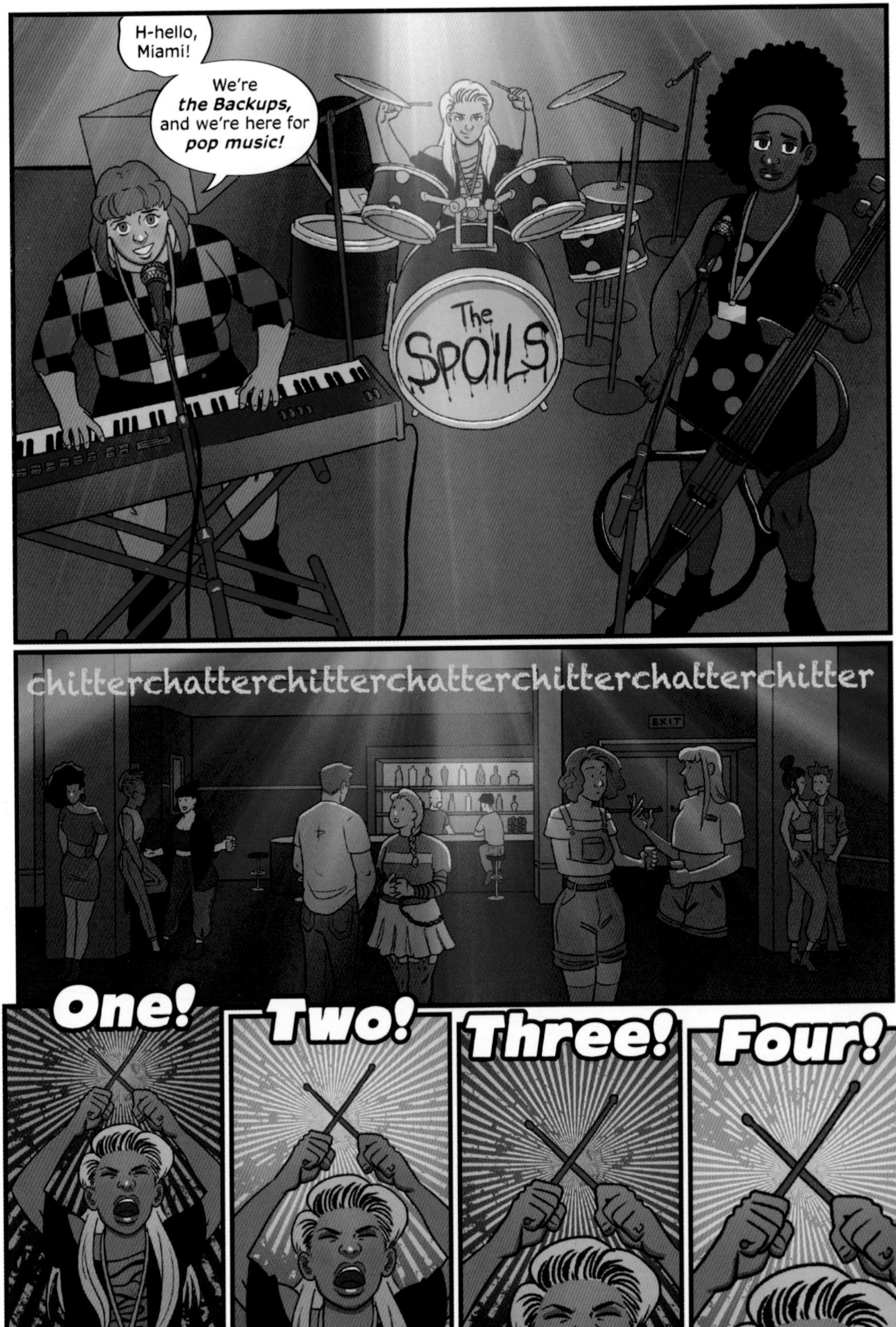
H-hello, Miami!
We're *the Backups,* and we're here for *pop music!*
The SPOILS
chitterchatterchitterchatterchitterchatterchitter
EXIT
One!
Two!
Three!
Four!

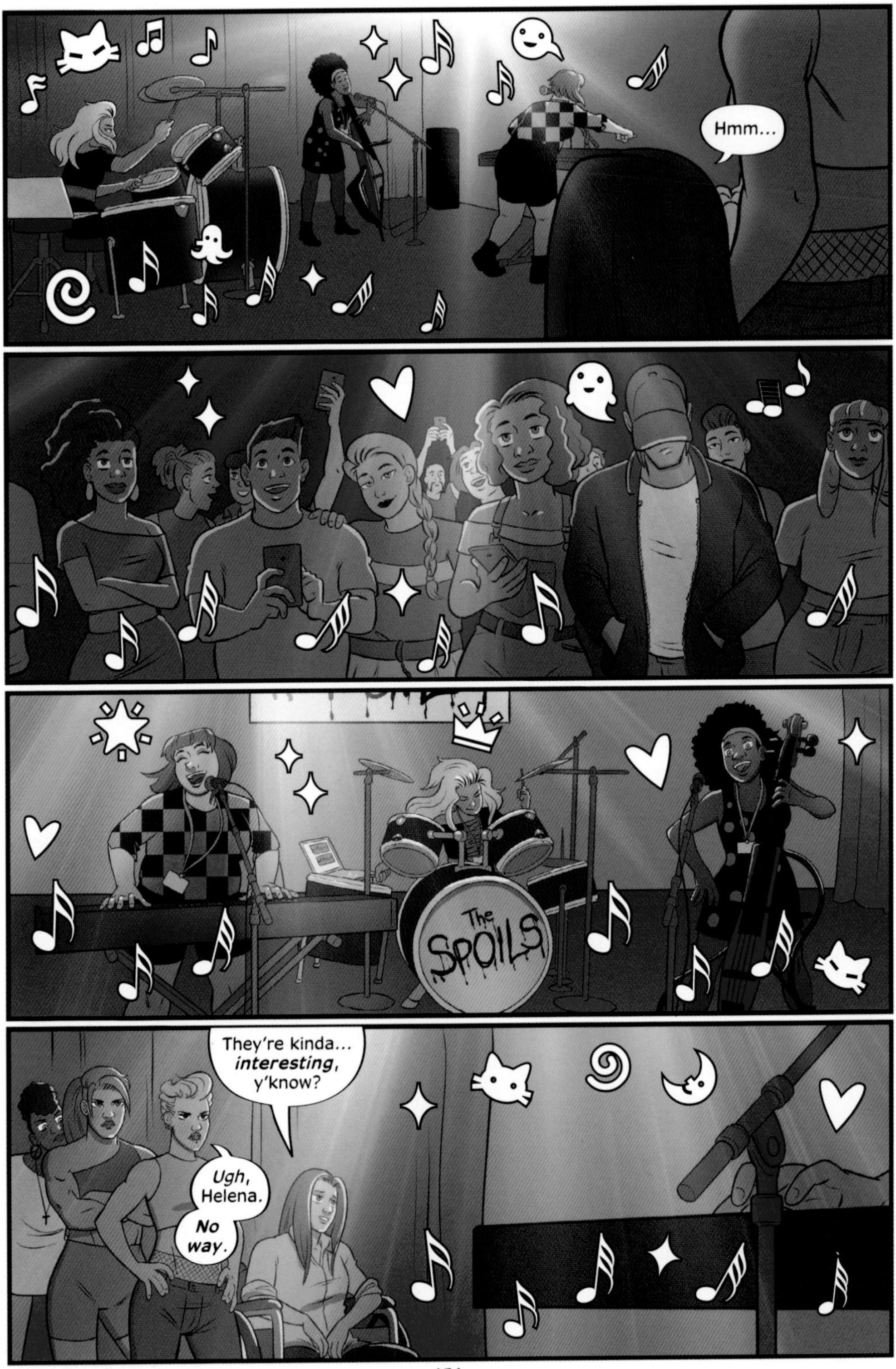
Hmm...
The SPOILS
They're kinda... *interesting*, y'know?
Ugh, Helena. **No way.**

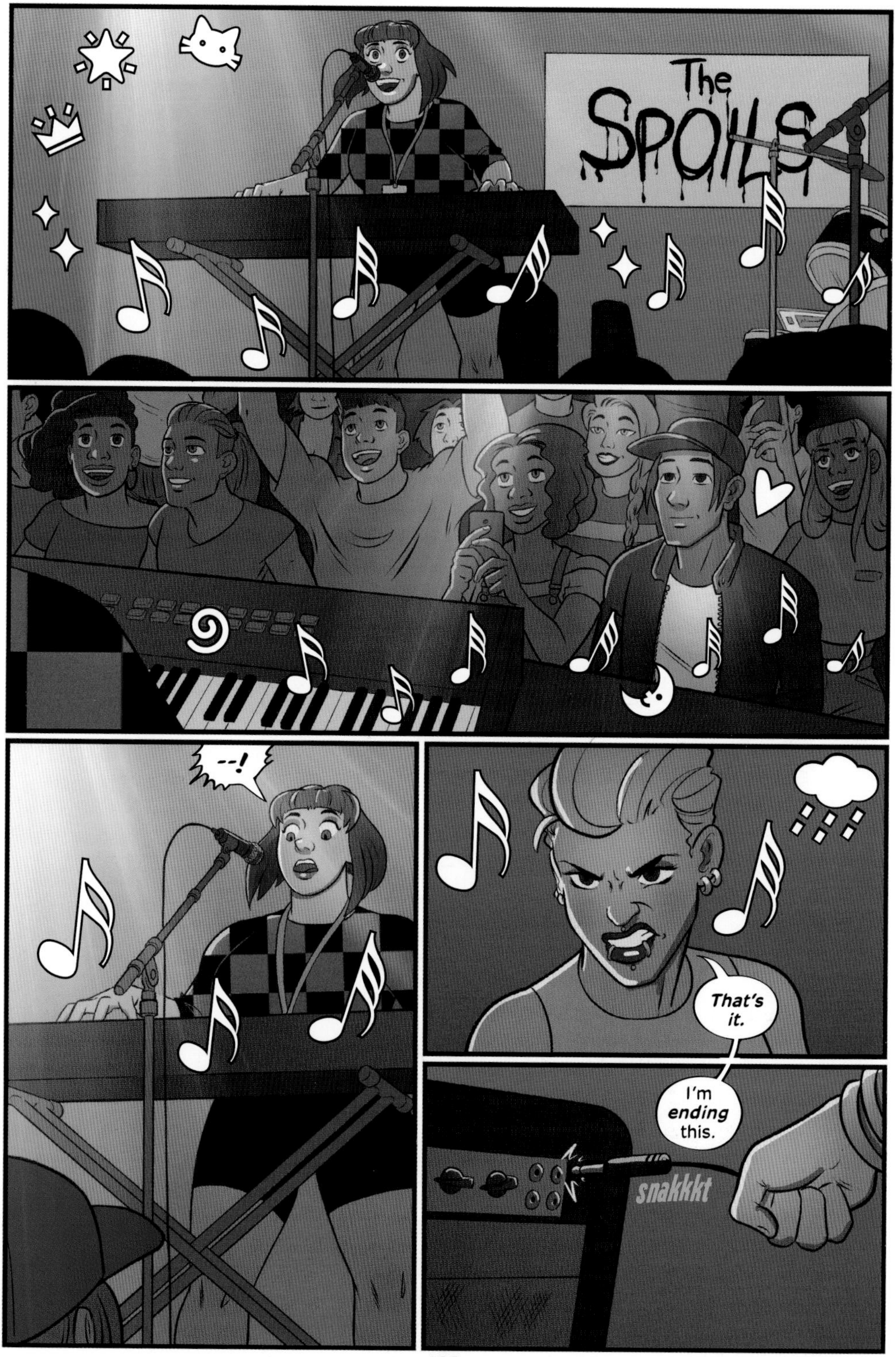
The
SPOILS
--!
That's it.
I'm *ending* this.
snakkkt

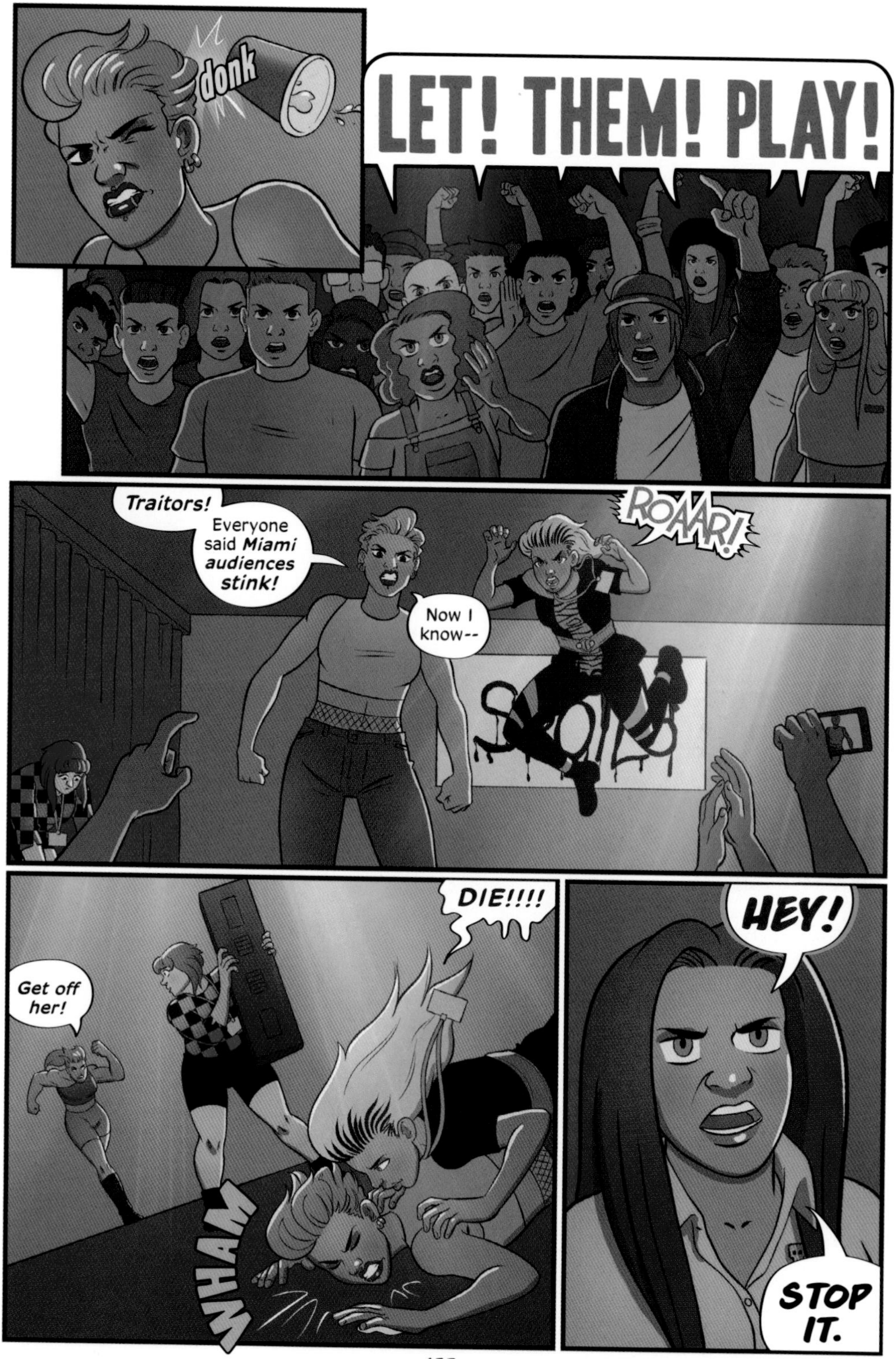
donk
LET! THEM! PLAY!
Traitors!
Everyone said *Miami audiences* stink!
Now I know--
ROAAR!
DIE!!!!
Get off her!
WHAM
HEY!
STOP IT.

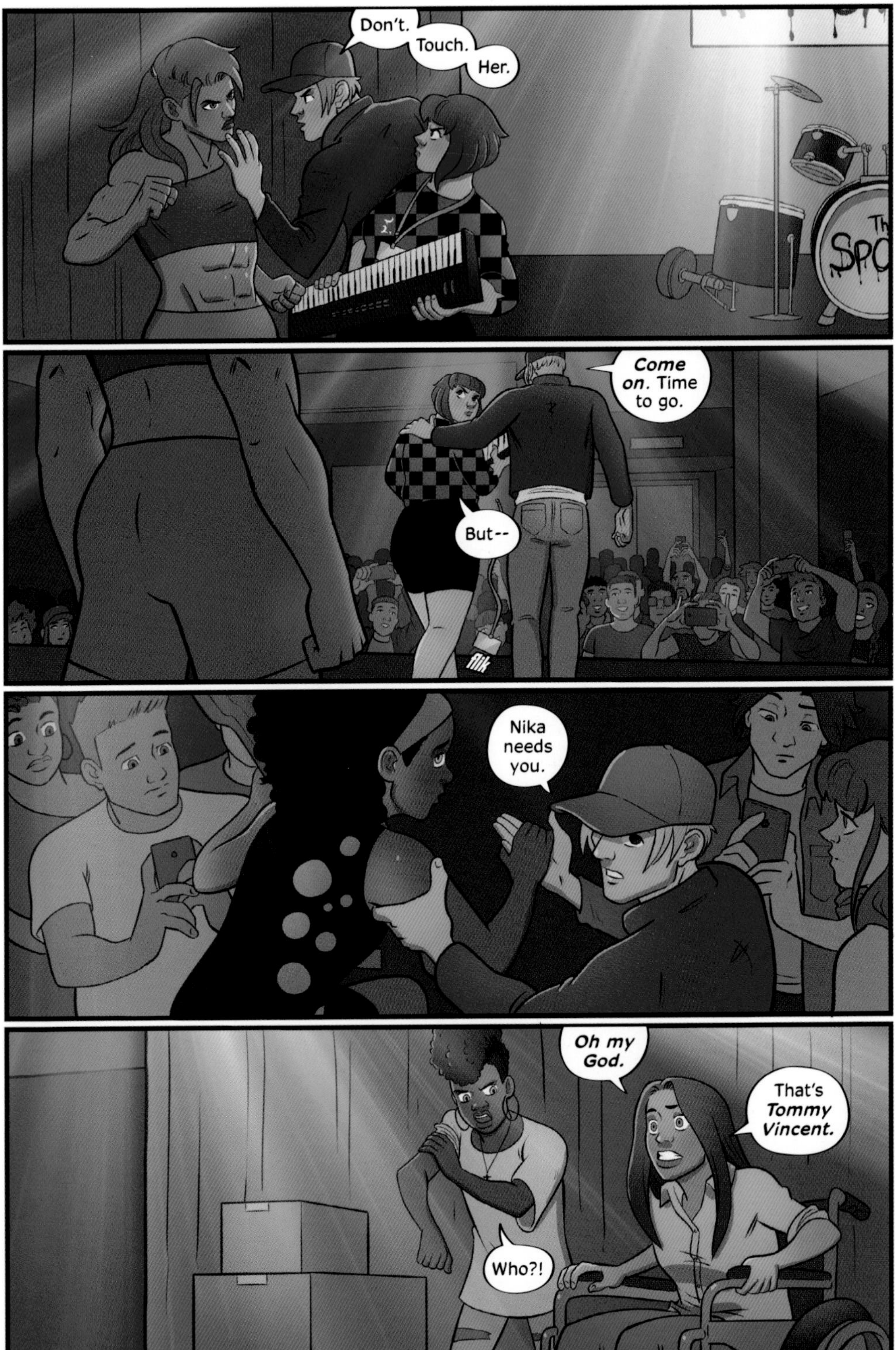
Don't.
Touch.
Her.
Come on. Time to go.
But--
Nika needs you.
Oh my God.
That's *Tommy Vincent.*
Who?!

159

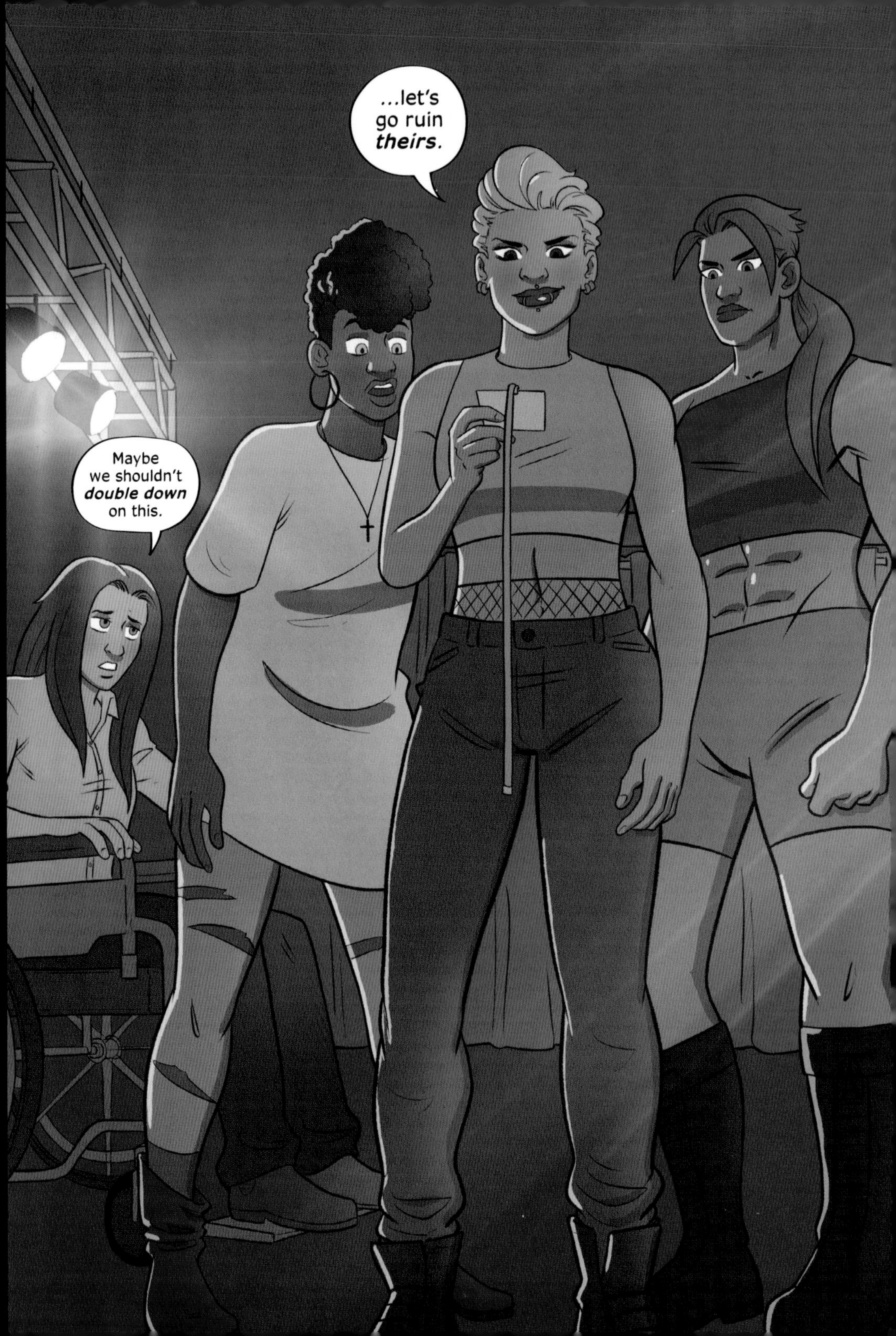
...let's go ruin *theirs*.
Maybe we shouldn't *double down* on this.

162

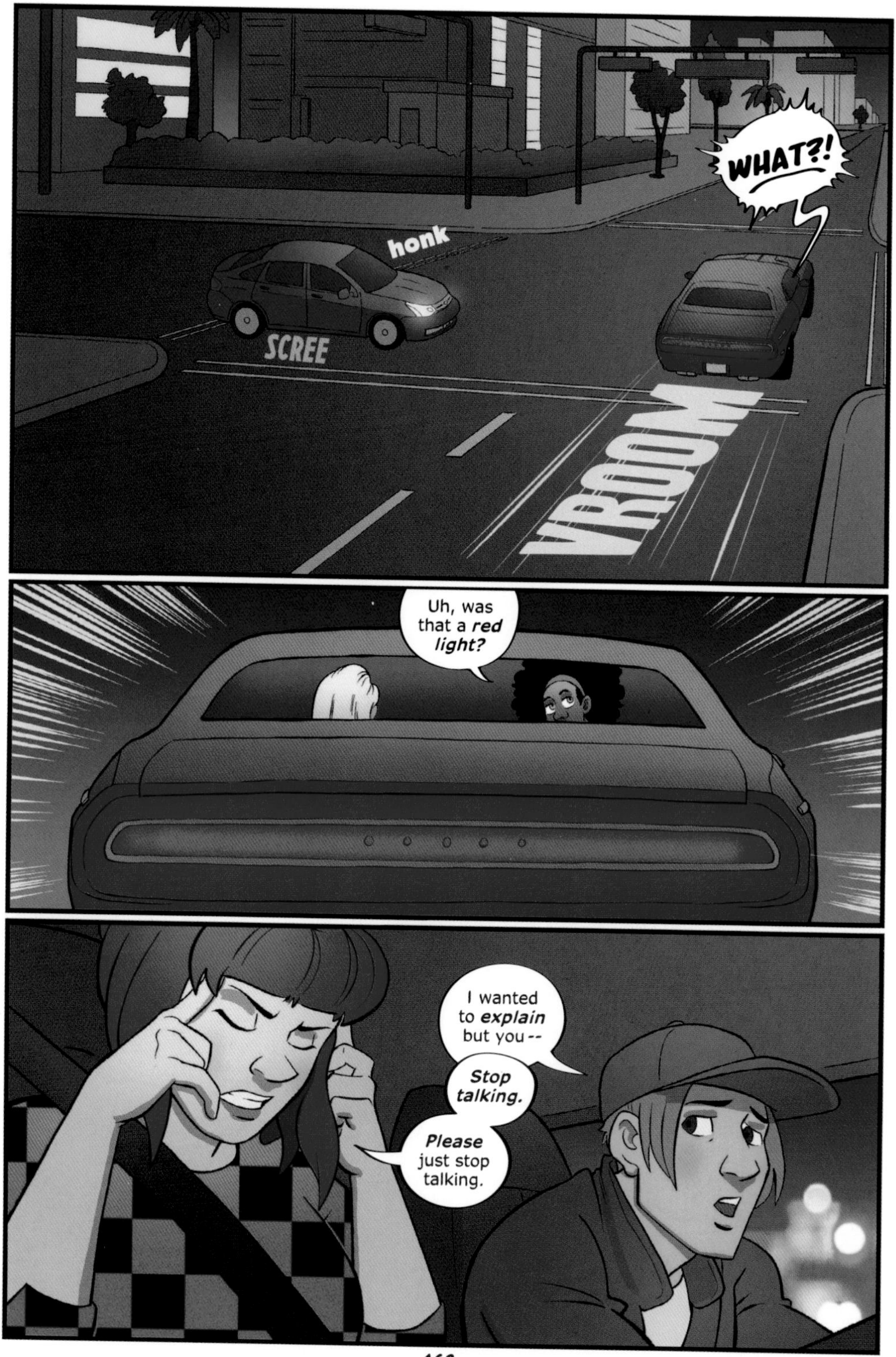
honk
SCREE
WHAT?!
VROOM
Uh, was that a *red light?*
I wanted to *explain* but you--
Stop talking.
Please just stop talking.

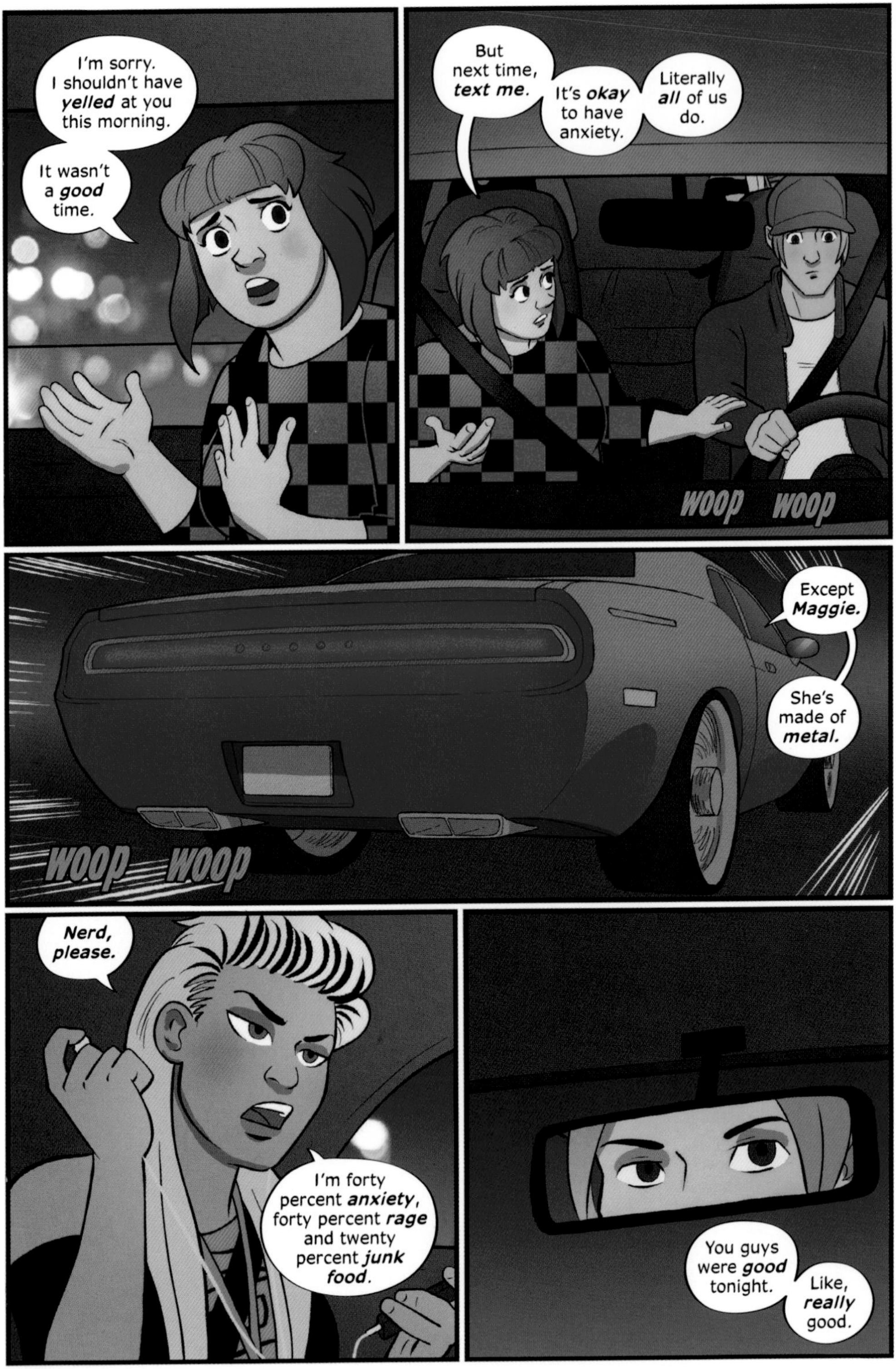
I'm sorry. I shouldn't have *yelled* at you this morning.
It wasn't a *good* time.
But next time, *text me*.
It's *okay* to have anxiety.
Literally *all* of us do.
WOOP WOOP
Except *Maggie.*
She's made of *metal.*
WOOP WOOP
Nerd, please.
I'm forty percent *anxiety*, forty percent *rage* and twenty percent *junk food*.
You guys were *good* tonight.
Like, *really* good.

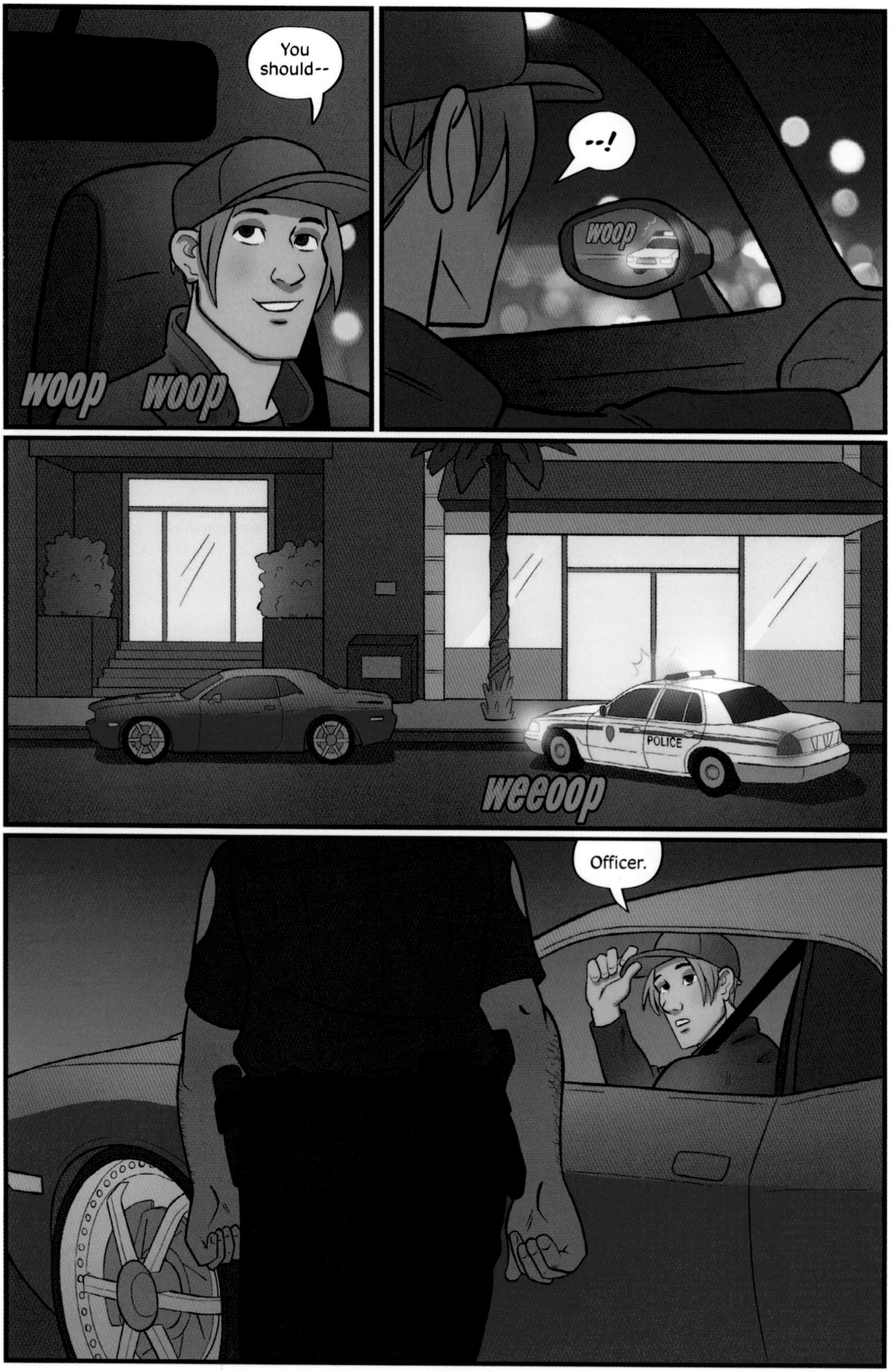
You should--
woop woop
--!
woop
weeoop
POLICE
Officer.

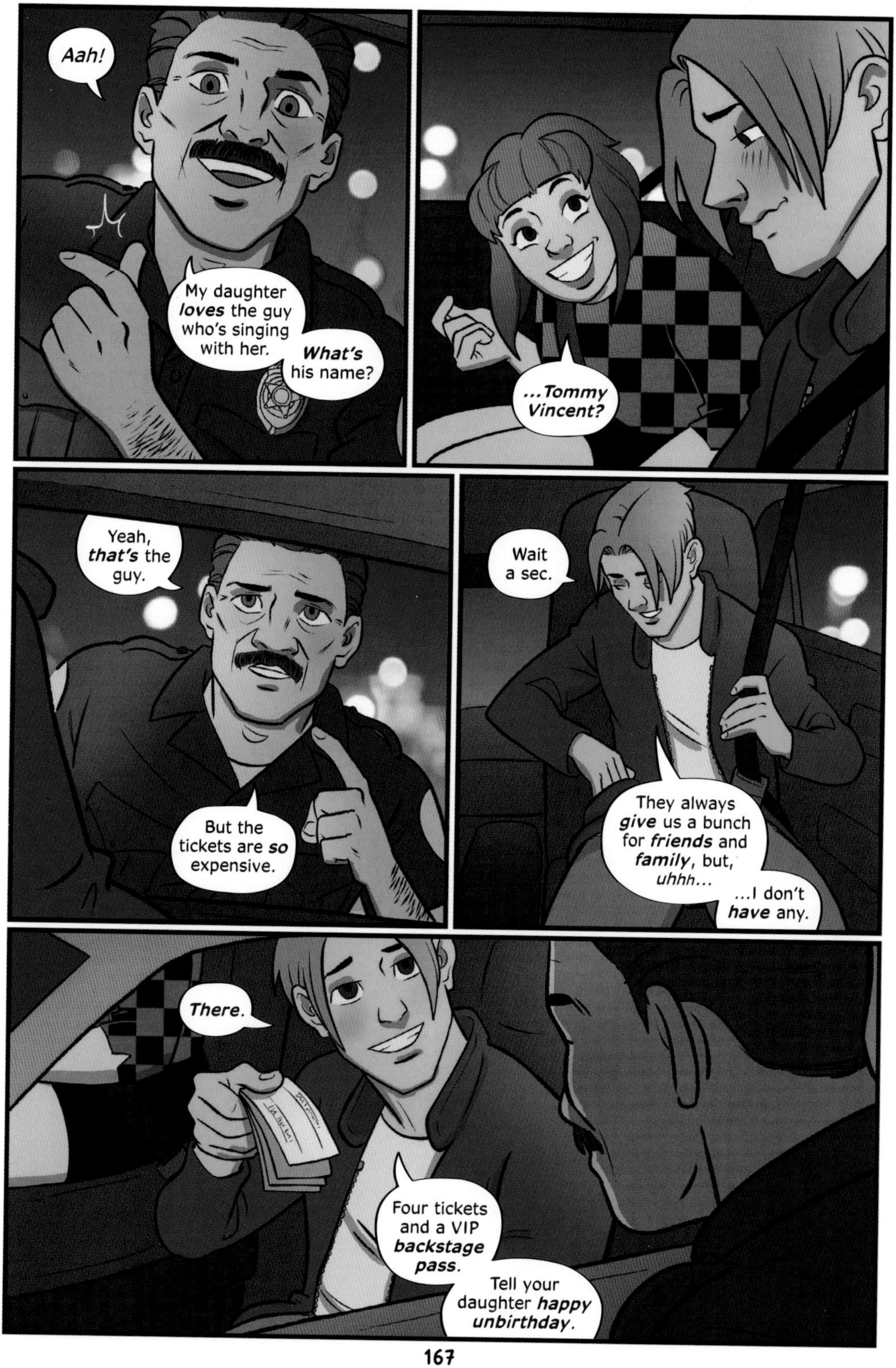
Aah!
My daughter *loves* the guy who's singing with her.
What's his name?
...Tommy Vincent?
Yeah, *that's* the guy.
But the tickets are *so* expensive.
Wait a sec.
They always *give* us a bunch for *friends* and *family*, but, *uhhh...*
...I don't *have* any.
There.
Four tickets and a VIP *backstage pass*.
Tell your daughter *happy unbirthday*.

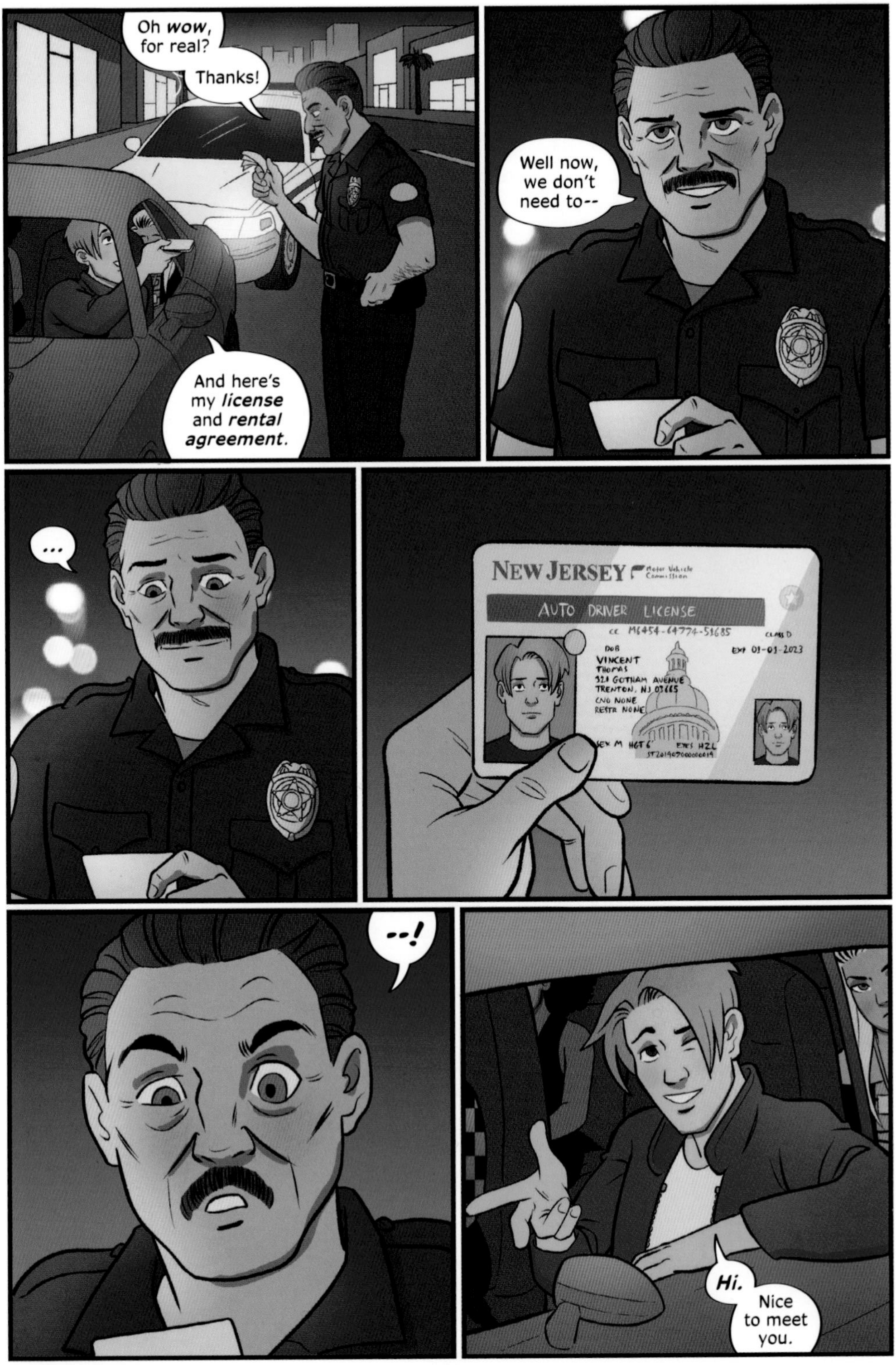
Oh *wow*, for real?
Thanks!
And here's my *license* and *rental agreement*.
Well now, we don't need to--
...
NEW JERSEY
AUTO DRIVER LICENSE
VINCENT
--!
Hi.
Nice to meet you.

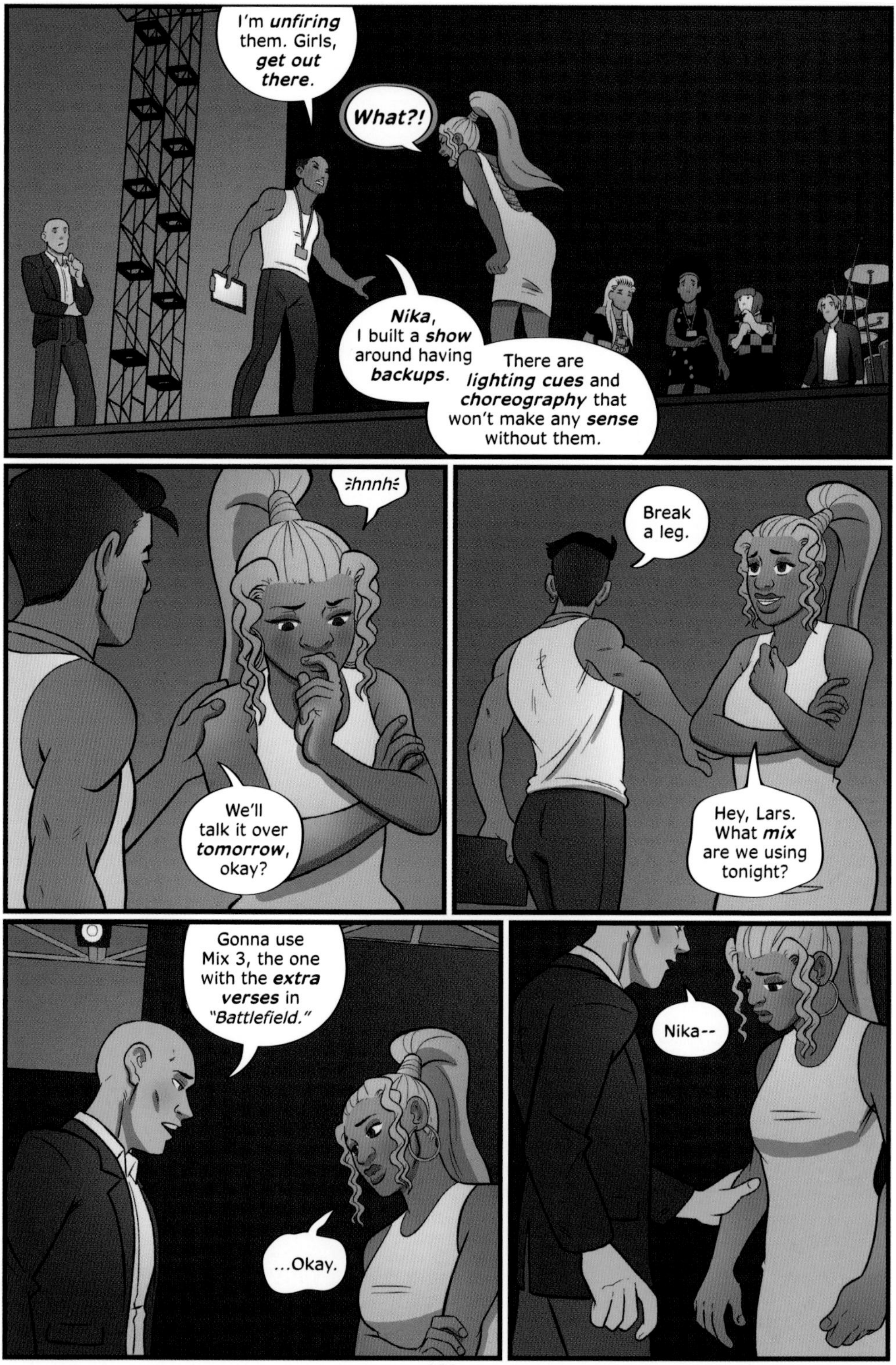
I'm *unfiring* them. Girls, ***get out there***.
What?!
Nika, I built a ***show*** around having ***backups***.
There are ***lighting cues*** and ***choreography*** that won't make any ***sense*** without them.
hnnh
We'll talk it over ***tomorrow***, okay?
Break a leg.
Hey, Lars. What ***mix*** are we using tonight?
Gonna use Mix 3, the one with the ***extra verses*** in *"Battlefield."*
...Okay.
Nika--

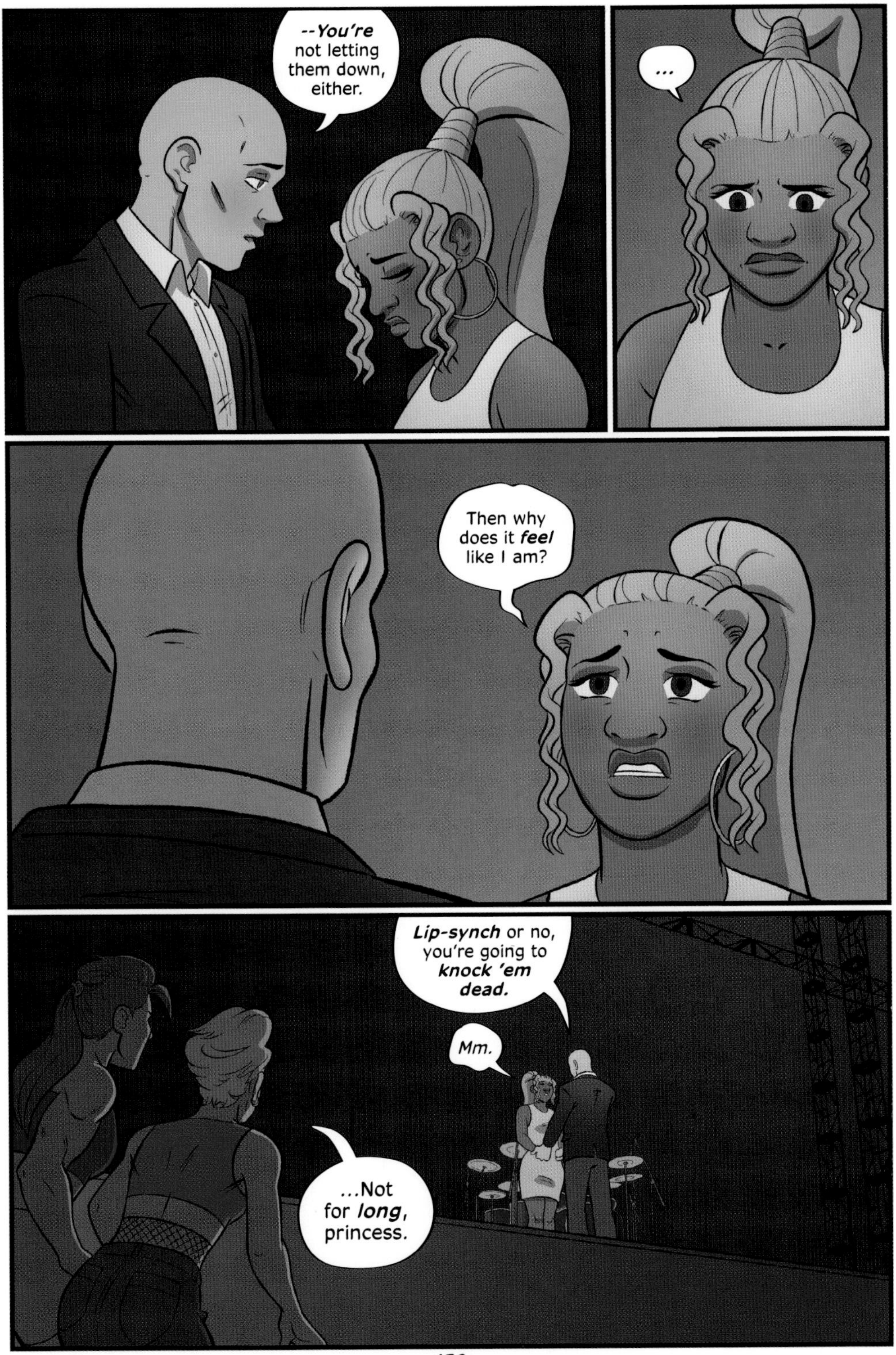
--*You're* not letting them down, either.
...
Then why does it *feel* like I am?
Lip-synch or no, you're going to *knock 'em dead.*
Mm.
...Not for *long*, princess.

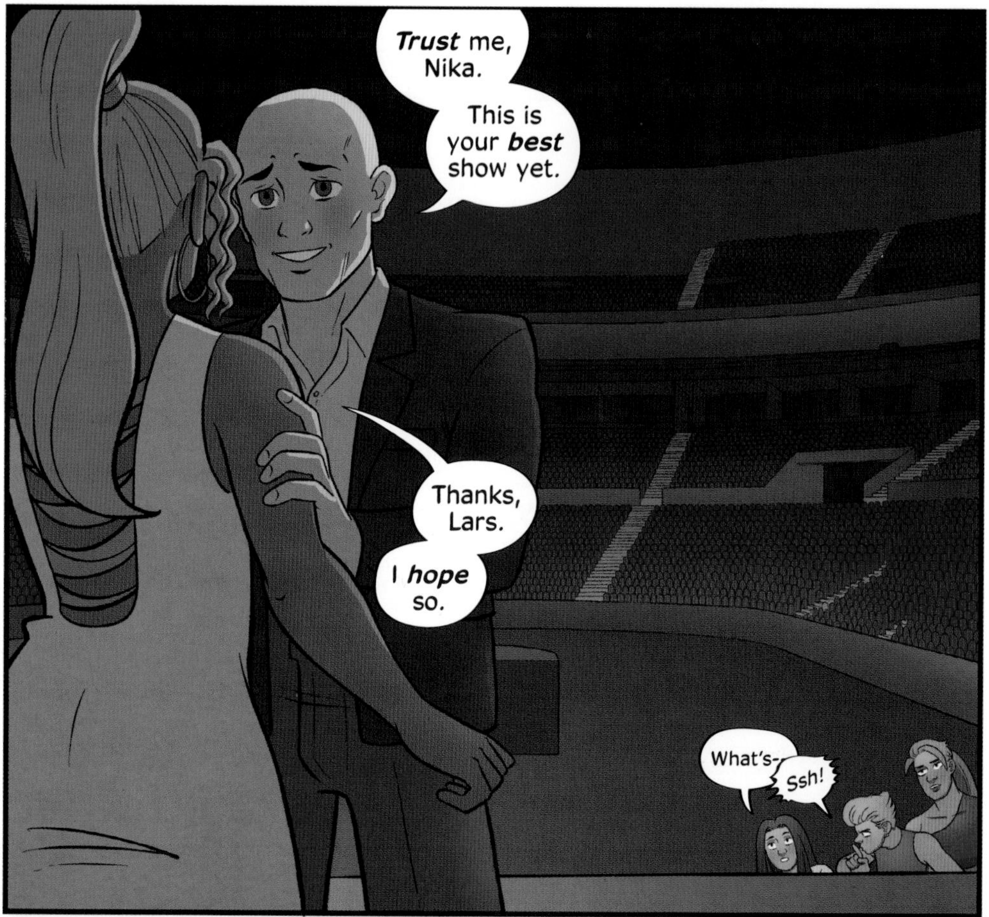
Trust me, Nika.
This is your *best* show yet.
Thanks, Lars.
I *hope* so.
What's-
Ssh!

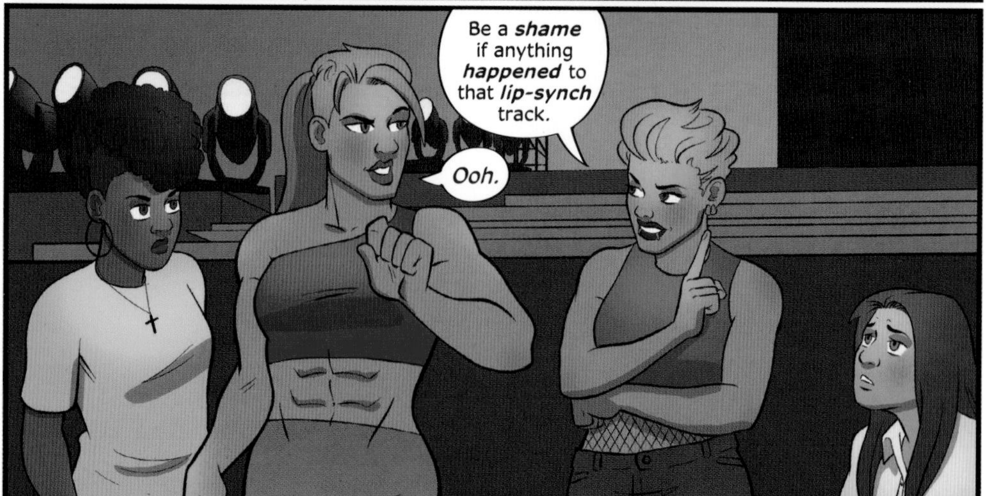
Be a *shame* if anything *happened* to that *lip-synch* track.
Ooh.

CHAPTER
6

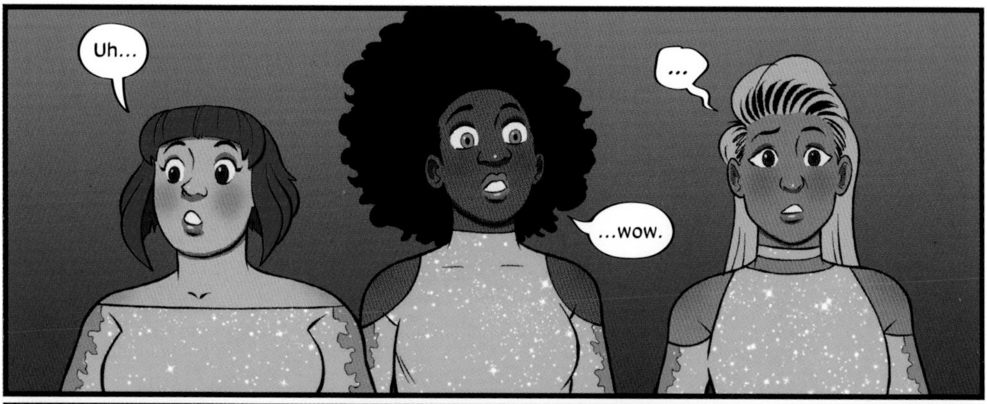
Uh...
...
...wow.

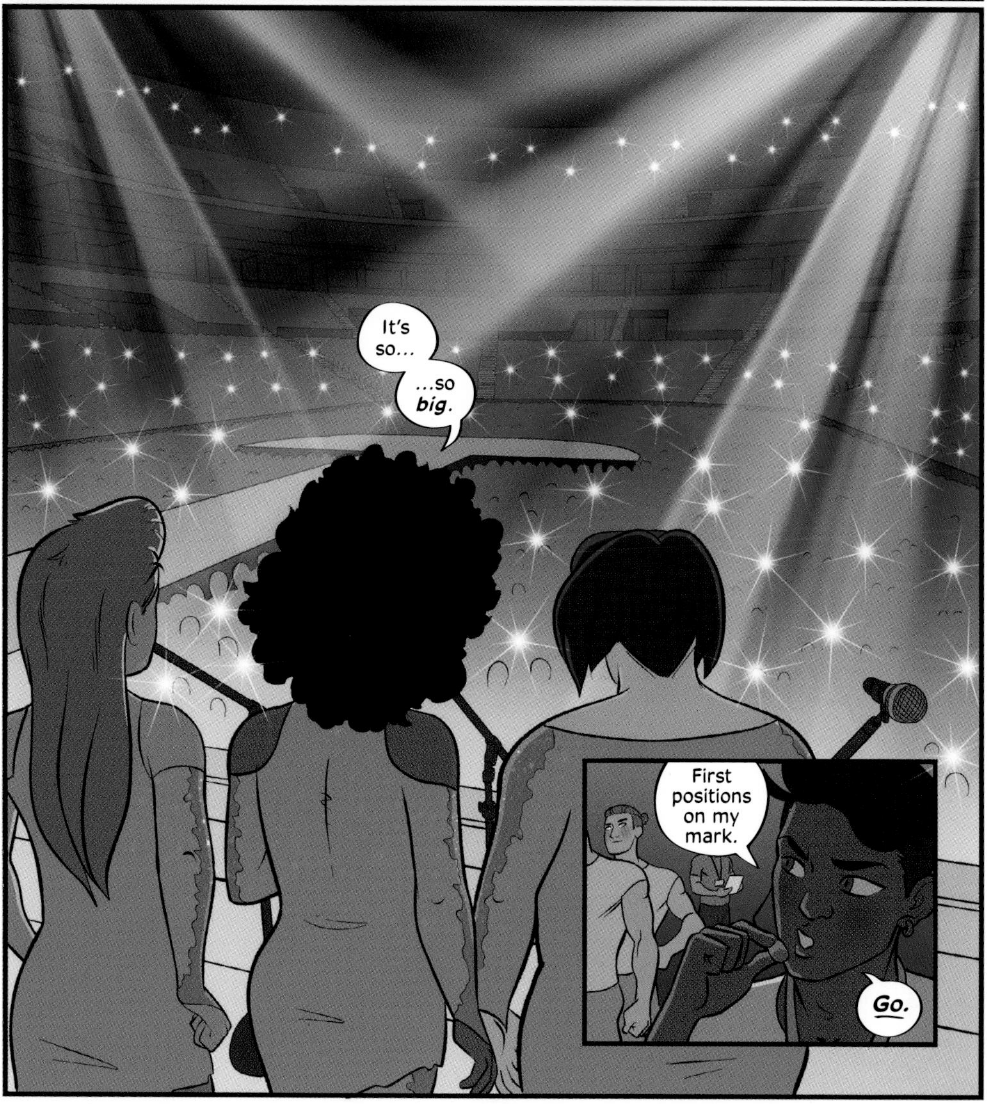
It's so...
...so *big*.
First positions on my mark.
Go.

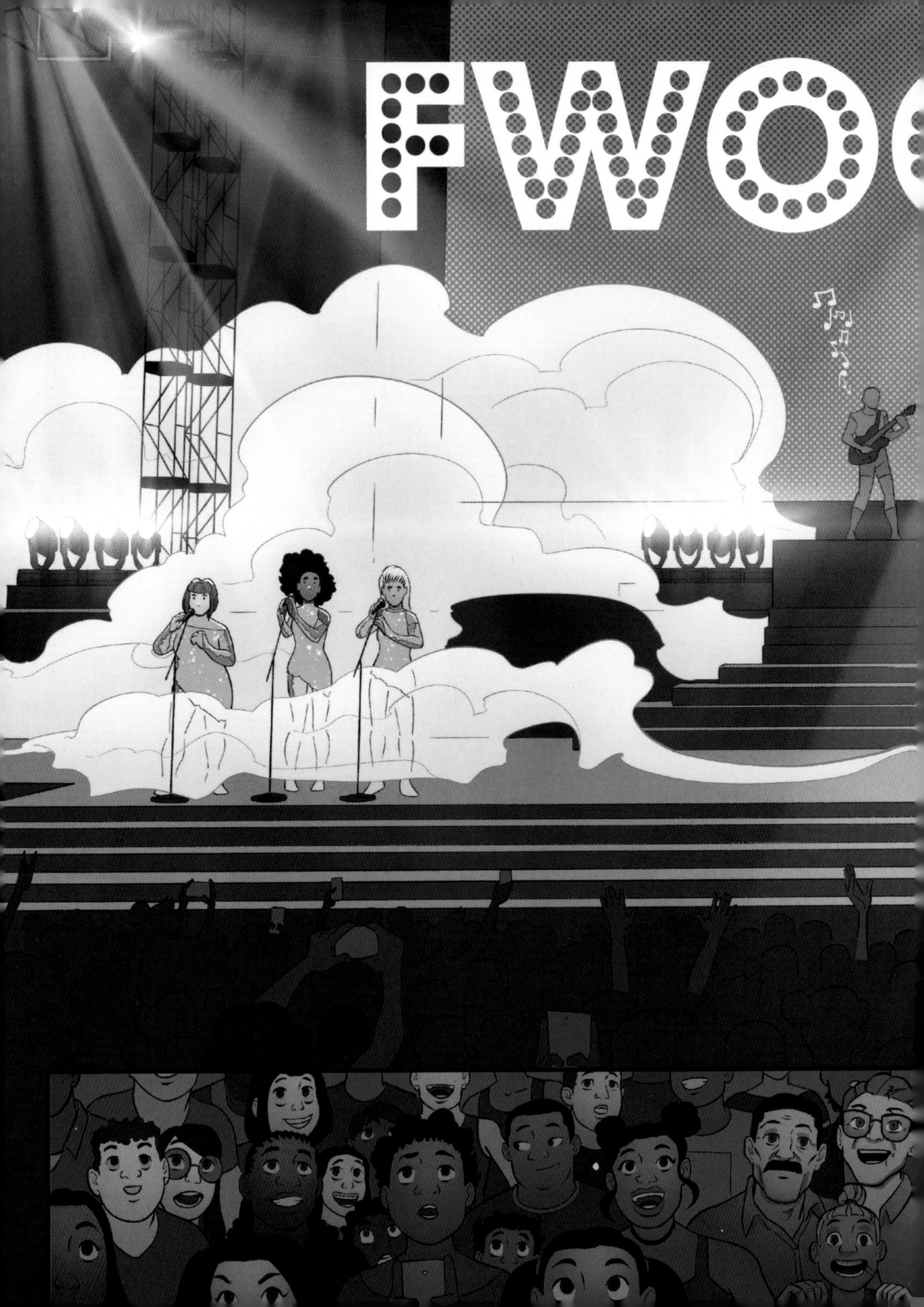
FWOO

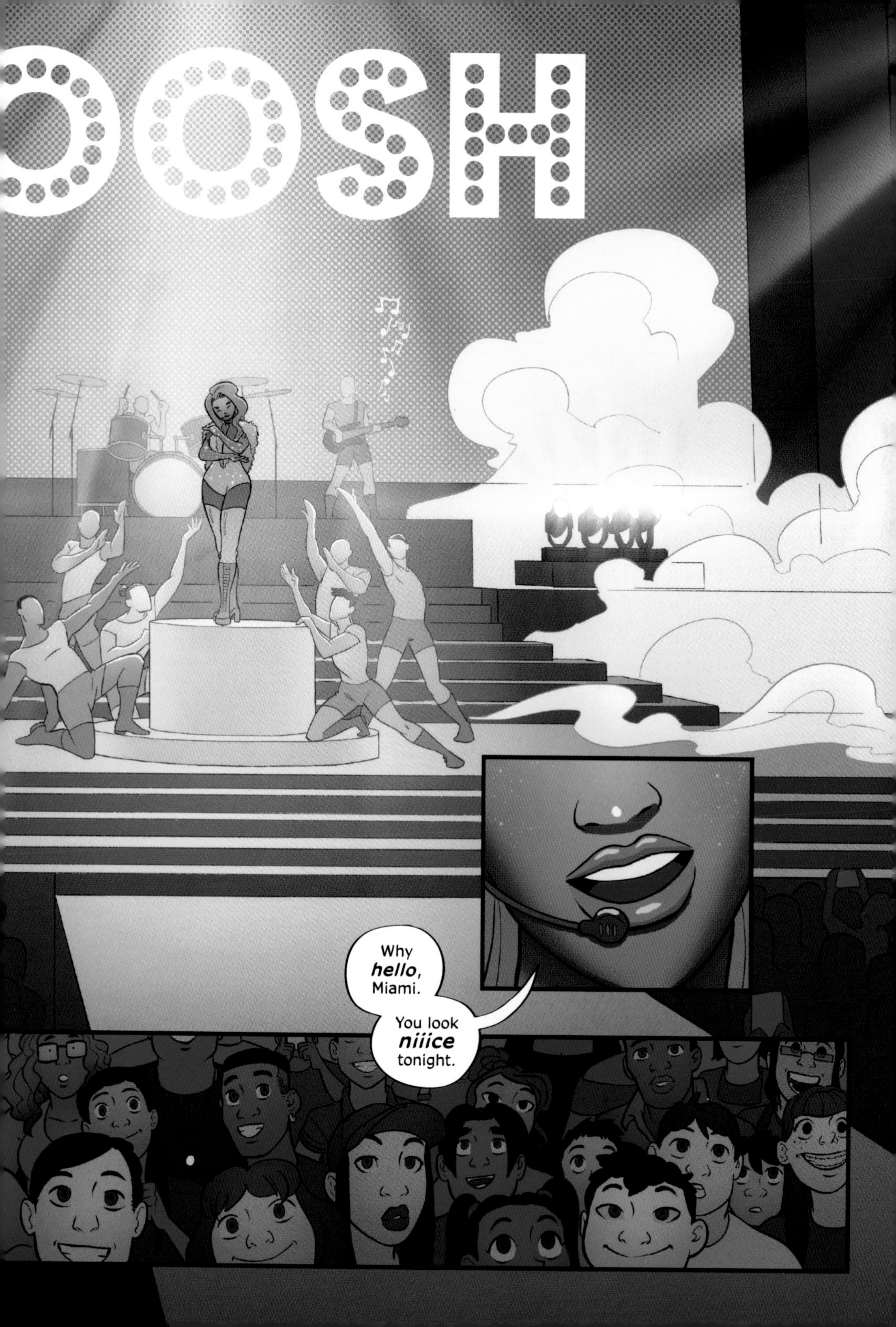
OOSH
Why *hello*, Miami.
You look *niiice* tonight.

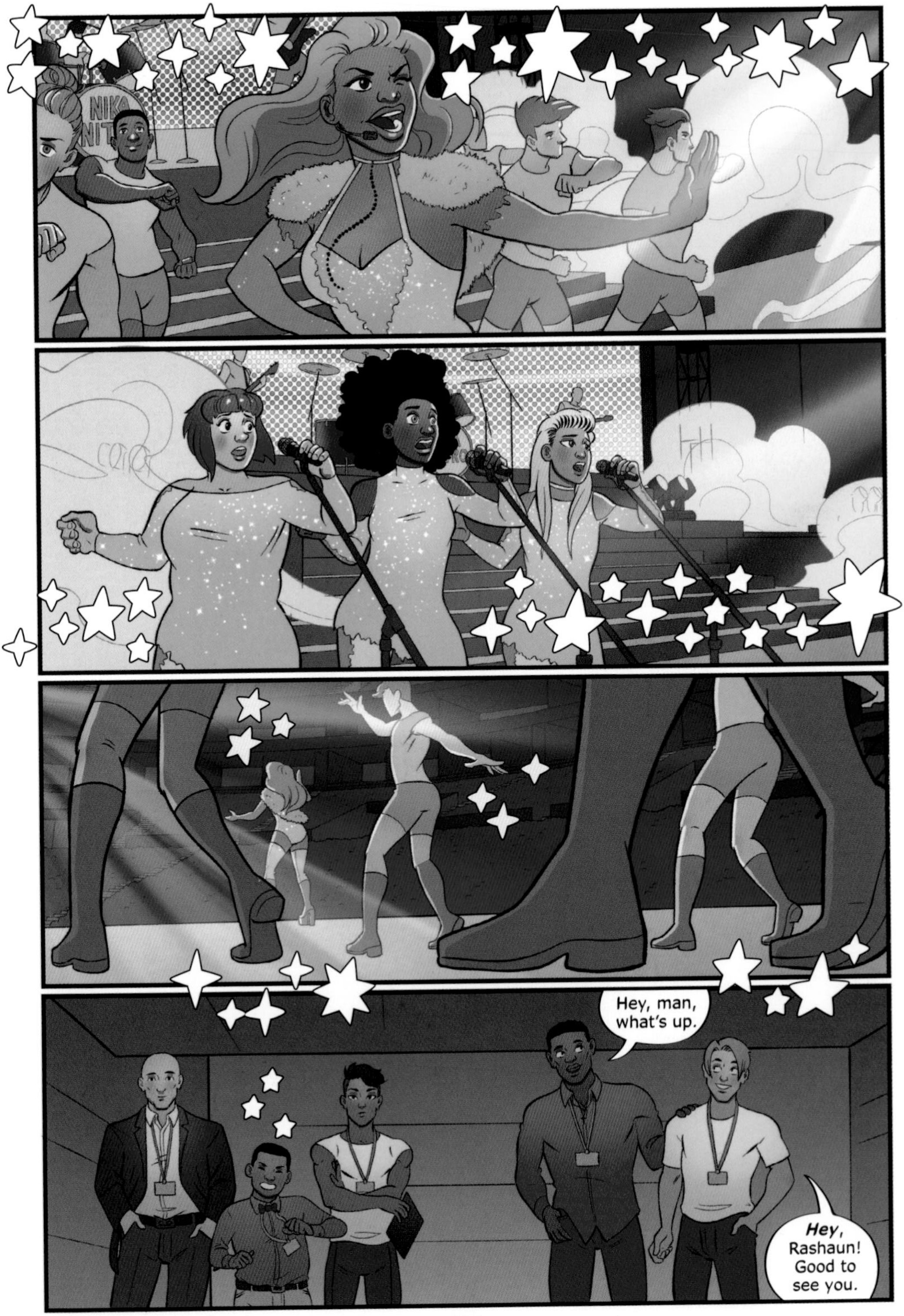
NIKA NITRO
Hey, man, what's up.
Hey, Rashaun! Good to see you.

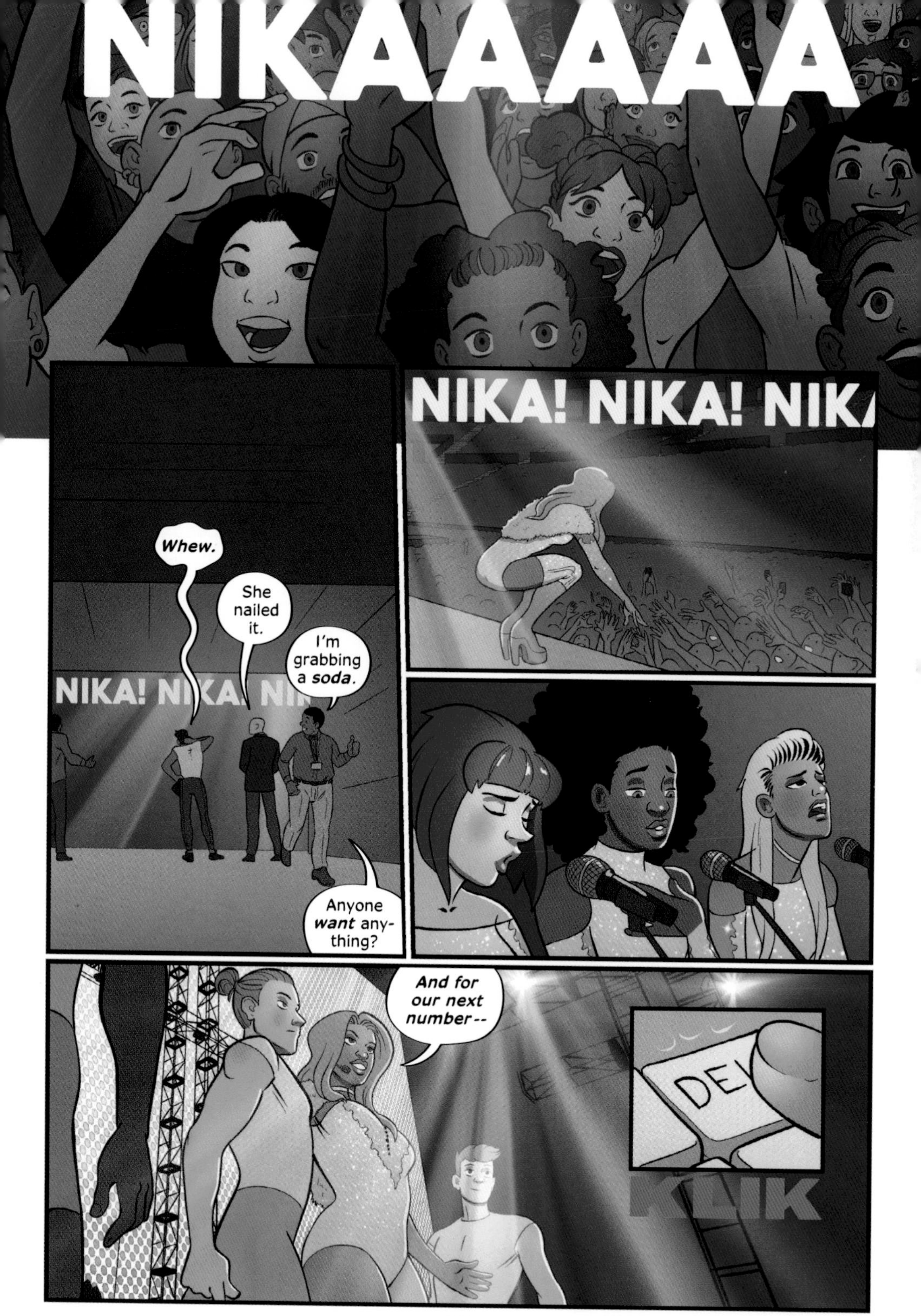
NIKAAAAAA
NIKA! NIKA! NIK
Whew.
She nailed it.
I'm grabbing a *soda*.
Anyone *want* anything?
NIKA! NIKA! NIKA
And for our next number--
DE
KLIK

182

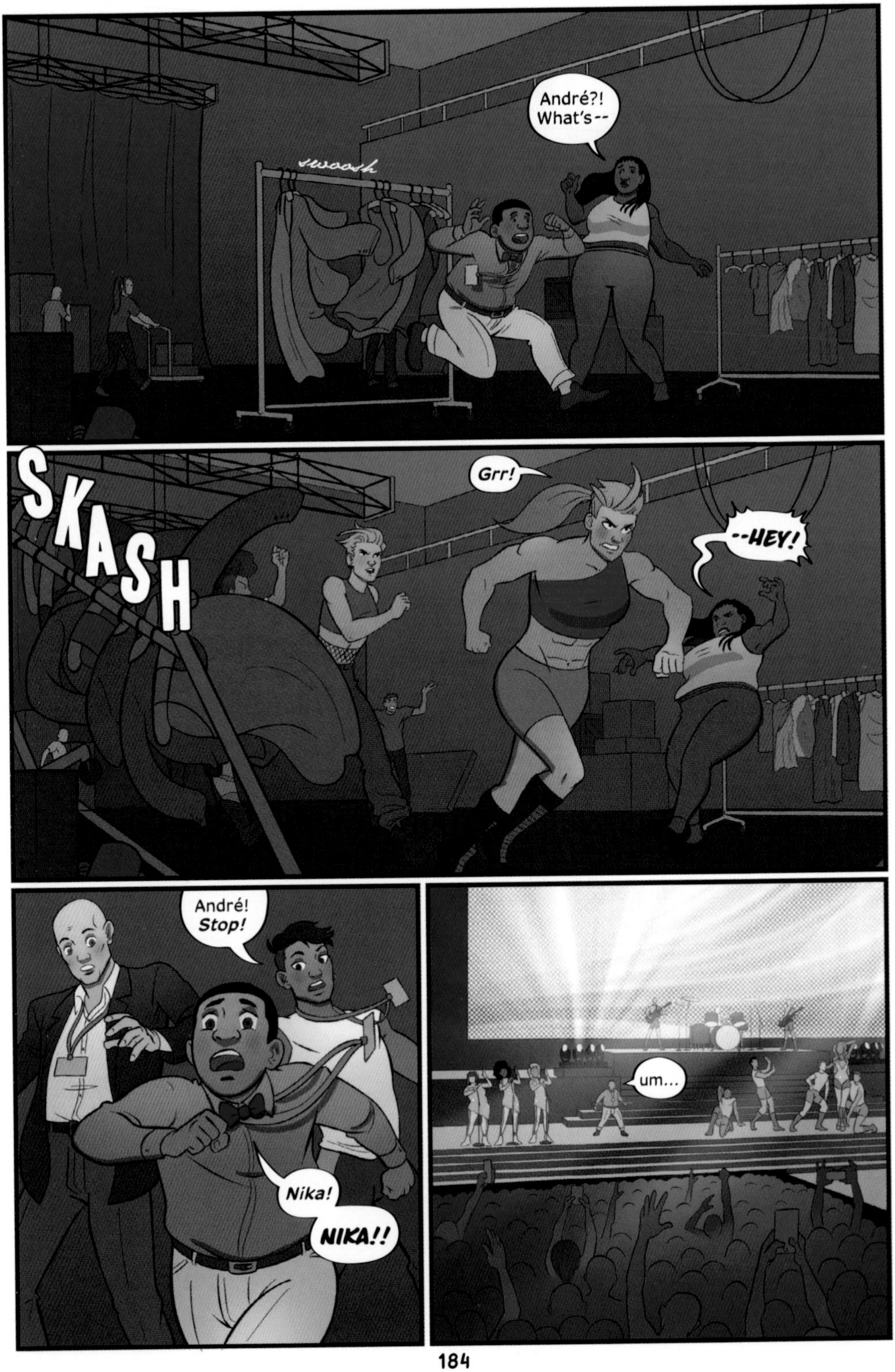
André?!
What's--
swoosh
SKASH
Grr!
--HEY!
André!
Stop!
Nika!
NIKA!!
um...

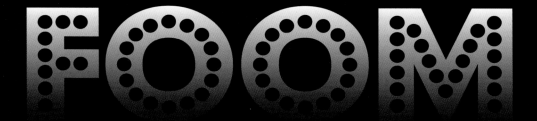

189

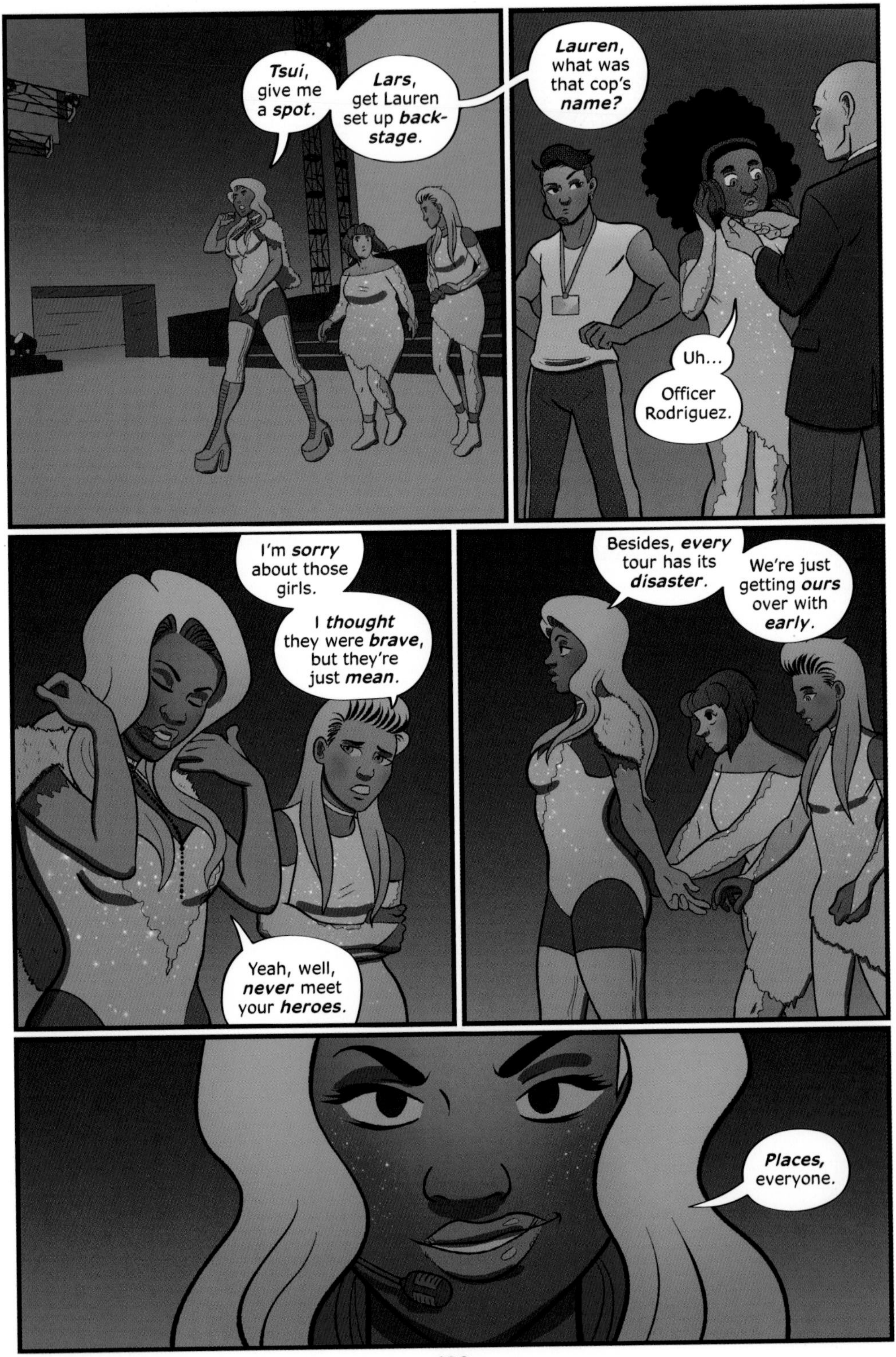
Tsui, give me a *spot*.
Lars, get Lauren set up *back-stage*.
Lauren, what was that cop's *name?*
Uh...
Officer Rodriguez.
I'm *sorry* about those girls.
I *thought* they were *brave*, but they're just *mean*.
Yeah, well, *never* meet your *heroes*.
Besides, *every* tour has its *disaster*.
We're just getting *ours* over with *early*.
Places, everyone.

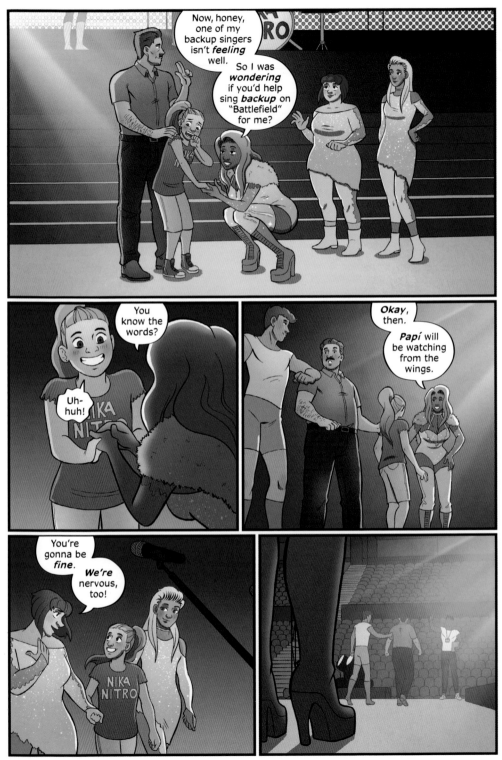

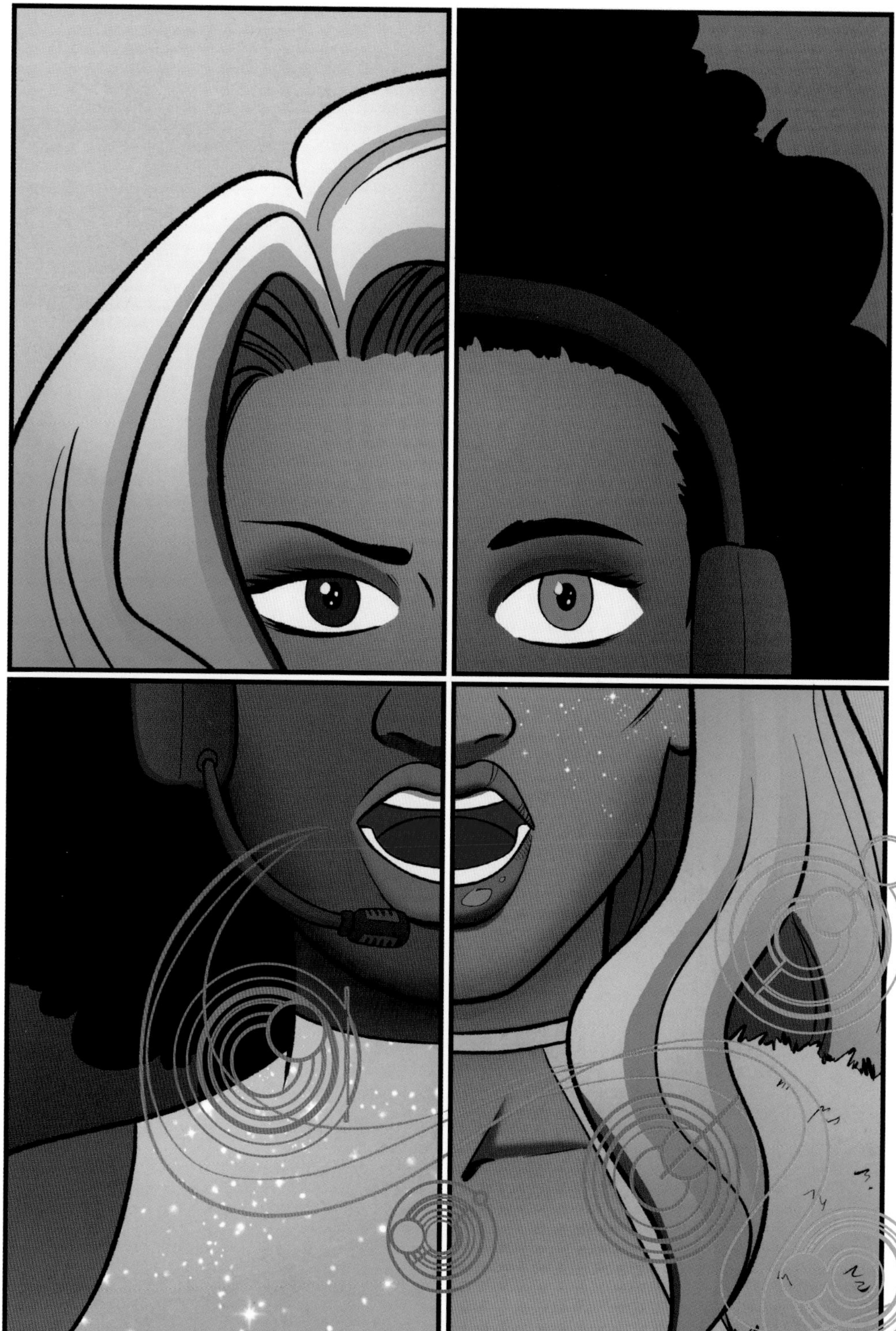

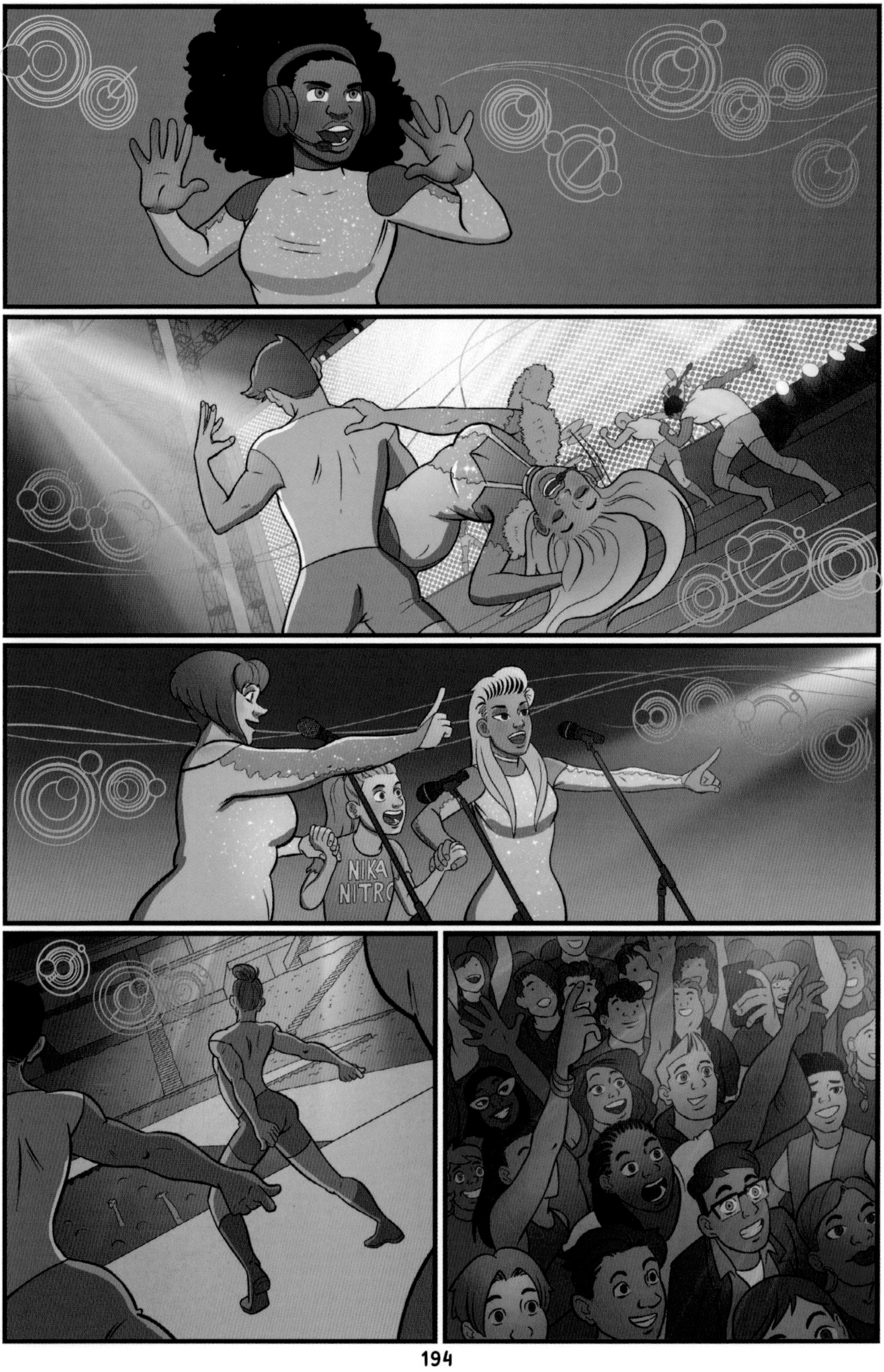
NIKA
NITRO

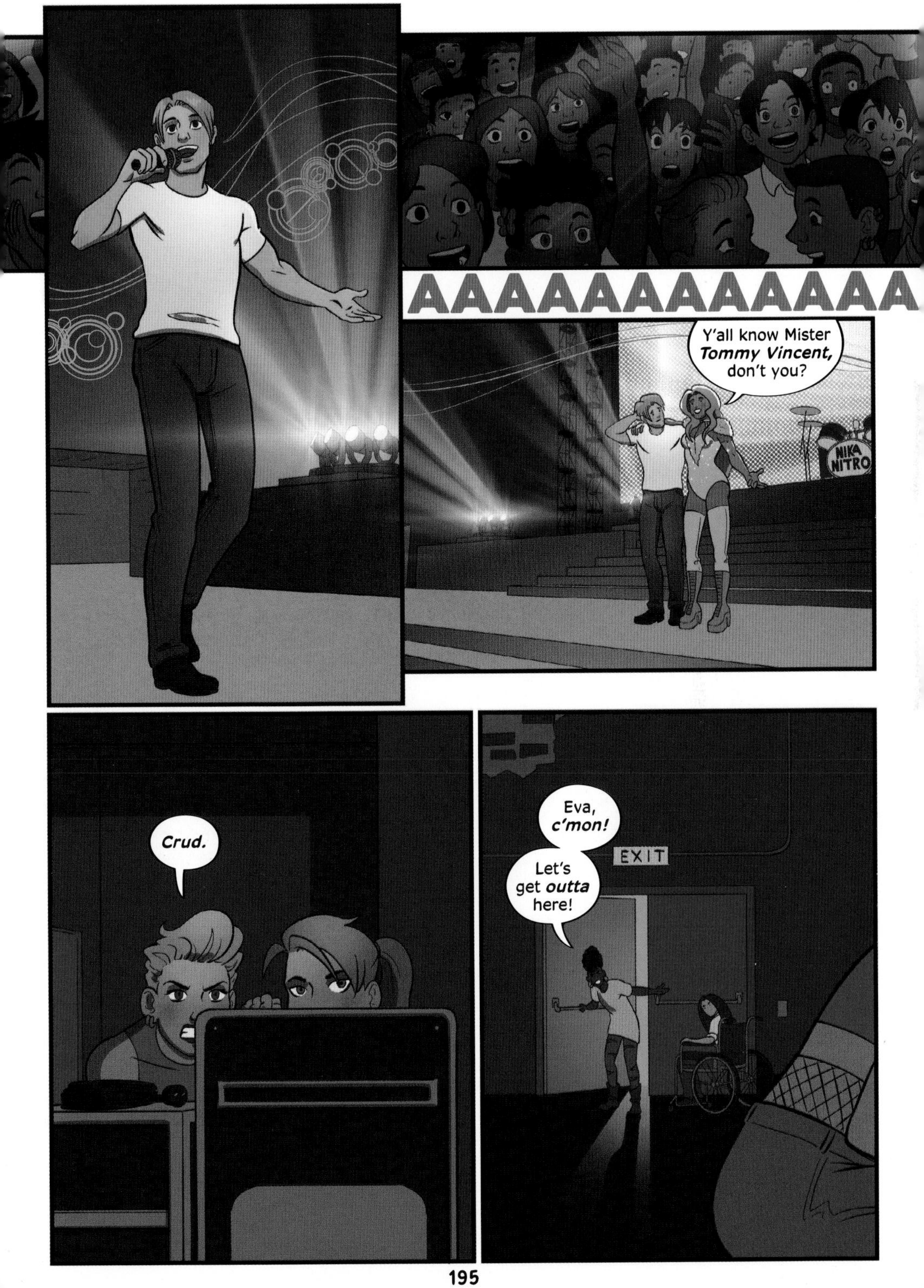
AAAAAAAAAAAAA
Y'all know Mister *Tommy Vincent,* don't you?
NIKA NITRO
Crud.
Eva, *c'mon!*
EXIT
Let's get *outta* here!

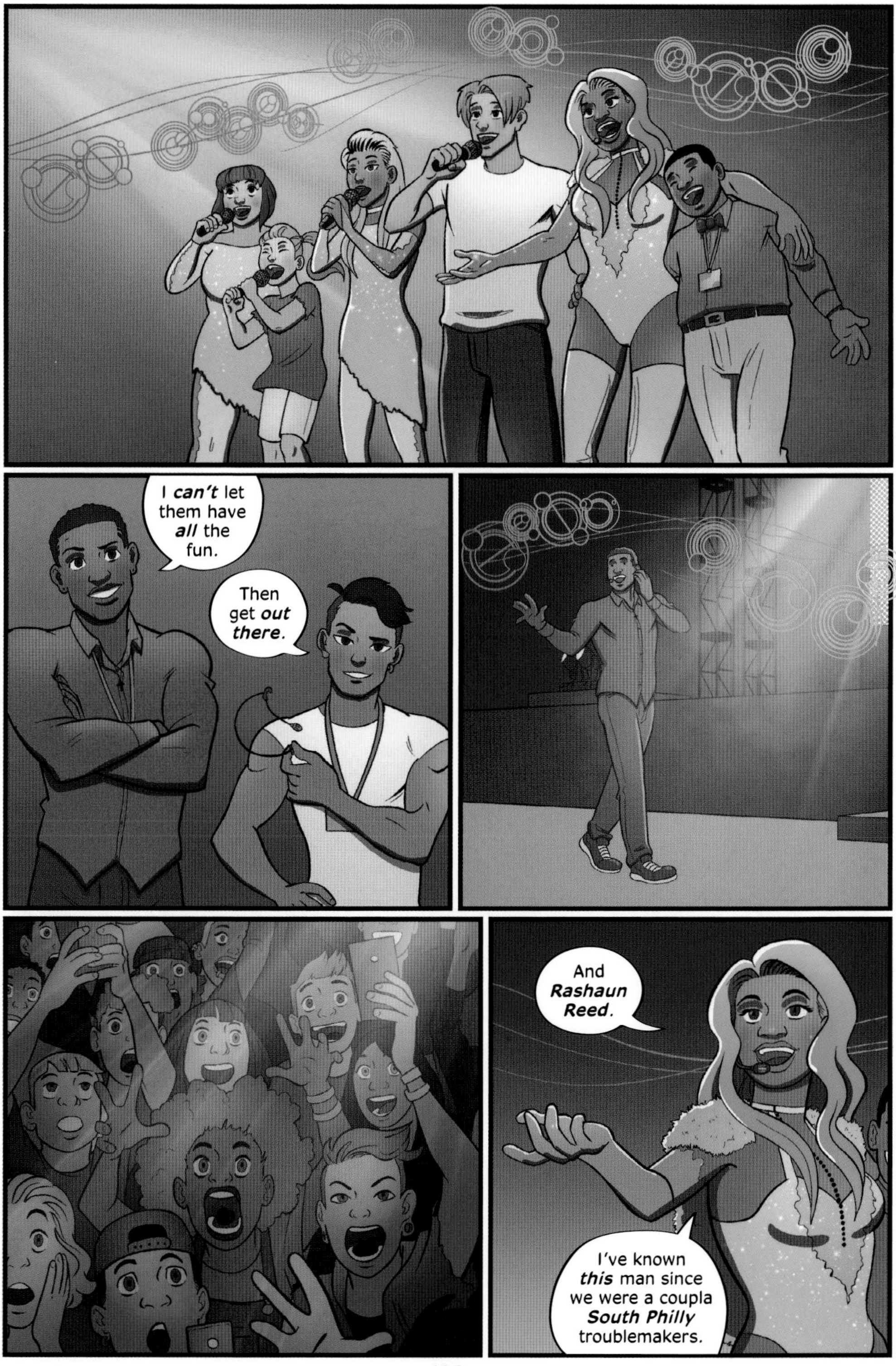
I *can't* let them have *all* the fun.
Then get *out there*.
And *Rashaun Reed*.
I've known *this* man since we were a coupla *South Philly* troublemakers.

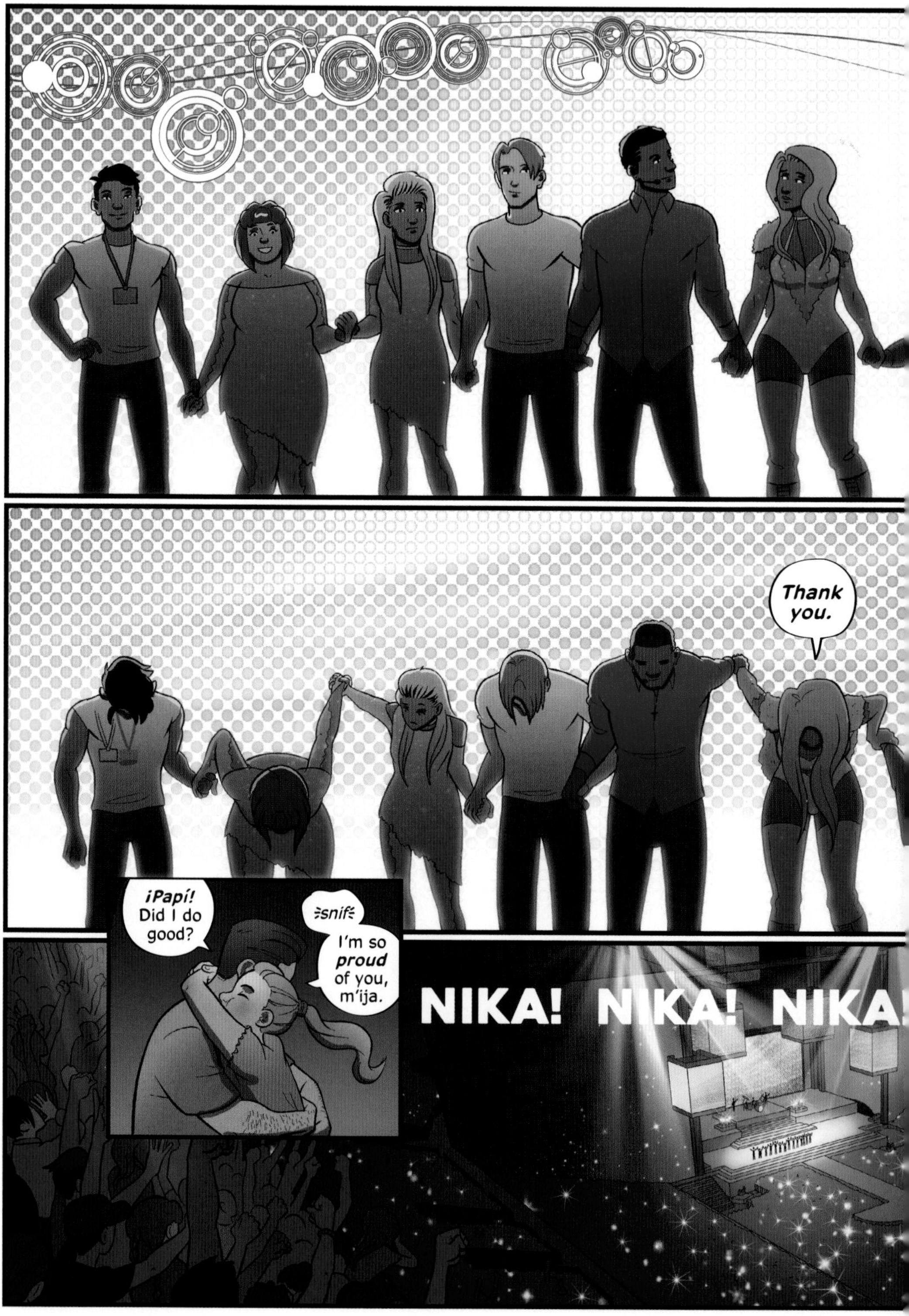

Thank you.
¡Papí! Did I do good?
≠snif≠
I'm so proud of you, m'ija.
NIKA! NIKA! NIKA!

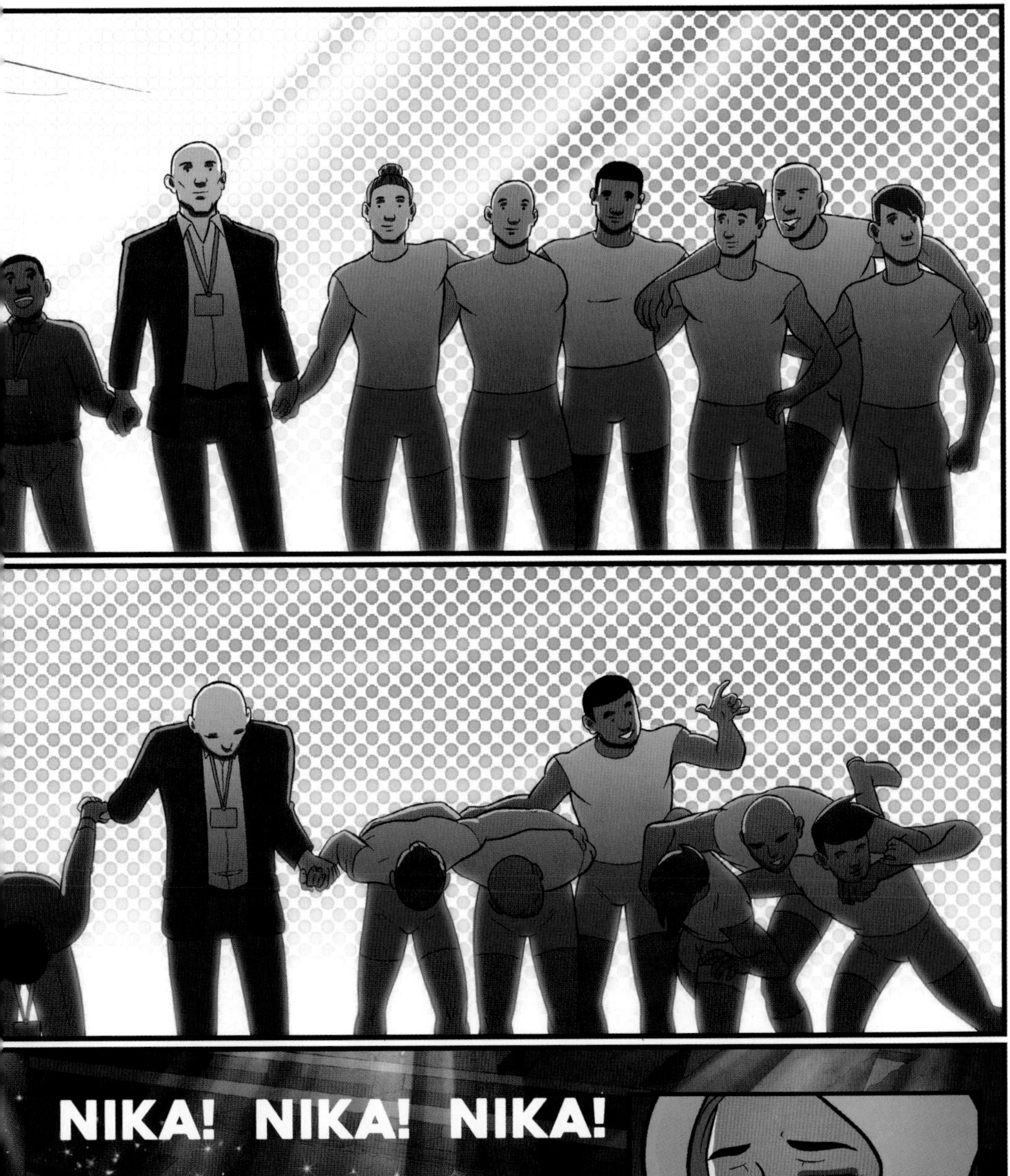
NIKA! NIKA! NIKA!
Now, I got a *confession* to make...

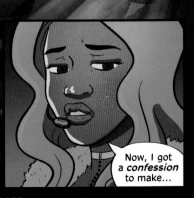

200

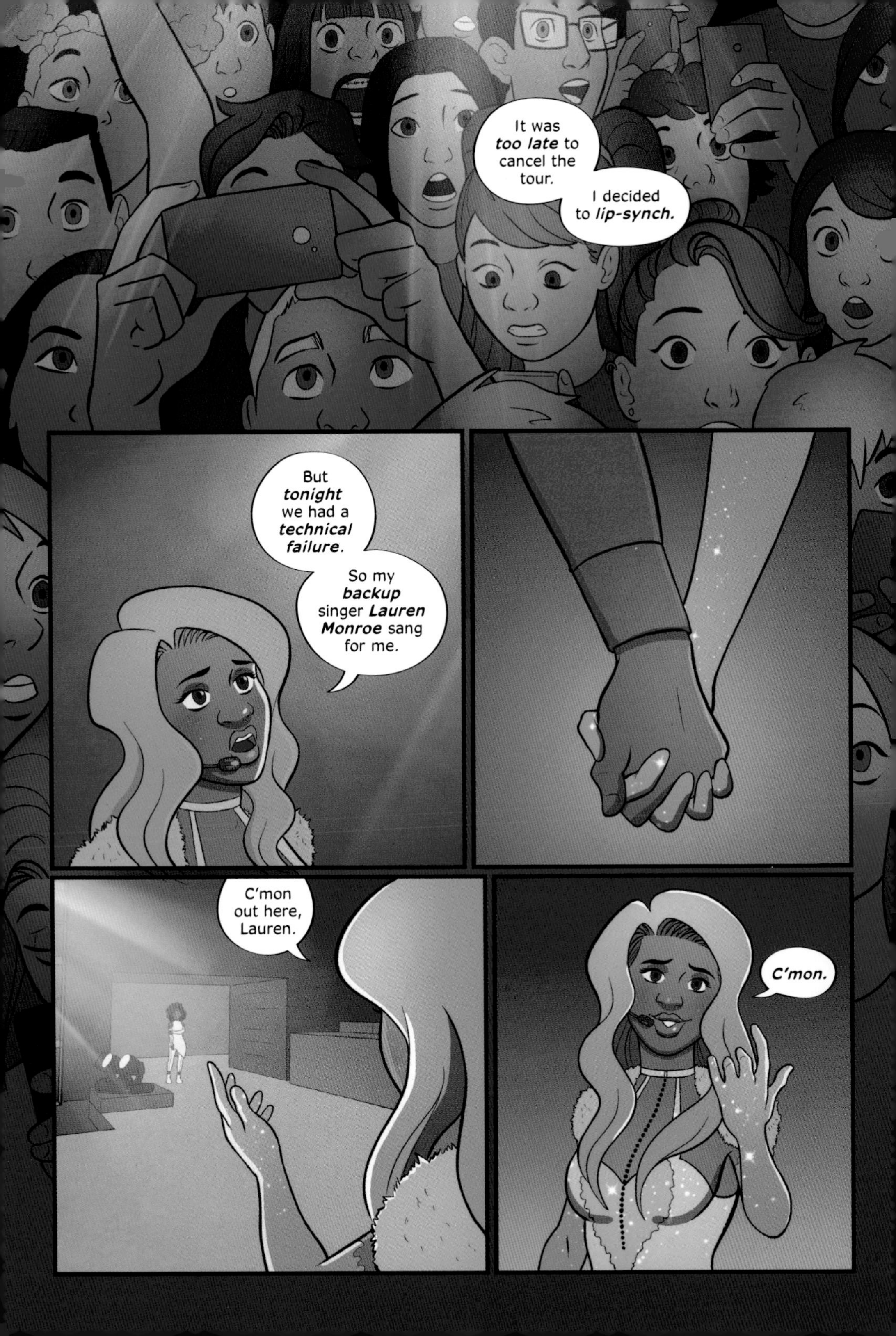
It was *too late* to cancel the tour.
I decided to *lip-synch.*
But *tonight* we had a *technical failure*.
So my *backup* singer *Lauren Monroe* sang for me.
C'mon out here, Lauren.
C'mon.

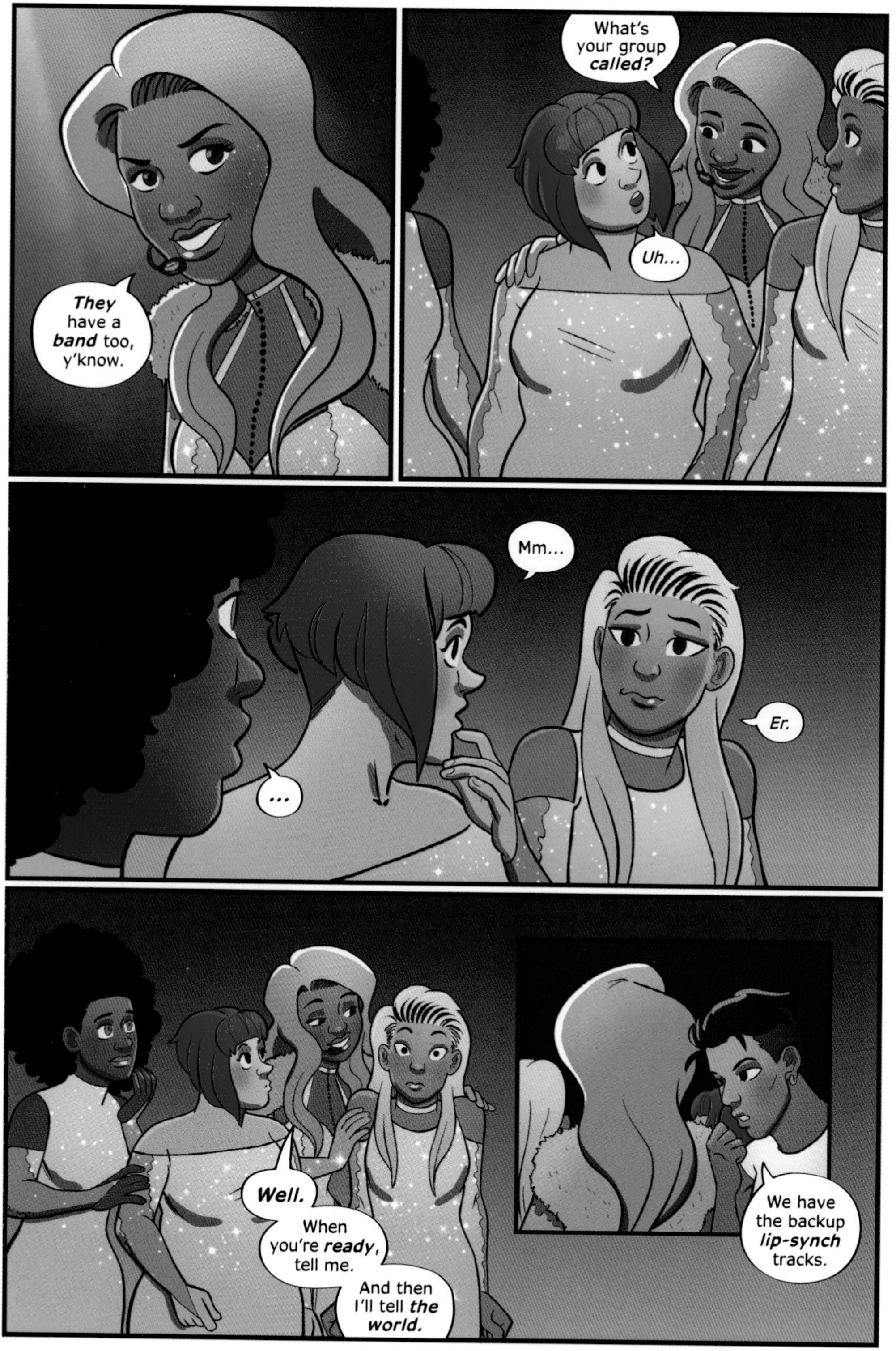
They have a *band* too, y'know.
What's your group *called?*
Uh...
Mm...
Er.
...
Well.
When you're *ready*, tell me.
And then I'll tell *the world.*
We have the backup *lip-synch* tracks.

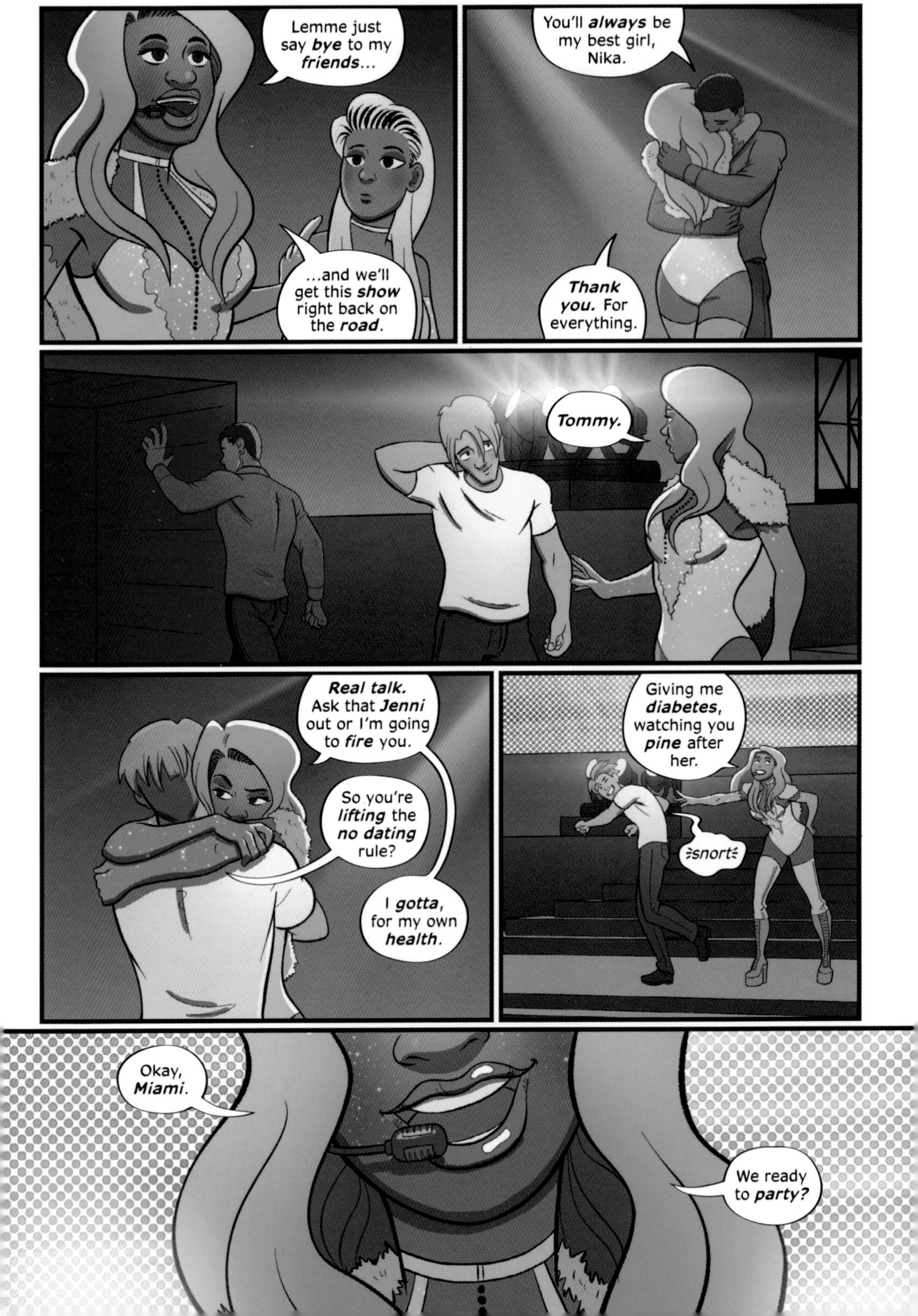
Lemme just say *bye* to my *friends*...
...and we'll get this *show* right back on the *road*.
You'll *always* be my best girl, Nika.
Thank you. For everything.
Tommy.
Real talk. Ask that *Jenni* out or I'm going to *fire* you.
So you're *lifting* the *no dating* rule?
I *gotta*, for my own *health*.
Giving me *diabetes*, watching you *pine* after her.
snort
Okay, *Miami*.
We ready to *party?*

205

THE END

PAPER DOLLS by Ashe Samuels

LAUREN

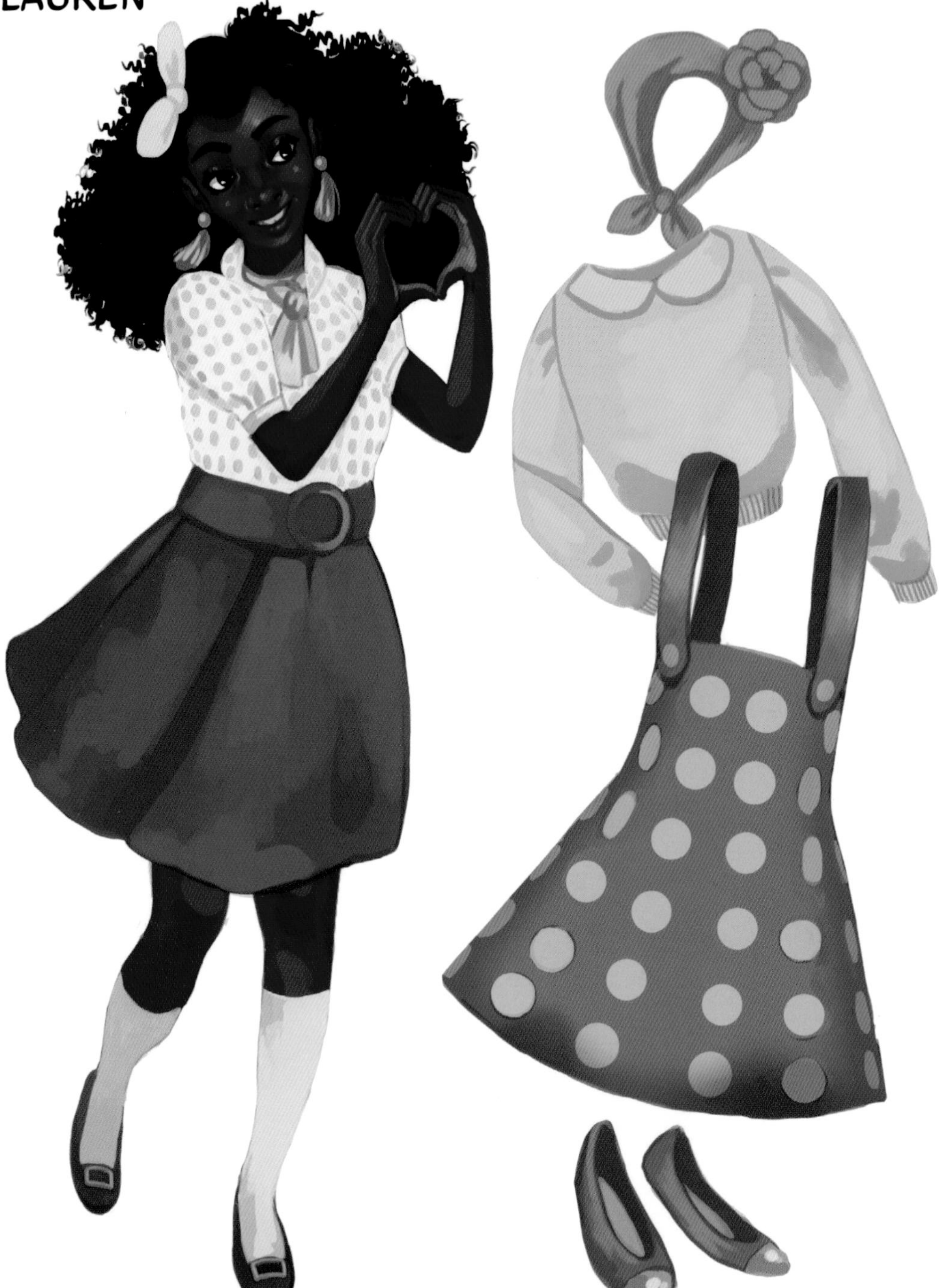

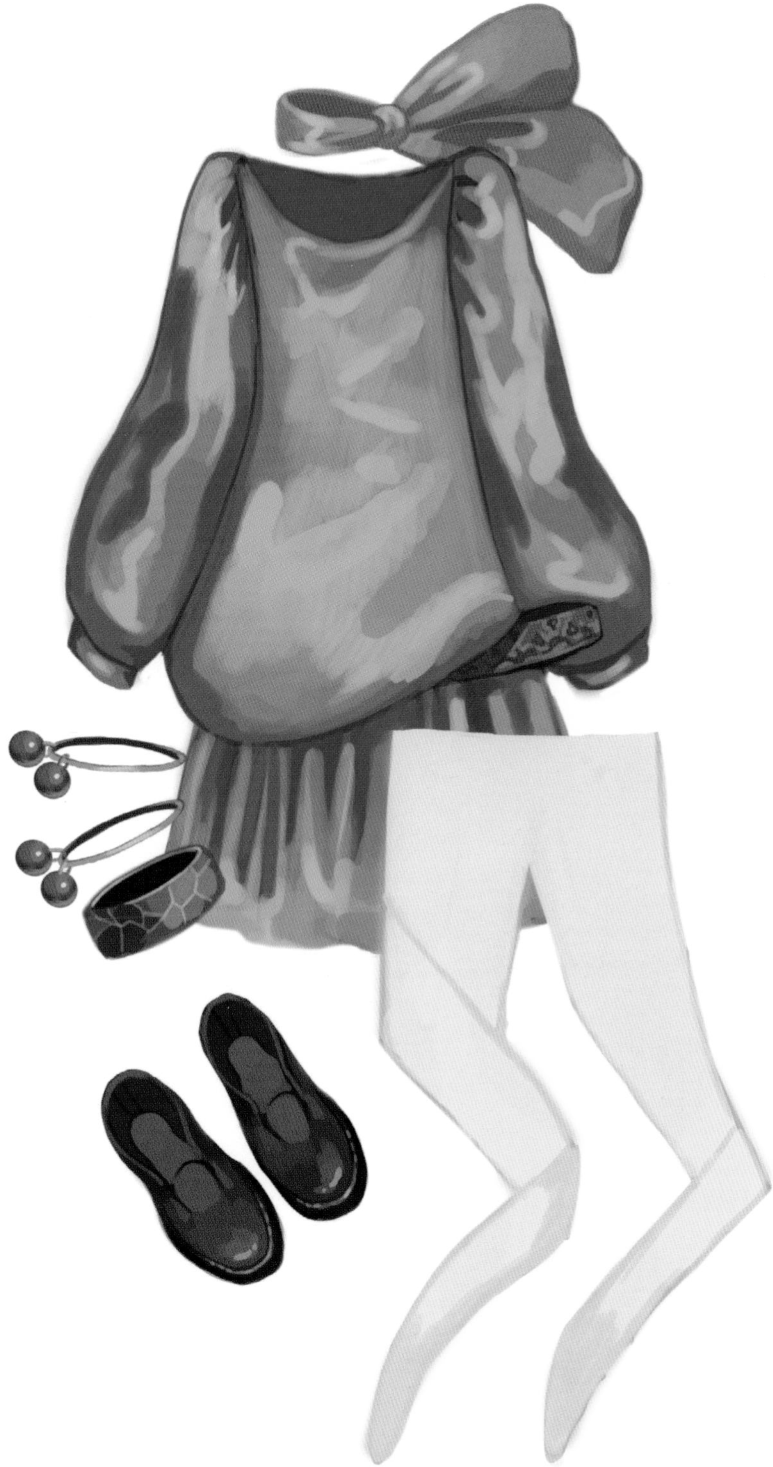

MAGGIE

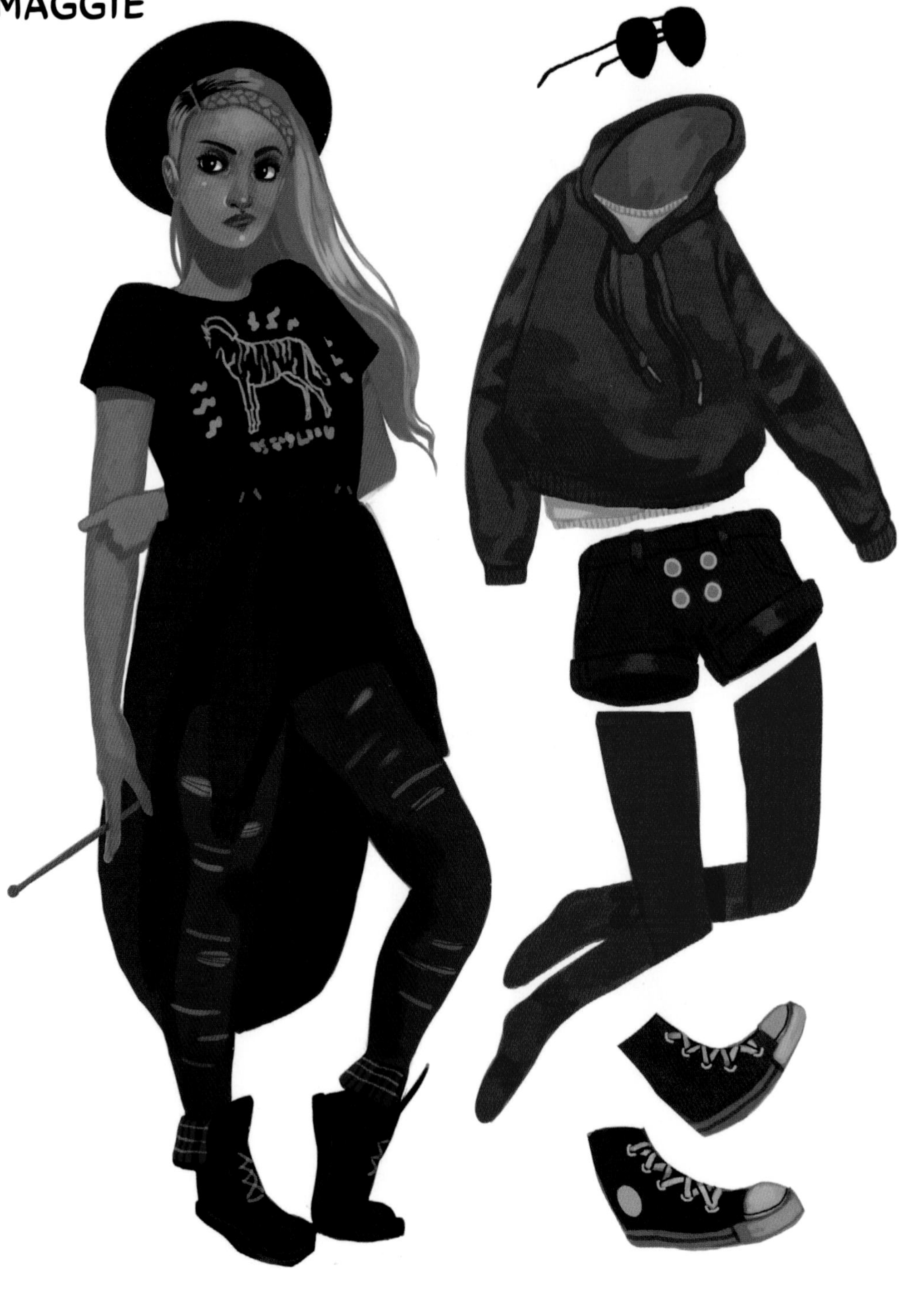

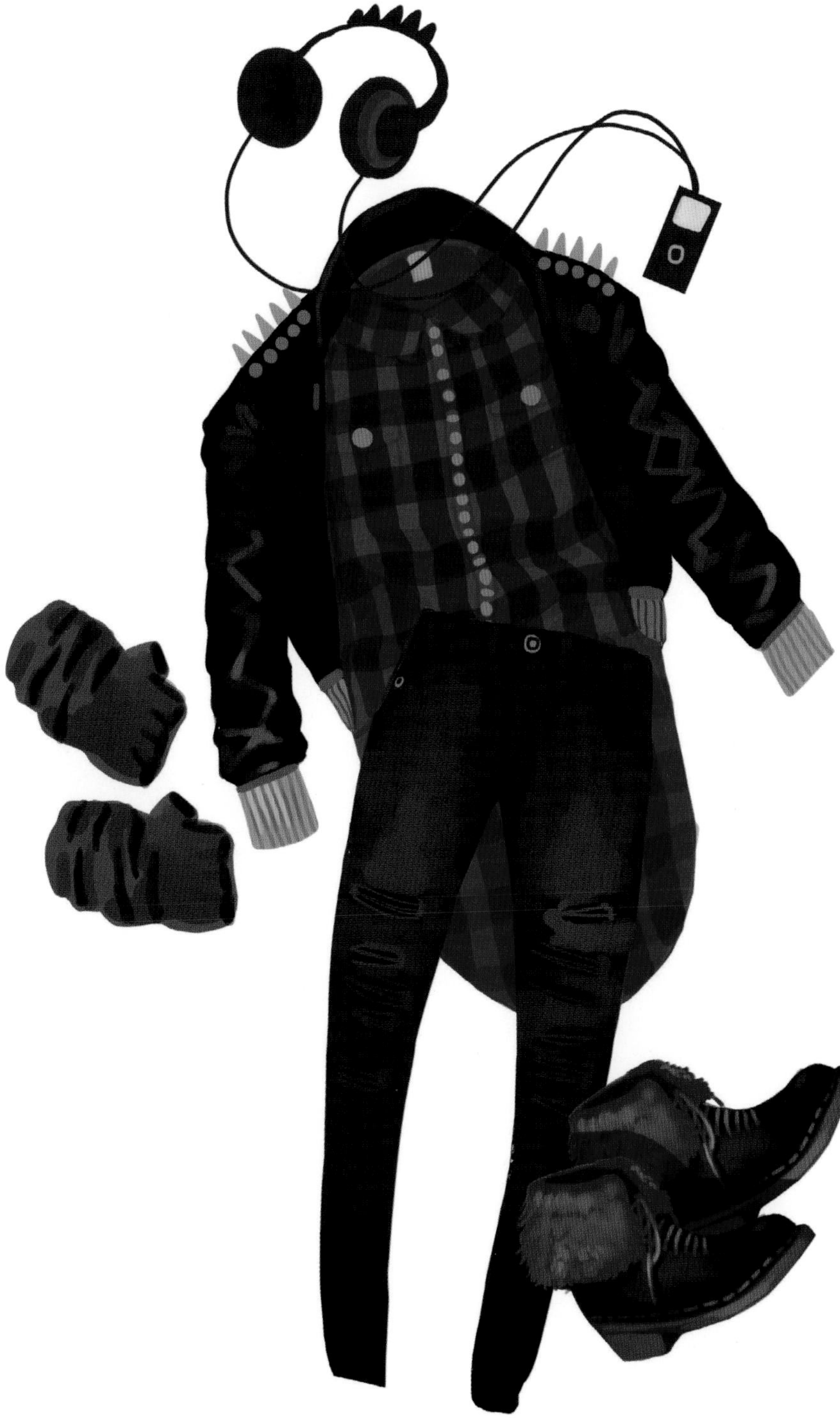

JENNI

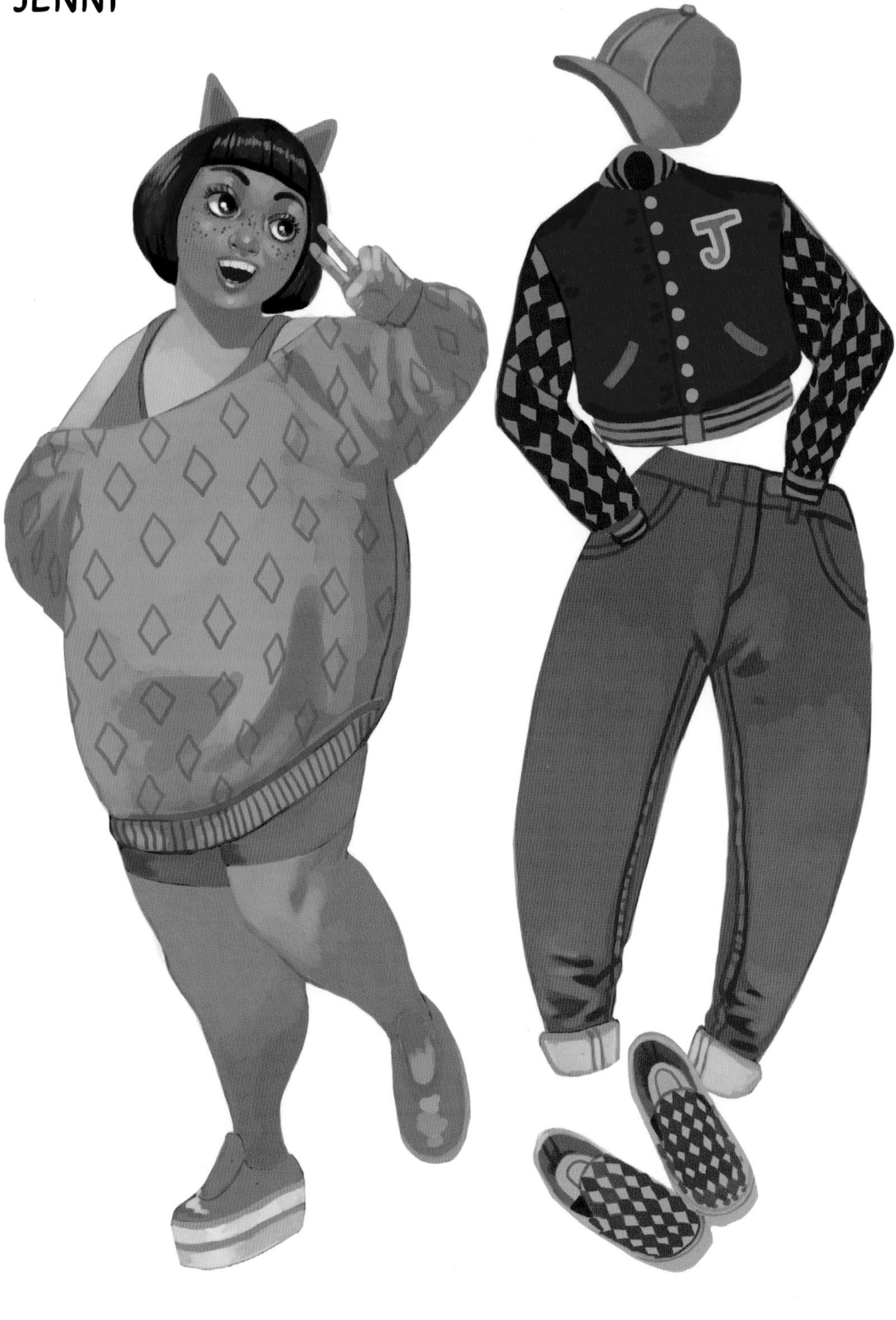
J

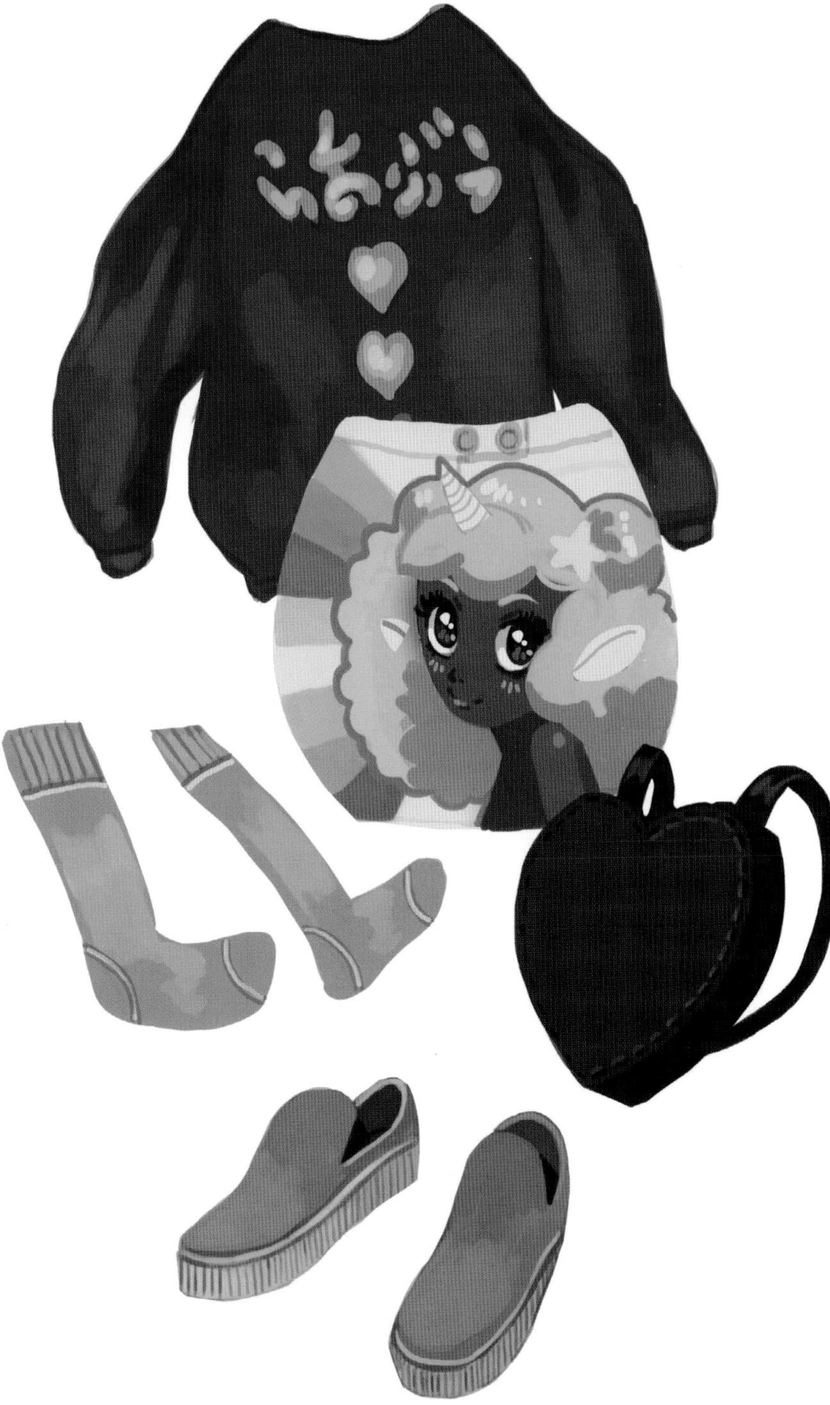

NIKA

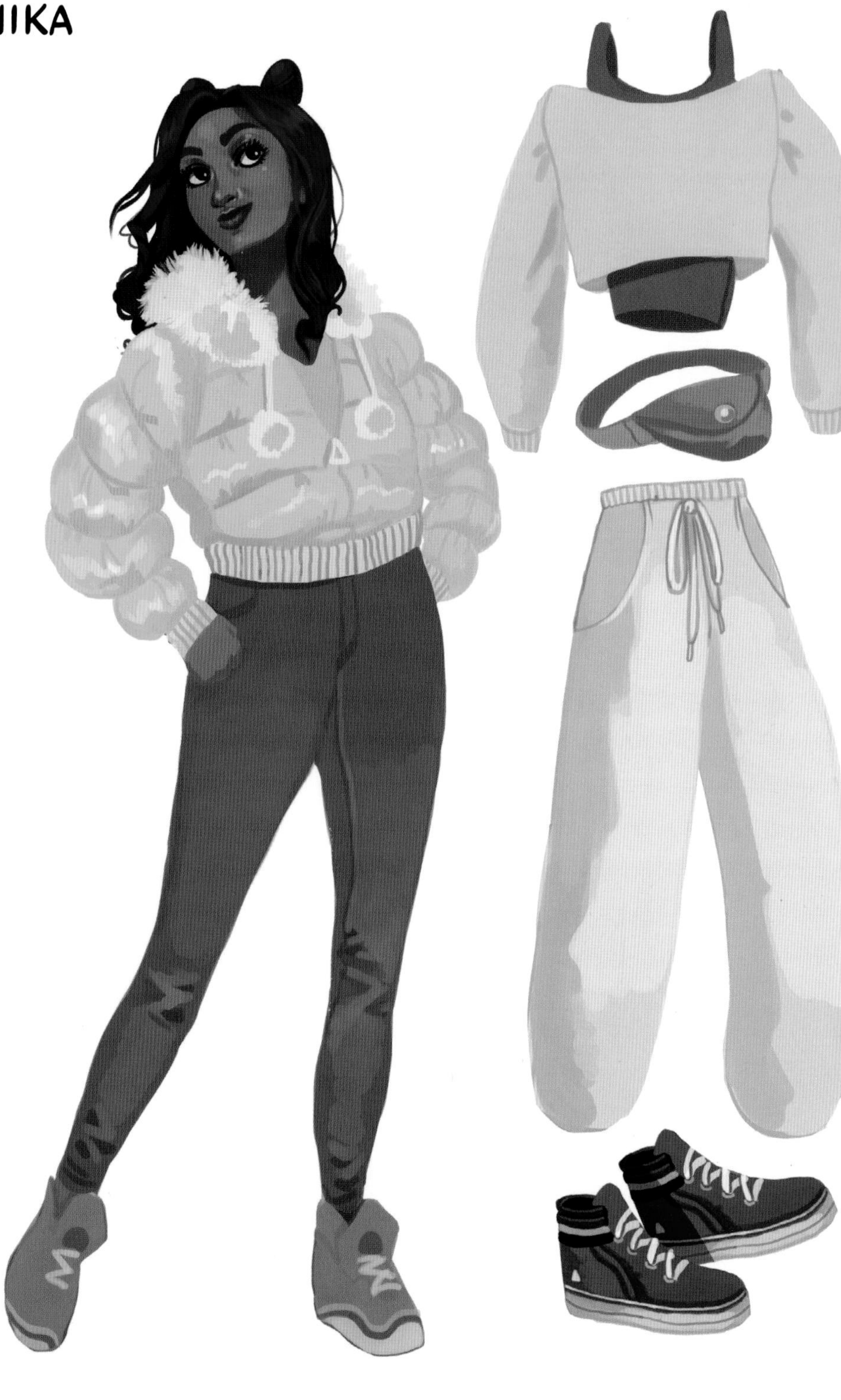

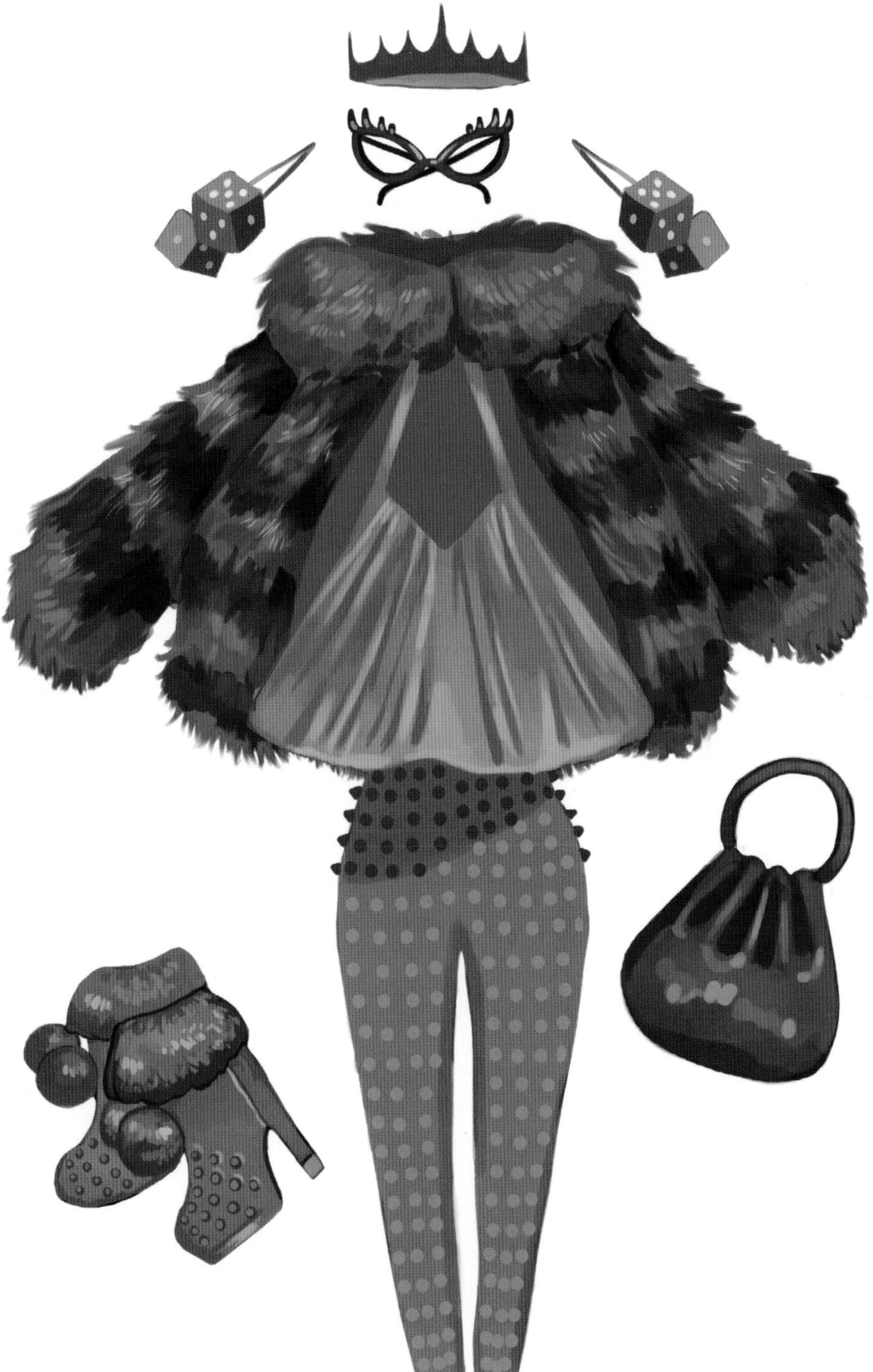

ABOUT THE CREATORS

Alex de Campi is a New York–based writer with an extensive backlist of critically acclaimed graphic novels including Eisner-nominated heist noir *Bad Girls* (Simon & Schuster) and *Twisted Romance* (Image Comics). Her most recent book was her debut prose novel *The Scottish Boy* (Unbound). Catch her YA adventure *Reversal* on her Patreon, and action-thriller *Bad Karma* serialized on Panel Syndicate. She is on most social media as @alexdecampi. She lives with her daughter, their cat, and a Deafblind pit bull named Tango.

Lara Kane is a freelance artist for animation and comics. Her career started with her participation in the short animated film *The Snowman and the Snowdog*, followed by various contributions as a storyboard artist for British animation studios such as Tandem Films, HIT Entertainment and Brown Bag Films. In comics she has worked with Dynamite, as well as collaborated with Alex de Campi on a short story for her *Semiautomagic* book. You can find her portfolio at larak.pb.gallery.

Dee Cunniffe is an award-winning Irish designer who worked for over a decade in publishing and advertising. He gave it all up to pursue his love of comics. He has colored *The Dregs* and *Eternal* at Black Mask, *The Paybacks* and *Interceptor* at Heavy Metal, *Her Infernal Descent*, *The Replacer* and *Stronghold* at Aftershock, Marvel's *Runaways*, DC's *Lucifer*, and *Redneck* at Skybound.

Dee Cunniffe is an award-winning Irish designer who
worked for over a decade in publishing and advertising.
He gave it all up to pursue his love of comics. He has
colored *The Dregs* and *Eternal* at Black Mask, *The Paybacks*
and *Interceptor* at Heavy Metal, *Her Infernal Descent*, *The
Replacer* and *Stronghold* at Aftershock, Marvel's *Runaways*,
DC's *Lucifer*, and *Redneck* at Skybound.

Ted Brandt is a UK-based inker, though he works mostly
in the American market. He has worked for Action Lab on
the acclaimed *Raven: The Pirate Princess*, as well as Marvel's
Mighty Captain Marvel and *Steve Rogers: Captain America*. His
most known work is the Eisner- and GLAAD-nominated series
Crowded, from Image Comics.

Ashe Samuels is a commercial illustrator with a heavy
leaning toward fantasy, sci-fi, and magical realism. She also
has a perfectly healthy obsession with fashion and yearns for
the good ol' days of thrift shopping. In between projects she's
either working on a novel or playing with her roommate's cats
in an effort to "stay productive, but not really."